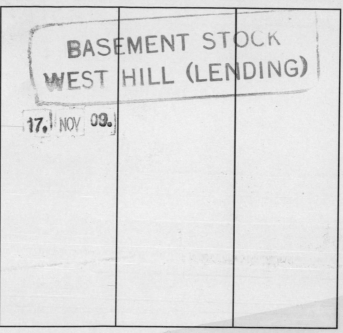

By Julia Gray

ICE MAGE
FIRE MUSIC
ISLE OF THE DEAD

The Guardian Cycle
THE DARK MOON

THE
DARK
MOON

Book One of
The Guardian Cycle

JULIA GRAY

An *Orbit* Book

First published in Great Britain by Orbit 2000

Copyright © Julia Gray 2000

The moral right of the author has been asserted.

A CIP catalogue record for this book
is available from the British Library.

ISBN 1 85723 993 8

Typeset in Erhardt by M Rules
Printed and bound in Great Britain by
Mackays of Chatham plc, Chatham, Kent

Orbit
A Division of
Little, Brown and Company (UK)
Brettenham House
Lancaster Place
London WC2E 7EN

This book is dedicated to the Jackson family
— to Gill, Max, Emma, Dicken and Fuchsia —
but especially to Juliet, my goddaughter,
with much love.

Prologue

It was a night when mountains ground their teeth, when islands moved like ships and the oceans boiled.

The birth of the Emperor's son had been prophesied many years before, but the court seers and advisors had left nothing to chance. The maiden selected to be the Emperor's seventh wife had been carefully chosen – from a noble family whose fecundity was legendary – and the required conception had been timed precisely nine median months in advance of the appointed day. All subsequent omens had been meticulously monitored and taken into account as the pregnancy progressed, and every contingency had been catered for. The midwives and physicians ~~~~~ equipped with potions that would induce labour if ~~~~~ ective.

In the event, and to the seers' delight, such measures were not required. The Seventh Empress of the Floating Islands knew her duty, and her young mind ordered her body into action.

Shortly before midnight on the fateful day, the Emperor's son was born. He was a plump and strangely

placid baby, who had to be coaxed into uttering his first
cry, but who nonetheless appeared physically normal. This
came as something of a relief, as many legends had spoken
of strange and hideous defects in children born when the
multiple lunar influence was at its strongest.

All those present were happily congratulating themselves on their success in fulfilling the prophecy when the
all but forgotten Empress screamed again, signalling that
her confinement was not over. The birth had been predicted by augury. What had not been foreseen was the
fact that there would be two imperial children born that
night.

Adina's second son could not have presented a greater
contrast to his twin. He was tiny, his skin mottled with
purple as if it were bruised, and he screamed incessantly –
without the need of any prompting – from the moment he
came into the world. Worse still, his right arm was withered – the hand little more than a tiny, grotesque claw –
and his right leg was twisted so that the foot was bent back
upon itself.

Dazed from pain and exhaustion, the Empress stared at
the baby as he lay howling in the arms of a nervous midwife. No one knew what this unexpected arrival portended,
least of all Adina, but she understood instinctively that it
was up to her to dispel the cloud of uncertainty that now
hung over the previously joyful occasion.

'Show him to me.' Although her voice was hoarse and
weary, the tone of command was unmistakable.

In spite of her own fears, the midwife held out the baby
to the Empress. When Adina saw the full extent of his
deformities, she could not hide the look of revulsion on her
face. She made no move to take the child, and the midwife
hesitated, waiting to be told what to do next. It was at that

moment that the baby chose to open his eyes for the first time, falling silent at last as he gazed at his mother's face. It was Adina's turn to scream.

'Take it away!' she shrieked. 'Take it away!'

As her attendants hurried to obey, wrapping the baby in a swaddling cloth and carrying him to the far side of the room, the Empress fought to regain her composure.

'Get that thing out of my sight,' she grated. 'And bring me *my son*.' In that instant she made it clear to everyone present that, in her mind, she had only one son – and the observers took their cue from her. The senior midwife brought the elder twin to the bedside, while minions cleared away the bloody sheets and tried to restore a semblance of normality to the scene. Adina cradled the child, looking at him with eyes that were full of relief as well as love.

'This is my son,' she whispered. '*This* is my son.'

In the antechamber where most of the court seers were gathered, the news that the Empress had given birth to twins was greeted with exclamations of disbelief. Their consternation increased when they learnt of the second boy's defects, and of the Empress's reaction to them. The hurried and anxious debate that followed was led, naturally enough, by Mirival, the Chief Seer. As the Emperor's closest advisor, he knew it would be his duty to report the unexpected event to his lord, but before he did so he needed a plausible explanation. In particular he had to explain the failure of their augury. Mirival prided himself on the fact that no one in all Vadanis knew more about the Tindaya Code, but his many readings of that ancient text had found absolutely no mention of twins. He had never even considered such a possibility, and nor had any of his fellow astrologers. How could their science have failed them so drastically, especially when their other predictions had all proved to be so accurate?

Mirival looked around at his colleagues, seeing his own fears reflected in their frowning eyes, and knew that they too were at a loss.

'Theories, gentlemen?' he prompted, without any real hope.

'There's nothing in the Code to even suggest—'

'I'm aware of that,' Mirival snapped. 'We've a great deal of work ahead of us, trying to seek out what we've missed, but that will have to wait. What I need right now is a way to present this to Dheran – and to the people.'

There was a long, awkward silence, as each of the seers contemplated just how foolish they were going to appear.

'Do the people have to know?' Kamin suggested timidly.

Mirival was about to tell his deputy not to be so stupid, but then he held his tongue, considering the idea.

'Should we not take our lead from the Empress?' Fauria enquired. 'Women's instincts do not contain the logic of astrology, but they cannot always be dismissed lightly. If Adina disowns the second boy, we can surely do the same.'

'Exactly,' Kamin said, more confident now that he had received some support from a fellow seer. 'Hide him away somewhere safe, and no one need know he even exists.'

'But the midwives will gossip, like all servants,' Shahan pointed out. He was the eldest of the group – and some said the least imaginative. 'We won't be able to silence all the rumours.'

'There will be some practical difficulties,' Mirival conceded thoughtfully. 'But silence can be bought or enforced if necessary.' He was beginning to warm to the idea. Keeping the second birth secret could save much embarrassment. Plans were already forming in his calculating mind.

'We'll still have our Guardian,' Fauria said. 'His destiny can unfold as planned.'

'And there's every likelihood that the second infant will die soon anyway,' Kamin added. 'He's clearly crippled, and who knows what damage may have been done to his internal organs.'

'Including his brain,' Fauria put in.

They paused again as the implications of that remark sank in.

'It would do the Emperor's standing no good if it were to become known that he had sired an imbecile,' one of the other seers observed.

'Seal the doors!' Mirival cried, suddenly decisive. 'No news, nothing at all, leaves these rooms without my express approval.' As guards hurried to obey his orders, he lowered his voice again and looked round at his colleagues. 'I will speak to everyone here before they leave the palace, to ensure their cooperation, but right now I must talk to Dheran. We can't hide the truth from him.' Much as I'd like to, he added silently. 'So, what should I tell him?'

Shahan, who had been silent throughout the discussion, his disapproval evident, now spoke again.

'Perhaps the second boy could actually be considered a blessing,' he said, then hurried to explain in the face of the incredulity displayed by his colleagues. 'Perhaps he was there to absorb the malign influences of the conjunction, so that his twin might be saved from any such afflictions and become the hero we all desire. Perhaps his role was to protect the Guardian.'

The old man watched as his fellow seers absorbed this idea, noting the eagerness that crept into their expressions, and wondered whether he actually believed his own theory.

'Coming from anyone else,' Mirival responded, smiling,

'I would take that as superstitious nonsense. From you it carries the stamp of authority.' And it'll certainly be good enough for Dheran, he thought privately. Dress it up in some suitably oracular language and he'll swallow it whole.

'It's almost midnight, sir,' a deferential voice reminded him.

Mirival nodded.

'Everyone is to remain where they are until I return,' he informed the gathering. 'It is time for my audience with the Emperor.'

Dheran was engrossed in a game of chaikra when Mirival entered the room. A glance at the board told the seer that the Emperor's position was hopeless, and that any competent opponent would force a win in a few moves. However, he also knew that Remi, the young courtier who was Dheran's adversary, would prolong the game for some time – and perhaps even contrive to lose, in spite of his clearly superior skill. That boy will go far, Mirival thought, as the young man looked up expectantly.

Dheran made the move that he had evidently been considering for some time, then glanced up at his advisor.

'Is it over?'

'Yes, Your Majesty. The Empress has delivered you a healthy son, exactly as prophesied.'

'Excellent.'

'Congratulations, sire,' Remi said.

'May I speak with the Emperor alone for a few moments, please.'

Although it had been phrased as a request, Remi was more than capable of recognizing an order when he heard one. He rose and left the room quickly, but in such a graceful manner that there was never any suggestion of haste in his movements. Mirival waited until the door closed softly behind him before speaking again.

'There was, however, one slight complication.'

'How is Adina? Is she well?' Dheran asked, genuine concern in his dark eyes.

'The Empress is in perfect health, although naturally tired and overwrought,' the seer replied, marvelling at the fact that Dheran actually cared for his seventh wife.

'Then what . . . ?'

'There was a second son,' Mirival said bluntly.

The Emperor stared at the seer in amazement. 'Twins? How can that be?'

'Fate has seen fit to present us with a mystery,' Mirival replied, 'but I can at least offer one possible explanation.' He went on to describe the second baby's abnormal appearance, and then expounded Shahan's theory about the infant's acting as a shield against astrological influences.

'So the child split in two?' Dheran asked. 'Good and evil, so to speak?'

'You could put it that way.'

'That should make the Mentor's job easier, eh?' the Emperor commented, smiling at his own cleverness.

'Quite so, Your Majesty,' Mirival agreed affably, though he knew it could not possibly be that simple. 'However, it does present us with something of a problem concerning the second child. Because he has already served his purpose, we must decide what to do with him.'

'Ah,' Dheran responded, and frowned to show that he was giving the matter serious thought. 'I see what you mean. What do you suggest?'

After that it was easy.

At the hour of midnight all the bells in the city of Makhaya began to ring in celebration of the birth of the

long-awaited imperial heir, and also to honour the alignment of the four moons of Nydus in the sky above. The
streets were thronged with people eager to witness this rare
event, something that only occurred every seventy-five
years and thus only once in most people's lifetimes. This
was a night when fates collided, when great events were
bound to happen, when history would be made, and everyone wanted to be a part of it. Not even the near-certain
threat of earth tremors would keep the onlookers in their
homes.

News of the birth of Adina's son was already spreading
throughout the city as the crucial moment arrived. As
everyone looked upwards, the thin crescents – which were
all that was visible of the Red, White and Amber moons –
grew thinner still. Then, at the exact moment of conjunction, they disappeared altogether behind the Dark Moon,
the 'sky shadow' that was completely invisible because it
reflected no light. Its observers only knew it was there
because it hid the stars beyond and occasionally produced
eclipses of the sun or, as now, its fellow moons.

The sky became a deeper black and the distant stars
shone brighter as the whole world seemed to hold its breath.
For a few moments the earth beneath their feet shook, as
the islands began to change course, but most people hardly
noticed. And then, as if by magic, the mirror images of the
three crescents appeared in the sky, growing brighter and
more substantial as the stately ballet of the heavens continued – and Makhaya's bells rang out in earnest.

Inside the palace the clamour of the celebrations could
barely be heard, and the mood was far more serious. The
impact of Mirival's words had been undeniable and – looking round the room at all the solemn faces – he felt a small
measure of hope. We might just pull this off, he thought.

Against all the odds, it might work. No one had asked what was to happen to the unwanted baby.

'One final thing,' the seer went on. 'I don't need to tell you how serious this matter is, nor how vital it is that our trust, both the Emperor's and mine, is not betrayed.' He had no need to emphasize just how important the events of the night were likely to be in deciding the future of the Floating Islands. Everyone present was aware of the importance of the arrival of the Guardian. 'No one outside this room, except for the imperial family themselves, must ever know of what we have witnessed here tonight. If our secret is revealed, you can be sure that I will discover the traitor – and that they and their family will be exiled.'

This barbaric threat had the desired effect. Duty would now be reinforced with fear – and if a few unsubstantiated rumours did persist, they could easily be dismissed as superstition. Mirival was already thinking ahead to the first public appearance of Dheran, Adina and their new son – their only son.

'I know I can rely on you all,' he concluded, allowing himself to smile. 'Now you are free to go about your normal duties – and to celebrate with the rest of Vadanis.' I, on the other hand, still have work to do, he thought grimly as he turned away and headed for his own quarters.

The city's revels lasted until dawn, and long before they were over the final part of Mirival's plan had been put into action. No one paid any attention to the unmarked carriage that slipped from the city under cover of darkness, and by the time the sun rose it was many leagues away.

Apart from the driver, the coach carried a man and a woman. In the woman's arms lay a tiny, misshapen baby, now wrapped warmly and fast asleep, but his companions did not know who he was or where he had come from – and knew better than to enquire. Their instructions had been passed on to them by people it would be unwise to double-cross, and had been quite specific.

'He's a poor scrap of a thing,' the woman remarked, looking down at the discoloured face.

'Don't get too attached,' her companion warned her. 'We deliver him as arranged, nothing more.'

'I know that.' They were both being paid enough to ensure they did not deviate from their orders. 'What would I be doing with a kid like this, anyway?'

'I'm just saying,' the man replied wearily.

The woman reached up and pulled back the heavy curtains. Early morning sunlight slanted in, falling across the baby's face. He slowly opened his eyes – and his temporary nursemaid only just managed to stifle a scream.

Sensing her shock, the man leant over to look for himself – and he too froze in disbelief. They stared, as if hypnotized, trapped by a mixture of fear and wonder.

The irises of the baby's eyes had seemed colourless at first, but now, in daylight, they were like pale diamonds, bright and glittering as if formed by crystalline facets rather than human flesh – with only a few irregular but quite brilliant flashes of colour in their seemingly infinite depths. It was the most unnatural sight either of them had ever seen.

'Moons!' the man whispered. 'No wonder they wanted to get rid of him.'

PART ONE

HAVENMOON

CHAPTER ONE

The last thing Terrel saw before the darkness found him again was the White Moon falling from the sky. The bright disc grew incredibly fast, filling his vision and threatening to crush him. Yet in his eyes the moon was somehow flat, like an enormous plate, even though he knew it should be a sphere – but this just made him feel curious, not afraid.

And then it was gone, extinguished without a trace, and he was enfolded by the suffocating darkness. Pain reached out with red fingers. He heard the thunderous rhythm of the sea – the sea in which he swam, but which he had never seen. Already he felt himself growing smaller.

Terrel recognized this phase of the dream. What had gone before was a broken-mirror rush of images, some strange and formless, others vaguely intimate, as if they were memories that belonged to someone else. Although the images had been real, as only dreams can be real, they had not frightened him. But what came next, although familiar, almost drowned him in fear. He knew that when he awoke he would be gasping for air and shivering, his skin cold and drenched with sweat.

It was not the pain that terrified him. He was used to pain. Nor was it the thought of drowning. This ocean would always release him. It was not even the fact that he was blind. His other senses more than made up for that lack. His fear was caused by the hatred that lay beyond the darkness, beyond the waves of pain; the remorseless enmity that was driven by something he did not – could not – understand. He felt it seep into every fibre of his body, like a slow-acting poison or some vile disease.

He fought against it instinctively, defending himself against his invisible foe. But the best he could hope for was to survive. He could never win. Like a hedgehog curling into an ever tighter ball, Terrel was drawing in upon himself. Drawing in, and drawing in, until there was nothing left.

This – as always – was when he woke up.

'It's odd that it was the White Moon,' Alyssa remarked. 'You'd have thought it would've been the Amber.'

Terrel sat up, blinking the last of the dream away. Alyssa was sitting, cross-legged, on the floor, and for a dazed moment he wondered how she had got in. Then he saw that the door to his cell stood open, and realized that he'd slept later than usual. He had not even heard the turnkey making his rounds.

'Do you think it's a sign of your destiny?' Alyssa went on. 'That's one of the meanings of the White Moon.'

'To have it fall on my head?' Terrel replied. 'I hope not.'

He no longer found it strange that Alyssa was able to 'see' his dreams. It was only one of her oddities, after all. When he had asked her about it, she had said that they floated near him, like a cloud, before they eventually faded and blew away. No one else could see these clouds, of course, but she had described his nocturnal visions with such startling accuracy on so many occasions that doubting her ability was no longer an option. Alyssa could do this with other people too – with anyone, in fact – but she had learnt not to speak of what she saw. Her strange talent had got her into trouble too often.

'Did you see anything after that?' Terrel asked.

Time didn't mean a lot in Alyssa's view of dreams, but she knew what he meant, and shook her head. Terrel hadn't really expected anything else. She always seemed to pick up on the early, trivial parts of his dreams, but never the end. What she saw was sometimes embarrassing, sometimes curious, but more often than not it was merely dull, because it didn't mean anything. He would have welcomed some insight into the fear, but she would never discuss that. Whenever he'd asked her about it she simply said that it wasn't really a dream, but was part of him. That was frustrating, but no amount of coaxing would make Alyssa admit to anything more, and Terrel had long since given up trying to force the issue. He wasn't even sure now whether she *had* anything more to say.

'Do *you* dream about the Amber Moon?' he asked now. All the moons had their own characters, their own spheres of influence, and the Amber moved in the realm of spirits, of intuition – and of dreams.

'I don't know,' she replied. 'I never remember my own dreams.'

'Never?' Terrel exclaimed in surprise, then realized that in all the times they had talked about dreams, he had never heard her discuss her own experiences.

Alyssa tipped her head to one side, a habit of hers when

she was thinking. It reminded Terrel of the action of a small bird.

'I remember the feelings sometimes,' she said, 'but never what caused them.'

'You're lucky.' Although his own dreams often faded quickly from his memory, even when he didn't want them to, some images remained all too clear.

'Maybe that's why I can see other people's.'

'Compensation, you mean?'

'If you say so. You're the one who knows all the big words.'

They were silent for a while then, neither feeling the need to fill the void with talk. They were nearly always at ease in each other's company. Alyssa brought a welcome warmth to the room, and Terrel realized that her presence had enabled him to recover from his nightmare almost instantly. His arm and leg still ached, but for once he had not woken struggling to catch his breath, and his skin was not even clammy. At times like this it was easy to imagine that he loved her.

Terrel had never quite been able to work out his feelings for Alyssa. He had known her for almost four years now, ever since she had first been brought to Havenmoon. She had just been a *girl* then, and because they were – as far as they knew – the only two inmates of a similar age, their friendship had seemed natural enough. It had only recently dawned upon Terrel that Alyssa was *female*, and thus different from him. His sometimes contradictory emotions when he was with her confused and embarrassed him, but if Alyssa was aware of any change in their relationship she gave no sign of it.

At fifteen Alyssa was a year older than Terrel, and at times she seemed the more mature of the two. Even the signs of her madness – which were real enough – were nothing out of the ordinary to her. She dealt with them in a calm, adult fashion that Terrel could not hope to imitate. Yet at other times she was like a child, laughing at things that he merely found idiotic, and skipping instead of walking.

This dichotomy was even echoed in her appearance. As Terrel looked at her now she seemed perfectly at ease, almost serene. Her shapeless grey shift covered a body that, while it was as tall as his own, was thin and frail – but which was now developing in ways that he found disconcerting. He felt somehow disloyal even thinking about it. In the last year or so her face had become more finely honed, as if she were growing into her own shape, and Terrel thought she was beautiful – although he had never mentioned this to anyone, least of all to Alyssa herself. And yet her deep brown eyes remained resolutely childlike, so large that the phrase 'wide-eyed innocence' might have been coined with her in mind. Her hair was another reminder of her relative youthfulness. It was blonde, the colour of sunlit straw, and cropped short in ragged, uneven clumps. She cut it herself – one of the few inmates allowed to do so – and although the results should have been comic, the style somehow suited her.

However, the most striking thing about Alyssa had nothing to do with her being caught between childhood and maturity, but was uniquely her own. Not only was she pale and thin, but there was also something altogether insubstantial about her, as if she might blow away in the slightest breeze. When she ran, it sometimes seemed as though she were floating – skimming over the ground like the ghost of a giant dragonfly. Alyssa's body, like her mind, often seemed only loosely tethered to the world.

'It isn't in my cell,' she announced now, looking puzzled.

Terrel was not surprised by this unexpected statement. Alyssa often began conversations in the middle, assuming that her companion had 'heard' her earlier thoughts on the subject. Many people found this extremely irritating, but Terrel was used to it, and even enjoyed the challenges it posed.

'Do you think someone might have taken it?' she went on, fingering her left ear in an abstracted fashion.

'I doubt it.' He already had a good idea of what she was talking about – she had few enough valued possessions – but he wouldn't spoil the game by asking her outright. 'Where did you last see it?'

'I took it off before we went to work for Ahmeza yesterday, but I don't know where I put it.'

Ahmeza was Havenmoon's head cook, a paradoxically stick-like and permanently angry woman who ruled her steam-filled domain like a tyrant. Terrel and Alyssa had both been on kitchen duty last evening, a chore they disliked.

'Well, if we don't find it we can always make another,' Terrel said. In fact he had already decided to make another earring to replace the one Alyssa had evidently lost. It would make him feel good to give her a present.

'When?' she asked abruptly.

'I don't know yet.'

This answer did not seem to satisfy her.

'I don't feel right without it,' she complained, looking crestfallen and touching her ear again.

The missing earring – Alyssa only ever wore one – had been made from a small, twisted piece of wood. She'd carved and polished it herself, and fixed a wire hook to the top, before making a hole in her earlobe using a tiny nail. The fact that this *hurt* and produced a short-lived flow of blood had seemed to surprise her. Terrel had found her crying, and comforted her as best he could, cleaning the wound and enlisting the help of one of the female warders, who wore earrings of her own. That had been more than a year ago, and since then Alyssa had rarely been without her only piece of jewellery.

'It could still turn up,' Terrel consoled her.

'I don't feel right,' Alyssa repeated.

As always, any hint of unhappiness in her face made Terrel want to go to her aid, to make everything all right for her. There had been so many huge tragedies in her life that any small ones seemed unbearable to him.

'What about something else?' he suggested. 'Until the new one is ready.'

'What?' she asked, her expression brightening immediately.

'Um . . .' Terrel mumbled, looking around his sparse furnishings for something he could fashion into a necklace, a ring – anything.

Alyssa fished a tiny piece of twine from her pocket and held it up.

'Could this help?' she asked hopefully.

The string was barely longer than one of her fingers and didn't seem very promising, but then Terrel had a flash of inspiration. A piece of thread had come loose from one of the seams of his nightshirt and he pulled this free, then held out his good hand for the twine. Alyssa gave it to him and watched, engrossed, as he began to weave them together.

'That too,' she said, pointing.

Terrel twisted round and saw one of his own brown hairs on the pillow. Feeling rather self-conscious now, he added this third strand to the plait, but then found he could not tie the necessary knot. He had adjusted to the limitations of his withered right arm for most things, but such delicate work was beyond him. He passed it over to Alyssa. Even she found it difficult, with the weave constantly threatening to unravel, but she succeeded eventually, and held up the new ring triumphantly.

'You put it on,' she said.

'Which finger?'

'That one,' she replied, indicating the third finger on her left hand.

Alyssa was smiling, looking directly into Terrel's eyes. She was the only one who ever did that. Even in Havenmoon, where the grotesque was commonplace, Terrel's eyes were a source of unease for inmates and staff alike. He understood why, and had developed something of a squint in his efforts to keep them hidden, but Alyssa actually seemed to *like* looking into them. And as she did so now, her own eyes – which could not have been more different from his, and which often seemed to be the only solid part of her – were as disconcertingly candid as ever.

Awkwardly, Terrel positioned the ring over the tip of her finger, then rolled it down until it fitted snugly at the bottom. Alyssa looked at it happily then glanced up again, smiling mischievously.

'That means you have to marry me now,' she said, and laughed in delight as Terrel blushed crimson.

CHAPTER TWO

'This stinks!' Elam complained, his voice filled with disgust.

'You don't say,' Terrel muttered.

The two boys had been assigned to mucking out the stables, a job they hated at the best of times – and these were definitely not the best of times. The day was hot, even for summer, and so still that there was no breeze to cool them or lessen the all-pervading stench. Dust from the straw irritated their throats and made their eyes water – and rubbing their faces with hands that were already filthy only made matters worse. There were flies everywhere.

'It's not fair,' Elam moaned. 'Why do *we* get lumbered with all the lousy jobs?'

Terrel could have told him why, but he was saving his breath – and he knew that the question had been rhetorical. Life within the madhouse was not fair, as they both had reason to know. In some ways, however, the two friends were luckier than many inmates.

'The sooner we finish, the sooner we can get out of here,' he said, lifting another shovelful of manure from the

stall and dumping it into the small cart. The handle of his
spade was wedged under his withered right arm, while his
left hand held the shaft lower down and guided the tool
back and forth. Lifting each new load meant that Terrel
had to bend his entire body, then straighten up and twist
to the side in order to reach the cart. To an observer who
did not know of his disabilities this would seem a particularly laborious method, perhaps even slightly comical, but
Terrel was used to it. Even so, it was heavy work, and he
was sweating profusely. Elam was toiling too, each new
effort causing him pain. He would never have admitted it,
but Terrel could see it in the way the other boy moved, in
his laboured breathing, and he felt another jolt of anger at
the injustice with which the world had treated both himself and his friend.

At just ten years of age, Elam had been committed to
the madhouse for stealing potatoes. Although the potatoes
in question had been left to rot in a muddy field, and
Elam's family were on the brink of starvation at the time,
his actions had been not only illegal but also in direct con-
travention of astrological lore. This stated that all root
crops must be sown only when two or more of the moons
were waning, and harvested only when two or more were
waxing. (The opposite was true for crops that grew above
ground.) On the night of Elam's arrest, all three visible
moons had been waning – which was why the potatoes had
been left to rot – and this flagrant disregard for the taboo
had angered the authorities. Under imperial law, the boy
had been too young to be imprisoned, but the seriousness
of his crime was such that the local magistrate had ignored
the mitigating circumstances and declared him insane –
justifying his own actions by claiming that only an addled
brain could have conceived of such a heinous act.

For the next two years Elam had languished in a cold,

damp cell in the lower reaches of the house, his limbs chained to the walls. His once lithe muscles had atrophied, and his joints had become stiff and painful. The appointment of a new Head Warden — who held slightly more enlightened views about heretical behaviour — meant that Elam was eventually released from this barbaric torment, but by then the damage was done. Although he had slowly regained some of his former strength, cold weather or any form of strenuous exercise brought the pain back, so that he often moved like an old man. When Elam and Terrel had first met, each had thought the other to be mocking his own graceless movements, and they had fought as enemies. Gradually, however, as they learnt the truth, they realized that they had much in common. Their eventual friendship was all the more devoted because of its troubled beginnings. Now, three years later, they were like brothers.

'How many more after this one?' Elam asked as they cleared the last of the soiled straw from the stall.

'Three.'

Elam swore softly, but with feeling. There were usually only a few horses kept in the stables. Most of the staff who did not live in the house walked to work across the moor that surrounded the estate. None of them could have afforded their own mounts anyway. But in the last few days there had been many more visitors than usual, and their animals required temporary lodgings. Neither Terrel nor Elam knew who the outsiders had come to see.

'*We* never get any visitors,' Elam muttered, 'but we still have to clean up after them!'

One of the things the two boys had in common was that they had both been abandoned by their respective families. Terrel had never known his, while Elam's had not lifted a finger to help him since his arrest. In truth there was little that they could have done, but they had not even tried to contact him and his resentment was simmering still. His bitterness was compounded by guilt, partly at having allowed himself to get caught, and partly because he had no idea what had happened to his family since his incarceration. For all he knew they might all be dead; in his darkest moods, he almost wished they were.

'No one would ever want to come here from choice,' Terrel pointed out. 'They're too afraid of us lunatics.'

'Hah! I sometimes think it'd be better if we *were* mad,' Elam grated. 'They don't make Old Timi shovel shit, do they?'

Old Timi was one of the most ancient residents of Havenmoon. He had been there for decades, and his peculiarities were legendary. He claimed to receive messages from other worlds every time he touched a green leaf or a blade of grass. He would refuse to eat any meal until some of the food had been smeared on each wall of the room – which did not endear him to the cleaning details – and at every full Red Moon he howled like a·wolf and tried to bite anyone who came too close. As he had no teeth left, he was no real danger, but he could make a nuisance of himself nonetheless.

Terrel shuddered at the thought of ending up like Old Timi, even though he knew Elam was not serious, and then banged his spade on the ground as another wave of anger swept over him. He and Elam were quite clearly sane – a fact that was tacitly acknowledged by Ziolka, the Head Warden, in the relative freedom he allowed them – so why should they remain incarcerated in this dreadful place? But Terrel was under no illusions that whoever had discarded him as a baby fourteen years ago would return for him now. He was not even sure he would want them to.

Two of the three remaining stalls were still occupied,

which meant spreading clean straw in new pens and then
swapping the mounts over. Terrel left this task to Elam
because his friend was indifferent to horses, having been
used to farm animals in his earlier life. Terrel disliked
horses, who grew nervous and fretful if he came too close.
He saw madness in their eyes – and, ironically, they probably saw something similar in his. Alyssa was the only one
who was quite at home with them. She never rode, but
could calm even the most fiery colt simply by talking to it
or stroking its neck. Although he was still smarting over
the trick she had played on him that morning, Terrel
wished that she were there now.

As the two boys went back to work, the warden who
had been watching over them went off duty and was
replaced by another. The stables were always guarded,
even though the only way out of the estate with a horse
was via the drawbridge over the moat and then through
the only gate in the wall. Because this was normally kept
locked, and the gatekeepers kept a constant watch there,
such an escape was impossible – but nonetheless a close
eye was always kept on any horses in the stables. The new
man, whose name was Ingo, strolled over now, a broad
grin on his face.

'Put your backs into it, lads. Got to have the place looking spick-and-span for tomorrow.'

'You could always lend us a hand,' Elam suggested caustically.

'I'd be glad to,' the warden replied, 'but I'm on duty.
Sorry about that.'

'Ha ha.'

'What's happening tomorrow?' Terrel asked.

'Some inspectors are coming,' Ingo informed them.
'From Makhaya. There'll be changes around here before
too long, you mark my words.'

'Yeah, well, when they make you Head Warden, don't forget to put in a good word for me,' Elam remarked sarcastically.

'Have this lot carted away by the end of my watch, and I might just do that.' Ingo wandered off again, whistling.

'That self-important clod has as much chance of becoming Head Warden as I do of being made Emperor,' Elam commented when Ingo was out of hearing. 'I've a good mind to bury him in a dung heap.'

'And what good will that do?'

'It'll make me feel better. Come on, I want to get this finished. For my sake, not his.'

Elam was still moaning as they struggled to complete the last stage of their task. Because neither of them had been able to face the thought of an extra journey, they had piled the handcart too high, making it even more cumbersome than usual and difficult to manoeuvre. Even with Elam pulling and Terrel pushing, their progress was agonizingly slow as they circled round the main house to the south. Going to the north would have been a much shorter route, albeit still circuitous, but it would have meant traversing the lower slopes of the small hill which was topped by the Necropolis – and the appalling prospect of the cart toppling over sideways.

'You'd have thought the people who built this place would've had the sense to put the stables and the kitchen gardens close to each other,' Elam grumbled breathlessly. 'Not on opposite sides of the house!'

The mansion had once been the home of a long-extinct noble family. When their line had ended, the Havenmoon Estate would have fallen into ruin had it not been for the need for a remote place to hide away the province's lunatics. Even the name had suggested such a use.

Havenmoon remained its official title – though the local people had other, more colourful names for the place – but in common parlance, and with an unconscious irony, the house was generally referred to as 'the haven'. The building's aristocratic past was all but forgotten now, but it was this that accounted for many of its eccentric features. Terrel knew its secrets better than most; he had spent his entire life there, after all. There were few rooms or corridors he had not visited at one time or another and – more importantly – he knew where *not* to go. Some of the dungeon cells, which had once been wine cellars, held sights he had no wish to see.

'I expect they didn't think of things like that,' he said now. 'That's what servants were for.'

'Slaves like us, you mean. Look out!'

They both winced as one of the cart's wheels struck a rut, and they had to move quickly to prevent it tipping over. Elam's litany of grievances continued, his increasingly fertile invective being directed at their task, the cart, the pain in his knees, the weather, fate in general, and even his own family.

'At least you *had* a family once,' Terrel said. His friend's embittered mood had infected him now, and he too was brooding. '*My* parents didn't even keep me long enough to give me a name!'

Terrel's name had been the choice of the wet nurse, a young woman from a nearby village who had been paid to come to the madhouse and tend to him after her own baby died. In the old tongue of the region, his name meant 'light of the new moon', and – even though the moons had all been *full* on the night of his birth – it seemed ecrily appropriate to anyone who looked into the child's uncanny eyes. The wet nurse had been paid for her services out of the 'donation' left with the baby – the anonymous blood money that the warden had accepted on the assumption that the infant was simply one more inconvenient off-spring of a well-to-do family. When Terrel arrived, no one had believed that he would live more than a few weeks, but he had proved them wrong. The human spirit ran strongly inside his twisted shell.

'Fate didn't deal either of us a particularly good hand, did it,' Elam muttered.

'I'm not sure we were given any cards at all,' Terrel replied sourly. 'Sometimes I hate the world so much I wish I could destroy it all.'

Their black mood lasted until the last of the manure had finally been offloaded at the vegetable garden. Then, because there was still more than an hour before sunset, they were free to please themselves for a while, a privilege that marked them out as luckier than most inmates. Their depression began to lift as, without the need for any dis-cussion, they set off back round the house, making for the lake that lay in the eastern part of the grounds. The heat of the day was still considerable, making the lure of the water irresistible. In spite of their weariness and aching limbs, the boys' pace quickened as they crossed the path that led from the haven's main entrance to the gate at the southernmost point of the wall. From then on the land sloped gently down to the lake, whose edges were clogged with reeds and lily pads. Swimming would have been dif-ficult if it had not been for an old wooden jetty, which had once been used for boating, and which still led out to rel-atively clear water.

'What's *she* doing here?' Elam asked. 'She doesn't even like the water.'

Even from a distance, the figure sitting at the end of the small pier was easily recognized. Alyssa had her thin arms wrapped around her knees, which were drawn up in front of her. She was staring out over the lake.

'Waiting for us, I guess,' Terrel said.

'Let's sneak up on her and push her in.'

'No!' Even though he was fairly sure that Elam wasn't serious, the very idea filled Terrel with horror. Alyssa always refused to go in the water, no matter how hot the day. She would never explain why.

'All right, all right,' Elam said, looking disgusted. 'I didn't mean it.'

It took Terrel longer than Elam to remove his filthy outer garments, because of the special boot that had been made to fit his crooked right foot. The boot's slanting sole was much thicker at the toe, and the long laces – which were tied well above his ankle – had to be fully loosened before the difficult job of pulling it off could begin. As a result Elam was already in the lake, having run past the unsuspecting Alyssa and dived in, by the time Terrel limped to the end of the jetty.

'Did he splash you?' he asked.

'Not really,' she replied, smiling.

'Made you jump though, didn't I!' Elam called, sounding very pleased with himself.

Alyssa stuck her tongue out at him.

Terrel slipped into the water, delighting in the sudden coolness on his grimy skin, and paddled out to join Elam. The lake was always cold, even in summer, and there were supposed to be fish in its murky depths, but Terrel had never seen any. Neither of the boys was a strong swimmer. Because of the weakness of his whole right side, Terrel would go round in circles unless he concentrated, and though Elam made dogged progress, the chill usually affected his joints before long. Terrel suspected that, if it hadn't been for her aversion to water, Alyssa would have been a better swimmer than either of them. After all – and much to their chagrin – she could easily outrun them both, and was so light that she would probably float easily.

'I think I'll swim to the island,' Elam stated boldly. 'Are you coming?'

'No. It's too far for me.'

The tiny island lay towards the northern end of the pear-shaped lake. Long ago, a small round tower – a nobleman's folly – had been built there, but now it was just a crumbling ruin, surrounded by spindly trees. It looked a peaceful enough place, though there were several quite gruesome legends connected with the island.

'What about you, Alyssa?' Elam called.

'No, thank you,' she replied demurely.

'Why not?'

'Because I don't want to.'

'Because it's haunted?' he teased.

'Everywhere's haunted,' she responded quietly.

Terrel knew that Alyssa frequently talked to ghosts; it was one of the reasons for her having been confined to the madhouse. Although most children grew out of their invisible companions, she had persisted in the one-sided conversations. According to her, she had learnt a lot this way, especially from her dead grandmother – including some things she couldn't possibly have known otherwise. Her strange behaviour had finally exhausted the patience of the living members of her family, and had eventually led to her being diagnosed as insane.

Terrel wasn't sure what to make of Alyssa's claims. He was sure she wouldn't lie deliberately, but he had never seen the faintest flicker of a ghostly presence even when – according to Alyssa – one was apparently standing right in front of him. Naturally they had talked about this a good deal, and she had told him – among other things – that some of the other inmates carried their ghosts with them, and that some ghosts were 'real' while others were 'made up'. He'd never been able to clarify this distinction in his own mind, but it was obviously significant to Alyssa.

A short while later Elam, who had set off towards the island but then wisely thought better of it, pulled himself out and sat down on the jetty to let the last of the day's sunlight warm him. He moved close to Alyssa, taking advantage of the strange fact that none of the clouds of mosquitoes, which swirled above the surface of the lake, ever went near the girl. Terrel was still in the water, washing himself as best he could and trying to get the smell of horses out of his hair. The coolness of the water did not affect the aching in his limbs – which was there all the time – and he revelled in its silken embrace.

'That's only true if you accept that it's the same everywhere,' Alyssa stated abruptly.

'What is?' Elam asked, obviously mystified.

'Maybe not all rivers run downhill in other parts of the world,' she added, ignoring him.

'What *are* you talking about?' he persisted.

'Perhaps islands don't float.'

'But islands *do* float,' Terrel said. 'So that they can move. They're supposed to.'

'That one doesn't,' Alyssa commented, pointing.

'That's different,' Elam said. 'It's only in a lake, not the sea, so it doesn't have to float.'

'All the islands of the Empire float,' Terrel added.

'How can anything as big as Vadanis *float*?' she asked. 'It's hundreds of miles long. And it's made of rock. Rocks sink.'

'I don't know,' Terrel admitted. He had often asked himself the same question, but in the end it came down to a matter of faith. He believed that the Floating Islands moved. This was partly because everyone – almost everyone – believed it, and partly because he'd seen it explained in a book, complete with maps and diagrams.

'It just does,' Elam said impatiently. 'Only barbarians live on land that doesn't move. Everyone knows that.'

'You can tell Vadanis is moving in the ocean by watching the stars,' Terrel added knowledgeably.

'But how can you be sure of that?' Alyssa countered. 'Have you ever even seen the sea?'

'You know I've never been *anywhere*,' he replied bitterly, hurt that she would even ask him such a question.

'Then how do you know the sea's moving past Vadanis? How do you know it even exists?'

Terrel couldn't think of any answer to that.

'Have you ever seen Makhaya?' Elam asked her.

'No.'

'Does that mean it doesn't exist either?'

'Perhaps.'

'So if you can't see something, it just doesn't exist?' he suggested incredulously. 'What happens if you close your eyes? Do I vanish?'

'Of course!' she exclaimed, all wide-eyed innocence. She was baiting him now.

Elam threw up his arms in despair.

'Well, I've *been* to Makhaya,' he told her. 'I know it exists.'

'Maybe you were dreaming.'

'I give up. You talk to her, Terrel.'

'Are ghosts like that?' Terrel asked thoughtfully. 'Is that why we can't see them?'

'Oh, good grief,' Elam groaned. 'You two are hopeless!' He stomped off to retrieve his clothes.

'Ghosts walk differently,' Alyssa replied placidly. 'For you they're always just around the next corner.'

'Will I ever be able to see round the corner?' Terrel asked.

Alyssa shrugged.

'I'm not a seer,' she said.

Some time later, as sunset approached, the trio were walking back up the slope towards the house when Terrel came to a sudden halt.

'Come on,' Elam urged him. 'If we're not inside by curfew, someone'll tell Ziolka and we'll be stuck in our cells for days.'

Terrel didn't move, his eyes unusually wide but unfocused.

'We should go in,' Alyssa echoed, but her concern was evident in her voice. 'Or we'll all get into trouble.'

'No,' Terrel replied flatly. 'We should stay out here. In the open.' Something deep inside him was trembling, but on the surface he was calm, and sure of himself for once.

'Why?'

'There's going to be an earthquake.'

CHAPTER THREE

The tremor did not last long, but it was much stronger than usual. If it had not been for Terrel's premonition, the three friends might have fallen as the ground beneath them shook and growled. As it was, they were badly disorientated, and staggered drunkenly for a few moments. Tiles fell from the roof of the house, adding their brittle crashing to the hollow rumbling noise that seemed to come from deep within the earth itself. Finally, just as it seemed that the quake was ending, a stone balustrade on a second floor balcony crumbled and fell to the ground, close to the door that the trio had been heading for. Heavy pieces of masonry thudded onto the paving below and shattered, peppering the surrounding area with flying splinters of stone.

'Moons!' Elam gasped. 'That was close. We could've been under that lot.'

A brief silence enveloped them as the world became still once more, then the sound of agitated voices drifted from inside the building. The earthquake had been completely unexpected, and had taken everyone by surprise.

'The seers must be losing their touch,' Elam commented, regaining some self-confidence.

Everyone who lived on the Floating Islands was used to the regular, minor tremors that occurred with a frequency determined by the aspects of the four moons. The astrologers had calculated the lunar pattern for many years in advance and, forewarned, the populace generally took the earthquakes in their stride. But this one had not been foreseen by anyone – except Terrel.

'You saw it coming, didn't you,' Alyssa said.

'How did you do that?' Elam asked.

'I don't know,' Terrel replied. 'I just . . .' He shrugged, incapable of describing what he had felt. 'I don't know.'

'A sort of tugging?' Alyssa said. 'I suppose so.'

The two boys looked at her.

'No, I didn't. At least I don't think so,' she went on. 'But Terrel might have.'

'What?'

'I wasn't talking to you,' she told him calmly.

'It's one of her ghosts,' Elam said, rolling his eyes.

'What I don't understand is how *you* felt it,' Alyssa added, ignoring Elam's derision. Then, after a pause in which she appeared to be listening intently to the silence, she said, 'All right. Farewell, Sevin.'

'Not him again!' Elam exclaimed.

'What was all that about?' Terrel asked.

'Some of the ghosts felt the warning too.'

'But they're in a different world,' Terrel objected, repeating what she had often told him.

'I know,' she replied. 'I don't understand it, and neither do they.'

'You haven't become a ghost and not told us, have you?' Elam asked Terrel facetiously.

'What did Sevin say?'

'That it was like the moons, but different.'

'Sevin's obviously as mad now as when he was alive,' Elam commented. 'No wonder they locked him up here.'

Alyssa gave him a pitying look.

'Like you, you mean?' she asked innocently.

'We'd better get inside,' Terrel said hurriedly. He was aware that the sun had set during their conversation, and their need to obey the curfew would forestall any argument.

As they went in, glancing up to make sure no more masonry was going to fall on them, Terrel saw the semi-circular shape of the Red Moon in the darkening sky. Nearer to the horizon the Amber Moon was a pale crescent rising in the east, and Terrel's final thought before he entered the shadowed world of the haven was to wonder what this night's dreams would bring.

Terrel was back in his cell well before he was locked in for the night, and no one made anything of the fact that he and his friends had broken the curfew. The turnkey made his rounds much later than usual that night, and Terrel assumed that the unexpected tremor had disrupted normal routines. To his annoyance, he found this unsettling.

The truth was that he found comfort in the regular patterns of his confinement. Because he was one of the inmates who had been classified as harmless, during the day he was free to wander within the boundaries of Havenmoon's self-contained world – unless he was being punished for something or was needed to work. Terrel knew that this privilege could easily be revoked, and because he did not want to end up like so many of the other inmates – who were permanently incarcerated in conditions that varied from the mind-numbingly boring to the downright horrific – he submitted to being locked up like a criminal each night without any thought of complaint. In one sense he had been alone all his life, and dealing with solitude came easily to him.

There had been times when he'd thought of trying to escape, but those times were long gone. In truth, Terrel was no longer sure that he would want to leave – even if he could do so as a free man. He had never known anything except the haven, never even seen beyond its high stone wall. His only knowledge of the outside world had come from books, and it seemed a strange and frightening place, full of inexplicable cruelties and daunting complexities. He was better off where he was.

He sometimes felt cowardly for thinking this way, but consoled himself with the fact that at least now he had the companionship of two people his own age – until he was ten his life had been almost entirely solitary – and that neither Elam nor Alyssa seemed to have any thoughts of escaping. The idea did not seem even to have occurred to Alyssa and, while Elam sometimes spoke of it, he – like Terrel – was aware that the chances of success were extremely remote. And failure would send him back to the dungeons, and to the tortures he had endured there.

Most inmates of the madhouse were either physically or mentally incapable of making an escape attempt, but anyone who tried faced almost insurmountable obstacles. Even if the wall and the moat which ran inside it were successfully negotiated without being seen by any of the guards, there was still the problem of having to trek across several miles of open moorland – which offered treacherous marshes and plentiful heather, but no food or shelter, and nowhere to hide. Anyone trying to use the only road, which ran south from the gate, would soon be recaptured, and taking any other route might mean days of fruitless toil. And even if all these hazards were overcome, each inmate had four concentric circles tattooed on the back of one of their hands — which marked them permanently as residents of the madhouse. Any stranger who arrived in one of the nearby villages and tried to hide his hands would be regarded with suspicion.

Terrel examined his own tattoo now. Someone had once told him that the circles represented the four moons, which seemed appropriate enough. Mental unbalance was not called 'lunacy' for nothing.

All around him, Havenmoon was strangely quiet. Even in the dead of night there were usually some sounds, especially when one or more of the moons was full, but the inmates were silent now, and even the old house itself was not producing its normal assortment of creaks and groans. It was as if the tremor had shaken everything into place and there was no need of more gradual adjustments.

And then, as if to challenge all Terrel's assumptions, Old Timi began to howl, giving voice to the wolf inside his feeble human frame. Although he sounded the same as always, the very fact that he was moved to howl at all was unnerving. Only half the Red Moon was visible that night; it would not be full for another eleven days.

It was just one more strange event, one more anomaly, in a day that had already seen too many for Terrel's liking.

Things are changing.

Terrel awoke with a start, unable to decide whether the words had been spoken aloud by himself or someone else, or whether they were just the tail end of a dream. Either way, the statement had a prophetic ring.

He was stiff and sore from the strenuous exercise of the previous day, but was relieved to find that any dreams that may have visited him in the night had left no mark on his memory. Sitting up, he saw from the sunlight in his cell's one high window that he had slept late for the second day in a row. Even so, he knew just from the feel of the room that the door was still locked. The turnkey was behind schedule again.

Terrel was feeling distinctly uneasy as he dressed, but then he remembered that the inspectors were arriving that day. Ziolka was probably keeping all his charges locked up while the official visit was in progress, to avoid any suggestion that his security was lax.

Once again the silence seemed deeper than usual, and as the morning drifted by Terrel could not help but recall his waking thought and Ingo's earlier words – *There'll be some changes around here* – and wondered what those changes might be.

Eventually, just before noon, he heard the clatter of several horsemen riding south towards the gate and, shortly after that, his door was finally unlocked. The turnkey offered no explanation for the change to his routine, but he did advise Terrel to make himself scarce unless he wanted to be pressed into service in the kitchen. Ahmeza's resources had been stretched to the limit by the recent influx of visitors, and she was on the warpath now, looking for 'volunteers' to help her make up for lost time.

Terrel took the hint gratefully. After checking on Alyssa's and Elam's cells – there was no sign of either – he made his way up to the second floor via a rarely used spiral staircase, and then climbed a ladder into the loft space beneath the tiled roof. Havenmoon's attic consisted of a large number of interconnecting rooms, all crisscrossed by beams and joists in apparently random patterns beneath irregularly placed stone buttresses. It was possible – if you were small enough, didn't mind cobwebs and watched where you put your feet – to traverse the entire length of the building from south to north. Terrel did so now. When he finally arrived at the trap door he was looking for, he paused, listening for a while before opening it. He had never known anyone else to come to the hidden room, and regarded it as his private preserve, but he didn't want to take any unnecessary risks. When he was convinced that all was safe, he pulled the door up and felt for the ladder he had left positioned below. Clambering down into the darkness always gave him a thrill of discovery, remembered from the first time he had come there. At the bottom he found the flint-box, and lit a taper and then two candles. In the still, musty air the flames burnt evenly, casting a yellow glow over the rows and rows of books.

Terrel had discovered the library several years earlier, and had been captivated at once. According to Ziolka – who either did not guess or did not care that Terrel had actually found it – the library had once belonged to an inmate who had died many years ago, and had not been used since then. Quite what a madman would have wanted with so many books had never occurred to Terrel; he had just taken advantage of the mouldering legacy, escaping to the library whenever he could, and laboriously teaching himself to read. He had become reasonably proficient, although some of the more erudite tomes were still beyond his understanding. He had returned now for two specific reasons, both related to the events of the previous day. The first, which stemmed from his conversation with Alyssa about the Floating Islands, was so that he could once more study the book that contained maps showing the islands' movement in the Movaghassi Ocean. The second was to see whether he could find some clue as to why there had been an earthquake yesterday when the islands were *not* changing course – which was the normal cause of such tremors.

He found the relevant volume quickly enough and, after studying several of the now familiar charts once more, he turned to the accompanying text.

For centuries, as long as human records have been kept, these linked islands have been adrift together in the Movaghassi Ocean, the largest of Nydus's seas. The islands move in stately fashion, on an irregular but predictable course, always steering clear of the various fixed land masses.

Why would anyone record such details, much less go to the trouble of plotting the incredibly complex patterns on the maps, if it wasn't true? Terrel read on.

Whether this admirable arrangement is due to mere good fortune or to some divine influence upon nature is beyond the scope of this treatise. However, the movement of the islands allows them to escape the rigours of geological and astrological disturbances that must plague other, less fortunate lands.

Were those 'disturbances' now somehow affecting the islands? Terrel wondered. And if so, why?

He went on reading for a long time, until his eyes grew weary and one of the candles guttered out. Although he had not found anything that would explain the abnormal earthquake, he had at least reconfirmed his belief in the nature of the Floating Islands. Whatever Alyssa said now, she would not be able to shake his conviction that the book's arguments – which were plausible and precise – were correct.

Terrel put the volume back on its shelf, snuffed out the remaining candle, and waited for his eyes to adjust to the almost complete darkness of the windowless room. Then he climbed the ladder and closed the trap door. Retracing his route back to the south wing, he emerged to find Elam waiting for him.

'Where've you been all day?' The boy looked weary, but there was a gleam of excitement in his eyes.

'Reading,' Terrel answered. Elam had never displayed any interest in the library, even though Terrel had often offered to show it to him.

'Lucky you. Some of us had to work,' Elam said, but without rancour.

'Did Ahmeza get you?'

'No, I escaped her clutches, but then Ingo dragged me off to help him cut wood.' The northern part of the estate was forested, and provided fuel for the kitchen and winter fires.

'And?' Terrel prompted, knowing that his friend's mood would not have been caused by the enforced collection of a few logs.

'That balcony wasn't the only thing the quake brought down,' Elam responded. 'Part of the fence round the Necropolis has fallen to pieces, and I was the only one who noticed.'

'So?'

'We could explore!' Elam exclaimed. 'Haven't you ever wondered what's up there?'

'It's only some old tombs.'

'Then why is it out of bounds?'

No one had ever *told* them as much, but the rusting iron fence, which was topped with nasty spikes, and the heavy locks on the only gate, had been eloquent enough. And the sides of the hill within the fence were so overgrown with low trees and shrubs – all of which seemed to bristle with thorns – that it amounted to another, jungle-like barrier. Only in winter, when the foliage was less dense, was it possible to catch a glimpse of stonework at the top of the slope.

'There's nothing up there,' Terrel said, trying to hide the unease he felt at the idea of entering that realm of the dead.

Elam was not fooled, and grinned eagerly.

'If you're scared, we can take Alyssa with us,' he said. 'If there are any ghosts, she can talk to them and tell them we're friendly.'

'She won't want—'

'She's already agreed,' Elam stated triumphantly.

Terrel had no choice now. He knew that he would find it unbearably humiliating if Elam and Alyssa went without him – even though he didn't think they'd find anything interesting.

'All right,' he mumbled. 'When?'

'As soon as we can get away. There's a rumour going round that Ziolka might be replaced soon, and we don't know what the new man will be like.'

The implication that their limited freedom might be further curtailed was not lost on Terrel.

'We'd better have some adventures while we still can,' Elam added, grinning.

CHAPTER FOUR

Their chance came the very next day. The news brought from Makhaya was clearly preoccupying Ziolka and his staff, and as a result Terrel and his friends found themselves left to their own devices. Taking advantage of this piece of luck, they set off as if heading for the lake, then turned north and skirted round the edge of the estate until they reached the far side of the hill. It was here that a section of the iron fence had collapsed – which would allow them to climb the slope without any possibility of their being seen from the house. Elam led them through the long grass and bracken to the spot where a small landslide had gouged away a section of the hill, destroying part of the fence in the process. Here they paused, already warm from their circuitous walk and the steadily rising heat of the day.

'Are you sure you still want to do this?' Terrel asked, looking at the dense undergrowth in the forbidden territory ahead of them.

'Of course,' Elam replied scornfully. 'No one up there's going to be any danger to us.'

'That doesn't mean we have the right to disturb them.'

'I doubt they'll even know we're there. Being dead means you don't generally notice very much.'

'There are no bad feelings here,' Alyssa stated in her dreamy fashion.

Elam raised his eyebrows and stared at Terrel as if to say 'You see! Even she agrees.'

'You'd know that if you listened properly,' Alyssa added.

All Terrel could hear were the songs of a few birds, and the faint rustling of leaves.

'Come on then,' he said, knowing that this was an argument he couldn't win. He wasn't even sure he wanted to; a little of the excitement that was obviously affecting Elam had belatedly rubbed off on him.

They clambered over the newly fallen boulders and loose soil, passed the twisted ends of the remaining fence, and entered an alien world. Any human influence had been lost long ago; even if this had once been an orderly graveyard, it was a wilderness now. Elam led them in single file, threading their way through rowan, ash and blackthorn, while trying to avoid the worst of the gorse and brambles. Their progress was slow and frustrating, with thorns snagging on clothes and scratching skin. On several occasions the undergrowth became so thick that they had to backtrack and try another route, while various birds scolded them from the branches above.

'I hope this is worth it,' Terrel said as he carefully disentangled himself from the latest thorns caught on his sleeve.

'Me too,' Elam muttered. The adventure had evidently begun to lose some of its appeal for him.

'We're nearly there,' Alyssa said.

'Where?' Elam queried. 'Oh!'

He had not even seen the tomb until he practically bumped into it. The monument was built of stone and had once been intricately carved, but the surfaces had been eroded to such an extent that the decorations or lettering were now nothing more than a random pattern of indentations. Even so, its size and solidity were impressive, and once the three friends had edged their way past it, they could see several more tombs dotted about the hillside.

The air about them was now perfumed with the heady scent of summer flowers. There were lots of rose bushes, which had run wild everywhere, and several other blooms that Terrel could not identify but which all added bright flashes of colour to the scene. Amid this floral profusion, the tombs lay in a state of disrepair, but by the time the trio had gone a little further they had forgotten about the graves. As they neared the top of the hill the trees thinned out, and in a glade at the summit was the most curious building any of them had ever seen.

It consisted of a single storey, built low to the ground – which was why they had not been able to see it from below. The roof of the square structure supported what had evidently once been a semi-spherical dome of some kind. This dome had split open and a good part had presumably fallen in, leaving a jagged shape like the edges of a broken eggshell. It gave the place a desolated, neglected air.

'Funny sort of tomb,' Elam remarked.

They had stopped on the edge of the clearing, and even though nothing more than bracken and furze lay between them and the building, they were all a little reluctant to move closer.

'It must've been for someone important,' Terrel guessed. 'It's much bigger than any of the others.'

'You'd have thought he'd have paid up for a better roof then,' Elam commented.

'This isn't a tomb,' Alyssa stated quietly. 'It was built for the living.'

'But there aren't any windows,' Elam objected. 'Who'd want to be in the dark all the time?'

'And who'd want to live *here*?' Terrel added. 'In the middle of a cemetery?'

'You don't need windows if you can open the roof. And if you're looking for peace and quiet, where better than among the dead?' Alyssa replied, answering both their questions in one go.

'What do you mean, "open the roof"?' Elam asked, looking at the crooked outline again.

'Come on,' she replied. 'I'll show you. There has to be a way in somewhere.'

They circled round and, just as Alyssa had predicted, found a simple wooden door. As they drew closer, Alyssa – who was in the lead now – came to an abrupt halt, and the boys soon saw what had made her hesitate. Next to the doorway, half hidden by long grass, was a skeleton. It had evidently been there a very long time; the bones were clean, bleached a pure white by the sun and rain, but it was still more or less intact. A few of the smallest bones had fallen away, but the larger ones were still in the positions they had assumed in life. The skeleton was sitting on the ground, its spine resting against the wall, with long legs stretched out in front and crossed casually at the ankles. The skull was tipped forward so that the jawbone rested on the breastbone, and what was left of the hands lay in what had once been its lap. More remarkable still, a small clay pipe was cradled within one of those hands.

'He looks as though he stepped out for a smoke and just fell asleep,' Elam said, his voice uncharacteristically solemn.

'Maybe he did,' Alyssa said.

'Not a bad way to go,' the young boy commented quietly.

Terrel wanted to ask if he was still there, if his ghost still inhabited the strange home that he had presumably occupied in life. But he found himself unaccountably moved, and unable to speak past the lump in his throat.

'He's moved on,' Alyssa said, answering his unspoken question. 'He has no reason to come back here.'

It was very quiet now on the hilltop. Even the birds seemed to have fallen silent.

'Well, are we going inside?' Elam asked eventually.

Alyssa nodded, and together they moved forward and began to push at the door. Although it was not locked, the wood had warped so that it scraped across the stone floor inside, making it difficult to open. As they pushed, Terrel squatted down next to the skeleton, and stared at the blank face. There was a macabre kind of peace in those empty eye sockets, but he sensed something more, some unfinished business, and was swept by another wave of emotion. It was not quite sadness, not quite regret, but a kind of unrealized longing. On impulse he reached out and took the pipe, slipping it into his pocket.

'Wow! Terrel, come and look at this!' Elam called. He and Alyssa had managed to open the door enough for them to squeeze by.

Terrel stood up and went in, seeing immediately what had excited Elam. In the centre of the large square room, dominating everything around it, stood a complicated metal apparatus supporting a long brass tube. The tube was set at an angle, its upper end pointing out towards the gaping hole in the roof.

'What is it?' Elam asked.

'I think it's a telescope.'

'A what?'

'The astrologers use them to look at the moons and stars. It makes them bigger. This must have been an observatory.' Terrel understood the roof's strange design now. Looking round, he saw another contraption off to one side, its winding handles connected via ratchets and chain pulleys to the curving doors that had once formed the movable roof. The roof had long since fallen into disrepair, and part of it had collapsed, adding to the litter strewn upon the floor.

'Will it make *us* bigger?' Alyssa asked.

'What?' Terrel was confused.

'The telescope. You said it made the astrologers bigger.'

'No, silly,' he laughed. 'It makes what you're *looking* at bigger, not you.' He thought about this, and added, 'Actually, it only makes it *seem* bigger, so you can see more detail.'

'Oh, you mean it bends light,' Alyssa said, her tone now matter-of-fact.

Terrel stared at her. His friend had virtually no education, could not even read, but every so often she came out with astonishing remarks like that one – and made him feel stupid.

'Does it still work?' Elam asked.

Terrel twisted himself into position, and put his eye to the lower end of the tube. All he could see was a circle of brightness.

'I think so,' he said. 'But we can't see anything during the day. I'd only be able to tell properly at night.'

'That's not much use then, if we're stuck inside with the curfew.' Elam replaced his friend and peered through the telescope briefly, then lost interest and went to examine the other contents of the room.

Terrel was still absorbed in studying the apparatus, and spent some time trying to work out what its various wheels and levers were for. It seemed obvious to him that they were designed to enable the operator to move the telescope – it wouldn't be much use if you could only look at one point in the sky, after all – but either he was doing something wrong or the entire construction was so corroded that the rust had set it solidly in place. He had no idea how long the rain might have been falling through the open roof, but suspected it was many years. Feeling disappointed, he joined the others in exploring the rest of the room.

There were bird droppings all over the floor, and a few small bones and feathers, as well as fragments of wood and metal. The remains of a narrow bed lay in one corner, its rotten frame patched with mildew and fungi. A once sturdy table had fared better. It was still standing at least, its surface even more cluttered and dirty than the floor. Among the debris Terrel picked out several tools, a small bottle stained with what might once have been ink, several pieces of wire, and what at first glance seemed to be a collection of curiously symmetrical pebbles. However, when he picked one of these up and rubbed a little of the grime from its surface, he soon discovered that it was a piece of clear glass or crystal, beautifully cut in facets. It might have been an experimental lens for a telescope, but Terrel had immediately thought of another idea for its use. He slipped the crystal into his pocket.

The only other item in the observatory to have withstood the depredations of time was a large, iron-bound chest, and it was this that now occupied Elam and Alyssa. There was apparently no lock, and the leather straps that must once have held it closed were now no more than a few mouldering tatters but, try as they might, they could not get the lid to budge at all. It was Terrel who solved the problem, finding two pieces of metal – one thin and sharp, the other a solid lump – and using them like a chisel and hammer. The blade was gradually driven into the crack below the lid, and worked round until, with a loud creak and a sudden exhalation of stale air – as if the chest were sighing – the lid shifted. The musty smell from inside was instantly familiar to Terrel and his sense of excitement intensified, but Elam's reaction to the contents of the trunk was quite different.

'Books!' he exclaimed in disgust. 'Is that all there is?'

'What did you expect?' Terrel asked. 'Gold and jewels?'

Elam shrugged.

'Something interesting, at least,' he said.

As Elam wandered off, Terrel pulled one of the volumes out of the trunk, handling it with great care. The leather binding was still in good condition, and the edges of the pages within weren't too badly discoloured. There was nothing on the cover to indicate what the book contained, but when Terrel gently prised it open he saw that the first page had been inscribed simply with a date – 'At17'.

'The seventeenth year in the reign of Emperor Ataman,' he translated, then thought for a moment. 'That's over four hundred years ago!'

'What's that down there?' Alyssa asked, pointing to a word scrawled at the bottom of the page.

'It looks like "Muzeni". Do you think that was his name? The man who lived here, I mean.'

'Could be.'

'And these are his journals,' Terrel concluded. 'This is incredible!' He turned to the next page, and found it covered with tiny but perfectly legible script.

'Read it to me.'

Terrel nodded and began.

'"History will prove me right. Just as the moons orbit Nydus, so this planet orbits the sun. (If this truth is damned as the 'belief' of a madman and I am confined here, so be it. Truth is not altered.) Our sun is a star like millions of others. It only appears so big and so bright to us because it is so much <u>closer</u> than any of the others. Yet it <u>is</u> big, far larger than this planet – and the rules governing the columns of attraction, that determine the motions of the stars, decree that the smaller object falls under the influence of the larger."' Terrel paused. 'In his time most people thought the sun went round Nydus,' he explained. 'Everyone knows it's the other way round now, but then it was considered blasphemy. History *did* prove him right.'

'What are "columns of attraction"?' Alyssa asked.

'I don't know. Maybe he'll tell us.' Terrel turned back to the journal. ' "The seers who call themselves scientists are nothing but deluded incompetents, as were the short-sighted fools who less than a century ago believed that only three moons existed, and refused to countenance the possibility of a fourth simply because they could not see it." '

'He sounds really angry,' Alyssa commented.

'And he couldn't hide it,' Terrel agreed. 'Which is probably why he ended up here.'

'I wonder how long he lived here?'

'Judging by the number of journals, I'd say quite a long time.' Terrel began turning pages and glancing at the contents. There were columns of figures, tables and charts, and diagrams of stars, as well as other, stranger notations. 'There's so *much* in here! If the others are the same, it could take years just to read them all.'

'Do you think we're the first to find them?' Alyssa asked. 'In all this time?'

'Probably.' It was a melancholy thought.

'So no one knows what else he discovered?'

'No. But I'm going to find out,' Terrel vowed.

Before he could read on, or look at any of the other volumes, he was distracted by a sudden shout which seemed to come from above.

'Get away from me!'

A moment later there was a loud thump, followed by another shout — and then a large chunk of the dome crashed down into the room. Terrel and Alyssa shrank back as bits of wood flew in all directions, and it was only when the dust had cleared that they saw Elam, lying quite still in the midst of the debris.

CHAPTER FIVE

Terrel and Alyssa hurried to Elam's side. He was breathing, but the fall had knocked him unconscious and a small cut just above his left eye was bleeding profusely. Terrel pressed a finger to the wound to stem the flow, and glanced up at the roof.

'We'd better move him in case any more falls in.'

By the time they had half carried, half dragged him to the side of the room, the bleeding had stopped. A few moments later, Elam groaned and opened his eyes.

'What hurts?' Terrel asked.

'Everything.'

'I don't think you've broken any bones, but try to move a little.'

Elam flexed his limbs gingerly.

'You're lucky,' Terrel concluded. 'Just bumps and bruises. What were you doing up there?'

'Just looking around. You can see over the wall from the roof.'

'How did you get up there?' Alyssa asked.

'There are rungs set in the wall outside, just round the

corner from the door.' Elam's eyes flickered and he raised an accusing finger. 'I was just looking, and then that *thing* attacked me.'

His companions glanced round. A large tawny owl was perched on the edge of the ruined roof, regarding them with intense black eyes. At the sound of Elam's angry voice it had raised itself up in alarm, but now it relaxed again, obviously deciding that he was no longer a threat.

'An owl?' Terrel exclaimed, trying hard not to laugh. 'I thought you'd seen a ghost.'

'The filthy creature flew in my face,' Elam said, remembering a sudden whirlwind of feathers and talons. 'I lost my balance.' He picked up a piece of wood and tried to sit up, meaning to hurl it at his assailant, but Alyssa caught his arm, and the renewed pain in his head made him think better of it. 'I'll get you next time,' he muttered venomously.

The owl did not move, but gave a long wavering hoot, followed by several sharp clicks.

'She was only trying to protect her young,' Alyssa said.

'How do you know?' Terrel asked.

'She just told me. The nest is in the other part of the dome, over there. Elam came too close, that's all.'

'How was I supposed to know?' Elam grumbled. Neither he nor Terrel doubted the nature of the communication between Alyssa and the owl. All animals reacted to her in remarkable ways.

'It's all right,' she went on. 'I've told her we mean no harm. As long as we avoid the nest, she won't attack again.'

The bird blinked twice, then flew off out of sight. Terrel turned back to Elam.

'How are you feeling?'

'Terrible.'

'Rest there a while. When you feel like moving, we'd better think about getting back.'

It was already past noon. Terrel knew that the longer they were away the more likely it was that questions would be asked about their absence – and he wanted the observatory to remain their secret.

Leaving Alyssa with their patient, Terrel retrieved Muzeni's book and leafed through it, reading occasional passages. It was hard to believe that it had been written so long ago, by the heretic whose skeleton lay just outside the door, but he couldn't think of any better explanation. Many of the sections he was drawn to were similar to those he had read in some of the books in the library, while others were quite new to him – and a few were quite frightening in their implications. One paragraph in particular, which was on a page opposite some indecipherable hieroglyphics, was very ominous in tone.

'I regret I will not live to see the Guardian born, for when that happens all our fates will be decided. If I am right, and conventional wisdom wrong, then the Code is predicting events that are astronomically impossible. So which is wrong, the prophecy or science? Either way, the consequences will be dire. (Even the court dullards see that!) It is hard to imagine destruction on such a scale.'

After that, Terrel lost his appetite for reading and became restless. When he glanced over at Alyssa, she smiled at him.

'Go on,' she said. 'The owl's asleep again. She won't bother you unless you disturb her.'

Terrel was no longer surprised when Alyssa knew what he wanted to do even before he did himself. He went outside, walked carefully round the skeleton, and found the metal rungs. Once he reached the top of the ladder, he kept to the edge of the roof, well away from the dome and the bird's nest. From his vantage point he could just catch glimpses of the roof of the main house, the far end of the lake, and parts of the grounds. But it was the view to the northeast, where the perimeter wall ran closest to the hill, that held his attention.

The open moor stretched away into the distance, a mixture of brown earth tones and purple heather, with bright patches of green in the wet marshes. In the hazy distance, Terrel could just make out the shapes of grey rolling hills. As far as he could see, there was no sign of any human influence on the land, which looked wild and forbidding even in the gentle sunshine. But it was still a source of wonder to him. It was his first sight of the outside world.

When he returned to his companions, Elam was sitting up, his back propped against the wall, and there was more colour in his cheeks. Taking one hand each, Terrel and Alyssa pulled him to his feet. Although he groaned again, he seemed reasonably steady, and they set off. Before Terrel left, he picked up the journal, wishing he could take all the books with him, and closed the lid of the chest.

'We ought to shut the door again,' he said once they were outside.

He and Alyssa managed to pull it to between them. The last part closed in a rush, so that the wood slammed into the door frame with a force that shook the walls. To their horror, this disturbed the skeleton and the skull toppled forward, taking the ribs with it like a ball scattering skittles. Then the spine and the arms collapsed too, leaving only a jumbled pile of bones on the ground.

No one spoke for several heartbeats. Then Elam cleared his throat.

'I guess his watch is over.'

Terrel nodded, knowing what his friend meant. The heretic's time was gone, and by coming here they had accepted the responsibility for his legacy. It weighed heavily on his shoulders.

'He wasn't much use as a sentry anyway,' Elam went on flippantly.

'Goodbye, Muzeni,' Alyssa said quietly, and with that the three friends began their journey back through the collection of crumbling mausoleums.

'If anyone asks, you were climbing a tree and fell out of it,' Terrel told Elam, as they entered the house. 'How are you feeling now?'

'Dizzy.'

Their roundabout route had taken them close to the stables, where one of the wardens had come out to enlist Alyssa's help in calming a restless pony, so the two boys had gone on without her. So far no one had paid them any attention.

'Are you sure you'll be all right?' Terrel asked, after he had helped Elam to his cell and on to his bed.

'Of course. Just leave me alone for a bit.'

Terrel did as he was told.

Two hours later, Terrel was sitting on the floor of the candlelit library, surrounded by books. Ever since he'd begun to study Muzeni's journal, he had wanted to compare it to things he'd already read. The sheer volume of the man's researches – even in a single journal – was astonishing. For the most part, his technical details about the lunar cycles, star maps, and the movements of the Floating Islands, were almost identical to the findings of other researchers – some of whom had made their discoveries much later. It was clear that Muzeni had been way ahead of his time.

However, he had also made many references to what he called 'the Code', which Terrel took to mean the Tindaya

Code. He had read about this before, though not in any great detail. He was not even sure he believed in prophecy – and anything so ancient seemed unlikely to have any bearing on his own life and times. However, because Muzeni obviously thought it was extremely important, Terrel's interest was renewed.

It took the boy a long time to make even the slightest progress, but he gradually worked out that Muzeni took a much more pessimistic view of the future, including some vague but horrible predictions about a massive upheaval, while most of the other scholars apparently seemed content to record that at some point in the future – Terrel could not work out when – the so-called Guardian would arrive, and hence all questions would be answered and all problems solved. Terrel was frustrated by the fact that all the books he had access to were at least sixty years old. He couldn't help wondering what the seers' latest conclusions were, but could think of no way to find this out.

The other thing that made Muzeni's writing stand out from the rest was his preoccupation with the Dark Moon. He kept returning to it, obsessively detailing his observations, and measuring the timings of its orbit in ever more exact terms. As far as Terrel could see, Muzeni had discovered nothing unusual, and this in itself had seemed to frustrate him. It was almost as if he *wanted* the moon to prove his calculations wrong. The heretic's words were usually precise and functional, but when dealing with the Dark Moon he became almost poetic, and occasionally incoherent. Reading some passages made Terrel wonder if Muzeni had actually been a little mad after all.

Eventually, deciding that he'd better go and check on Elam, Terrel left the library by his normal route. The labyrinthine roof space seemed even gloomier than usual, but it was only when he reached the south wing that he realized – to his horror – that it was dark outside. He had lost track of time in the library, and now it was long past curfew.

He crept along the empty corridor, wishing that he had left the journal in the library. If he was caught he would be in dreadful trouble, and having to explain the book tucked inside his shirt would only make the situation worse – not to mention the fact that the wardens were sure to confiscate his find. He reached his own door, not knowing whether he wanted it to be locked or not. If it was, the turnkey might have assumed he was inside, but then he wouldn't be able to get in and so would have to hide all night. If it wasn't, he could slip inside, but this would mean that his absence had definitely been noticed. He was likely to be in trouble either way.

The handle squealed as Terrel tried it, sounding horrifyingly loud in the silence, and he froze, but no one came to investigate the noise. The door was locked.

Terrel stood where he was for a few moments, paralyzed by indecision, until he was struck by a new idea – an idea that both excited and terrified him. Might as well be hung for a sheep as a lamb, he told himself. Although he was familiar with the phrase, he had never seen a sheep or a lamb, and had only the vaguest idea of what they looked like. The only animals he'd ever seen were horses, Ahmeza's goats, and a few feral cats who roamed the grounds at night. I could do with cat's eyes now, he thought, and grinned, even though his heart was racing. Moving as stealthily as he could in the darkness, he set off again.

Terrel had never been outside alone at night before. The darkness did not bother him as much as the fact that there was so much of it. It had no limits. The sky above was full of stars, but even familiar objects on the ground looked just as distant, just as alien. It was a silver-grey world, bleached of all colour, the only contrasts provided by the variations of starlight and shadow.

He almost turned back, afraid to venture out into this void, but he forced himself to run, heading towards the lake. At the water's edge he paused, confident now that he was not being pursued, and looked around. Having moved away from the bulk of the house, he could see the half Red Moon in the western sky and the slender curve of the Amber Moon high above – two beacons of pale colour in the dark emptiness. He took reassurance from their presence, and began to walk towards the hill.

By the time he reached the observatory Terrel was breathless and covered in scratches, but he hardly cared. Trying not to look at the pile of bones, he pushed the door open and stepped inside. Somewhere overhead an owl hooted mournfully, but he was growing used to the noises of the night. Stepping up to the telescope, Terrel crouched down and looked through the eyepiece – and saw nothing.

The view it offered him was blank, so completely black that he wondered – absurdly – whether someone had covered the other end of the instrument. Then he thought – more rationally – that perhaps it was not working after all, that the long exposure and falling debris must have damaged it in some way. Fighting his own dismay, Terrel returned his eye to the lens, more in hope than expectation – and saw a star blink into life.

As he watched, mesmerized, more stars appeared – brighter and more beautiful than he had ever seen them before – until the entire circle was filled with their lustre. By then he knew what had hidden them and he looked up at the sky with his own eyes to confirm it, even as the hairs on the back of his neck stood on end.

The fact that he had chosen to look through the immovable telescope at the exact moment when the Dark Moon was passing directly in front of it seemed to him to be an omen. Muzeni had dedicated his cloistered life to studying that mysterious black object – and now fate had passed the task on to another. Terrel swore a silent oath there and then, vowing that he would do everything in his power to be worthy of his long-dead mentor.

In the darkness above, the owl called again, bearing witness to the boy's promise.

CHAPTER SIX

Terrel had decided to spend the rest of the night on the hill, using the same sheep-and-lamb reckoning that had taken him there in the first place. Because his days were regulated by the sun, he would usually have been asleep by now, but because he had no idea when he would be able to visit the observatory again, he was determined to make the most of this opportunity. However, he could not get the telescope to move – its mounting was indeed rusted solid – and watching the slow procession of a few stars across a fixed point in the sky soon began to pall, especially as to do so he had to crouch in an awkward position under the lens.

He became even more frustrated when he discovered that he would not be able to read. Even though the White Moon – which was waning but still three quarters full – had now risen and was spreading its 'cold light of logic' over the scene, there was not enough light for him to be able to decipher Muzeni's tiny handwriting. When he tried, Terrel's sensitive eyes – which were already tired – soon began to hurt, and what he thought he had read made little or no sense. He gave up, settled down on the floor with his back against the wall, and wondered what to do next. His body was beginning to crave sleep, but he was determined not to give in to it, afraid that he might not wake in time to get back before the haven began to stir in the morning. On the other hand he did not know whether he was capable of staying awake all night, in spite of the cold and discomfort. Terrel finally decided that if he *was* going to sleep it would be better to do it now rather than later.

Curling himself up on the hard floor, he closed his eyes and tried to relax, only to find himself distracted by the unfamiliar sounds of night. He was soon able to identify the calls of at least three different owls, but there were many other noises – the wind soughing in the broken roof, various rustlings and tiny squeals – and he could not even guess where some of them came from. Although these signs of unseen nocturnal activity no longer frightened him, he was accustomed to the relative silence of his cell and so grew *less* sleepy as time passed. Eventually he gave in and sat up again, stretching his stiffening limbs. For a few moments he thought about going outside, where the grass would at least make a more comfortable bed, but the idea of sleeping in the open, amid all the rustlings, was too much for him. He needed walls around him, even if the roof gaped open to the stars.

The pale moonlight was now falling on the cluttered table where Terrel had found the crystal, and this made him reach into his pocket and take it out. He spent some time polishing the stone, using his own spit and the cloth of his shirt, until the facets all seemed to glow with a light of their own. Inspired now, he rose and limped over to the table, found two strands of wire and cleaned them in the same way. Then, taking up a pair of small brass pliers and finding – to his surprise – that they moved easily enough, he began to twist the wire into a tiny cage, imprisoning the newly polished stone. This too was delicate work in the half-light, but he persevered, working as much by touch as by sight, making minute adjustments until he was finally satisfied. As he crafted his simple design, his mind flitted back and forth. He would have preferred the warmer light of the Red Moon for his purpose. It was not only the harbinger of violence and blood, but of fire as well, both in the literal sense and as a metaphor for passion – and for this task he wanted love, not logic. However, he could no more control the passage of the moons than he could control the flight of the wind, and the chaste light did at least bring out the inner brilliance of the stone. He thought of Alyssa, of her fragile health and unworldly manner, of her awkward grace and lambent eyes. And he wondered what she meant to him, and what he meant to her.

Finally, he inspected the new earring, balancing the end of its hook on the tip of one of his fingers, and felt a glow of satisfaction. He had created something that made the night's adventure worthwhile. And on that thought he lay down again, and promptly fell asleep.

Terrel dreamt of the sea – not the sea of his recurring nightmare, but of a huge, grey-green expanse, seen from the air as if he were a bird in flight. Under the varied moonlight the ocean seemed endless, transmuting the colours above to a restless shimmering of silver, pink and gold.

He watched, knowing that he was not the only one who did so, as a city of glass and crystal rose from the waves. It was not real; even he knew there could be nothing like this in the physical world. It was all in his mind, but it was *important*, though he couldn't work out why.

He desperately wanted to go there, but no matter how hard he tried, the sparkling illusion remained out of reach. The city was beautiful but flawed, with obvious fractures running through the patterns of light. Without thinking, Terrel tried to mend them, to heal the wounds, but met with only partial success.

Other forces were at work now, and he grew afraid. A sword was hurled into the heavens by an unknown hand – his own? – and, as if in response to this challenge, the sky answered with a cluster of radiant meteors that hurtled down from above. The first few crashed into the sea in bursts of hissing spray, but then the fiery missiles began to hit the city, spreading an explosive chaos deep into its crystalline structure, crushing its ethereal beauty. Within moments it had collapsed, splitting into shards that sank beneath the waves, until all that was left was the sea, the sound of distant mocking laughter – and a scream.

'*No!*'

Terrel woke with the sound of his impotent denial still echoing within the observatory walls, and felt himself shivering. The wanton destruction of the crystalline city had been bad enough, but even more horrifying was the fact that the last thing he had seen had been Alyssa's eyes, trapped within the sinking ruins. Worse still was the knowledge that he had been able to do nothing to save her.

He scrambled to his feet, feeling chilled inside and out, and staggered to the door. There was no telling exactly how long he had been asleep, but he was relieved to see that there was no sign yet of the morning's brightness on the eastern horizon. Even so, he knew it was time to go.

Some time later, Terrel was crouched in the dark sanctuary of the spiral staircase near his cell. Sneaking unnoticed into the house had been easy enough; the difficulty now would be getting back into his own room without being caught. Everything depended on the turnkey unlocking the door without bothering to look in, but there was nothing Terrel could do about that. He just had to wait – and hope.

He had already been hiding there for more than an hour, and the journal tucked inside his shirt was beginning to irritate his skin. He had formed a vague plan to bring *all* the journals back from the observatory and take them to his library, but their combined bulk would mean several trips – and on this occasion he had felt it was too risky to take more than one. Now, as he sat wishing the last of the night away, he could only wonder when his next chance to climb the hill would come.

He gradually sensed the house come to life around him until, at last, he heard the measured tread of the turnkey on his morning round. Moving as stealthily as he could, Terrel crept down to the bottom of the stairs and then along to the junction of his corridor. Peering round, he saw the turnkey already past his own door, in the act of unlocking another. The man was whistling softly, and did not seem to have noticed anything out of the ordinary. When he went on his way, Terrel slipped round the corner and was in his cell a few moments later. It had been so easy, he almost laughed aloud – and then a new idea began to form in his mind.

He had only just had time to hide the journal and the earring, and to lie down on his bed, his eyes closing of their own accord, when the door was thrown open again. Ahmeza stood there, hands on bony hips and fire in her eyes.

'You'll do,' she declared loudly. 'Up! Up!'

Terrel was not the only one the cook had pressed into service that morning. Elam and Alyssa were there too, but he saw little of his friends because they were stationed at the far end of the long, noisy kitchen. Terrel felt as though he was sleepwalking, and was even more clumsy than usual – which led to harsh words and the occasional slap. In the end he was so desperate to escape and get some rest that he deliberately knocked a pile of plates from the draining board so that they smashed on the tiled floor. It was a risky stratagem, which earnt him a stinging blow to the side of his head with an iron ladle – but it did serve his purpose.

'Clear that lot up and then get out!' Ahmeza screamed at him. 'You're more trouble than you're worth.'

Half dazed and in considerable pain, Terrel did as he was told, then fled back to his cell. He fell onto the pallet gratefully and was asleep in moments.

When he awoke it was well past midday, and he was thankful that no one had disturbed his delayed rest. His head still throbbed, but he felt more alert now. Reaching under his thin mattress, he retrieved the journal, unable to resist the temptation to read while he was still being left in peace.

This time, rather than flicking through the pages as he had on previous occasions, Terrel decided to work through the book systematically, hoping to get a feel for the work as a whole. In that he was frustrated, because the journal was in itself fragmented – leaping from astronomical observations to personal commentary, from theories about the past and future to vitriolic venting of the author's spleen. Muzeni had ranged over a wide assortment of topics, apparently at random, as the mood took him. There were some passages that Terrel could make no sense of, especially those dealing with concepts such as 'the invisible metallic flux which passes through all things' – and there were others that made his blood run

cold, such as the one describing something called a 'vol-
cano', which apparently involved fire spewing up from the
earth below. Such an event sounded highly improbable to
Terrel, but Muzeni's description of it was horribly convincing. There was even one page detailing the effects of
such a fire *under the ocean* – which seemed even more
absurd to Terrel – and which resulted in giant waves 'big
enough to sweep away whole towns from the coast of
Vadanis and, possibly, to alter the course of the entire
group of Floating Islands'.

Easier to understand, though they still made for uneasy
reading, were the parts relating to Muzeni's contempt for
anyone who did not think as he did. ('Perhaps that is why
they have put me here, hidden among their ancestors. The
people in these graves make more sense than most of the
living!') But, as Terrel had realized earlier, the subject
that roused the heretic to his greatest bouts of passion was
the Dark Moon. Reading one paragraph in particular left
Terrel almost breathless.

'I imagine its darkness not as an absence of light but as
some indescribable amalgam of all the forces of nature,
condensed into that single ominous sphere. But how can a
sphere contain such awe-inspiring potential? Surely it is
but a curled shape that masks another. The Dark Moon is
a bird of prey, black wings stooped in a hunter's silent
flight, black eyes fixed upon her target, talons outstretched,
slicing the sky above her unsuspecting victims. No rules
confine her; no defences can turn her away. When she
strikes, her speed and savagery will be unmatched,
unmatchable. We will not even feel the death blow.'

Before he could even try to consider what this all meant,
the sound of footsteps came from the corridor and Terrel
hurriedly pushed the book under his pillow. He only
relaxed when Elam put his head round the door.

'Skiving as usual,' his friend remarked. 'While we do all the work.'

Alyssa came in after him, and immediately went to inspect the lump on the side of Terrel's head.

'Does it hurt?'

'Of course it hurts!'

'Don't listen to him,' Elam advised. 'He's got such a thick skull he probably hardly noticed.'

'There are still dreams here,' Alyssa said, sounding surprised.

'I was asleep until an hour or so ago,' Terrel explained. 'I was up most of the night.' Having remembered none of his daytime dreams, he was curious to know what Alyssa could see, but she said nothing.

'You cut it fine with the curfew last night,' Elam remarked. 'I didn't see you at dinner. Or afterwards, come to that.'

'I missed the curfew. I spent the night at the observatory.' He enjoyed seeing the shock on his friends' faces, quickly followed, in Elam's case, by envy.

'You were outside?' he exclaimed. 'At night?'

'Not so loud,' Terrel said, grinning. 'Someone might hear.' He went on to tell them about his adventure, omitting only one episode. Both Elam and Alyssa were suitably impressed.

Eventually, when he had finished answering Elam's many questions, Terrel produced his final marvel.

'There's one last thing I have to show you. Close your eyes, Alyssa.'

'Why?' she asked, smiling.

'Just do it. And hold out your hands.'

When she obeyed, he lifted the mattress again and took out the earring. In daylight its crude construction was more obvious, but the crystal sparkled nicely. Elam rolled his eyes but refrained from comment as Terrel dropped it into Alyssa's outstretched palm.

Her brown eyes opened then – and grew wider when she saw her gift.

'For me?' she whispered, holding it up to the light.

Terrel nodded, enjoying his friend's childlike pleasure.

'It's like your eyes,' Alyssa said in wonder, then turned to Terrel and kissed him.

It was a spontaneous action, shy and gentle, her lips brushing against his cheek, but he felt colour rise in his face – and his blush deepened as they gazed briefly into each other's eyes.

Behind Alyssa, Elam was pretending to stick a finger down his throat and making retching noises. For a moment Terrel was angry, then he burst out laughing as Alyssa turned round and gave Elam a friendly shove.

'If you two have quite finished . . .' the boy muttered, staggering across the room in theatrical fashion.

'It's beautiful,' Alyssa said, ignoring his interruption and turning back to Terrel. 'Did you make it?'

He nodded.

Alyssa slid the hook through the hole in her earlobe, and grinned delightedly.

'How do I look?'

'Like a fairy princess,' Elam replied instantly, though with less sarcasm than Terrel would have expected. He himself could think of nothing to say.

At that moment the door opened again, and Ingo shuffled in.

'I might have known I'd find you three together,' he remarked in his habitual offhand manner.

'We've done our stint for today,' Elam told him. 'In the kitchens.'

'That's not what I'm here for,' the warden replied,

turning to look directly at Terrel. 'Ziolka's looking for you, lad.'

'Why?' Terrel asked, finding his voice at the same time as his heart sank, thinking that his night-time absence must have been discovered.

'You may find this difficult to believe, after fourteen years,' Ingo replied. 'But you've got a visitor.'

CHAPTER SEVEN

In the silence that followed Ingo's announcement, Terrel's immediate reaction – one of stunned disbelief – turned slowly to a flood of contradictory emotions that made him feel quite nauseous. *We* never get any visitors, he thought, recalling Elam's words.

'Well, come on then,' Ingo urged. 'They're waiting.'

'Who is it?' Terrel whispered, asking the first of the many questions that had crowded into his head.

Ingo merely shrugged and turned to leave the cell, unwilling or – more likely – unable to enlighten him. With a last bewildered glance at his two friends, Terrel followed.

As soon as Shahan saw Terrel's eyes, he knew there could be no doubt about the boy's identity. Others might share the misfortune of broken or twisted limbs, but anyone who had glimpsed those bright, colourless orbs in the baby's face would know that they could not be duplicated. It was a moment he had been waiting and hoping for for more than two years, and now that it had arrived he felt a mixture of relief and excitement – and a little dread. He had begun to fear that the child might be dead. This was not because he thought Mirival would have had the infant killed – the scandal caused by such an action, should it ever have become public knowledge, would have shaken the Empire to its core – but because the baby's health had seemed so delicate, making him vulnerable to any number of perils. However, the boy had survived – and that spoke well of his courage and tenacity.

When Shahan had begun his secret investigation – at first tentatively, but then with increasing conviction – he had decided that the child was most likely to have been hidden away in some sort of institution. If his true identity was ever discovered, this course of action would be eminently justifiable. The boy's strange eyes, together with his obvious deformities, would have been reason enough for him to be cast out from any family of social standing. And having embarked upon such a course, the selection of this particular madhouse had been a logical choice. It was a long way from Makhaya, and few people – including, until recently, Shahan himself – even knew of its existence. Its position in the broad moorlands of Saefir Province, which was sparsely populated even in its more fertile and hospitable regions, guaranteed its obscurity. By definition, its inmates were the unwanted flotsam of Vadanis, and as such they attracted little attention – although that might change soon, given recent developments.

The fact that Shahan had found his quarry at all was a testament to his obstinate determination. The only person whom the seer could be reasonably certain knew of the boy's whereabouts was Mirival, and – for obvious reasons – Shahan could not ask him. The Chief Seer still held the pre-eminent claim to the title of Mentor, and certainly had the ear of Emperor Dheran. He was clearly not a man to be trifled with. However, Shahan had been prepared to take some risks as his doubts concerning the latest interpretations of the Code grew stronger. Discreet enquiries among Mirival's known associates had eventually led to a woman who – for a suitable fee – had remembered being told of a child being taken from the city at the time of the lunar confluence.

That trail was long cold, of course, but – inspired now – Shahan had made excuses to leave Makhaya and travel widely, following his hunches. He had lost count of the number of hostels, sanctuaries, orphanages and prisons he'd visited, asking at each about a foundling who would have arrived soon after the alignment of the moons. Although that date was easily remembered, he had always received a negative answer – until now.

'Is this the one?' Ziolka asked curiously.

'Yes.'

'Should I . . . ?'

'Leave us, please,' Shahan instructed tersely.

They were standing in the Head Warden's spacious office, which Terrel had just entered. The boy was so nervous he was shaking. Ziolka, his deference to the visitor obvious, hurried from the room, and this raised even more questions in Terrel's mind. On the way there he had been in a daze, his thoughts full of ever more outrageous ideas. Could this stranger be a member of his lost family – perhaps even his father, come to reclaim him? Would they recognize each other? In the end he had simply followed Ingo, his heart filled with a mixture of hope and foreboding.

When he'd been ushered into Ziolka's inner sanctum, and seen the visitor for the first time, Terrel had been shocked. He had never seen anyone who looked so ancient. Not even Old Timi was as venerable and worn as this grey-haired man, whose straggly beard partially hid a wrinkled, angular face with a great hooked beak of a nose and pale grey eyes. He looked far too old to be Terrel's father.

'Your name is Terrel, is it not?'

The boy nodded, then – surprising himself – he found his voice.

'Who are you?' he blurted out.

'I am called Shahan.'

That told Terrel nothing, but the old man's intimidating presence and intense stare prevented him from speaking again.

'We should sit.' Shahan waved the boy to a chair, and took another for himself. 'I am tired from my journeying.'

Where had he come from? Terrel wondered as he did as he was told, his legs practically giving way beneath him. He seemed to have lost the use of his tongue again, and could only wait to see what would happen next.

'Have you heard of the Tindaya Code?' The question came out of the blue, adding a further layer of confusion to the boy's already disordered thoughts. After a long pause, Terrel nodded briefly.

'And do you know anything about it?'

Again the boy hesitated, but then his memories provided him with something solid to grasp – even if he couldn't yet see what possible relevance it might have – and he was able to speak again.

'It was written on stones that were found in the ruins of a great temple in the Central Mountains,' he said. 'It's supposed to be a prophecy.'

Shahan nodded, a look of surprise on his previously impassive face.

'Where did you learn this?'

'From books,' Terrel replied without thinking, then fell silent, afraid that he might be forced to reveal his secret library.

'So you can read?' Shahan queried, wondering how the boy had found such books in this out-of-the-way place.

'Yes,' Terrel replied quietly.

It was the seer's turn to fall silent, considering. He could not help comparing Terrel to the prince, the twin brother whose existence was presumably unknown to this boy. There was a certain similarity between the facial features of the two, but otherwise they could hardly have been more different.

'Do you believe in prophecy, Terrel?' the old man asked eventually.

'I don't know,' he replied warily.

'I wondered, because you said the Code was *supposed* to be a prophecy.'

'If we knew what was going to happen all the time,' Terrel responded, 'what would be the point of doing anything?'

Good question, Shahan thought. What indeed?

'It's rarely as simple as that,' he said aloud. 'Augury is not an exact science, especially when you are working with information that's incomplete.'

'The missing stones, you mean?'

The seer nodded.

'Yes, plus the ones that are broken or eroded, not to mention the parts that are in a language no one understands.'

Some of Terrel's earlier qualms were beginning to fade. He had not known what to expect of the meeting – but it had certainly not been this. Although he did not know what to make of Shahan, he was intrigued. He'd never been able to discuss such things with anyone before.

'It's very old too, isn't it?' he said.

'It certainly is. The Code was discovered a little over five hundred years ago, but no one knows how long it had been up there on the mountain. Some people say it could even have been there for thousands of years.' Shahan expected the boy to be amazed by such a notion, but Terrel only nodded solemnly. The seer wished he could know what was going on behind those strange eyes.

'So is the Guardian coming soon?' Terrel asked, surprising Shahan again.

'He's already here.'

That silenced the boy for a while, and Shahan was content to wait for the next question.

'Do you think he'll save us?' Terrel asked eventually, remembering a line from Muzeni's journal: 'It is hard to imagine destruction on such a scale.'

'Let's hope so,' the seer replied, smiling. 'We'd better give him all the help we can, eh?'

If Terrel paid any attention to the choice of pronoun, he gave no sign of it. He was deep in thought again.

'Does all this have anything to do with the Dark Moon?'

This time Shahan could not hide his astonishment at the boy's perspicacity, and felt a bubble of elation.

'Yes, it does.'

'Tell me,' Terrel demanded, eager now.

'All right.' Shahan leant forward in his chair and began ticking points off on his fingers. 'As you know, the Code describes a great hero, who we've chosen to call "the Guardian". Although it also tells us a great deal about his life and work, a lot of this is very vague, and there are all sorts of possible interpretations. But one thing is clear. Unless he fulfils his destiny, there will be a worldwide disaster of unimaginable proportions. There's also mention of another character, the Mentor, who is variously described as a teacher, a go-between and an interpreter, and who is supposed to guide the Guardian throughout his life. No one knows who that is yet, but his main task seems to be to help the Guardian choose between good and evil.'

'Why would a hero choose evil?' Terrel asked.

'I'm not sure,' the seer replied, 'but we all have the capacity for both, don't you think?'

'I suppose so.'

'The important thing at the moment is that, according to all the interpretations, the Guardian is born at the time of one lunar conjunction, and will become our saviour by the time of the next.'

'Seventy-five years later.'

'That's right. Or at least that's what it should have been.'

'What do you mean?'

'No one is sure now when the next conjunction will be.'

'But surely . . .' Terrel began, then faltered, new light dawning. 'The Dark Moon?'

Shahan nodded.

'It's changed its orbit. That should be impossible—'

'"Astronomically impossible",' Terrel quoted.

'Exactly, but it's happening, no matter how hard some people have tried to deny it.'

' "So which is wrong, the prophecy or science?" '

'Does it have to be one or the other?' Shahan asked, puzzled now.

'Yes. The Code predicts that astronomically impossible things would happen.'

'It does?' The seer was astounded. 'I've never—'

'Have you heard of someone called Muzeni?' Terrel cut in.

Shahan thought for a while, then slowly shook his head.

'He was a heretic, who was sent here over four hundred years ago,' the boy explained. 'I've been reading—' He stopped abruptly, his eyes narrowing suspiciously. The sudden change in his appearance and attitude was startling, and Shahan wondered what he had done to provoke it.

'Why did you come here?' Terrel demanded abruptly. 'Why now?'

'It's complicated.'

'Why are you asking *me* these questions?' He was agitated now, and Shahan saw, for the first time, flashes of colour deep within those translucent eyes. 'What's all this about?'

Shahan did not answer immediately. Their conversation had reinforced his conviction that the boy was important, but how was he to explain this to Terrel? How would he react to the news that he was the Emperor's discarded son, or that he might have a part to play in the fulfilment of the prophecy? He might reasonably conclude that the man telling him such tales was mad. If their roles were reversed, the seer would not believe any of this without some proof – and what proof did he have to offer?

For a moment, Shahan considered simply taking the boy back to Makhaya, and confronting the court with his existence. Such a confrontation would be dangerous, potentially explosive, but surely the truth could not be denied then. However, such a course of action would hardly be fair to Terrel. What would the boy actually *do*? What was his role supposed to be? And his physical appearance would not help his cause. Indeed, it would undoubtedly make him the subject of ridicule and hostility. There was also the certain enmity of those, like Mirival, who had a vested interest in keeping Terrel's origins a secret. They were powerful men, who would do their utmost to discredit the boy. How could Shahan subject him to all that with so little preparation? Given the confined nature of his life so far, Terrel had made remarkable strides, but he was still an innocent.

'Well?' Terrel demanded, growing impatient at the old man's silence.

'Do you know when you were born?' Shahan asked eventually.

'Not exactly. About fourteen years ago. Someone left me here as a baby.' He stopped, his expression changing again. 'Do you know who left me? Was it you?'

'No, it wasn't me,' Shahan replied heavily. He was aware of being drawn into deeper and deeper waters now, and didn't know whether he would sink or swim – only that he had to try. Whatever he said next might have repercussions even he could not foresee.

'Are you . . . ? Do I have a family?' Terrel asked quietly.

The decision about how to answer that question was suddenly taken out of Shahan's hands, as the door to the office was thrown open and a soldier in the flamboyant uniform of the Imperial Guard strode in. The seer rose to his feet, infuriated by the intrusion, while Terrel seemed to shrink into his chair, his eyes half closed as if in fear.

'What's the meaning of this?' Shahan protested.

'I'm glad to meet you finally, Seer,' the newcomer stated. 'You've led us a merry dance.'

'Do you know who I am, Captain?' the old man enquired, still bristling with indignation.

'Most certainly, Seer Shahan,' the soldier replied.

'Then please leave at once. I have important business here.'

'I'm afraid that won't be possible,' the captain stated. 'You are under arrest.'

The old man was clearly taken aback.

'Arrested? On what charge?'

'Treason.'

CHAPTER EIGHT

The interview and its abrupt conclusion left Terrel shaken and bewildered. After the captain's dramatic announcement, two more soldiers entered the room and took Shahan away. The old man protested at first, but then he glanced at Terrel and fell silent, allowing himself to be led from the room. The soldiers simply ignored the boy, obviously considering him to be of no importance. Terrel was grateful for this small mercy, terrified by the guard's evident self-confidence and brazen air of authority. He was left alone in Ziolka's office for some time, apparently forgotten by everyone, and he dared not move from his chair.

His thoughts were dazed, with another set of questions added to those already raised by the visitor. Who exactly *was* Shahan? The captain had called him 'Seer', but the deference such a title should have commanded had been completely lacking from his tone. Was the old man really one of the astrologers? Or had the soldier just been mocking him? And what had he done to warrant the accusation of treason?

There were so many unanswered questions, but the most puzzling of all – the one that Terrel's mind returned to again and again – was the one he had asked earlier and to which he had received no reply. Whatever Shahan's status or his crimes, he had been Terrel's first visitor from the outside world after fourteen years of isolation. And all he had wanted to talk about was an ancient prophecy. That, like so much else, made no sense at all to the young boy. His whole life had been spent within the confines of Havenmoon's walls, and no prisoner could possibly be expected to know about such things. So why had Shahan come to see *him*?

Recalling the old man's last fleeting glance in his direction, Terrel could not escape the sudden conviction that it had been his own presence that had silenced Shahan's protests. It was almost as though he had not wanted to draw the soldiers' attention to the boy – and the possible implications of that were frightening as well as unfathomable.

Terrel jumped as the door opened again, startling him out of his uncomfortable reverie, and Ziolka came in. The Head Warden's florid face was sheened with perspiration, and there was a hunted look in his porcine eyes.

'What happened?' he asked Terrel.

'They arrested him.'

'I know that. What did he come here for? Why did he want to see you?'

'I don't know,' Terrel replied truthfully.

'He must have told you *something*!' Ziolka exclaimed. He was clearly worried, afraid that he might somehow be unwittingly implicated in the visitor's unknown crimes.

'We just talked about prophecies and astrology,' Terrel told him. 'None of it made much sense to me.' He stared up at the warden steadily, refusing to be drawn further.

Like most people, Ziolka could not hold the boy's gaze for long, and he soon looked away.

'This is all getting too much for me,' he muttered.

Me too, Terrel agreed silently. Me too.

Alone in his cell once more, Terrel gave up trying to make sense of what had happened. The guard who had escorted him back to the south wing had tried to question him, but he had kept his council, not wanting to add to the gossip that he knew would be spreading through the house. The other cells had already been locked, even though there had still been more than an hour to go until sunset – another sign of Ziolka's panic. As a result Terrel had not had the chance to confide in Alyssa or Elam – the only people he *would* have liked to talk to – before he was confined himself.

Some time later, after exhausting himself in pointless circles of speculation, he finally fell asleep.

It was hardly surprising that Shahan would figure in Terrel's dreams that night, but the old man's fleeting appearances told him nothing, and were only one element in a chaotic mixture of sounds and images. He dreamt of fire bursting from the earth in great red waves, heard music drifting over distant, misty hills and saw horses crashing through the undergrowth beneath gigantic trees. He saw the world overlaid with gleaming lines and translucent particles that shifted constantly, forming and reforming into patterns that were both beautiful and precise. He dreamt of Alyssa's eyes looking out from the face of an owl before it flew away, leaving him alone with only the stars for company – until the Dark Moon obliterated them too. He felt the red hatred, as malevolent as ever but further away this time, so that it was a remote presence, lacking any real threat as long as he did not try to oppose it.

It was only at the very end of his ephemeral journey, in the twilight time before he awoke, that Terrel sensed the rush of violence, the sudden impact of short-lived pain which soon gave way to oblivion. He was both the hunter and his prey, and the chase filled him with an unruly jumble of emotions; malicious satisfaction, cold horror, utter confusion and a lingering frustration that not even the final darkness could swallow. He knew all the time that he was not the master of his own fate, that he – like those around him – was being driven by forces outside himself. The dream ended with a familiar mocking laughter ringing in his ears, laughter that made his blood run cold.

Several miles away, as the first pale glow of dawn crept across their camp, two soldiers of the Imperial Guard stood looking at the body of a third man who lay on the ground between them. A crossbow bolt protruded from between the corpse's shoulder blades.

'What were you thinking, Marik?' the captain asked.

The younger man hesitated, his face a picture of uncertainty and fear.

'He . . . he was trying to escape,' he replied eventually.

'Rivas and Zanelli didn't think so,' the captain said, naming the two men who had been on sentry duty for the latter part of the night. 'They say he was just going to take a leak in the trees.'

'But . . . but I saw him, sir.'

'From inside your tent? When you were asleep?'

'I woke up. I saw him and I knew.' Marik sounded stubborn now. 'He was getting away.'

'An old man? On foot?' the captain asked pointedly.

'How far do you think he'd have got before we caught him?'

'I did what I had to do, sir.'

'We were supposed to bring him back to Makhaya, not kill him!' the officer shouted angrily. 'How am I supposed to explain this to Mirival?'

'I don't know, sir,' the soldier replied, after a pause in which he seemed to be considering the possible repercussions of his hasty action for the first time. 'I was only following orders.'

'Oh, really?' The captain's voice was dangerously quiet now. 'And precisely whose orders were they?'

Marik did not answer, his confusion obviously deeper than ever.

'I suppose they came to you in a dream,' his commander remarked sarcastically, then became brisk and businesslike. 'Hand over your weapons. For the rest of this mission you are to consider yourself under arrest. I'll deal with you properly when we get back to the city.'

'Yes, sir,' Marik responded, doing his best to hide his dismay.

As the young man was led away by two stony-faced colleagues, the captain looked down at the seer's body. The old man appeared to have been shrunken by death and already seemed to have become part of the forest, his grey hair like some exotic lichen growing next to the moss and ferns. Marik's shot had been deadly accurate – he'd always been one of the unit's best archers – and Shahan had hardly bled at all. The captain sighed wearily. This incident was not likely to do his own career prospects any good, but what was done was done. By all accounts the seer had been a traitor, and would have met with a similarly unpleasant end sooner or later. Even so, it was a shame to see such a life snuffed out in this ignominious manner. During the time he had pursued him from one end of Vadanis to the other, the captain had come to feel a grudging respect for his quarry. This was not the final scene he had envisaged for their duel.

'Truss him up and sling him across one of the pack horses,' he ordered, beckoning to some of the men nearby. 'He'll be as stiff as a board soon, so make it quick.'

Terrel had never seen Alyssa react in this way before. As soon as she entered his cell her eyes grew wide, the colour drained from her face, and she seemed to stare at nothing, gazing into the distance. All his anxious questions were waved away impatiently as she gestured for quiet, watching the echoes of his dreams – the echoes only she could see.

When, at last, she blinked and lowered her gaze, Terrel was bursting with curiosity. His own fragmented memories of the night's adventures were already beginning to fade, despite his efforts, but when he saw the expression on his friend's face he began to wonder if he really wanted to remember them.

'What is it?' he whispered. 'What have you seen?'

'It's very real,' Alyssa replied. 'Too real.'

'What do you mean?'

'It wasn't all yours, either,' she went on, adding to his misgivings.

'Just tell me what you saw,' he pleaded.

'The man who came to see you, did he have grey hair and a nose like a beak?'

'Yes,' he said, thrown by the apparent change of subject. 'Why?'

'He's dead.'

'What! How can you know?'

'You were there, in your dream.'

Terrel remembered the sensation of sudden violence and the confusion that had followed. He felt the cold horror again.

'How . . .' he began.

'Dreams are sometimes meant to show us things,' she explained.

'And I saw . . . ?'

Alyssa nodded.

'The soldiers were camped overnight in a forest. He was walking away when one of them shot him with a crossbow. His spirit left then.'

'But it was only a dream,' Terrel protested helplessly. 'It doesn't mean it was real.'

'No.' Alyssa sounded quite certain. 'It happened. Others saw it too.'

'Others? Who?'

'I don't know. They were too far away to see − apart from the soldier, of course.'

'*He* was dreaming too?'

'That's why he acted as he did,' Alyssa confirmed.

'In his sleep?'

'No,' she replied patiently. 'He woke up.'

'And killed Shahan?'

'Yes.'

'Why?'

'He had to. Someone made him.'

'Who?'

Alyssa thought about this for a moment. For the first time her expression became uncertain − and unhappy.

'You,' she told him quietly.

CHAPTER NINE

'This is madness!' Lathan bellowed, his outrage rising above the uproar in the Seers' Chamber.

'Not madness,' Kamin replied evenly. 'Indisputable fact.' He had known his announcement would create a furore, but he was surprised to see Lathan leading the opposition. There were other seers who could generally be counted on to provide a far more reactionary response to any new idea. Lathan was widely respected for his keen intellect and open-minded stance on most issues, and the fact that he had been roused to fury was an indication of just how deeply the council was divided.

'But what you claim to be true is simply *impossible*,' Lathan stated bluntly, provoking several cries of agreement. 'To accept it is to throw away all that we believe, all that we trust, to discard not only our lives' work but the legacy of all the seers who have gone before us.'

'The history of science is full of so-called impossibilities that have eventually been proved correct,' Kamin countered. 'If we do not question our assumptions, we can never progress.' Like his adversary, Kamin was quite sure of his own opinion, and the rest of the seers – an almost unheard-of gathering of the full council – grew quiet again, content to follow the debate between the champions of the two sides.

'That is mere semantics,' Lathan retorted sharply. 'Your claims make a mockery of centuries of observations, of countless volumes of empirical evidence, and of every axiom we hold dear. You are asking us to accept that everything we have ever known – every star chart . . .' He waved an arm at the incised diagrams that adorned the walls and domed ceiling of the circular chamber. '. . . every prophecy, the very *essence* of our science – that all this is wrong. That even the sacred symbol of our vocation is nothing but a lie!' He pointed dramatically at the orrery which stood at the centre of the room, the four coloured moons revolving slowly around the model of Nydus.

'What I am saying is that we are faced with an exceptional event,' Kamin responded. 'One which we cannot yet explain.'

'So exceptional that it is beyond reason!' Lathan exclaimed.

This outburst provoked another exchange of argument and insult from their respective supporters, and Kamin had to wait impatiently to be heard again.

'The fact remains that the orbit of the Dark Moon *has* altered,' he repeated doggedly, when the hubbub had abated.

'No! This is some aberration, a defect in your observations.'

'The observations have been verified independently by several of us. You've all seen the results, you've all checked the calculations. There is no mistake. Unless you would class myself and all my colleagues as incompetent charlatans, our findings are undeniable – so what is the point of trying to deny them?'

Behind his deputy, seated in the Chief Seer's ceremonial throne, Mirival nodded, his face set in an impassive mask. He had followed the debate with an increasing sense of unease, aware that what was being discussed was more than a simple matter of astrology. The whole future of the Empire was at stake.

Lathan's self-evident disgust at not being able to shake Kamin's certainty had silenced him temporarily, but one of his supporters took up the challenge.

'Is it not possible that your observations have been skewed by the unusual changes in Vadanis's own position?'

This question provoked another furious argument, because some of Lathan's followers did not accept that the islands had been diverted from their normal course.

'We have compensated for these variations,' Kamin replied eventually, when he was able to make himself heard. 'You know that.'

'That's why you're in error, then!' another dissenter cried. 'The islands have *not* changed course, any more than the Dark Moon has.'

'Yes, they have!' shouted a seer who had just returned from one of the coastal monitoring stations. 'I've seen the proof with my own eyes.'

'Why do you think that is?' another man asked. 'If the Dark Moon is in the wrong place, it would naturally pull us off course too.'

'Rubbish! Even if it was, the variation could not be enough to cause such a change. We have *two* inexplicable events here, not one.'

After that the argument grew even more fragmented and chaotic, until Mirival judged it time to intervene. He had tried to remain aloof for as long as possible – as befitted his status – leaving the main burden of presentation to his deputy, but now he felt he should exert his authority.

'Gentlemen!' He held up a hand for quiet, and was soon rewarded with the council's undivided attention. 'I am satisfied that the reports of the alteration to the Dark Moon's orbit, which Kamin has explained so succinctly, are indeed true. I expect no man to accept this on trust,' he added, glancing at Lathan, 'but ask only that each of you repeat the experiments for yourselves. There is no denying the proof of one's own eyes. I hope then that we may reach a consensus, for there is much work to be done. Even though our opinions do not coincide at present, my colleague Lathan has made several very important points. The first is that this is an aberration. Nothing in the past could have prepared us for what is happening now. Our challenge therefore is to determine the *cause* of this anomaly. If something has happened, it cannot be impossible. That is self-evident. What is crucial now is that we must discover why and how it happened. But this is only the first part of our task. The second is to evaluate the consequences of these changes. Lathan stated that we must now doubt everything we have previously taken for granted – and he is right.' He was deliberately twisting the other man's words and everyone knew it, but no one challenged him. 'All our predictions of earth tremors, all our assumptions concerning seasonal and meteorological conditions and the variations in the course of the Empire itself must be examined anew. I don't need to remind you that the movements of the Dark Moon are woven into the very fabric of our society. Moonlore does not just affect the people in this room. The laws, taboos and traditions of our land depend upon it. If we are to avoid legal and constitutional chaos, then we need to act quickly.'

He paused, letting them think about that for a few

moments. The Dark Moon did not wax and wane in the sense that the other moons did — it was always black — but its unseen cycles were still included in the astrological calculations that ruled the people of Vadanis and the outer islands. If this were suddenly to become ambiguous, chaos did indeed threaten.

'I am certain,' he went on, 'that by working together we can soon clarify the position and give a clear lead to every magistrate, every farmer, every physician — in fact to every person in the land. The changes to the orbit are currently small, but they are significant, and if you project them over the next sixty-one years, their significance becomes both critical and dramatic.'

He had no need to tell any of the seers what he was referring to. In sixty-one years from now, the four moons had been due to align once more — and the Guardian was supposed to fulfil his heroic destiny.

'You're surely not questioning the validity of the Code?' Lathan asked incredulously.

'Of course not,' Mirival replied. 'Only our interpretation of it. It is now possible that the four moons will not line up every seventy-five years. Indeed, another conjunction may never take place. Or if it does,' he continued, raising his voice over the howls of protest, 'we do not yet know when it will be.'

'We must all return to our studies of the Code!' Kamin cried, re-entering the debate now that Mirival had made its outcome inevitable. 'There is much that could stand to be re-evaluated if we are to help the Guardian achieve his purpose.'

'We are privileged to live in interesting times,' Mirival declared. 'Great events are upon us, gentlemen. Let us not shirk our duty to the Empire, to Nydus and to the future!'

That, he thought, should end the gathering on a suitably

rousing note. He stood up, hoping that the time for words was over and the time for action had begun. Moments later his hopes were dashed when one of the elderly seers, a man named Batou, rose unsteadily to his feet and waved his scarecrow-like arms.

'It's worse than you all think!' he shouted in a wavering but piercing voice. 'The Dark Moon has not only speeded up — it's got bigger!'

As most of his colleagues rounded on him, pouring scorn on his absurd ideas, a few began to voice their tentative agreement — and the chamber filled with noise again.

'That was all we needed,' Mirival groaned. 'What did that old fool think he was up to?'

'Actually, he may be right,' Fauria said resignedly. 'Batou's not the only one to note an apparent increase in the size of the sky shadow.'

'But why did he have to raise it when he did?' Kamin complained.

The three men had retired to the Chief Seer's quarters to discuss the situation in quieter, more private surroundings.

'It doesn't really matter,' Mirival sighed. 'Sooner or later everyone will have to accept that changes *are* happening, whatever they are. What we have to do is decide what practical measures to take in order to deal with them.'

'And what to do about Jax,' Kamin added.

Mirival nodded. In his position as leading contender for the title of Mentor, it had fallen to him to act as the boy's principal tutor. However, it was common knowledge that the prince's education was not proceeding as well as it might.

'He's been even more obtuse than usual recently,' he

admitted wearily. 'I can't imagine what he'll make of all this.'

'I suppose we've no doubts that Jax *is* the Guardian?' Fauria said tentatively.

'He has to be,' Mirival stated firmly. Allowing himself to think otherwise was out of the question. Like all of his colleagues he was aware that the Code referred to the Guardian variously as a king, a prophet and even – apparently – as a god, but other passages seemed to describe 'him' as some sort of creature. This inconvenient detail had been ignored by most of the seers, and the timing of Jax's birth had removed such doubts as were left.

'Perhaps it's a good thing the conjunction might come sooner than expected,' Kamin remarked, only half joking. 'Many of us don't live to be seventy-five, and even if he did, Jax would be an old man by then. Batou's only seventy-one, and he doesn't exactly cut a heroic figure.'

'You don't think Shahan might be right?' Fauria prompted.

'About the twin, you mean?' Mirival answered. 'No. You saw the baby. How could we show people *that*, and tell them he was their saviour?'

Shahan had shared his theories with only a few people, all of whom had rejected them outright.

'He's probably been dead long since,' Kamin added.

'Has there been any word on Shahan's whereabouts?' Fauria asked. 'Or on what he's doing?'

'Not yet,' Mirival replied. 'But I wouldn't put it past the old cretin to be looking for the twin.'

'If the twin was still alive,' Kamin ventured, 'do you think bringing him back to Makhaya might make Jax buck his ideas up a bit? Perhaps the two of them *combined* somehow make up the Guardian. We still haven't explained the double birth, after all.'

Mirival thought about this idea for a few moments. It had some attractions, but in the end they were far outweighed by the disadvantages.

'No. Forget him,' he said. 'Can you imagine what Adina would say if we even suggested it?'

The three men laughed uneasily.

That evening Fauria slipped quietly through the maze of darkened corridors that linked the various apartments of the inner palace, until he reached the quarters of the Empress Adina. He was ushered inside, without any need of knocking, by her personal chamberlain. As Mirival had predicted many years earlier, Remi had risen rapidly through the court ranks and was now the senior aide of the most powerful woman in the Empire. Some said Adina was even more powerful than the Emperor himself.

'Go right in, Seer,' Remi told Fauria. 'She's waiting for you.'

As always when summoned to Adina's presence, Fauria experienced a not unpleasant tremor of fear. She was indeed as formidable as she was beautiful, attributes which had caused one court wit to remark, 'She's like the sun. It's best not to look at her for too long.' The Emperor had taken no more wives, and there had been no more children since the birth of Jax and his twin. As tradition and augury decreed, Dheran's offspring from his earlier marriages had long been discounted in the matter of court power and politics, and Adina's ambitions for her son had not been dented by his unremarkable talents.

'It's good of you to come and see me in person, Fauria,' the Empress said in greeting. So much of their communication was, by necessity, carried out through discreet messengers.

'It is always a pleasure, Your Majesty.'

'Tell me, what did you and Mirival talk about after the council?'

From the blunt nature of the question, Fauria assumed that Adina had already been briefed on the debate in the Seers' Chamber, and that she probably had a fairly good idea of the topics that would have arisen afterwards.

'The specifics of practical measures to be taken now,' he replied.

'And do any of these concern my son?'

'Naturally. As Guardian, the Prince is central to our plans.'

'And no one is being swayed by Shahan's preposterous ideas?'

'No, Ma'am.' Then, choosing his words carefully, he told the Empress about Kamin's half-hearted suggestion concerning the missing twin, and Mirival's reaction to it.

Adina's face darkened.

'You say Mirival hesitated before rejecting this idea?'

'For a few moments only,' Fauria replied blandly, knowing that this would be enough to set her blood boiling. Publicly she had never even acknowledged the existence of Jax's brother, but in private it was another matter. Fauria's own clandestine alliance with the Empress allowed him to see the hidden side of her nature — which added to the risks and to the possible rewards of their relationship.

'Mirival is the only one who could possibly know where the twin is, and after all this time I doubt he could find the boy even if he tried,' he said now.

'But Shahan is trying anyway?'

'So it would seem.'

Adina did not respond immediately. After a few moments' thought, she spoke again.

'Do you still harbour the ambition to be named Mentor?'

'It would be an honour, Ma'am,' Fauria replied smoothly, 'but destiny will choose the right man.'

The Empress smiled, knowing that they understood one another.

'Of course.'

A short while later, after Fauria had left and Remi was pouring her another glass of wine, Adina looked up at her chamberlain.

'Tell me, Remi. Where in the Code does it say that the Mentor has to be a *man*?'

The next day, Makhaya was shaken by several unexpected earth tremors. None was particularly strong, and little damage was done, but the cumulative effect was to raise the level of apprehension in the city. Almost all the seers had been involved in furious calculations during the night, but even taking into account the putative new orbit of the Dark Moon, these quakes could not be explained. News also reached the city that day from Vadanis's central mining district. It had apparently been hit by a similar series of tremors, which had seriously disrupted operations. No one there could find any explanation for what was happening.

Evening found Mirival at the end of a largely unproductive tutorial with Jax. He was about to bring the lesson to an end when Dheran entered the room unannounced. The Emperor had a vague, unworldly air about him these days, and he just waved a hand as his Chief Seer rose in greeting.

'Carry on, carry on.'

'We've finished,' Jax said, and stared defiantly at Mirival, daring his tutor to contradict him.

No wonder no one has yet laid claim to the title 'Mentor', Mirival thought wearily. If they knew what I have to put up with, no one would even *want* to. Even so, he knew many seers who still aspired to an important role in history, while others – perhaps with better judgement – sycophantically declared that the Mentor must be the Emperor Dheran himself, the Guardian's father. Looking at the two of them now, Mirival could not help feeling doubtful about either's claim. But what were the alternatives?

'Bad business, this. With the Dark Moon, I mean,' Dheran remarked. 'Complicates things.'

Mirival was saved from having to respond to this fatuous comment by the entrance of a servant who announced that there was a Captain Yesko outside, waiting to have a word with the Chief Seer.

'Can't you see I'm in the middle of an audience?' Mirival said, irked by the soldier's presumption – and by his timing.

'Yes, Seer, but the captain said it was urgent.'

'Oh, let him in, Mirival,' the Emperor said. 'I'm not going to stand on ceremony.'

The seer nodded his assent and the servant left, to be replaced a few moments later by the captain, who bowed low before the Emperor.

'Am I to assume you have located Seer Shahan?' Mirival enquired.

'Yes, Seer.' The officer's colourful uniform was stained from several days' hard riding, and his face bore the signs of worry and fatigue.

'Where is he now?'

'In the garrison quarter-room. He's dead.'

'Dead?' Mirival exclaimed.

'One of my men was forced to shoot him as he tried to escape.'

'*What?*'

'And what was Shahan doing gallivanting off round the country?' Dheran asked.

'He was on a wild-goose chase, Sire,' Mirival replied. 'Following some heretical beliefs he'd been deluding himself with. It seems he has paid for them with his life. Where did you catch up with him, Captain?'

'At a madhouse in Saefir Province.'

At this Mirival could not help stiffening a little in surprise. Behind him, interest sparked in Jax's eyes.

'You may go now, Captain,' Mirival said, recovering his self-possession, 'but I shall expect a full report in the morning.'

'Yes, Seer.' Yesko bowed again and departed, leaving Mirival to his own thoughts.

Before she retired for the night, Adina went, as always, to bid goodnight to the prince. He was lying on his bed, still fully clothed, with a satisfied expression on his round face. When the Empress enquired about what had pleased him so, he told her about Shahan's death.

'That's good, isn't it, Mother?'

'Yes, it is,' she replied, smiling sweetly. 'Very good.'

CHAPTER TEN

Terrel woke to the acrid scent of dried sweat mingled with fear – the smell that always pervaded his cell now.

The last few days had been among the most unsettling of his life. Not only did he now have to share his sleeping quarters with two strangers, but when he had last seen Alyssa and Elam it had been for no more than a few moments – and that had been more than two days ago. With the coming of the new regime, the inmates had been spending much more time locked up, and most of the freedoms they had enjoyed had been revoked. It was only now that they had gone that Terrel realized just how valuable they had been.

The new Head Warden was a man called Aylor – a man who already commanded both fear and hatred. He was a captain of the provincial militia and, although small in stature, his air of self-confidence and ruthless determination meant that his authority was unquestioned. Ziolka had disappeared, and no one knew whether he had been sent packing or had left of his own volition. He had last been seen engaged in a heated argument with Aylor, and there were several rumours circulating about his fate. Even though Ziolka had been his gaoler, Terrel found that he missed his reassuring presence. Some of the old staff remained on duty, but the majority had been replaced by soldiers of the captain's troop. Many of these men clearly regarded the inmates with disgust, treating them as no better than animals, and there had been several violent incidents. Terrel had even heard a rumour that some inmates had been killed, as well as reports of beatings and the rape of some of the female prisoners. He had managed to avoid any direct confrontation himself, but was almost frantic with worry about Alyssa, imagining all sorts of unbearable horrors being inflicted on her fragile body and gentle mind. He was worried about Elam too. His friend's headstrong nature and acerbic tongue had often got him into trouble in the past – and it did not take much to provoke the soldiers to anger. The fact that Elam still seemed to be suffering from the after-effects of his fall from the observatory roof only made him more vulnerable. Terrel wished that his friends could have been the ones to share his cell. He found that not knowing what was happening to them was the hardest thing to bear.

The reason for the arrival of the soldiers, and the subsequent upheaval, had been a sudden influx of new prisoners – many of whom were no more insane than Terrel, but who were all obviously terrified. This in turn had led to considerable overcrowding in the cells, which was why Toresh and Rian had been billeted in Terrel's room. They were both older than him, though still young, and although they displayed a certain amount of bravado when none of the militiamen was around, it was obvious that they were frightened and bewildered by what was happening to them.

As far as Terrel could tell from the little they had said

so far, their only 'crime' was to have unwittingly broken
one of the astrologically defined taboos, but it wasn't
clear why such a minor infringement should have merited
such severe punishment. They both protested their innocence, and Terrel could not help wondering whether the
mysterious alteration in the orbit of the Dark Moon was
making such legal matters even more complicated than
usual. This might go some way to explaining why so
many more 'lunatics' had been committed to the haven
recently.

Terrel sat up in bed now and glanced at the two newcomers, who still lay on thin blankets on the floor,
twitching occasionally in their sleep. He would have been
no match for either of them in a fight, but they seemed
afraid of him – in awe of his strange eyes, his twisted limbs
and his supposed madness. This was why Terrel had not
lost the use of his bed, as many of the other long-term
inmates had done.

Toresh groaned and clenched his fists, his eyes moving
rapidly beneath his still-closed lids. Terrel wondered what
he was dreaming about. Rian stirred, opened his eyes and
looked around in confusion, as if he did not know where
he was. Then his gaze fell upon Terrel and he grew still as
the demoralizing memories of the last few days came back
to him.

'Will we get any breakfast?' he asked.

'I'm not sure,' Terrel replied. Food had been in short
supply recently and meals, such as they were, had come at
odd times. All the inmates were constantly hungry now.

Toresh muttered something in his sleep, and Rian
glanced at him anxiously.

'He's dreaming again. Ever since . . .' He left the
thought unfinished, rubbing absently at the crudely
daubed mark on the back of his hand. It was an indication

of the haste with which events were moving that there had been no time for proper tattoos.

'Do you know what he dreams about?' Terrel asked curiously.

'It doesn't make any sense,' Rian replied. 'We've never even seen the sea.'

'Neither have I, but I still dream about it.'

'Do you see waves the size of mountains, and all the islands breaking into pieces and sinking?' Rian asked, a haunted look in his eyes.

Terrel did not know what to say to that.

'It's all because of those stupid rumours,' Rian went on. 'He's been having the same nightmare ever since they began.'

'What rumours?'

'Someone said Vadanis has changed course, that we're going to collide with one of the barbarian lands. It's non-sense, of course, but there are so many strange things happening nowadays . . .' His voice trailed off again, leaving Terrel to contemplate his own recent dreaming.

He too had seen horrors, though nothing on such a scale. His dreams had been more personal, constantly replaying the scenes of Shahan's death and reminding him of what Alyssa had said about his own part in the murder. That was something she had not been able to explain properly. She had become confused when he tried to question her, and Terrel had been left to hope that it simply wasn't true. Even so, he was plagued by vicarious guilt, and kept wishing that the old man would return to Havenmoon – alive and well. In his heart he knew he was wishing in vain.

Toresh gasped and woke up, his ruddy face sheened with sweat and his eyes full of terrors.

'Moons!' he breathed. 'When is this going to stop?'

'It's all right. It will all be sorted out soon and we'll be able to go home,' Rian told him with patently false optimism. 'You'll be fine then.'

Toresh looked at him with a mixture of scepticism and hope, then shook his head in despair.

'We're never going to get out of this place,' he said. 'Never.'

Aylor gazed out over the hastily assembled throng, not bothering to hide his contempt, and cursed the day he had drawn this assignment. Where was the honour in standing guard over this mismatched collection of criminals and madmen? Most of the faces that looked back at him were fearful, though a few were so addle-witted that their expressions were merely curious or completely vacant. Aylor would soon change that. Even a lunatic could learn the meaning of fear.

'Things are going to be different here from now on,' he declared, wondering how many of his wretched audience could even understand what he was saying. 'I've no time for shirkers. You either earn your keep or you get thrown in the dungeons with nothing to eat but the rats. Unless they eat you first, of course.' Several of the soldiers who were standing guard around the edges of the courtyard grinned at this, but Aylor's face remained coldly malevolent. 'We have another consignment of misfits and freaks arriving tomorrow,' he went on, 'and we have to make space for them – unless you want to sleep six to a room. So the first thing we're going to do is clear out the north wing. Get to work!' The new Head Warden turned on his heels and strode back through the haven's main entrance, leaving his deputies to organize their conscripts.

Until that moment Terrel had been feeling better than he had done for some time. When he and his cell mates had been summoned to the gathering, he had correctly assumed that this would be his chance to see Alyssa and Elam again. When he had located his friends among all the other inmates in the courtyard he had been overjoyed to find them both unharmed and in reasonably good spirits. They had not been able to exchange more than a few words, but their mere presence had done wonders for his own state of mind. Now, however, the news of yet more prisoners, and the opening up of the previously abandoned north wing had made the day seem less bright. His library, with all its treasures, was in the north wing.

'Come on, come on. Stop slacking. Get a move on there!'
    The shuffling procession of inmates ignored Ingo's exhortations. Even though it was only a few hours old, the operation to clear out the north wing had already degenerated into a shambles. A generally unwilling and inept work force, together with the nature of the old building – with its narrow passages and doorways, its steep staircases and sloping floors – had combined to produce chaos. A great deal of uncoordinated effort had produced endless delays and only limited progress, and Terrel had begun to hope that the library might be safe for a while yet. The second floor had hardly been touched so far, because even the relatively accessible first storey was proving to be so much more trouble than expected. Doors were locked, with no sign of any keys; others were so warped or swollen that they could not be opened; and the rooms they managed to reach proved to be cluttered with so much junk that each one took an age to empty. Thick dust, grime and cobwebs made the job dirty and unpleasant, and falling debris had already caused many delays and a few injuries. Although the soldiers didn't seem to care about any of this, Ingo was obviously trying to curry favour with his new

masters and kept shouting and urging his charges on, waving his arms about and offering unwanted advice.

'Turn it sideways, you morons!' he yelled. 'Or do I have to throw you in the dungeons?'

Terrel and Elam, who were labouring to manoeuvre a three-legged table down a twisting flight of stairs, took no notice of the warden's threat, knowing that he was no longer in a position of power. The soldiers clearly regarded him as something of a joke.

'We could break off the other legs,' Elam suggested. 'They're half rotten, and the table's already useless. It'd be easier to carry then.'

'Keep moving!' Ingo shrieked. 'And no talking.'

Elam shrugged, biting back a sarcastic retort, and the two boys continued their slow and awkward journey. When they finally reached the ground floor, they were directed towards one of the doors at the rear of the house, only to find the way blocked by others who were waiting to go the same way. Eventually their intermittent progress took them close to Ahmeza's kitchens and it was there, as they waited in line, that they could not help but overhear an argument between the cook and Aylor.

'Listen, you scrawny bitch, *my* orders come directly from the Governor of Saefir Province, and I have all the authority I need to do *anything* I like here. And that includes stringing you up from a tree if necessary.'

'Then you and those hulking great brutes of yours had better learn to cook your own meals,' Ahmeza replied, undaunted by the threat.

'We'll do that if we have to,' he shot back, then appeared to have second thoughts. 'Just get on with your job, woman.'

'So you expect me to feed twice as many people with the same resources as before?' she demanded.

'You'll just have to be more efficient, won't you.'

'And now you tell me there's a whole load more coming tomorrow?'

'Yes. And they won't be the last,' he snarled. 'Shall I tell you what's happening? Shall I?' His vehemence had finally cowed Ahmeza, and she said nothing. 'The Dark Moon's not where it's supposed to be,' Aylor stated angrily. 'So every idiot who doesn't know that is breaking the law without even realizing it. And our revered Governor has instructed his magistrates to play it safe. They're condemning anyone who violates a taboo with the Dark Moon in its new position *and* those who would have done so if the damned thing was in the right place. And they're all coming here. *Now* do you understand?'

'I still can't do the impossible,' the cook responded, but she spoke more quietly now.

'If you can't do your job,' the captain told her bluntly, 'I'll find someone who can.'

By then Terrel and Elam were moving forward again, and they heard no more.

'What was all that about?' Elam asked.

'They don't know what to do,' Terrel replied, speaking as much to himself as to his friend, 'so they're making these people scapegoats.' He was dismayed by this confirmation of what Shahan had told him and of his own subsequent speculation.

They were outside now, and a soldier directed them to throw the table onto the large bonfire that was burning just beyond the vegetable gardens. Smoke from another blaze at the front of the house drifted above the roof on the gentle breeze, making the already sultry air even harder to breathe.

Having completed their task, they were about to return for their next load when Terrel's attention was caught by some shutters being thrown open on the second floor. Moments later various objects were thrown out, so that they crashed to the ground below.

'Now why didn't we think of that?' Elam commented. 'It's an awful lot quicker than lugging stuff down the stairs.'

Terrel did not reply, his gaze fixed on some of the flying debris. A few of the smaller items seemed to flap and flutter like wounded birds and he knew, with a sinking heart, exactly what they were.

'What's the matter?' Elam asked.

'They've found the library,' Terrel whispered.

Already some of the books were being collected, carried over to the fire and unceremoniously dumped into the flames. He could hardly bear to watch.

'I'd've thought you'd have read them all by now,' Elam remarked casually.

How can they? Terrel wondered miserably. How can they just destroy all that knowledge, all that learning, as if it means nothing? He could not believe that he would never be able to return to his sanctuary and lose himself in the wisdom of men from an earlier time.

'Come on,' Elam urged. 'They're only books.'

Terrel was about to respond, his sadness mixed with outrage, when all thoughts of the library and its doomed contents were driven instantly from his mind. A high-pitched scream echoed from within the house, followed by several angry shouts. Terrel had no idea who the man's voice belonged to, but the other one was immediately familiar.

As he began to run, Alyssa screamed again.

CHAPTER ELEVEN

Desperation lent Terrel a strength and agility he did not normally possess. Instinct as much as the sound of Alyssa's voice led him to a narrow hall beneath the ground floor of the north wing. Elam had tried to follow him but hadn't managed to evade the sentries at the kitchen door. Terrel had got inside, but he was brought to a halt as soon as he entered the vaulted chamber by a group of soldiers standing just inside the door. One of them simply thrust out an arm as Terrel tried to lurch past, and shoved him to the floor. When he looked up, he saw the men grinning as they watched one of their colleagues at the far end of the gallery. They were obviously looking forward to some entertainment – and when Terrel saw what they were watching, his heart froze.

Alyssa was backing away from the soldier. One side of her grey shift was ripped so that it hung off her bare shoulder, and there was a look of undisguised terror in her innocent eyes.

'Get away from me.'

'You little cat,' the man hissed, touching the scratches

on his face, then inspecting the blood on his fingertips. 'You'll pay for that.'

As he advanced menacingly, Alyssa took another step back, only to find herself trapped against the wall. One of her hands came up briefly, trying in vain to rearrange her torn garment, and her attacker flinched.

'Come on, Keth!' one of his comrades called jovially. 'You afraid of a crack-brained girl?'

The man glanced round, scowling, and made an obscene gesture.

'Is this going to take all day?' another soldier asked, provoking more amusement. 'We're supposed to be on duty, you know.'

'Aye, Barca's right. The captain'll be here soon, and he don't like us wasting time.'

As Keth turned his attention back to Alyssa, Terrel tried to stand up, but he was pushed to his knees again and his protest died in his throat as Alyssa chose that moment to fight back. Her hand flicked out, like a snake striking, her fingers extended and stiff. She was evidently aiming for her assailant's eyes and, judging from his reaction, she found her target. Keth howled and staggered back, clutching at his face, while his colleagues roared with laughter.

Watching helplessly, Terrel could only admire her bravery, even as an icy fear still held him in its grip. The eventual outcome of the encounter seemed inevitable.

Keth's rage now far outweighed his lust, and he wrenched his sword from its scabbard. One of his eyes was shut, a mixture of blood and tears running down his cheek, but he was intent on murder nonetheless. Raising his sword, he lunged forward, swiping the blade in a vicious, downward arc.

'No!' Terrel screamed, struggling against the hand that

still held him down. The next few moments seemed to last for an age, but even after it was all over, no one was able to describe what had happened. The light in the hall grew bright and then dimmed, as the air itself seemed to crackle. The stone walls shivered and moaned as the entire scene became a blur. Only the sword remained in focus, flashing with a light that came from nowhere as it began its deadly curve.

Quite how its course was diverted remained a mystery. One moment it was heading unerringly for Alyssa's unprotected throat, the next it was flying sideways, wrenched from the soldier's grip and striking the wall with a harsh grating sound. At the same time, even though she had not been touched, Alyssa collapsed in a dead faint and Keth, caught off balance by his weapon's aberrant behaviour, also fell to the floor.

Silence returned, and for a few incredulous heartbeats nobody moved. Then three soldiers ran forward. Two of them knelt by their fallen comrade, while Barca went to investigate Keth's sword. This was now sticking out of the wall, a part of its blade – the length of a man's forearm – embedded in solid rock. When Barca tried to reach for it, a bright blue spark jumped from the hilt and stung his fingers, making him cry out and jump back. When he found the courage to try again, he was able to grip the sword but could not move it. The steel was fused to the stone. He was so astonished by this extraordinary phenomenon that he had not noticed his companions' increasingly frantic efforts to revive Keth, but now their words registered.

'He's dead! The bitch killed him.'

'Well, it looks like she paid with her own life,' Barca replied, glancing over to where Alyssa lay, perfectly still.

'We'll make sure of that,' the other soldier growled venomously as he rose to his feet and drew his own sword. He strode towards Alyssa, intent on avenging his comrade, but as he did so his blade flew out to the side and caught Barca a sharp blow on his kneecap.

'Hey, watch what you're doing!' he yelled.

'I didn't do anything,' the other man protested. 'Someone grabbed my arm.'

'And who was that? A ghost?'

'Something did. I swear.'

'Give me that,' Barca muttered. He grabbed the weapon and approached Alyssa, only to have the hilt almost torn from his grasp as an invisible force twisted the blade to one side.

Barca stopped, staring first at the sword, then at the seemingly lifeless girl.

'She's a witch,' he breathed.

For a while no one spoke, and for the first time they all saw that the girl was not dead. Her chest rose and fell, almost imperceptibly, but otherwise she lay motionless, her eyes closed.

'We ought to get her out of here,' Barca said.

'I'm not going near that mad witch,' his companion answered quickly.

'Then we'll get one of the loonies to do it,' Barca decided, his own reluctance obvious.

Terrel, who had been watching all this with wildly fluctuating emotions, came forward quickly when the soldier beckoned to him. It seemed to him that there was an unnatural darkness around Alyssa, a shadow that masked her from the world and, in spite of his longing to see that she was all right, he felt nervous as he approached. His skin tingled, and blood pounded in his head, but nothing untoward happened as he knelt beside his friend and took her gently in his arms. She felt cool and soft to the touch, but her breathing was so slow and shallow that it hardly seemed enough to sustain her. The pulse at her neck was equally faint, and she was obviously deeply unconscious.

'Alyssa,' he whispered. 'Alyssa, wake up.'

There was no response. Wherever she had gone, she was beyond his reach. Terrel consoled himself with the fact that at least she was still alive.

'What's going on here?' Aylor demanded as he strode into the chamber.

The soldiers all snapped to attention, but no one answered.

'Barca, stay where you are. The rest of you get back to work. Now!' The captain waited while his men hurried to obey, then turned back to the one who remained. 'Well, soldier?'

Barca gave a brief, halting description of the strange events that had taken place in the gallery. His commanding officer's evident disbelief was only overcome when he was shown Keth's sword embedded in the wall.

'Keth paid for his stupidity, didn't he,' Aylor concluded, glancing down at the dead man's bloodied face, and noting that his chest seemed to have caved in, as if it had been crushed by a great weight. 'Detail some men to bury him.'

'Yes, sir. What about the girl?'

'She needs a healer,' Terrel blurted out from where he knelt, still cradling Alyssa's head in his arms.

Aylor laughed.

'No healer's going to waste his time on her.'

'Some of the men think she's a witch, sir,' Barca said nervously.

'I doubt she poses much of a threat,' the Head Warden replied, smiling. 'But just so you can all sleep easier in your beds tonight, have her locked in one of the dungeons. She can starve to death for all I care.'

*

That night Terrel lay awake long into the hours of darkness. He could not stop his thoughts from returning to Alyssa and the hopelessness he had felt when the solid prison door had been closed upon her small, huddled form.

Finding a strength he had not known he possessed, he had carried her limp body from the hall and into the dungeons. His pleas to be allowed to stay with her had fallen on deaf ears and, as soon as she had been incarcerated, he had been forced back to work. By the end of the day he had been exhausted, his limbs stiff and sore, but even now – hours later – sleep would not come.

Who or what had saved Alyssa from Keth's murderous attack? Had it been her ghosts? And why had she fallen into a coma, even though she had not been injured? Her life had always been touched by madness, but now it also seemed to have been affected by some form of magic. And yet little good had apparently come of it. Aylor intended simply to leave her to her fate, and she could surely not survive for very long alone in that damp, dark cell. The thought of Alyssa dying slowly in that friendless void tore at Terrel's heart. He wanted to lash out, to shout and scream against this latest injustice. And yet what could he do? Even if he was able to steal the key, evade the guards and get to her side, she would still be beyond his reach. She was trapped somewhere, in a world of her own – and Terrel could only hope that it was a better world than the one he inhabited.

He could not imagine his life without her, and began to weep at the very thought.

By the time morning came Terrel, who had not slept at all, was in a terrible state. But he had pushed self-pity aside, and had resolved to save Alyssa or die trying. Although he didn't yet know what he was going to do, he was determined not to stand idly by and let her life waste away in silence.

He had noticed that her dungeon cell had a tiny barred window near the ceiling, which must look out from the base of the haven's northern wall. Although it was far too small to present any possibility of escape – even if the bars could somehow be removed – it would at least allow him to see her, to talk to her, perhaps pass her food and water if she recovered consciousness. He would also find out all he could about her gaolers' routines, to see whether it might be possible to gain access to her cell. Then, if one of the travelling physicians who periodically visited Havenmoon could be persuaded to . . .

His thoughts were interrupted by the turnkey opening the door of his own, comparatively comfortable cell, and rousing him and his roommates. As he levered his aching body from the bed, his head swam from lack of sleep.

The day passed in a haze of exhaustion. The clearance of the north wing was progressing faster now, and Terrel was forced to witness the total destruction of the contents of the library. Although he was sickened by the appalling waste, Alyssa's plight had put the conflagration into perspective. As Elam had pointed out, they were only books.

It was only at the end of the afternoon, when the promised arrival of yet more prisoners reduced the proceedings to near chaos, that Terrel was able to slip away and find the window to Alyssa's cell. His eyes took a few moments to adjust to the gloom inside and when they did he saw, to his dismay, that she still lay exactly where he had placed her on the cold floor. There was no reaction when he called her name, and it was only after staring at her for some time that Terrel was finally able to convince himself that she was still breathing. By then he had been spotted by one of the soldiers and ordered back to work.

'I haven't forgotten you, Alyssa,' he told her before he stood up. 'I'll get you out of there, I promise.'

In all the years he had known her, Terrel had never once dreamt about Alyssa. But that night, when he collapsed onto his pallet, too tired even to undress, he felt her presence at once. Sleep claimed him, and she slept beside him. There was warmth and comfort in her closeness, a peacefulness in her slow breathing that calmed his fears and let him rest. He understood.

Terrel smiled in his sleep.

CHAPTER TWELVE

'You're going to trust in a *dream*?' Elam exclaimed.

'"Dreams are sometimes meant to show us things",' Terrel quoted. 'Alyssa said that herself.'

'But how do you know *this* one did? Don't you think it might just have been wishful thinking?'

The comfort Terrel had felt during the night – and which had still been there when he awoke – was slowly dissipating in the face of Elam's persistent scepticism. But he needed to cling to the hope that the dream had been a message.

'She heard my promise,' he said obstinately. 'She's going to be all right.'

'I hope you're right,' Elam responded, his own doubts clear.

The two boys were once again part of the team clearing the disused rooms. They were both very weary but, because Aylor was overseeing the operation that morning, the soldiers kept them under almost constant supervision and there was no chance of rest. Even when Elam suffered another bout of dizziness – something that had been happening occasionally ever since his fall – he was forced to struggle on. The task seemed endless and, for once, they were glad when Ahmeza came and commandeered their help. For the next hour they took turns drawing water from the well so that the kitchen could continue with the thankless job of providing food and drink for the expanded population. Ahmeza still gave the impression of being angry with everyone and everything around her, but now she seemed subdued as she went about her business. Because her store cupboards, vegetable garden and orchards were already much depleted, she had made arrangements for supplies to be sent in from the nearest villages in order to make up the shortfall. Her resentment at being forced to do this was palpable.

While they were in the kitchens Terrel managed to steal a few scraps of food, hoping to be able to take them to Alyssa later. He even managed to escape briefly and made his way down into the dungeons, hoping to reach her cell, but was forced to turn back when he encountered some of Aylor's men. As he fled, he almost ran into two of the captain's deputies, but they were deep in conversation and paid him no attention as he stepped to one side.

'This is ridiculous. How are we supposed to cope with so many? This place isn't even a proper gaol. Security's hopeless.'

'I know. The old man's going crazy. He's even decided to clean out some building up at the necropolis and use it to lock away troublemakers.'

'Moons! I hope I don't get that assignment. The place is supposed to be haunted.'

The two men went on their way, still complaining, but Terrel had already heard enough. He crept back to the kitchens and joined Elam again.

'We have to go back to the observatory,' he whispered.

'Are you *crazy*?' his friend exclaimed.

'We have to,' Terrel repeated. 'Aylor's going to have it cleaned out and use it as a prison.'

'So?'

'So they'll burn all Muzeni's journals. We can't let that happen.'

'Why not?' Even as he spoke, Elam knew the answer. He had seen how badly the loss of the library had affected Terrel.

'Because they're priceless. And besides, I made a promise.'

'What promise?'

'To Muzeni.'

'But he's been dead for hundreds of years!'

'That doesn't mean his work's not important. There's so much in those journals. I can't let it all be destroyed.'

'You *are* crazy,' Elam said, but the heat had gone from his voice now.

'I was meant to find those journals, Elam. I'm sure of it.'

'Don't get all mystical on me,' his friend complained. 'Just how do you propose getting up there?'

'At night.'

'Oh, great! We get to break the curfew as well.'

'We can slip away up to the loft before the turnkey makes his rounds,' Terrel explained. 'There are so many people here now the soldiers won't miss two. I just heard one of them say their security's hopeless. We'll wait a bit and then sneak out after dark. I did it before, remember?'

'That was before the charming Aylor and his men arrived,' Elam pointed out. 'They don't have the same relaxed attitude to people breaking the rules.' The boys had already seen two inmates beaten almost senseless for minor transgressions.

'It'd be worth it if we get the journals out safely,' Terrel claimed.

'That's easy for you to say. You weren't chained up in the dungeons for two years.'

'They won't do that. Even those rooms will be in use as sleeping quarters soon. The worst we'll get is a thrashing.'

'Oh, that's all right then,' Elam remarked sarcastically.

'Besides, we're not going to get caught,' Terrel went on. 'Once the curfew's past, the soldiers'll be relaxed. No one'll be expecting us to get out – and they certainly won't expect us to go up the hill.'

'That's true,' Elam conceded, 'but I still can't believe you think it's worth it.'

'I'm going to do this,' Terrel replied calmly. 'On my own if necessary. I just thought you might like another adventure.'

Eventually Elam returned his friend's grin.

'All right,' he said. 'When do we go?'

'Tonight.'

'How did I know you were going to say that?'

'So now what?' Elam asked as he and Terrel lifted the iron-bound chest that contained Muzeni's journals. 'What are we going to do with them?'

Terrel had given this some thought – but beyond the obvious fact that the books had to be rescued from the observatory, he had not come up with many ideas. There must be lots of possible hiding places in the overgrown cemetery, but choosing one of them in the dark wasn't going to be easy.

'Let's get them outside first,' he said.

'Why not put them in one of the tombs?' Elam suggested, as they edged towards the door. 'Half of them are falling down anyway – and no one's going to investigate their contents too closely.'

'I thought of that,' Terrel replied. 'I'm just not sure we'll find one with enough space for the chest.'

'We could take the journals out.'

'No. They'd rot away in a few days. The chest is the only thing that's preserved them for so long.'

They had managed to manoeuvre the heavy trunk out of the half-open door by now, and set it down next to the forlorn pile of bones. In the varied moonlight the necropolis was a place of whispering shadows and half-seen movement. It made both boys nervous, although neither was prepared to admit it.

They had waited beneath the roof timbers of the haven for several hours, taking it in turns to snatch what sleep they could, before leaving the house some time after midnight. By then all had been quiet – and if any sentries were still on duty, they hadn't noticed two small figures creeping away from the south wing. Elam had adjusted to being outside at night more quickly than Terrel had done on his earlier escapade, and they had reached the top of the hill without incident. They had planned to spend as little time there as possible, then return to their hiding place inside the house while the night was still at its darkest, but now their indecision was threatening to delay them.

'All right. Let's split up and investigate,' Elam suggested. 'If you find anywhere suitable, come back here and call.' He hooted in a passable imitation of a tawny owl. In the distance a real owl hooted back, and the two friends laughed nervously. 'You see, even she agrees,' Elam said.

They set off in opposite directions, picking their way through the long grass.

It was Terrel who found the ideal hiding place. The sepulchre was surrounded by brambles except on its lowest side, so that it could not be seen from above, and one end of the stone construction had crumbled to dust, leaving a gaping black hole. Terrel investigated gingerly, and then, as he emerged into the starlight again, a large shape flew past, gliding in perfect silence until a wavering cry made him jump. Then he smiled. It seemed that the owl approved of his choice.

Actually getting the chest inside proved straightforward enough, but it was still hard work and took much longer than the boys had hoped. When it was finally done, they were both smeared with dust and their arms were covered with scratches. However, as their clothes were already filthy from the work they had been doing for the last few days, this did not concern them too much. They left quickly, hoping their efforts had not left too obvious a trail.

'Don't worry,' Elam commented as they made their way down towards the gap in the fence. 'By the time the soldiers have found their way up here and looked around a bit, there'll be grass flattened all over the place.'

'I still don't like the thought of them invading Muzeni's home,' Terrel replied.

'*We* did,' Elam pointed out.

'That's different. We were meant to find it.'

Elam refrained from comment, concentrating on making his way through the dense undergrowth. Once they were outside the fence, he turned right without thinking, intending to retrace their circuitous route back to the house, but Terrel caught his arm.

'I'm going this way,' he said, nodding in the opposite direction.

'Why?'

'I want to see Alyssa.'

'It's dark! You won't be able to see anything.'

'No, but if she's awake, I can talk to her,' Terrel said optimistically. 'Now we're out here anyway, I'm going. I don't know when I'll get another chance.'

'If we go that way we'll be in the open for much longer,' Elam pointed out.

'That's a risk I'm prepared to take.'

'All right.' Elam gave in, realizing that this was not an argument he was going to win. 'I'll come with you.'

'You don't have to,' Terrel said.

Elam just looked at him. A few moments later, they set off together.

As they rounded the northwest rim of the hill and saw the great bulk of Havenmoon looming before them, it was impossible not to imagine eyes peering out at them from all those blank and shuttered windows. Crouching down, they watched for a while, but saw no movement anywhere. Clouds were covering the moons now, and the only light on the scene came from the smouldering embers of the two great bonfires to either side of the house. The dull red glow gave the huge house an almost demonic presence.

The two boys glanced at each other and nodded, then ran down the slope and across the open space beyond until they reached the deeper shadows beneath the north facade. The remains of the fire were out of sight now, around the corners to either side. Crouched down and breathing hard, they listened for any sound of an alarm being raised, but the silence was almost complete.

'Go find her window,' Elam whispered. 'I'll keep watch.'

Terrel nodded and set off immediately, moving with as much stealth as his awkward gait allowed, while his friend crept towards the corner at the front of the house.

When Terrel finally reached the skylight of Alyssa's cell, his earlier hopes soon faded. Elam had been quite right, of course; he couldn't see a thing. Calling her name softly — he dared not raise his voice — produced no response, but he persevered, lying down and pushing his face right up against the bars to peer into the darkness. Eventually he thought he could make out a slightly paler patch within the gloom — and if it *was* Alyssa, then it seemed that she still had not moved. But he couldn't be sure that it was not just his imagination playing tricks on him. He was about to call one last time when a sound broke the stillness of the night and he glanced up fearfully.

The voices were coming from around the corner to the rear of the building, but they were too far away for Terrel to make out what was being said. However, he was soon able to pick out the noise of footsteps, and the distant conversation became intelligible.

'Looks safe enough to me,' the first voice said.

'It's not going to flare up now, is it,' the second replied. 'I reckon it'll probably rain soon anyway.'

'This is a waste of time. Let's get back inside.'

'I'll just check the other one.'

'Suit yourself.'

Before Terrel realized what was happening, a man came round the corner of the house. Although he was only visible in silhouette, he was strolling nonchalantly and whistling to himself — and Terrel knew immediately who it was. However, that did nothing to make his predicament any less dire. Any movement now would give him away instantly, and yet if he stayed where he was, Ingo would pass so close he would probably stumble over him! Paralyzed by fear and indecision, Terrel could only wait for the inevitable.

The next thing he knew a small shadow was sprinting across the lawn towards the woods that lay to the north.

'Hey!' Ingo shouted, pausing for a moment in shock, before giving pursuit. 'Stop there!'

Terrel almost cried out, simultaneously grateful to Elam for providing a diversion and horrified that his friend was taking such a risk. However, he held his tongue and watched anxiously as first Ingo and then the other guard set off after their prey. And then, because he knew Elam would never forgive him if he didn't take advantage of the opportunity, he crept round the shadows at the side of the house until he was able to get inside and make his way up to the loft. Once there, all he could do was wait and hope.

CHAPTER THIRTEEN

It was almost dawn when Terrel finally heard footsteps on the spiral staircase. From the quietness of the approach he guessed it must be Elam – any soldiers looking for him would have no need of such stealth – but it was still an enormous relief when his friend reached the loft.

'Over here,' Terrel whispered.

In the near darkness it was impossible to tell how Elam looked, but it was obvious from his slow tread that he was very weary.

'Are you all right?' Terrel asked as his friend slumped down beside him.

'Fine.'

'You got away all right?'

'Of course. I'd kill myself if I couldn't outwit that idiot.'

'Did he recognize you?'

'I don't think so,' Elam replied. 'He didn't get close enough to see my face. With a bit of luck they won't even report it. Having to admit they lost me wouldn't make them look too good, would it.'

'But if they do,' Terrel said, 'they might check all the cells when the turnkey makes his rounds.'

'Well, there's nothing we can do about that now,' Elam remarked. 'I didn't see any signs of movement anywhere inside. Besides, we can always say we were caught in another part of the house at curfew and had to sleep where we were. That should confuse the issue, if nothing else.'

They were silent for a while.

'Elam,' Terrel said eventually. 'I . . . I . . .'

'Forget it,' his companion replied, not wanting any thanks.

'I . . . I just hope I can be as good a friend to you some-time,' Terrel said awkwardly.

'You already are,' Elam replied. After another pause, he added, 'It just made sense, that's all. Ingo couldn't have missed you where you were, but I had the chance to get away clean. Even if you'd escaped, they were bound to rec-ognize you.'

That was certainly true, Terrel thought, but it didn't stop him feeling both guilt and gratitude. However, he knew that saying as much would only embarrass them both.

'Was there any change with Alyssa?' Elam asked.

'Not as far as I could see.'

'Well, at least we got the journals safe.'

Terrel said nothing. Even that minor victory no longer seemed worth the risks they had taken. He had no idea if he would ever get the chance to read them.

Because the turnkey made his rounds at the normal time, with no sign of unusual activity, both Terrel and Elam were able to slip quietly back into their respective cells. Toresh and Rian regarded Terrel curiously, but said noth-ing, and he did not think they would betray him.

The soldiers soon ordered everyone from their rooms, as

they had done for the last few days, and as Terrel wearily prepared himself for another round of toil, he began to feel safe at last. However, the inmates were all herded towards the courtyard at the front of the house rather than to the north wing. The morning was cool and overcast, with a dampness in the air that promised the first rain in several days, but the sudden chill that Terrel felt as he stood in the midst of the crowd had nothing to do with the weather. Aylor emerged from the main entrance and stood at the top of the steps there, but it was not the captain's appearance nor his stern expression that made the boy's heart pound. It was the fact that Ingo was at his side. And at the Head Warden's first words, Terrel's fragile confidence evaporated altogether.

'It has been brought to my attention that the curfew was broken last night,' he stated bluntly, then turned to Ingo. 'Pick him out, warden.'

Terrel almost panicked then. He had seen Elam on the far side of the courtyard, but had deliberately not gone to join his friend. Now he could not help but glance in his direction, hoping against hope that Aylor was bluffing. However, as Ingo and two other guards pushed their way through the gathering, it was soon obvious that Elam was their target and then Terrel did not know whether to go to his friend's aid or call out for him to run. In the end he did neither, and merely watched in horror as Elam was dragged, unprotesting, to the steps.

Aylor looked the prisoner up and down as if he were inspecting a particularly noisome piece of garbage, but Elam's expression showed no fear. Indeed his eyes were quite blank, and Terrel realized that his friend was experiencing another of his dizzy spells.

'Were you outside the house last night?' the captain asked, his voice deceptively mild.

Elam shook his head, but the movement seemed to dis-
orientate him, and the guards who were holding his arms
tightened their grip as his legs buckled. Terrel knew that
they would take his sudden weakness as the result of guilt
and fear.

'It's him, sir,' Ingo volunteered. 'I know the way he
runs.'

Aylor glanced at the warden, and the contempt in his
eyes silenced any further comment.

'How did you get out?' he asked, returning his gaze to
Elam.

'I didn't,' the boy replied, finding his voice.

'Then why weren't you in your assigned cell when it
was unlocked this morning?'

'I was . . . No . . .' Elam's confusion seemed genuine. 'I
missed the curfew. Had to sleep in another room.'

'Where?' Aylor demanded. 'Who were you with?'

Elam struggled to make sense of these questions, his
mind still spinning.

'Well?'

'I'm not sure,' he mumbled. 'I didn't know them.'

The Head Warden turned to the watching crowd.

'Did any of you share your cell with this boy?'

No one answered. Terrel thought about speaking up,
but it was common knowledge that he and Elam were
friends. And he was not sure that Toresh and Rian could
be trusted to back him up.

'You were outside,' Aylor stated flatly. 'Were you
alone?'

'Yes . . . No. I wasn't outside.'

'You're lying. What were you doing out there? Trying
to escape?'

Elam shook his head.

'You're a fool, boy,' Aylor told him. 'You think to deny

my authority? The punishment for that is harsh. Just in
case anyone else gets any stupid ideas, I'm going to have to
make an example of you.'

The dagger appeared in the captain's hand as if by
magic.

'No!' Terrel screamed. 'No! It was *my* idea! I . . .' But
his voice was lost among the other cries that Aylor's sudden action had provoked.

And by then it was too late. Aylor struck so fast and
with such clinical brutality that no one could doubt that
the blow was fatal. Elam looked down at his chest, the
expression on his face not one of pain but of sheer surprise. The blade had sunk in up to the hilt, and it was only
when the captain wrenched it out again that the boy felt a
short-lived shiver of agony. Then his legs gave way altogether and he fell into an endless darkness.

After their initial outburst, the onlookers all fell silent,
aghast. Even Ingo looked horrified. Terrel felt as though
his own heart had been pierced; he could not move, or
breathe, and his mind simply refused to accept what he
had just seen. An anguished voice inside his head shouted
endless, hopeless denials. Doubling up, his eyes temporarily blind, he shook uncontrollably, his stomach heaving. He
did not hear Aylor's terse final words as he told the
inmates that this was the justice they could expect, and
that security would be tighter from now on. It was only
when Aylor had gone and the crowd was dispersing that he
was able to move at all. Ignoring the orders of the guards,
he staggered over to where Elam's lifeless body had been
thrown down on the steps. Terrel wanted to comfort him,
to tell him that he loved him, that he was sorry . . . to
bring him back to life. But before he even got close one of
the soldiers grabbed him.

'Where d'you think you're going, son?'

'He was my friend,' Terrel gasped, aware for the first time of the tears running down his face.

'Well, he ain't no more,' the soldier said. 'And you'd better not make too much fuss unless you want the same treatment. On your way.'

Terrel stopped struggling then, still staring at the untidy pile of flesh and rags that was all that was left of his friend. And then he glanced up and saw Ingo looking back at him. There was a smile on the warden's face – and in that moment, Terrel knew that at least one person had heard him cry out. His own life was now held in Ingo's treacherous hands.

Terrel expected them to come for him all morning, but it was only when the inmates were allowed a break for their frugal midday meal that his fears were confirmed. The preceding hours had passed in a fog of pain and self-recrimination, but when he saw Ingo in conversation with Toresh and Rian, both of whom looked understandably fearful, he knew his time was up. Ingo and the soldier with him turned away and began to walk towards Terrel – and it was then that he saw what the warden held in his hands. It was Muzeni's journal, the one that had been hidden beneath his pallet.

In spite of his fear, Terrel suddenly felt quite calm. He was in no doubt now that his overnight absence had been discovered and – even though no one could possibly know where the journal had come from – his mere possession of such a book would serve to confirm his guilt. Given recent events, he could expect little mercy from Aylor. Part of him was almost glad. Alyssa's coma and Elam's death had deprived him of both the people he loved; there seemed little left worth living for. But as Ingo and his doom moved closer, such fatalism was replaced by the instinctive need for self-preservation and he glanced around, assessing his chances of escape. The hall was crowded, with all the doorways guarded, so the prospects were not good. There was nowhere to run.

And then an inhuman howling split the air, with a cry that was born in the wild mountains. Many of those in the room clapped their hands to their ears to keep out the fearful din, while others were so startled they almost fell from their benches. At the same time a bowl, full of the thin soup that was the main part of the meal, was hurled at Ingo, splattering him with broth and forcing him to duck aside. A moment later, the source of the awful noise was on the move. With unbelievable agility for one so ancient, Old Timi leapt first onto a trestle table and then from there at Ingo. The madman's hands were curved into claws, and his toothless mouth was open wide in a mad snarl. His moon was full and he was a wolf again.

Ingo tried to swat him away like a bothersome insect, but the wolf possessed a strength that Old Timi did not, and the two men went down in a tangle of limbs. Several other long-term inmates decided to give vent to their own inner demons, shouting or laughing in turn. Many of them climbed up onto the tables, sending crockery flying in all directions. The more recent arrivals were either frightened or bemused by these antics, but most of them stood up too, adding to the confusion. The watching sentries hesitated, unable to make any sense of what was going on, then began to force their way towards the howling at the centre of the disruption.

Terrel didn't know what had brought on this lunatic demonstration, but he wasn't going to wait to find out. Instead, he dived to the floor and began to crawl on all fours through the mêlée towards the nearest exit. When he reached the door it was unguarded and he slipped out, hobbling as fast as he could down the corridor. He had no idea where he was going, and only wanted to put as much distance between himself and Ingo as possible – so it came as something of a surprise when he bolted through another open doorway and found himself in the kitchens.

'I might have known it'd be you causing all that commotion,' Ahmeza remarked. She was standing in front of him, with her arms folded and a fierce look in her eyes. Having discharged her most recent duty, she was alone, her domain otherwise deserted for the time being.

'They're going to kill me,' Terrel gasped.

The cook's eyes hardened. She had not witnessed Elam's execution, but she'd heard all about it, and the news had only confirmed her opinion of Captain Aylor.

'Then you'd best not let them catch you,' she said. 'In here.' She pulled the lid off a barrel, normally used for storing apples but empty now, the fruit having gone to feed the many extra mouths.

Terrel hesitated, staring first at the barrel, then at the cook, wondering why she had decided to help him.

'Come on!' she snapped. 'Get in.'

He did as he was told, and squashed himself down inside the sweet-smelling wooden struts. As Ahmeza replaced the lid the darkness was almost complete, and the heady scent of fruit was overwhelming. Trying to still his convulsive shaking, Terrel listened hard for any signs of pursuit, but all he could hear was the thumping of his own heart. It was so loud that he thought the soldiers must hear it if they came too close. However, the next activity in the kitchens came not from the militiamen searching for the fugitive but from Ahmeza's helpers returning with dirty plates and bowls, and the usual bustle was restored. Terrel remained perfectly still, even though his muscles were beginning to cramp, and prayed to all the moons and stars for deliverance.

Some time later he heard voices raised above the clatter of pots and pans, and knew that the soldiers had come. Their search did not last long under Ahmeza's scolding tongue.

'You think I wouldn't know if he was in my own kitchens?'

When they had gone Terrel relaxed a little, and for the first time began to wonder what he was supposed to do next. If he stayed at the haven he would soon be captured, and so it seemed that he had no choice but to try to escape to the outside world. This thought frightened him almost as much as that of facing Aylor – and he had no idea how to make such an attempt.

Time passed and, drunk on fermented apple fumes, Terrel dozed. The kitchens grew quieter again, and then Ahmeza greeted a newcomer.

'Jon! About time too!'

'Hello, sister,' the man replied. 'I came as fast as I could.'

'I'm glad you're here,' she told him, with as much warmth in her voice as Terrel had ever heard. It had never even occurred to him that the cook must have a family somewhere.

'Did you bring all I asked for?' she said.

'Almost. Come and see.'

The voices retreated for a while, then returned.

'As soon as the unloading's complete, take the ponies and the cart over to the stables,' Ahmeza told her brother. 'It's too late for you to head back tonight, so you'd better stay here and head out in the morning.'

'All right.' Jon sounded reluctant, but obviously saw the sense of the idea.

'I'm sorry I couldn't get Aylor to meet your full price,' she added. 'We'll all starve before that man sees sense.'

'It's not so bad, if I get the firewood we agreed on,' he replied.

'It's the one thing we have plenty of,' Ahmeza said. 'Till the winter, at least. I'll get some of the lads to load the cart up tonight, so you can leave at first light.'

'Fair enough.'

'Just make sure none of the loonies try to leave with you,' the cook advised him, laughing. 'Our captain doesn't like anyone who breaks his precious rules.'

Hidden in his fragrant refuge, Terrel realized that the cook had staged the conversation near the barrel for his benefit.

'They're looking for one poor kid now,' Ahmeza went on. 'Going through the whole house, room by room. I wouldn't want to be in his shoes when they find him. Come on, let's find you a bed for the night.'

That was as clear a warning as he was ever going to get, Terrel thought. He had to get out of the house soon, because even the kitchen could not remain a safe refuge for much longer. He needed to hide somewhere in the grounds, and then – somehow – get himself aboard Jon's cart in the morning. It sounded simple enough, put like that, but the frightened boy had no idea how to go about it.

Where could he go – always assuming that he was able to leave the kitchens undetected? The observatory? That seemed like tempting fate, and the memories of his disastrous visit there with Elam were still painfully fresh in his mind. Could he hide in the stables? No, that was too obvious, too risky. Where then? The woods? Down the well? Don't be absurd, he told himself angrily. When it came to him at last, the answer was frightening, but he knew it was his best chance. No one would think of looking for him there – if only he could make it that far.

The kitchens had been quiet for some time now, but Terrel knew they would not remain so for long. If he was ever going to leave, it had to be now. He carefully pushed the lid of the barrel aside and stood up, almost crying as the pain lanced through his stiff legs. Climbing out proved difficult, especially as he was terrified of making a noise, but he managed it, and then limped over to the door that led out to the gardens and peered through. It was dusk, with a light drizzle falling from a leaden sky, and no one seemed to be about. So Terrel forced his protesting limbs into action again and ran crookedly into the cover of the vegetable patch. Crouching there among the tomatoes and beans, he heard no sound of any alarm. So far, so good.

Inside the haven there were far more lights than usual, and he knew that the soldiers were carrying lamps as they went through the house, presumably looking for him. It was a distinctly uncomfortable feeling, and reinforced his determination to get away.

He ventured further from the building, then slipped from the garden into the southern orchard. After waiting there and still seeing no signs of any pursuit, he trusted himself to the increasingly gloomy evening and set off into the wide open spaces, circling round to the south of the house in an irregular arc. Eventually he crossed the path and continued down the hill to the lake. Once there he found the jetty and, without hesitation, lowered himself into the water.

Long before he reached the haunted island he was gasping for breath, afraid that he might drown, but he made it at last and pulled himself, shivering, onto the shore. When he had recovered a little, he got up and staggered towards the tower, hoping to find some shelter. As he did so he

could not help remembering some of the legends connected with the place. The most famous of these was of
the young maiden who, when she refused to marry the
lord of the time, was walled up inside the tower to starve.
But she was only one of the ghosts reputed to dwell there.
If all the stories were to be believed, this small island had
seen more murder, rape and treachery than many cities –
and it took all Terrel's dwindling supply of courage not to
jump out of his skin at every small noise.

To his surprise the lower part of the ruin proved quite
hospitable. It was like a small cave, and the floor was covered in several years' worth of dry leaves. Forgetting that
he would need to get them wet again in order to leave the
island, he stripped off his dripping clothes in the hope that
they would dry out a little overnight. Then he tried to rub
some life back into his tortured limbs before lying down
and making himself a cocoon of leaves. Before long, exhausted in both body and mind, he slept.

Terrel had expected his own paralyzing feelings of guilt
and remorse over Elam's death to turn into nightmares,
but his dreams that night were calm, almost soothing. He
floated on a bed of light, like an eagle soaring weightless
on the wind. He saw nothing, felt nothing. It was as
though the ghosts of the island were watching over him,
spreading a protective veil over his mind. It was only at
the end that he heard her voice and began to struggle. He
knew it was Alyssa and fought to see her, to be with her,
but she remained disembodied and remote, and it was
only when he had come to terms with his frustration that
he could actually hear what she was saying.

'It's all right. I know you have to go. I'll wait for you.'

The dream was fading now, its purpose served, and
there was nothing Terrel could do about it.

'Don't worry. I'll wait for you.'

Terrel woke feeling a mixture of reassurance and terror. For the first time he realized the full implications of his escape. If he were to succeed it would mean abandoning Alyssa – and he was not sure he could bring himself to do that. It was one thing to leave her for a few days while he was planning ways to help her; it was quite another to contemplate fleeing from the estate altogether. He would not be able to return in the foreseeable future, perhaps ever. He would not be able to see her, speak to her . . . And yet in the dream she had given him her blessing, her promise – almost as if she wanted him to go. Dreams are sometimes meant to show us things. But could he trust them?

Looking out of the entrance of his man-made cavern, he saw the Red and Amber Moons, close together and low in the sky, both full. Love and dreams, he thought. Or violence and the spirit world. Who was to know? The gap in the cloud cover closed, and the moons were hidden again.

What choice do I have? he wondered. I can't stay. After this Aylor is bound to 'make an example' of me – and then I'll have abandoned Alyssa for good. At least this way there's the possibility of coming back.

He got up and dressed in his damp clothes, took one last look around, and thanked the island spirits for their welcome. Then he waded into the cold, black water, knowing that before he went to the stables – however stupid it was – he had to visit Alyssa's cell one last time, to bid her farewell.

Daybreak was still some hours away, and in the darkness he nearly missed the jetty and got entangled in the reeds. When at last he heaved himself out of the water and started back towards the house, the benefits of his night's rest already seemed to be slipping away and he began to doubt himself once more. His natural caution made him wait and watch at some distance from the haven, but he could detect no movement and there were no lamps burning now, so he moved forward and came to the window at the base of the north wall.

Peering in, it seemed to him that her pale shape was brighter than before – even more ethereal – but she still had not moved.

'Alyssa?'

There was no response, but he had expected none.

'Goodbye, my love. I *will* come back for you. I swear it.'

And then, tearing himself away as tears threatened to blind him, he headed for the stables, knowing that he would keep his promise. All he could hope for was that she would be able to keep hers.

PART TWO

THE WANDERER

Chapter Fourteen

Terrel and the cow stared at each other. It was probably true to say that neither had ever seen anything like it before.

Certainly Terrel had never seen a cow before – although he had heard them lowing earlier in the day, and had been wondering what sort of creature could possibly make such a loud and yet so mournful a noise. Having come face to face with the animal as he pushed his way through a narrow gap in a hedge, he was relieved to find that although its sheer bulk and stubby horns were intimidating, it seemed placid enough.

For her part, the cow – in as much as she was able to tell the difference between humans – probably recognized that this ragged figure was unusually shaped and that his eyes were strange. However, as he did not seem to be either a threat or a possible supplier of food, her natural curiosity was soon exhausted and she returned to her grazing.

This was not true for the others in the small herd. They had been further away when Terrel emerged into their field, and thus had not been able to see who or what he was. One of the nearest cows decided to investigate, and began to walk towards him slowly, and that piqued the interest of the rest. Soon all the cows were converging on him, some of them breaking into a lumbering canter, until they came to a halt a few paces away, forming a semicircle of curious stares. This renewed the inquisitiveness of the first animal, and she looked up again. One of the others mooed plaintively, and there was some slight jostling and shuffling of hooves as those at the back pushed forward to get a better view.

Terrel's first instinct had been to retreat, to put the hedge between himself and the herd, but now, faced with this attentive audience, he felt the urge to put on a performance for them, to dance or sing. That in turn made him want to laugh – and he acknowledged the unfamiliar impulse with gratitude. In the end he did nothing, and simply gazed back at the row of large eyes and slow-moving jaws.

He was thinking, for perhaps the hundredth time since leaving the haven, that the world was full of such commonplace wonders, when a wordless but obviously human cry sounded from the far side of the field.

'Heeey-yup!'

On hearing the remote voice the cows lost interest in Terrel and turned away, ambling across the meadow in the direction of the newcomer. As they thinned out, Terrel saw a figure – presumably the herdsman – walking towards him, and once again his first thought was of flight. Hard experience had taught him that he was unlikely to find much of a welcome among his own kind.

The farmer was a big man and he was carrying a heavy stick, with which he gave several of the cows almost friendly taps as they passed by. Should he choose to wield it as a weapon, Terrel had no doubt that it could land a crushing blow, but in spite of this he lingered, hoping that on this occasion his instincts would be proved wrong. It had been a long time since he had held a conversation with anyone, several days since he had even heard another voice, and the need for some sort of human contact was strong.

The man was obviously aware of Terrel's presence now and, although he moved in an unhurried fashion, his long stride covered the ground quickly, and there was a stern expression on his weather-beaten face.

'You're trespassing, boy. This is my land.'

Then he fell silent, and Terrel knew that this was because he was close enough now to have seen his eyes. He had become used to the reaction, and sought to deflect it as best he could.

'They're just eyes,' he said. 'They don't do anything special.' He half expected the farmer to make one of the surreptitious signs which were supposed to ward off evil, but he just stood where he was and met Terrel's gaze in steadfast manner, evidently assessing the stranger.

'What are you doing here?' he asked eventually.

'Nothing,' the boy replied, then realizing that this was not a sufficient answer, he added, 'I'm travelling . . . looking for somewhere to stay.' He was painfully aware of his own appearance. His clothes were torn and stained, and he was filthy. The only advantage to this was the fact that the dirt hid the tattoo on his left hand. He had grown thinner, and living rough had worsened the constant aching of his deformed limbs, so that his face had developed a gaunt and desperate look. It took little imagination to predict the way most people would react to his presence. Such a stranger would have been unwelcome in most places, even if his eyes had not been so unusual.

'Well, you can't stay here,' the farmer told him flatly, dashing any faint hopes that Terrel might have harboured about this encounter turning out differently.

'I know,' he replied meekly. 'Is there . . . Do you have any work I could do?'

The big man laughed.

'You don't look much like a farm hand to me,' he said.

'I've worked in stables.'

'I've all the help I need.'

Terrel accepted the rejection stoically. He had expected nothing else.

'I can read and write,' he said, refusing to give up all hope. 'Do you know of anyone—'

'You'd best try in the village,' the farmer cut in, his dark eyes betraying none of the incredulity that Terrel's claim had provoked elsewhere.

'Where's that?' In truth Terrel had no idea where he was.

'No more than half a league, over there,' the farmer replied, pointing across the field. 'There's a path through the woods that's easy enough to follow.'

'Do you mind if I cross your field then?'

'Not if you clear off afterwards,' the man said gruffly. 'And don't come back. I've got enough troubles with my beasts without you bothering them.'

'Thank you.'

The farmer turned away without another word and stomped off after the herd, which was heading towards a gate at the edge of the woods. Terrel followed at a distance. By the time he reached the far side of the meadow and had spotted the path to the village, the animals had gone through the gate and turned in the opposite direction, obviously following a well-established routine. They were now trudging into a steep-sided gully between two boulder-strewn hills. As he ushered them onwards, the farmer abandoned his earlier cries of encouragement and spoke in an easy, conversational tone.

'Quiet now, girls,' he told the herd. 'We don't want to wake up Old Runeshanks, do we.'

Terrel watched them until they were out of sight, wondering who or what Old Runeshanks was, then turned and plodded on his way.

Terrel had lost track of how many days had passed since his escape. All he knew was that he couldn't go on as he was for very much longer. Unless his fortunes changed, he would soon become too weak to look after himself – and then it would only be a matter of time before he starved to death. There had already been times when he'd been tempted to give up, to lie down in a ditch somewhere and go to sleep, hoping never to wake up again. The only reason he had not done so was his promise to Alyssa.

From the moment he had found himself in the freedom of the world outside the haven, the boy had been torn. He had wanted to stay as close to his former home as possible, in the forlorn hope of getting news of Alyssa – and of eventually returning to her – but the dangers of doing this were obvious. Terrel had no idea whether Aylor would decide to pursue him in open country, but even if he did not, the problem of his tattoo being noticed – or of his being recognized as a fugitive – was much greater in and around the villages at the edge of the moorland. And so, reluctantly, he had begun to wander further afield.

It was not long before he realized that although his earlier life had been restricted, it had been simple in many ways, and surprisingly protected. He had been sheltered by the very routines that confined him, with a roof over his head, a bed to sleep on, food on a regular basis, and the company of friends. He had none of those things now.

From the outset he had been forced to beg or steal food, and each time he succeeded – whether through a rare act of kindness or because of his own dishonest stealth – he felt guilty and ashamed. He was not a natural thief, having an instinctive knowledge of right and wrong, and most of the people he encountered were themselves poor and could hardly afford to share their meagre provisions. It was true many of them treated him horribly, and that the insults and threats his appearance often provoked were hurtful, but in Terrel's mind that did not give him the right to rob them. He only did so out of desperation. If no one was willing to give him the chance to earn some sustenance lawfully, what else could he do? He knew almost nothing of scavenging for food in the wild, and was as likely to poison himself as satisfy his hunger that way.

He had slept in the open on many occasions – thankful for the relative warmth of summer – as well as in barns or outhouses whenever he could sneak into them undetected. On one occasion he had even stayed overnight in a cave he'd stumbled upon late one evening. He'd left in a hurry the following morning when he had seen that the floor was littered with bones. He had no wish to meet the hunter whose lair he had usurped.

This comfortless way of living had done nothing for Terrel's physical wellbeing, and he often woke to find himself bruised and stiff from another cramped night. But this was not the worst aspect of the hours of darkness. His dreams were often horrific and exhausting, so that he hardly seemed to get any rest at all. And even when he could not interpret their elusive images – or could remember only part of the disturbing visions – he inevitably linked them to recent events, and tortured himself with his waking thoughts and feelings.

Foremost among these was the corrosive regret that was eating him up from inside. His own actions at the haven – insisting on the visit to the observatory, and then forcing Elam to go with him to Alyssa's window – had led to his friend's death and his own self-imposed exile, and thus his enforced separation from Alyssa. His memories were made even more bitter by the fact that the entire expedition had been to no purpose. He would probably never even get the chance to read Muzeni's journals now, and his presence outside Alyssa's cell had achieved nothing. He still clung to the obstinate belief that she would somehow survive her ordeal, but when he thought about it rationally, he knew that her situation was terrible, especially as Havenmoon was in such turmoil. He had even less justification for his fervent belief that he would see her again one day.

Terrel also knew that trouble was brewing in the outside world, and this made his own prospects that much less promising. It was clear that great events were taking place, and that they were beyond the control – and the understanding – of ordinary men.

He was still in the process of learning just how large and how amazing the world was. Two days ago he had caught his first glimpse of a distant mountain range, and had stared at it in awe. The first time he had seen a large river he had been similarly amazed – and the first town he had come to had left him breathless and afraid. How could there be so many people, in such a small place? No amount of reading could have prepared him for such sights, and every day brought new wonders – and new terrors. Through it all his predominant emotions were bewilderment and fear, but there had been a few moments of exhilaration too, when he realized that all of Vadanis had been opened up to him. Whether it would ever offer him anything other than his current miserable existence remained to be seen.

Now, as he limped along the woodland path and saw a clearing where several trees had been felled, his thoughts returned to the morning of his escape.

It had still been dark when he had crept into the stable yard, but he had been able to see that Jon's cart was there, piled with corded wood, just as Ahmeza had said it would be. There did not seem to be any sentries on duty – or if there were they must have found a comfortable place to sleep away their watch – so Terrel moved fast, knowing that he did not have much time. Climbing up on to the cart, he began to clear a space in the centre of the pile of wood, placing bundles round the sides so that they built 'walls' around him. Then he climbed down into the hole he had created and began to cover himself over, starting with his legs. It was a painful and awkward process, and he had to dislodge the last few bundles and let them fall on top of him. When he had finished, the boy was lying inside a wooden tomb. It was incredibly uncomfortable, and he was not even sure that he could not be seen from outside. There was nothing he could do about that now – and it was only at this point that he had felt the finality and the anguish of leaving Alyssa behind. He wept silently for all the losses he had suffered, then composed himself to wait, motionless in spite of his discomfort and the cold embrace of his wet clothes.

Light came slowly, revealing a few small gaps in the wooden framework around him, but no one seemed to notice anything untoward. Terrel heard voices, including Jon's, and, shortly afterwards, he felt a gentle rocking as the ponies were harnessed to the shafts. Then they moved off, jolting and swaying over the yard and then along the rutted

path towards the gate. This part of the journey seemed endless, and at one point the wood shifted around him, digging
into his chest and arms and making him think it might fall
and expose his hiding place, but Jon continued on his way.
Eventually the cook's brother halted the ponies and exchanged greetings with the gatekeeper – who sounded bored
and sleepy – while Terrel held his breath. Moments later he
heard the sound of the iron-clad gates creaking open and felt
the cart begin to move forward again.

Even though he couldn't see anything, Terrel knew
that – for the first time in fourteen years – he was outside
the walls of the estate. He could hardly believe it. Excitement made his heart race, but he remained hidden,
knowing that staying on the cart was his best – perhaps his
only – chance of crossing the moor. His thoughts turned to
the end of the journey. The nearest village was Cotillo,
which was where he assumed Jon lived, but he did not
know what his reception would be there. Could he trust
Jon? Ahmeza had helped him evade capture, but had she
told her brother anything? Would it be better to try to
break away before they reached the village?

In the end the decision was taken out of his hands.
After about an hour of steady travelling, Jon spoke.

'You can come out now.'

Terrel froze, not sure whether the unexpected words
had really been addressed to him.

'We're well out of sight of the haven, and no one's following us,' Jon added, reining in the ponies. 'You must be
uncomfortable in there.'

A short while later, with Jon's help, Terrel had extri-
cated himself from the wood pile and was sitting next to
the driver as they continued on their journey. Jon had
been taken aback by the sight of Terrel, but he recovered
quickly enough.

'Did Ahmeza tell you I was going to try to come with you?' Terrel asked.

'No. She talked about you a bit, but she probably thought it best I didn't know your plans,' he replied. 'I knew they were searching for you, though, and when I saw that the wood'd been disturbed, I put two and two together.'

'Why didn't you give me up?'

'And risk my sister's anger? No thank you! She's sharp enough when you're on her good side, and she liked you.'

Terrel took some time to digest this surprising news, and they rode in silence for a while. Before they reached the edge of the moor, Jon told the boy that he'd be better off not going all the way into Cotillo.

'There's some who don't think the way I do. And the way things are now, anyone with one of those . . .' He indicated Terrel's tattoo, '. . . isn't likely to get much of a welcome round here. You'd be better off heading west a way.'

Terrel nodded, seeing the sense of Jon's argument. He also knew that going into the village with Jon might get his rescuer into trouble, and he had no wish to see that happen. They parted company where the track divided, some distance north of Cotillo.

'Thank you,' Terrel said simply. 'Thank you.'

'Good luck,' Jon said, before he drove away. 'I hope you find what you're looking for.'

Terrel turned and began his journey into the unknown.

Since then Terrel had travelled a long way, without really knowing where he was going. But in one sense he was no further forward at all. He still had no idea what he was looking for.

CHAPTER FIFTEEN

When Terrel finally reached the village, he saw that it was little more than a hamlet, a scattering of single-storey wooden houses built at the crossing of two trails. From a distance it seemed almost deserted, but as he drew closer he could see several old people sitting in groups around their doorways, and a knot of small children playing at the far end of the main thoroughfare, watched over by a trio of women. There were no young men anywhere, and although Terrel wondered what had taken them from their homes, he also felt some relief at the thought that he was less likely to have to face any violence.

Mindful of the hostile reactions his appearance often provoked, he had already done what little he could to improve matters. He had washed his hands and face in a small stream, run wet fingers through his hair and brushed down his ragged clothes as best he could, before rubbing some dirt on to the back of his hand to mask the tattoo again. Now he simply walked into the village, squinting in part because the sun was strong, but also to minimize the effect the sight of his eyes might have on the inhabitants.

He meant to approach one of the groups outside the houses, hoping to receive some sort of welcome, however reluctant, from the village elders, but before he could reach them his attention was drawn to a notice nailed to a post at the central crossroads. He went up to it, aware that he was now being watched by several pairs of eyes, and saw that it was an official proclamation, issued in the name of the Governor of Saefir Province. He began to read, already reasonably certain of what it would be about, but was interrupted by a voice behind him.

'Can you read that, young man?'

Terrel turned round to see a man who was clearly very old but who held himself upright and with pride. Only his eyes, which were so clouded they were almost white, betrayed him. He was holding the hand of a small boy, who was presumably acting as his guide, and it was the child who reacted to the sight of Terrel's eyes. His gasp was accompanied by an expression of fear and horror, and the old man clearly sensed the boy's unease.

'What is it, Rico?'

'His eyes,' the child whispered.

'Are they worse than mine?' the old man asked, smiling.

'They're full of stars!'

'Really? Well, that's good, isn't it? The stars—'

'No! It's horrible,' the boy exclaimed. 'And his arm's all bent.'

'Rico!' the elder admonished. 'You mustn't say such things. It's wrong to judge a person by their appearance.' He turned back to Terrel, who had waited uncertainly throughout the exchange, and added, 'Please excuse my grandson. He's very young.'

'I've been called worse things,' Terrel replied. 'And I'd be the first to admit my eyes *are* strange. But they're just eyes,' he added, glancing at the child. 'They won't hurt you.'

'Apologize to our visitor, Rico.'

'Sorry,' the boy mumbled unconvincingly.

'Now say it like you mean it.'

'It doesn't matter,' Terrel said quickly. There had been times when children had pelted him with stones and adults had threatened him with far worse, simply because they didn't like the way he looked. Rico's childish dislike was nothing by comparison.

The old man frowned, but did not press the issue, returning after a moment to his original question.

'So you can read the proclamation?'

'Yes.'

'You see, Rico. This is a man of learning, someone to be respected. What is your name, young man? I am called Efrin.'

'Terrel.'

'Ah. Light of the new moon. Your parents were familiar with the old tongue, I see.'

Terrel saw no point in telling the old man that he had never met his parents – whoever they were – and that they had certainly not had anything to do with his naming.

'I used to be able to read such things, but my eyes are going,' Efrin went on. 'It's just a blur now, and soon I won't be able to see anything at all.' There was no self-pity in his voice, simply an acceptance of what was. 'Of course I don't suppose I'd have been able to make much sense of this. Even our underseer can't seem to sort it all out.'

'Your underseer?' Terrel queried. He had never heard this term before.

'A lad called Chenowith. Clever, but still wet behind the ears, if you know what I mean. Two years in Makhaya and he thinks he knows everything. Ha! Well, this proclamation soon gave the lie to that.'

'Grandpa?' Rico said, tugging at the old man's sleeve. 'Can I go and play?'

'I don't see why not. If Terrel here will let me take his arm on the way back to the house.'

'Of course.'

Rico ran off, his relief obvious. Terrel watched him go, knowing that soon all the village children would hear about the peculiar stranger in their midst.

'So will you read this to me?' Efrin said. 'We might make sense of it together.'

Terrel did as he was asked. After a pompous preamble, the text of the notice contained vague references to 'changes in the patterns of the heavens', and then listed a series of dates concerning the cycles of the moons. Particular emphasis was laid on the Dark Moon and the alterations in the periods when it was waxing and waning, especially in comparison to the other moons. It was unnecessarily complicated, and by the time Terrel had finished he was not in the least surprised that the underseer had been confused.

'Well, I *think* I've got it straight now,' Efrin said doubtfully. 'But what's going on? How could the seers have got it so wrong before? I thought it was all fixed years in advance.'

'Something's different,' Terrel replied. 'Something no one can explain.'

'And it's always us – the farmers and country folk – who are supposed to change our ways because of it,' the old man complained. 'Planting and harvesting aren't things you can do on the whim of some prophet in the city. Look what's happening here!'

'What do you mean?'

'Chenowith is making us run round in circles. That's where the men are now, out in the fields before the corn is even ripe. If we go on like this we'll all starve. And I'll wager it's the same in others places too. The soldiers said they were posting these proclamations in every village in the province. There's only a few of us can read, so that leaves us at the mercy of the underseers, and half of them are incompetent charlatans. It won't be long before the fanatics are spying on everything, making life difficult for ordinary people. What do I care where some eclipse falls as long as there's food on my family's table?' The old man paused and took a long breath. 'At least we've not come to that yet,' he said, calmer again now, 'and I'm forgetting my manners just like a six-year-old. Would you like something to eat and drink?'

'I'd like that very much,' Terrel replied.

Some time later, replete from the best meal he had enjoyed since leaving Havenmoon, Terrel felt his spirits rising. Having been welcomed by Efrin – who was clearly regarded with respect by the villagers – he also seemed to have been accepted by the rest of the depleted community. Gallia, Efrin's daughter and the mother of Rico, had provided the food, and several other adults had slowly gathered to hear him talk. Gallia would not look him in the eye, and most of the others seemed nervous in his presence, but the longer they conversed with the traveller the more comfortable they felt. Only the children remained unconvinced, creeping up to get a peek at the now famous star-filled eyes and then running away, shrieking and laughing at their own daring. For his own part, Terrel was simply grateful to rest and eat without fear or guilt, enjoying the hospitality of Efrin's household. Despite the villagers' evident curiosity, he talked about himself as little as possible, lying only when he had to, and excusing his lack of knowledge of the world by saying he had lived a sheltered life as a servant in a big house until he'd been forced to go out and seek his own fortune.

'You should go to Makhaya,' Gallia suggested. 'They say there's always a need for scribes and suchlike there.'

'Perhaps I should,' Terrel said, half serious.

'Talk to Chenowith, then,' someone else advised. 'He's been there.'

'Much good it did *him*,' Efrin remarked sourly.

'I'd like to talk to him,' Terrel admitted. 'Will someone show me the way to the fields?'

'Rico will do it,' Efrin said, then turned away and yelled to his grandson.

'Are you sure, Father?' Gallia asked. Her disquiet was obvious.

'Just tell me where to go,' Terrel said quickly. 'I'll manage on my own.'

Gallia nodded, not bothering to hide her relief, then led Terrel to the edge of the village and gave him directions.

'Thank you, Gallia.'

She still would not look at him directly and he felt a pang of sadness, wanting to overcome her reluctance.

'I'm very grateful for your kindness to a stranger,' he said, 'especially one as unusual as me.' He wanted to ask her why she was so afraid of him, but lacked the courage.

Gallia merely nodded in response, her gaze fixed on the ground, then hurried back to her house. Terrel watched her go, then turned and went to look for the underseer.

The scene in the cornfield was like a moment frozen in time. Half the crop had already been harvested, with much of it gathered into sheaves and stacked in neat piles, but all work had stopped now. A dozen or so men plus a few young women were standing about, their scythes and sickles idle. They were all watching two men who faced each other in the centre of the cleared area of stubble. One of these was tall and well built, and his rugged face was red with anger and his muscles taut, as if he were only restraining himself with some difficulty. The other looked tiny by comparison, and had the smooth complexion of youth. They were arguing and, although the younger man was clearly afraid of his adversary, he too was standing his ground. Their voices, one deep and hoarse with rage, the other light but passionate, were loud enough to carry easily to where Terrel stood, unnoticed, at the edge of the field.

'First you tell me to start cutting even though it won't be ripe for several days yet – and now, halfway through, you tell me to stop?'

'If you don't, I'll have to condemn the *entire* crop and have it burnt,' the younger man – whom Terrel assumed to be Chenowith – replied, with equal fervour.

'But it's madness! How can you tell such things from a *book*?' He gestured angrily at the ledger that Chenowith held open in his hands.

'I'm sorry, Leman,' the underseer replied. 'I wish it wasn't so, but the moons don't lie. You know the law.'

'But we planted at the correct dates. You know that. How can it suddenly all be out of kilter?'

'Things have changed,' Chenowith told him, less confident now. 'You've seen the proclamation. It just took me a little time to work out the implications.'

'So what you're saying is that the seers got it wrong in the first place? That the almanac is wrong?'

'There must have been some errors, yes.' The young man was obviously embarrassed.

'Then how do we know you're not making an error now?' Leman demanded. 'None of us can even read that damned proclamation. Maybe the moons don't lie, but men can.'

The insult clearly cut deep, and Chenowith's face grew pale with anger.

'I am your underseer,' he said sharply. 'And until either the Governor or one of my superiors in the Seers' Council tells me otherwise, my word is law here.' He paused, aware of the hostility all around him but prepared to stand by what he'd said.

Leman's fury was still running high, but Chenowith's words had clearly had an effect on him.

'Can we not keep what we've already cut?' he asked. 'We can't afford such waste.'

The younger man shook his head determinedly.

'The Dark Moon changed aspect during the night. This corn is tainted and must be burnt. Can you afford to eat poison?'

'During the night?' Leman exploded. 'You had all night to work this out? And yet you let us begin this morning? Your incompetence . . .' Words failed him.

'I was up all night trying to finish my calculations,' the underseer replied defensively. 'This is a most complex matter. It's not only the Dark Moon that's—'

'I don't want to hear your excuses!' Leman snapped.

'The rest of the crop can be saved,' Chenowith said placatingly. 'You only have to wait another two days and the White Moon will begin to wane. There will be time then—'

'Unless something else changes in the meantime,' the big man remarked caustically.

The underseer did not reply, and the silence stretched as the villagers' anger began to turn to sullen resignation. Their lives had always been ruled by the unseen forces of the skies, and they were not about to start breaking their taboos now – no matter how much they resented the hardships this would bring. They might despise Chenowith, but in the end they would obey him.

Terrel had listened to the debate, aware of the tensions all around but fascinated by the underseer's arguments. He very much wanted to talk to him and to study his almanac – but he was destined never to get the chance. One of the villagers had finally spotted the stranger, and when he took note of Terrel's appearance he cried out in alarm.

'Enchanter! An enchanter!'

Suddenly Terrel was the focus of everyone's attention – and it was a distinctly unpleasant feeling. Whether because of the already inflamed atmosphere, or because younger men are naturally more belligerent, his reception here was quite different from the one he had received in the village. Tools began to seem like weapons in the harvesters' hands, and every face wore a hostile or fearful expression as they began to gather round the outsider. Terrel had no idea why he had been called an enchanter – in fact he did not even know what an enchanter was – but he heard other, equally ominous whispers on the lips of some of the men.

'He has the demon eyes.'

'Look! There's his rune-sign on his hand.'

'. . . steal our souls.'

Only one man was prepared to confront him directly and that, predictably, was Leman.

'Who are you? What are you doing here?'

'My name is Terrel.' He was very frightened now, and angry with himself for having fallen into such a dangerous situation. 'I came here to talk to Chenowith.'

A further rumble of unease ran through the watchers.

'How do you know my name?' the underseer asked, obviously taken aback.

Terrel hesitated before replying, wondering whether his best chance might be to play on their evident superstition and pretend to have magical powers, but in the end he decided to stick to the truth.

'I've been to your village.'

This provoked another outburst from the onlookers, and Terrel hurried to calm their fears.

'Efrin invited me to eat with him.'

'That old fool,' someone muttered.

'And Gallia gave me directions here,' Terrel added.

At the mention of the woman's name one of the harvesters stiffened, his knuckles showing white as he gripped his scythe.

'If you've harmed her,' he declared, 'I'll kill you!'

'Why would I want to harm her?' Terrel answered, bewildered. 'Or anyone? I'm no enchanter or demon. I'm just a man.'

'Then why are your eyes like that?' Leman asked.

Before Terrel had a chance to reply, another villager stepped forward.

'Perhaps he's the reason for all this!' he shouted wildly. 'He's put a curse on our fields!'

'No!' Chenowith cried. 'There is no curse. This is astrology. Science!'

The underseer was having to compete with voices raised in anger, and Terrel wasn't sure the harvesters were paying him any attention.

'We want no enchanter here.'

'Put his eyes out. He won't be able to harm us then.'

'Why would an enchanter be dressed in rags?' Leman asked. 'Or walk with a twisted leg?'

'His evil has crippled him,' someone suggested. 'We should finish him off.'

Several of the men began to advance menacingly, and Terrel was about to threaten them with magic – desperate enough now to reconsider the ploy he had rejected earlier – when Chenowith spoke up with the beginnings of real authority in his voice.

'Have you taken leave of your senses?' he shouted. 'You would consider murder on account of your superstitions? This is no more than a boy. He has no power. That resides in the heavens. Leave him be.'

The villagers hesitated, many of them looking to Leman for leadership, while Terrel was glad he had kept quiet.

'Would you have us just let him go free?' Leman asked, glancing at Chenowith.

Before the underseer could reply, the man whom Terrel had taken to be Gallia's husband interrupted.

'He goes nowhere until we know he's done no harm in the village.'

'That is fair,' Chenowith decreed. 'All you have at the moment are suspicions. If there is proof of wrongdoing, then that is another matter.'

'Yatil, you're the fastest,' Leman said. 'You go.'

The man ran off, and the rest returned their gaze to Terrel. Secure in the knowledge that there was nothing wrong at the village, the boy took a few paces towards Chenowith, hoping to be able to talk to his unexpected ally. To his surprise, the harvesters and the underseer all moved back. They were still afraid of him. Deciding to act in the least threatening way possible, and giving up any thoughts of a conversation, Terrel simply sat down in the stubble and waited.

In due course Yatil returned with the news that all was well, but although the mood relaxed a little, it was clear that the antagonism towards the stranger persisted. Chenowith came over to Terrel as the boy rose to his feet.

'You'd better leave,' he said quietly. 'While you still can. These peasants have no education and are prone to violence.'

'I meant no harm to anyone.'

'I know. I'm sorry.'

Terrel went, limping as fast as he could, heading away from the village. He knew he was being watched by everyone there, and did not feel safe until he was some distance away. He had been granted several insights into the ways of the world that day, but the one that caused him the most pain was the fact that, for all his supposed sympathy, not even Chenowith had been able to look him straight in the eye.

That night, alone again, Terrel slept on a bed of moss beneath a thatch of leaves. The woodland seemed unnaturally quiet, lacking the normal assortment of rustlings and nocturnal cries, and he felt uneasy.

When sleep finally came, he dreamt of burning cornfields and choking drifts of smoke. Then he was caught in a whirlwind so that he was spun round and round, grasping at fleeting images. Endless pages of script, that he knew he must read somehow, were blowing in the wind, but no matter how hard he tried, he could not catch them. When stillness returned, Terrel looked into a mirror and saw his own face, but his eyes were opaque, milky white. The mirror shattered, leaving him blind. Then he was high above a great city, looking down upon hundreds of magnificent buildings. He heard bells ringing – and he felt contempt and a sense of boredom, feelings that were alien to him and yet somehow familiar, even comfortable. Then they too vanished into the echoing thunder.

The end came, as he knew it would, in the unreasoning terror of the crimson sea – the sea that reduced him to nothing, and left him drained and sweating in the cold darkness of the forest.

CHAPTER SIXTEEN

'What are you doing up here?'

Jax turned from his airy contemplation and stared at his father. It was hard to tell which of them was the most surprised. The whole court knew that the prince liked to sleep late in the mornings, and Dheran seemed as frail as he was absent-minded – and yet here they both were, atop the highest tower of the imperial palace at dawn.

'Nothing much,' Jax replied, then grinned. 'Actually, I was trying to find somewhere Mirival won't think of looking. His lessons are getting more and more boring.' He had no intention of telling his father about the dream that had propelled him out of bed to their current lofty perch. 'What are *you* doing here?'

'Oh, I don't sleep much these days,' the Emperor said. 'I wander about, you know. Probably drive the servants mad, popping up all over the place.'

'Probably,' Jax agreed, still grinning.

'I come up here when I want to look out over the city and think.'

'Think about what?'

'Oh, the responsibilities of being Emperor, how the people regard me, that sort of thing.'

'Sounds a bit too serious for me,' the prince commented. Whenever he looked out over Makhaya he felt only irritation that he knew so little about its more interesting districts, and he regarded his father's subjects with disdain.

'They *are* serious matters,' Dheran said gravely. 'You may joke about your education, but it's the foundation of what you must learn before you are fit to become Emperor.'

Jax groaned inwardly.

'I thought my lineage made me fit to be Emperor,' he said, his voice sulky.

'Eligible,' his father replied. 'Not fit. That is a privilege you must earn if you are to command respect.'

People will respect me, Jax thought. They won't last long if they don't. His surprise at meeting his father was turning to annoyance, and he was beginning to wish he could think of some way to escape. At the very least he had to find a way to change the subject of their conversation.

'Did you hear the bells this morning?' he asked.

'Of course,' Dheran replied. 'They're another reason I wasn't able to stay in bed. Do you know why they were ringing?'

Jax realized that he had fallen into a trap he'd unwittingly set for himself.

'No,' he admitted.

'They were marking the full of the White Moon,' the Emperor told him, using the patronizingly 'adult' tone that his son found so infuriating. 'You would know that if you paid attention to your studies. Every man on Vadanis has to be aware of the lunar cycles. You, more than anyone, should realize that.'

Here we go, Jax thought helplessly. It'll be the fate and destiny speech now.

'The moons prophesied your fate from the moment of your birth,' Dheran said on cue, but then he fell silent and when he spoke again a few moments later his tone had become melancholy, and his thoughts had evidently ranged out in new directions. 'Your destiny was supposed to be fulfilled when you're seventy-five. That's a long time to wait, and I wouldn't live to see it, of course. I mean, I'd be . . .' He struggled with the sum for a while, then gave up. 'Over a hundred, anyway. So it's not likely, is it?'

Moons! I hope not, Jax exclaimed silently. Few people even lived to the venerable age of seventy-five – which in itself seemed impossibly ancient to the fourteen-year-old prince. A hundred was just ridiculous.

'But now I hear it might be earlier,' the Emperor went on, staring dreamily at some distant clouds that the newly risen sun was painting a delicate coral shade.

The sooner the better, Jax thought. He knew he was supposed to become a hero in due course, and liked the status this conveyed upon him, but no one ever told him how he was to go about it. All he got were yet more tedious lessons.

'Mirival told me that,' the prince said, feeling that he ought to make some contribution to the conversation.

'Ah, so you pay attention to *some* of the things your tutor tells you,' his father remarked, smiling.

'Of course I do. It's just that so much of it is so *dull*, and I can't see what any of it's got to do with me – or my destiny.' Jax remembered his last lesson, when his impatience had boiled over into an ill-tempered outburst. He'd informed Mirival that because he was in the prophecy, he was going to be a hero whether he knew all these boring facts or not. The seer had replied that he certainly hoped so, but his tone had been so insolent that the prince had been enraged, and had stormed out of the lesson in disgust. He hoped the incident had not been reported to his father, or Dheran would no doubt embark on another lecture.

'Most people think he's the Mentor,' the Emperor said. 'He's there to guide you.'

'I suppose so,' Jax replied, pretending to agree meekly in the hope that Dheran had finished.

'Of course, you weren't the only one born that night.'

This remark caught the prince completely off guard, and he could think of nothing to say. Nor could he work out why his father had chosen this moment to raise a topic that was usually forbidden.

'I often wonder if I did the right thing,' the Emperor added vaguely.

'About the baby, you mean?'

Dheran nodded.

'I suppose he must be dead by now.'

Jax could have told him otherwise, but he decided to hold his tongue. The explanations would be too complicated and, besides, he didn't want the old fool talking to Mirival about his twin. Shahan's interfering had been bad enough – although it had presented a challenge.

'Mirival said at the time that there wasn't much hope for him,' Dheran went on, 'but perhaps if he'd stayed here in Makhaya, with all that our physicians and healers could have done . . .' He left the thought unfinished.

'Do you know where the baby was taken?' Jax asked.

'No. Mirival arranged all that. I thought it best to keep out of the way. Maybe I should have spoken up.'

'I'm sure you and Mirival did what was best for Vadanis,' the prince said. Not that you had much choice, he added silently. Adina had told Jax about his twin – and had made it perfectly plain that it was *her* influence that had ensured the exile of the deformed infant.

'I suppose so,' Dheran responded quietly.

'Just as I will when my turn comes,' Jax said, hoping that this loyal statement of intent would satisfy his father.

'It weighs heavily sometimes,' Dheran said portentously.

'What does?' the prince asked, then wished the words back as soon as he had uttered them.

'The imperial crown. Ruling all this.' The Emperor spread his arms wide, indicating the panorama before them.

Having learnt his lesson, Jax chose not to comment, and contented himself with looking suitably solemn. Inside he was railing against such morbid thinking. What was the point of ruling all this if you never *did* anything? His father just moped about the palace, making everyone miserable. He did not deserve to be Emperor. For a moment Jax considered pushing Dheran over the parapet, but it was only a fleeting impulse. He would not reach the legal age for inheritance for another two years, and the prince shuddered at the thought of Mirival as Regent.

'Excuse me, Your Majesty.'

The timid voice belonged to a young maidservant. As the Emperor and his son turned to see what she wanted, she curtseyed stiffly, looking down at the floor.

'What is it, my dear?'

'Chamberlain says the papers are ready for your signature, Your Majesty, and cook says your breakfast is ready now.'

The girl curtseyed again, obviously nervous. She was one of the many servants who had been sent to look for the

Emperor, and she had not really expected to find him here.

'I'll be down presently,' Dheran told her, smiling to reassure the shy creature.

Jax smiled at her too, though for different reasons. She was one of the pretty ones, and he was imagining what she would look like with no clothes on.

'You see, Jax,' Dheran said when the maid had left. 'You're not the only one who is forced to complete mundane but necessary tasks. There have been so many new decrees recently my wrist aches from signing them all. Will you join me for breakfast?'

'No, thank you, Father,' the prince replied, thankful for the interruption. 'I think I'll stay up here a bit longer.'

When he was alone again, Jax tried to concentrate on some of the things he had learnt that morning, but his mind refused to cooperate. He kept thinking of the maid-servant. After all, he was nearly a man now, he told himself. It was time to complete the transition. He knew Adina was already making plans for his marriages once he came of age, but in the meantime . . . What was the point of being in a position of wealth and power unless you could use it to enjoy yourself? He wondered idly if he could get away with ordering one of the younger maid-servants to come to his rooms. Or maybe, he thought, his pulse quickening at the idea, he might even be able to find one with a mind like Marik's.

'Go away!'

Mirival waited patiently as Lathan's servant knocked again at the door of his master's study.

'Chief Seer Mirival is here to see you, sir.'

'Well, tell him to go away.' Lathan's voice cracked halfway through the sentence so that the last two words were little more than a croak.

The servant glanced nervously at Mirival, who decided to take matters into his own hands.

'Open the door, Lathan. If you don't I shall bring the guards to break it down.'

There was silence for a few moments, then the two men heard the sounds of footsteps shuffling across the room and bolts being drawn back. However, Lathan did not open the door but retreated again, so that by the time Mirival had turned the handle himself and entered the chamber, he was slumped at his desk once more.

'Come to gloat?' he muttered venomously.

'No,' Mirival replied briskly. 'I have a job for you.'

Lathan grunted in disbelief, and turned to face his unwanted visitor for the first time. The seer's face was puffy, and his eyes were red-rimmed from lack of sleep, but it was the despair Mirival saw within those eyes that caused him the most alarm. Lathan's belated acceptance of the facts had shaken him deeply, as Mirival had known it would, but it was also clear that the very foundations of Lathan's world had crumbled to dust, leaving him almost broken. This was a waste of talent the Chief Seer could not allow.

'As you can see, I am fit for nothing,' Lathan announced with evident self-loathing. He gestured round the room, at the desk that was littered with papers covered in much amended calculations, at the untidy pile of books and the shelves cluttered with various chronometers and optical instruments of all kinds. It was the den of a recluse, a fanatic – and of someone who had reached the end of his tether.

'You've always been the best mathematician on the council,' Mirival stated firmly. 'That hasn't changed.'

'I thought so once,' Lathan mumbled despondently. 'But now . . .' He picked up some of his workings, crumpled them into a ball and tossed it casually across the room.

Mirival knew that his fellow seer had finally confirmed to his own satisfaction that the Dark Moon had changed orbit, and – even more mystifyingly – that it had actually increased in diameter. However, no one had yet come up with a feasible explanation for why – or how – these events had occurred.

'We're all confused,' the Chief Seer admitted. 'You're not alone in that.'

'Confused? Confused!' Lathan exclaimed bitterly. 'Either we're all insane, or the heavens themselves have gone mad. Which do you prefer?'

'We're making progress,' Mirival declared. 'We'll understand it eventually.'

The first part of this statement was indeed true. The immediate consequences of the change had been calculated with reasonable accuracy and, through the network of underseers and with the help of the army, these had now been proclaimed in all the provinces. What had once seemed a hopeless task, with administrative chaos just around the corner, was now at least under control – and those local authorities who had overstepped the mark in dealing with the situation on their own had been reined in. In addition, estimates of the timing of the next four-moon conjunction were now being refined. Although the calculations varied, it was reasonably certain that it would take place some sixty-four years after the last one, eleven years earlier than expected and fifty years from now. Reinterpretations of various relevant sections of the Tindaya Code were also well under way and, reassuringly, the early results indicated that disruption to the prophecies would be minimal.

The one area in which the seers' combined efforts had met with almost no success was in evaluating the movements of the Floating Islands. According to all their calculations, the alterations in size and movement of the Dark Moon should have had an almost negligible effect on the islands' course – far less than had actually taken place. It was this worrying discrepancy that Mirival wanted Lathan to work on.

'However,' the Chief Seer went on, 'we only have a chance of understanding it if we all work together.'

Lathan shook his head, but he looked weary now rather than incredulous.

'What do you want me to do?' he asked, a small measure of his professional pride resurfacing.

'Make some accurate observations about the course of the islands. The ones we're getting now are contradictory, and it's vital we clear up the mess.'

'You trust me to do that?'

'I do. Pick your own team. Travel wherever you need – the Imperial Guard will provide transport. But you must move quickly. Ludicrous rumours are already beginning to spread, and we must stop them. Will you do it?'

Lathan hesitated for only an instant before nodding.

'Good. I'll let you get on then.' Mirival turned to go, but the other man's voice halted him in his tracks with an unexpected question.

'You weren't at Shahan's funeral, I noticed. Why was that?'

'I had pressing issues of state to attend to.'

Shahan had been buried with no ceremony and little fuss. He had had no family, and many of his fellow seers had felt it politic not to attend, preferring to disassociate themselves from the dead man's rumoured heresies – although no one seemed to know exactly what these were. Others, including Lathan, had felt that they should pay their respects to a senior colleague.

'A sad end for a man of his learning, don't you think?' he said now. 'To be murdered like that.'

'Sad indeed,' Mirival agreed. 'But murder is too harsh a word. The court martial found his killer guilty only of a lesser crime.'

'Yes, because his fellow soldiers closed ranks and stuck to their story. But didn't you find the idea of Shahan trying to escape like that a little far-fetched?'

'Who knows what lengths a man in his state of mind would be driven to,' Mirival replied.

'Do you know what misguided path he was following?'

'I have some idea, but I don't see the point of sullying his reputation now. He is gone. Best to forget the follies of his last days.'

Lathan nodded. He seemed to be on the point of prolonging the conversation, but then thought better of it, and Mirival went on his way.

That afternoon a small group of like-minded men met in a spacious courtyard near the Seers' Chamber. They did so deliberately, reasoning that the best place to hide a conspiracy was out in the open. Men in their positions would naturally have much to discuss, especially concerning their latest research, and no one would think twice about seeing such a debate take place. And in that particular spot, which they had chosen with casual-seeming care, they would be able to spot any interloper long before he was within earshot.

The subject of their conversation was rather more delicate than the movements of moons or islands, and it went on for a long time. In the end a consensus was reached, but not before every conceivable repercussion of their actions had been meticulously dissected.

'So, we're agreed then?' said the man who, though he would have denied the title, had become their leader by default. 'An anonymous letter to Mirival. If he shouts treason from the rooftops, then we'll find another way. If he stays silent, we take our plans a stage further. Will you all accept my wording for the letter?'

'Provided you keep to the exact points we agreed,' one of the others replied. Like the rest, he was glad to be relieved of this particular responsibility. The delivery of such a letter would require stealth and cunning.

'Of course.'

There were nods of agreement all round.

'Then our message will be delivered this evening,' the leader stated, and with that the conspirators went their separate ways.

The night brought with it an oppressive heat and a heaviness to the air that promised storms. By the next morning the skies were at war, with purple-black clouds rumbling over Makhaya and violent short-lived squalls of drenching rain across the rooftops. Lightning spread across the heavens, sometimes in a single blinding arc of brilliance, sometimes in apparently endless branching networks that stretched from one horizon to the other. There was even one horrifying moment when the lightning took the shape of a glowing ball, which rolled down the centre of a street on the outskirts of the city before disappearing in a sudden explosive thunderclap. Many fires were started, while at the same time flash floods ruined several properties.

Because it was situated on high ground, the imperial palace seemed to its inhabitants to be uncomfortably close to the turmoil above.

'I have such a headache!' Adina cried, holding her hands over her ears as another clap of thunder followed hard on the heels of a nearby lightning strike. 'When is this storm going to end?'

Jax watched his mother with barely concealed amusement. He loved Adina dearly, but she had always been fond of dramatic gestures, and her acting talents – while considerable – could hardly be considered subtle. He was actually rather enjoying the violence of the weather. It made an exciting spectacle, and did at least provide an interesting diversion from his daily routines. In fact, he realized now that the elements had been doing their best to keep him amused for some time. The weather that summer had been the most changeable he'd ever known, with several storms, unseasonable cold spells and even – so it was reported – tornadoes in the southern provinces. Jax wished one of these whirlwinds would visit Makhaya; he would have liked to see the effect it would have had on the buildings here.

There had also been a number of unexplained earth tremors recently, and while none of these had been serious, Jax had enjoyed watching the consternation of the seers when one of them struck. It was almost a surprise when they predicted a tremor accurately nowadays.

'You could always go down to the wine cellars,' he suggested. 'It would be quieter down there.'

'Don't be ridiculous!' the Empress snapped, glaring at her son.

In a lull between the peals of thunder, someone knocked at the chamber door.

'What now?' Adina groaned, then called out to whoever it was to come in, assuming it would be one of her servants. When Fauria let himself in she cursed inwardly, realizing she had forgotten their appointment. For his part, the seer was obviously taken aback to see Jax sprawled in one of the chairs, but he recovered his poise quickly enough.

'I'm sorry, Your Majesty. I did not wish to intrude.'

'He should have been at his lessons by now,' the

Empress replied, knowing full well that Fauria had been aware of this when choosing the time for their meeting.

'I'm not going till he sends for me,' Jax declared. 'I'm not a glutton for punishment.' He had noted Fauria's unease and was now speculating on its cause. Had his mother acquired a secret admirer? He wouldn't blame her if she had. Dheran wasn't up to much these days – but then Fauria could not really be said to be much of an improvement. It was more likely to be a matter of court politics, which was much more interesting. What are you hiding from me, Mother? he wondered, looking at the Empress and impudently raising his eyebrows.

'Should I return later?' the seer asked.

'Perhaps . . .' Adina began. 'No, stay a while and talk. It'll take my mind off this infernal weather. Sit down and tell me the latest gossip.'

'The rumour-mongers have surpassed themselves recently,' Fauria said after a moment's thought. 'There's some story about a monster deep within the mines of Betancuria.'

'A monster?' Jax sat up, his interest ignited.

'Yes. No one's seen it properly, of course, but it's been described as an unnatural, malevolent darkness.'

'Darkness in a mine. How unusual,' Adina commented facetiously.

'Does it kill people?' Jax asked eagerly.

'Apparently it does. Gossip credits it variously with swallowing men whole, turning them to stone, melting them like wax candles, or vaporizing them into smoke.'

'How bizarre,' the Empress remarked in disgust.

'It's all nonsense, of course,' Fauria conceded.

'But there must be *something* down there,' Jax said.

'Even rumours have to start somewhere,' the seer conceded.

'So what are they going to do about it?'

'Given that it's almost certainly some natural geological force,' Fauria told him, 'they've tried to block it off.'

'And has that worked?' Adina asked.

'Apparently not,' the seer replied. 'But then all of this is only hearsay. The only thing we can be sure of is that the mining engineers now have the perfect excuse for being well behind on their production schedules. I suspect—'

He was interrupted by another knock at the door.

'That's probably your summons, Jax,' Adina said, much to her son's obvious displeasure. 'Enter.'

Remi came in, took in who was present at a glance and bowed his head to the Empress.

'I'm sorry to interrupt, Ma'am.'

'What is it, Remi?'

'I have grave news,' the chamberlain replied. 'Seer Mirival has been found dead in his home.'

CHAPTER SEVENTEEN

Terrel had been wandering aimlessly since he'd been driven from the cornfield. The strength of the antagonism provoked by the sight of his eyes had left him feeling utterly desolate. He had only been welcomed by Efrin because the old man was blind. Terrel wondered whether he might fare better if he were to bind his own eyes with cloth and pretend to be blind himself, like a beggar he had seen earlier in his travels, but he did not want to be accepted because of a lie – and the practical difficulties would be almost insurmountable. There must be someone, somewhere, who would give him a chance. But he had no idea how to find them.

After a while, he realized that he must have been going round in circles, because he was back at the field where he had encountered the cows. The herd was there again, and so was the farmer. This time Terrel remained hidden within the foliage of the tall hedge, mindful of the fact that he had been told to keep away. He watched as the cows headed once more for the gate, which already stood open.

The warning began, as it always did, as a trembling deep inside him, but this time it was stronger than ever. Terrel was used to the sensation by now, and as the premonition grew to certainty, he simply accepted it. Then, as he looked around to make sure he was in as safe a place as possible, he remembered something the herdsman had said two days ago.

Before he realized what he was doing, Terrel set off across the meadow in his lopsided run, calling at the top of his voice.

'Don't go into the ravine! Don't—'

The farmer turned to look at him, his face darkening with anger, but the boy's words made him hesitate.

'I thought I told you—'

'There's going to be an earthquake!' Terrel gasped as he came to a halt under the man's stern gaze.

'There's nothing due for days,' the herdsman replied, but there was doubt in his eyes. Like every other farmer in Saefir, he was aware that several recent tremors had not been listed in the almanac. 'What are you talking about?'

'Old Runeshanks,' Terrel replied. 'What is it?'

'What do you . . . ?' The farmer set aside his surprise and answered the question. 'She's a witch who was buried inside the hill over there,' he said, pointing to one side of the ravine. 'Behind that cliff face.'

'The cliff's unstable, isn't it?' Terrel guessed, seeing immediately how rockfalls could lead to a legend about a vengeful witch.

'Yes.'

'The earthquake's going to wake her up,' Terrel went on, knowing he was right. 'Don't go in there. Not yet anyway.'

During this discussion the cows had been ambling on,

following their usual routine, and most of them had now passed through the gateway and were heading towards the gully. They obviously did not sense anything out of the ordinary, and their owner knew that animals were often much more sensitive to such things than any human. And yet there was something about this strange boy . . .

He whistled loudly and the cows all stopped, turning their large heads to look at their master. They displayed no surprise, merely the curiosity that Terrel had seen before. Nothing happened for a while, and time seemed to slow to a crawl. Terrel's certainty did not diminish, but he could see the doubts building up in the herdsman's mind.

'If this is some sort of trick . . .' the farmer said threateningly, glancing round as if he expected the boy's accomplices to emerge from their hiding places at any moment.

'It's not. I swear.'

Most of the cows had now begun to graze on the sparse vegetation next to the trail, glancing back at their herdsman every so often. They still seemed quite content. Terrel saw the farmer draw in his breath to send them on their way again, and made one last despairing effort to convince him.

'*Please* don't go in there. It'll be soon now.'

The man frowned, his hand tightening on his stick, but then the trembling inside Terrel grew to a crescendo, and he knew the waiting was over.

'It's coming!'

The herd clearly agreed with him. Several of them began lowing in alarm, and a few had become skittish, shifting and stamping nervously.

The earthquake struck. Terrel was thrown to the ground, a victim of disorientation as much as the sudden vibration, but the farmer remained on his feet, staring in horror. The cows panicked and, although none of them fell, they charged in all directions, some crashing into the hedge, while others thundered back down the trail towards the men so that Terrel feared he might be trampled. The sound of their terrified lowing was joined by an ominous crashing from the ravine – and beneath it all was a deep growling that seemed to come from the bowels of the planet. The whole thing lasted only a few heartbeats, but it was the strongest tremor there had been in a long time.

When it was over, the herdsman called to his charges in a voice that shook, calming them as best he could. Then, as Terrel picked himself up, he glanced at the boy.

'How did you know?'

Terrel shrugged.

'I can't explain it.'

'Is it over?'

'Yes.' As with any earthquake there was the chance of some lesser aftershocks, but the boy could sense nothing else coming this time – and the animals all seemed calm enough now.

The farmer went round the herd, rescuing one of the beasts who had become entangled in the hedge, and patting each animal on their neck, talking to them softly all the while. Then, beckoning for Terrel to follow, he went to inspect the ravine. It was still passable, but the trail was strewn with rocks, some of them large enough to crush either man or cow. The farmer was white-faced with shock. He knew that without Terrel's warning he would have lost some of his herd at least, perhaps even been killed or injured himself.

'She woke up all right,' he said to himself, looking up at the cliff face above, then turned to Terrel. 'Can you always do that?'

'I think so.'
'Then maybe I have some work for you after all.'

Terrel was to spend almost two median months at the farm, and during that time he came as close as he had ever done to being part of a real family. The farmer, whose name was Ferrand, had overcome the initial qualms of his wife, Magana, and their two sons with the simple yet forceful argument that – no matter how odd he seemed – Terrel had probably saved not only his own life but those of half the herd as well. And, he had added, even if it was not for the debt he owed the boy, such a remarkable talent could prove very useful in these troubled times.

As always, it was Terrel's appearance that caused the most unease. Jehar – who, at twenty, was two years older than his brother Vizquel – remained suspicious of the newcomer for quite some time. However, as Terrel asked for nothing more than a place to sleep and enough food to live on – and in return did whatever he could to earn his keep – even Jehar eventually grew accustomed to the strange outsider. And when Terrel correctly predicted another tremor – less severe this time – he proved his worth to them all. He was also able to help Ferrand make the necessary amendments to his almanac by interpreting the various proclamations that were posted in the nearby villages.

As the days passed, Terrel began to learn the ways of the farm: the daily migrations of the cattle to pasture and back for milking; the slower rhythms of planting and harvesting various crops; the careful preserving of food in preparation for the harsher months ahead; the rituals involved in the feeding and care of goats and hens; and the regular trips to the nearest villages to barter produce for whatever else they needed. He discovered how the milk yield of the herd varied according to the aspects of the moons, and how the irregularities of the Dark Moon had caused several animals to become fretful or even barren. And through it all he felt an internal tug of war as his new-found contentment battled against the idea that he was betraying Alyssa.

He dreamt of her often – without ever being able to see her face – in between his regular nightmares, and each time he visited her that way he woke feeling strangely reassured, still convinced she was alive and waiting for him. When fully awake he was not so sure, tormenting himself with his own imaginings. But he had wandered so far from the haven that he no longer knew in which direction it lay – and even if he was to return, he had no more idea about what he could do to help her than he'd had when he left. Until he could answer that question he saw no point in moving on, and the attraction of having found a place where he was accepted, where his life had become stable, was undeniable. He had no wish to return to the outright hostility of his earlier wanderings, and chose not to accompany any of his hosts on their visits to nearby settlements. He was happy to remain a part of their small community, and they in turn had no wish to advertise his presence to the outside world.

There were three other people who lived and worked on the farm; a burly labourer called Ty, his wife Mia and their daughter Sarafia. At eleven years old, Sarafia was the closest to Terrel's age, and once she had overcome her initial shyness – and her nervous parents had come to terms with Terrel's presence – they spent a lot of time together. It was from the young girl that Terrel learnt of the legend of the enchanter, a story that was part of local folklore.

'He lived in a castle made of glass, on top of a mountain,' she told him. 'But sometimes he would come down among us to practice his sorcery. He had eyes that drew you in like a whirlpool. When you looked into them, all you could see was a faraway light, like the sun or a thousand stars – and if you did that you were lost. He could make anyone do anything he wanted then, especially the women.' She blushed at this, but Terrel didn't notice.

'My eyes don't have that effect,' he said. 'Rather the reverse, in fact.' But he could see now why his appearance caused such discomfort – and why Gallia's husband in particular had been so concerned.

'I don't believe all the stories,' Sarafia remarked, 'but I like hearing them.'

'You're good at telling them too,' he told her.

'Do you think so?' She smiled in genuine pleasure at the compliment. 'I'd like to be a travelling player, going to all the villages and putting on shows and telling stories. But I don't suppose I ever will,' she added, suddenly downcast. 'I'll probably be stuck here for ever.'

'There are worse places to be stuck,' Terrel said.

Terrel's time at the farm coincided with a number of strange sights in the sky. Shooting stars became an almost nightly occurrence, their short-lived beauty counterbalanced by their reputation as harbingers of conflict. When the stars fall so do the dreams of men, as the old saying put it. For several nights a distant comet was also visible, an ice-blue streak making its slow progress across the heavens – and that too was seen as an ominous event. There were also several eclipses of the sun by various moons. Regardless of the fact that all of these – even those caused by the Dark Moon on its altered course – had been accurately predicted by the seers, the unusually close grouping was seen as significant. The unnatural periods of reduced light filled the people in the shadows below with a sense of unease.

All this only served to intensify the rumours that were spreading throughout the countryside, concerning various upheavals in Makhaya, of dissent among the seers themselves, and of the imminence of unspecified disasters. This speculation was made worse by the undoubted fact that a split was developing between those who were guided by the heavens in all things, and those who saw themselves as more practical men – to whom most of the recent developments made no sense. In a situation where neighbours might take to spying on one another to make sure that no taboos were being flouted, and where soldiers constantly patrolled the countryside, tensions were bound to run high.

For the most part, the inhabitants of the farm were not directly affected by this uneasy state of affairs, but even in their relative isolation they could not remain unaware of it. Terrel in particular was frustrated by the fact that he did not know more. He thought longingly of Muzeni's journals, and wondered whether those hidden pages might contain answers to the mysteries that were currently engulfing Vadanis. But they too were beyond his reach, as remote as the Dark Moon itself.

'It's twisted too far,' Vizquel muttered, caught between frustration and panic.

'We can still do it,' Ty said, although his voice betrayed his lack of confidence. 'Come on, old girl. Keep trying. This'll be over soon.'

The cow bellowed as she strained helplessly. There had been several difficult calvings recently, but this was proving to be the hardest so far. To make matters worse, Vizquel's parents and Jehar were away at market when the labour began unexpectedly early, leaving the birthing in relatively inexperienced hands.

The cow had produced several calves over the years, and she knew – from the pain and the length of time this one was taking – that something was seriously wrong. She was growing weak now, and if she went down there was a good chance they would lose her and the calf. Sarafia, who had been holding the cow's head while the men laboured, was in tears, distressed by the animal's protracted ordeal.

Terrel, watching from the barn door, wished there was something he could do to help, but he usually kept well out of the way on these occasions. This was not mere squeamishness on his part – although he did find the process vaguely repulsive – but because he still believed that his presence made animals nervous. That was the last thing they needed now.

With another agonized groan the cow ducked her head, then raised it sharply, catching Sarafia off guard and sending her sprawling on to the straw. Ty glanced at his daughter in alarm, saw that she was unharmed but in no state to help any more, then shouted over his shoulder.

'Terrel! Get in here! Hold her still, or we'll never have a chance.'

Terrel limped across as fast as he could, and took hold of the muzzle that had been fitted to the cow's head. Dark brown eyes regarded him dolefully, madness sparking in their depths. Instinctively he stroked her hard, wide nose and whispered in her ear.

'Be calm. It's going to be all right.'

To his amazement he felt the animal relax a little, and it was soon clear that Ty and Vizquel were aware of it too.

'I don't know what you're doing,' the farmer's son gasped, 'but keep doing it. It's coming.'

'Come on, old girl,' Ty repeated, a little more hopefully this time. 'Nearly there.'

Terrel found himself in a waking dream, fighting pain

that for once was not his own, and even though he didn't really know what he was doing, the process seemed natural enough.

When the calf was finally born, emerging into the world in a sudden ungainly rush, its mother moaned with exhaustion and relief. Terrel still held her head, murmuring soothing words, while Ty and Vizquel tried unsuccessfully to coax the unconscious new-born creature into life.

'It's no good,' Ty said eventually. 'It's dead.'

'At least the old girl's all right,' Vizquel said. He sounded sad, and utterly weary.

Ty went to his daughter and picked her up.

'Are you all right, little one?'

Sarafia nodded, snuffling, and he carried her out of the barn. Vizquel came to give what comfort he could to the cow, and Terrel left him to it. He too felt exhausted, even though he had only been directly involved for a very short time. Looking now at the bloody corpse on the ground, he thought it was too small, too pitiful, to have been the cause of such turmoil. He was about to turn away when he stopped, sure that he had seen the calf's eyelids flicker.

He quickly knelt at the creature's side. Ignoring the gore that matted its coat, he put a tentative hand on the small head. It was still warm, and Terrel knew – without knowing how – that there was still a spark of life somewhere. This time he fought not against pain but against a morbid apathy, willing the flickering spark into flame. The calf coughed weakly, then shivered. Breath bubbled around its nostrils. Finally its legs began to move, scrabbling against the floor until it rose unsteadily to its feet and stood trembling for a while before tottering over to its mother.

Terrel watched as the calf began to suckle, feeling an exhausted delight – until he glanced at Vizquel and saw that the farmer's son was staring at him with an incredulous mixture of awe and terror on his face.

That evening, when everyone had been told what had happened and had been to see the miraculous calf, Terrel was treated like a hero, but he knew that there was also an element of disquiet in the way they regarded him. He began to wonder if perhaps they thought he really was an enchanter after all. Only Sarafia seemed to be unreservedly delighted by what had happened; all the rest seemed to think he'd somehow brought the calf back from the dead. He tried to explain that it had been alive all the time, that it had simply needed someone to convince it to make the effort, but he was not sure they believed him. Everything Terrel had done had been instinctive, without the need of conscious thought, and in the end even he began to wonder what exactly had taken place. He went to bed that night later than usual, feeling a confused mixture of emotions, and expecting to relive the day in his dreams. In the event he slept soundly, and when he woke he couldn't remember any dreams at all.

Staggering out of the barn in which he slept, he went over to the well, intending to draw some water to wash and try to revive his sluggish brain. He saw Jehar standing by the gate at the end of the yard, staring at the distant horizon. There was something about his unnatural stillness that worried Terrel.

'Are you all right?' he asked as he came up behind the farmer's son.

Jehar did not turn round, but must have recognized the voice because he flinched, even as he continued to gaze into the distance.

'I've thought something was wrong for a few days,' he said quietly. 'Now I'm sure of it.'

'What's the matter?'

'It's moving much too fast,' Jehar replied, 'and too far. Look.'

Terrel looked, and saw the orange glow as the first curve of the sun rose into the sky. For a few moments he saw nothing untoward, then he got his bearings and finally realized what Jehar meant. Even the heavens were defying the laws of nature.

The sun was rising in the north.

CHAPTER EIGHTEEN

'The islands must be spinning,' Terrel said. He knew enough about astronomy to be fairly sure that this was the only explanation that made sense.

'And they don't normally?' Jehar asked, obviously confused.

'No. As far as anyone can tell, the Floating Islands act like an enormous lodestone. Regardless of where we are in the ocean, or which way we're heading, we keep our orientation more or less the same – even when we change course.'

'So the sun always rises in the east and sets in the west?'

'Exactly.' Terrel recalled a passage from Muzeni's journal concerning the invisible metallic flux. According to the heretic this was connected to the lodestone theory, but Terrel had not been able to work out how.

'But the place it rises changes during the year,' Jehar objected.

'That's mostly because the entire planet is tilted on its axis,' Terrel explained. 'And our position in the ocean affects it too.'

'But not as much as this.'

'No,' Terrel agreed. Here was yet another sign that all was not well with the world.

'What does it mean?' Jehar said. 'What's happening?'

'I wish I knew.'

They were silent for a while as the sun's light grew brighter and they felt the first warmth of the day.

'How do you know all this stuff?' Jehar asked eventually.

'I read about it in books.' Terrel had told his hosts much the same story as he had told Efrin, portraying himself as a homeless orphan. It was as close to the truth as he had been able to come.

Jehar, who could not write more than his own name and was able to read only enough to decipher the necessary signs and dates in the farmer's almanac, accepted Terrel's answer without comment.

'First the Dark Moon, now this,' he said quietly. 'The seers will probably change the rules again now, won't they.'

Terrel, who had no way of knowing, said nothing. He had no doubt that similar comments were being made all over Vadanis, and he was thankful he was not a village underseer. Chenowith and his colleagues were going to have a lot of explaining to do – and were probably as much in the dark as everyone else.

'I thought the gossip we heard at market yesterday was crazy,' Jehar said. 'Now I'm not so sure.'

'What gossip?'

'Some madman was saying that the islands had gone off course. That it was a sign.'

'A sign of what?'

'That the day of reckoning was coming. The end of the world.'

'That *is* crazy,' Terrel said, but then he remembered

another sentence from Muzeni's journal. *It is hard to imagine destruction on such a scale.*

'Maybe not,' the farmer's son replied. 'If the islands can start spinning, why can't they head the wrong way too?'

Terrel had no answer to that. All he could do was hope that the reasoning was wrong.

'That's not all,' Jehar went on. 'Somebody else was talking about a monster in the mines somewhere that eats people or makes them disappear. A monster! Sometimes I think the whole world's going mad.'

Terrel, who had more than a passing acquaintance with true madness, found it hard to disagree, but did his best to reassure his companion.

'Gossip like that's hardly reliable though, is it?'

'Maybe not,' Jehar conceded. 'To tell you the truth I pretty much dismissed it at the time – and I forgot about it altogether when we got back last night and found out what had been going on here.'

The look he gave Terrel then was full of doubt and fear. It seemed that Jehar was connecting the improbable events surrounding the birth of the calf with all the other fantastical tales he had heard recently. Suddenly the apparent normality of the last two months counted for nothing. Once again, Terrel was the boy with the eyes of an enchanter.

The day passed in typically industrious fashion. Whatever else was happening in the outside world, cows still had to be milked and crops tended. If there was less banter than usual between those who worked on the farm – especially when Terrel was nearby – it was merely a reflection of the thoughts they were keeping hidden. Outwardly, everything went on as normal. The islands might be spinning like a top, but there was nothing this small community could do about it. The sun rose and set, like any other day. The only difference was that today it set in the south.

Terrel did not linger after the evening's communal meal, aware of the tensions round the table, and of the fact that many of them centred on his presence. Glancing up at the sky as he crossed the yard, he saw all three visible moons, the Amber almost full, the White and Red almost exact semicircles. All three were waxing, growing more powerful amid the stars that decked the night sky with delicate necklaces of light. Somehow the air seemed more potent, as if there were revelations just waiting to be discovered. Terrel knew that this was a night when dreams would come.

Inside the fragrant darkness of the barn, he felt his way to the ladder and climbed to the loft where his blankets were spread out on a shifting mattress of hay. He undressed and lay down, wrapping himself against the growing chill, and stared at the rafters above him. The triangular ends of the barn beneath the eaves were open to the air, which would make it a cold place as autumn drew in, and Terrel wondered if the time had come for him to move on. The thought dismayed him, but he had known all along that he could not stay at the farm for ever. He fell asleep, wishing he had someone to tell him what he was supposed to do with his life.

He did not know what had roused him, but suddenly he was wide awake.

Hello, Terrel.

An incredible surge of joy catapulted the boy from his makeshift bed. Then he staggered and almost fell as his twisted leg buckled.

'Alyssa? Alyssa!' He would have known her voice anywhere. 'Where are you?'

I'm here, silly, she replied, sounding amused.

Her voice seemed to be coming from above him, but that was ridiculous. The only way up to the loft was the ladder, and the top of that was right next to his bed. Terrel searched the hayloft and the darkness below, but could see nothing.

'Where?' he cried, desperate to see her.

Up here.

Looking round again, he saw a barn owl, its pale, heart-shaped face shining in a patch of moonlight. It was ignoring the sound of mice skittering on the floor below, and continued to stare directly at Terrel – who was beginning to wonder if he was dreaming.

It's not a dream, she told him. *It's really me. I'll come and peck your nose, if you like.*

'But you're an owl!' he said stupidly.

No, I'm not, she retorted. *I'm just using her so I can come and talk to you.*

'But . . .' Belatedly, it occurred to Terrel that there was something strange about Alyssa's voice. The only sound was that of an owl hooting, and yet he heard every word clearly – inside his head. Still stranded in disbelief, he could only stare at the bird.

Look. I haven't become *an owl,* Alyssa explained patiently. *I'm just borrowing her body for a while. That's not so very strange, is it? I'm not the first to do something like this, and I certainly won't be the last.*

It seemed very strange indeed to Terrel, but he did not know what to say.

My own body is sleeping, Alyssa went on. *At the haven. I'm all right. I said I was going to wait for you, and I will.*

'You said that?' Terrel exclaimed. 'It wasn't just a dream?'

Dreams are real too, you know, she replied. *And I can still see yours. In fact it's easier now.*

The reality of what was happening still seemed insane to Terrel – he was talking to an owl! – but he was beginning to accept it now. And the fact that Alyssa had told him she was all right was the reassurance he had longed for. His mind raced with questions.

'How did you find me?'

I've got your ring, she replied. *It will always guide me to you.* As she spoke the owl raised one foot, and Terrel saw the 'ring' wound around one of her talons. What had begun as a joke now seemed infinitely precious, linking them together as if it had been a real wedding band. His last doubts were cast aside.

'Are you still in the same cell?'

I told you. My body is. I'm here.

'But . . . your body . . . it's unharmed?'

Yes. I am protected.

From the way she said this, Terrel knew he would get no answer to the obvious question. He remembered the soldier's blade being dashed aside by some invisible force, and decided that all he could do was trust in what she said.

'I *am* going to come back for you,' he swore.

I know, Alyssa replied softly. *But not yet. Aylor's still in charge there, and he'd kill you if he caught you. Besides, there are other plans being made for you.*

'Plans? What plans?'

I don't know. The others will tell me when they're ready.

'What others?'

I can guide them to you, but I'm not sure you're ready to look round the corner yet. Do you want to try?

Terrel was about to ask her why she was talking in riddles, when for the second time that night he was presented with a literally incredible sight. To his amazement and terror, three faintly luminous figures appeared in the loft. The nearest of them was instantly recognizable, even though he was transparent, and Terrel's already racing heartbeat became even more frantic. Elam was sitting casually on a beam, whittling at a piece of wood with a knife that was evidently as sharp as it was translucent. It seemed such an extraordinarily mundane thing for a ghost to be doing that Terrel almost laughed, but then he noticed the small dark stain on the front of Elam's tunic, and the reality of what he was seeing sobered him again. His friend looked bored, and was paying no attention to his surroundings.

'Does he know I'm here?' Terrel whispered.

Not yet, Alyssa replied. *None of them do.*

One of the other two ethereal figures was also familiar and, although it was a shock to discover that Shahan really was dead, the seer's presence provided another link to Terrel's former life. He too did not seem to notice where he was, being deep in conversation with another old man, who was dressed in outlandish clothes. Both were gesticulating and seemed to be speaking at once, but Terrel could hear no sound. As he stared in awe he became aware that there was something different about the unknown ghost. He was somehow less distinct, the features of his face and hands less sharply defined than either Elam's or Shahan's.

'What are they arguing about? Why can't I hear them?'

You will. When they need you to, Alyssa replied, answering only his second question.

'Who's the one in the red cape?'

That's Muzeni.

'Really?' Terrel was beyond astonishment now. 'He doesn't look the same as the other two.'

He died a long time ago, Alyssa explained, *so he's faded a bit. In fact the only reason he's still here is because he thinks he has unfinished business.*

'And has he?'

The owl seemed to shrug, and blinked solemnly.

I don't know. There's another reason for him being different. Muzeni died peacefully, just as we guessed, but the other two died suddenly and violently. That always makes it harder for the spirits to adjust, and they're more likely to stay in this world.

'More unfinished business?' Terrel guessed.

Coming to terms with the change, Alyssa agreed. *That's why you can see them more clearly.*

'Can they see *us*?' he asked. So far the ghosts had ignored his presence completely.

If they choose to.

Terrel looked at Elam again, and was enveloped by a sudden longing to talk to his friend, to tell him all the things he had been unable to say in life . . . to tell him he was sorry.

As if in answer to his unspoken plea, Elam looked up then and their eyes met.

Not much of a place you've got here, Elam commented. *At least we had proper beds at the haven.*

Tears sprang into Terrel's eyes at the sound of another longed-for voice, one he thought had been lost for ever. But he smiled at the same time, thinking that this was just the sort of acerbic remark Elam would have made if he had still been alive. Then the guilt he felt returned in full measure, so that he almost choked on it. When he spoke it was barely more than a whisper.

'I'm sorry. I never meant—'

The funny thing is, Elam cut in, speaking with uncharacteristic calm, *I was going to die anyway. It seems that the fall from the observatory roof did something inside my head. They explained it to me, but I didn't really pay much attention. But as it turned out, Aylor did me a favour. At least that way it was quick.* He paused, spectral eyes twinkling. *And it forced you to* do *something for a change. I almost died laughing when Ahmeza stuffed you in that apple barrel.* Realizing what he had said, he grinned.

'You saw that?' Terrel exclaimed.

I was wandering round the haven for a bit, Elam replied. *I even met Sevin! He's really peculiar, even for a ghost, so it's no wonder he and Alyssa got on so well.*

I heard that, Alyssa warned him.

Throughout the conversation the owl had been perched on the same rafter, remaining quite still, but now she flexed her talons.

Whoops! Elam said in a stage whisper. *Mustn't annoy the bird-girl. She has friends in high places.* He did not sound particularly worried, however, and before Terrel could ask him about Alyssa's 'friends', he went on with a question of his own. *What made you go to the island? That place still gives me the creeps.*

'I knew no one would look for me there,' Terrel replied.

You're not as daft as you look, are you, Elam remarked approvingly. *I've got the feeling we're going to have some more adventures together, after all.*

Abruptly, before Terrel even had time to respond, Elam vanished. Shahan and Muzeni were gone in the same instant, leaving Terrel breathless and wide-eyed. Only the owl remained.

'Where did they go?' he asked, not sure whether he ought to be disappointed or relieved.

They walk differently, Alyssa told him. *We'd have been here earlier otherwise. I must go too.*

'No!' Terrel cried urgently.

She needs her wings back.

'Why don't you come in your own shape?' he asked, overcome with longing to see her again.

Because I'm not dead yet! Alyssa replied indignantly.

That silenced Terrel. He knew she would go soon whatever he said now.

Farewell, Terrel. I will return. I have your ring, remember?

'Farewell, Alyssa,' he said softly.

The owl left her perch and swooped out of the open end of the barn. As Terrel watched her go, flying on silent wings into the night, he felt as though his heart was being torn in half. Then, knowing that the wonders of the night were over, he lay down again and tried, in vain, to go to sleep. Below him the sounds of the night returned as the small creatures who inhabited the barn resumed their nocturnal activities.

Jehar crouched in the darkness, keeping quite still for a while, then crept into the yard. Now that he was outside, he found that he was trembling so badly he could hardly walk.

Roused in the night by his own disturbing suspicions, he had come to the barn and had heard Terrel talking to a bird. The owl had replied in the wavering calls of its own kind, but the boy had somehow seemed to understand it. There had been something else too, something half seen, hidden within the patches of moonlight that mottled the hayloft, but Jehar had no idea what it might have been. Nor did he want to know.

He was sure now of only one thing. His family had given sanctuary to a sorcerer.

CHAPTER NINETEEN

'Terrel. Terrel! Wake up. You've got to get away.'

Someone was shaking his shoulder and whispering urgently. He felt as if he'd only been asleep for a few moments, but in spite of his confusion at being roused again, he knew that the voice was real this time – and that it was not Alyssa's.

'Sarafia?' he mumbled. 'What is it?'

'Jehar's gone crazy,' she exclaimed. 'He said he heard you talking to an owl!'

Terrel's heart sank as he realized he'd been overheard, and he saw now that Sarafia was genuinely worried.

'He was shouting so loud it woke everyone up,' she went on breathlessly. 'I could hear everything through the wall! Ferrand calmed him down, and sent Vizquel to Mandia to fetch the underseer. If they wait for him you'll have plenty of time, but I'm not sure Jehar's going to leave it that long. I've never seen him so angry. Magana even gave him some apple brandy – and they only get that out at the moon festivals – but I think it might have made things worse. He was yelling about killing you. You must get away.'

This was all too much for Terrel. On top of everything else that had happened that night, this latest development threatened to overwhelm him. He felt paralyzed, unable to move or even think.

'Come on,' Sarafia urged. 'Get up.'

'I've got almost no clothes on,' he objected, knowing that he was being ridiculous, but unable to stop himself. He had had no thoughts of modesty in front of Alyssa or the ghosts, but now, with a real girl beside him, it seemed important.

Sarafia let out a groan of disbelief.

'I'll get down then,' she said, 'but hurry.'

She disappeared from sight as she climbed down the ladder, and Terrel pulled on his clothes. The special boot took time as always, his fingers fumbling with the laces. Why am I doing this? he thought. Why don't I just explain? But he knew that Sarafia was right. He had to get away, at least until Jehar had calmed down.

'Hurry up!' Sarafia called softly from below. 'I can hear them shouting again.'

By the time Terrel had half climbed, half slid down the ladder, he could hear them too, but was unable to make out what they were saying.

'This way,' Sarafia said, taking his arm and almost dragging him towards a side door.

They went out into the night, skirting round behind the goat pens and the slurry pit, then climbed over the gate that led to the lane the cows used every day. Terrel had begun to unlatch it, but Sarafia stopped him, knowing that its hinges squeaked – and it was this more than anything that brought home to Terrel just how frightened she was.

Crouching down behind the wall, they listened to the voices, which were growing louder again. A swaying yellow light came from the yard, making it obvious that someone had carried a lamp outside, and Terrel risked peeking over the top of the wall. He saw Jehar striding towards the barn, with Ferrand and Ty close behind him.

'I told you to wait, boy!' the farmer roared.

'I'm not a boy,' Jehar replied angrily, rounding on his father. 'I'm going to finish this.'

He turned back and Terrel saw, to his horror, that Jehar was carrying an axe.

'Don't you think—' Ty began.

'Shut up,' Jehar snapped and marched towards the barn again, only to be pulled back when Ferrand grabbed his arm.

Jehar shoved his father away, and the older man fell to the ground heavily.

'If you're too blind to see what's happening under your own nose, just keep out of my way!'

Terrel was horrified at the venom in Jehar's words. He had almost begun to think of himself as part of this family, but now it seemed he was responsible for tearing it apart.

Jehar had only gone a few paces when a high-pitched scream stopped him in his tracks. All three men looked round as Mia came running from the cottage that adjoined the main farmhouse.

'Sara's gone!' she wailed. 'She's not in her bed.'

'He's got her,' Jehar exclaimed, glancing at Ty. 'Are you convinced now?'

As Ferrand struggled to his feet, the two younger men began to run towards the barn, both calling Sarafia's name. The girl herself reached up and pulled Terrel down beside her.

'Stop gawking,' she hissed. 'They'll see you.'

'You should—' he began, but she silenced him with a wave of her hand.

'Once they realize we're not there, they'll start looking further afield,' she said, sounding remarkably calm. 'If we can get to the woods, they'll never find us. Come on.'

Without giving him a chance to respond, she set off down the trail, bent low to the ground. After a moment's hesitation, Terrel followed, doing his best to keep up with her. As he ran, he heard the men calling her name again.

When they reached the woods, Sarafia led him into the deeper shadows until they found a dendron tree, whose low, overhanging branches formed a sort of living cave. From there they could watch the lane while remaining invisible themselves. Neither spoke for a while, as they got their breath back and assured themselves that they had not been followed.

Eventually, Sarafia let out a long sigh and sat down on the bare earth. Too dazed to even think of doing anything else, Terrel sat down beside her. She turned to him then, and he saw that her eyes were bright with excitement as well as fear.

'Who *were* you talking to?' she asked.

There was a long pause before Terrel answered, his hesitation betraying him even as he tried to think of what to tell her. A dozen different explanations flashed through his mind, ranging from outright denial to fanciful invention, but each seemed more unlikely than the last – and the truth was the most absurd of all. In the end he chose the one that seemed the most mundane, and hoped that Sarafia would not question him too closely.

'A girl,' he said at last.

'Oh.'

He heard the disappointment in her voice, and could not fathom the reason for it.

'She's called Alyssa?'

'Yes. Look, your parents must be worried. Shouldn't you—'

'I don't know anyone around here called that,' she said, refusing to be sidetracked.

'She's not from around here.'

'She's from where you used to live?'

'Yes, but—'

'So she's been with you all the time?'

'No.'

'Where is she now? How did she get away?'

'Look, Sara, I can't explain. Just—'

'Why not?' she demanded. 'I thought we were friends.'

Terrel could see moonlit tears brimming in her eyes now, and felt terrible about deceiving her.

'We are,' he claimed.

'I don't understand this,' Sarafia declared, sounding almost angry now. 'Jehar said no one could have got up there without him seeing – and it was an *owl* he heard. He was outside until he heard you call out her name, and you sounded surprised.'

'I *was* surprised,' Terrel said truthfully.

'And then you said "But you're an owl!", ' she went on. 'What did that mean?'

'I didn't . . . Jehar must have been mistaken.'

'No. He was very sure about what he heard. He kept repeating it over and over. There wasn't a girl with you at all, was there?'

'Yes, there was,' Terrel said desperately.

'Why are you lying to me?' She was crying openly now. 'I helped you escape. I hate you.'

This was more than Terrel could bear. It seemed not only pointless but cruel to try to maintain the deception – and Sarafia was right. He owed her the truth.

'Alyssa *was* there,' he said quietly, 'but she was in the shape of an owl.'

The relief he felt at this admission was qualified by Sarafia's reaction. There were no tears now, and she stared at him with a wide-eyed expression that he could not decipher.

'So you *are* an enchanter!' she breathed.

'No,' he replied earnestly, shaking his head. 'I didn't do anything. She's the one—'

'An enchantress?' the girl gasped in wonder. 'Has she put you under a spell?'

'No,' he said, trying not to smile. Not the sort of spell you mean anyway, he added silently.

'Do you love her?' she asked unexpectedly.

'Yes,' Terrel replied when he had recovered from his surprise. 'Yes, I do.'

Sarafia nodded, her expression grave and a little sad.

'Will you go to her now?'

I wish I could, he thought ruefully, but before he could respond, they heard Ty calling his daughter's name. The fear and anxiety in his voice obviously made an impression on the young girl.

'I'd better go back.'

For the first time, it occurred to Terrel that Sarafia might have imagined the two of them as rather more than friends. He had never considered the idea that any girl – apart from Alyssa – might find him attractive, but now he realized that his very strangeness was probably what had appealed to Sarafia's romantic nature. It was even possible that she had thought of running away with him when the opportunity arose, following her dream of becoming a wandering storyteller. But the sound of her father's tormented cries had brought her back to a harsher reality.

'Will you be all right?' Terrel asked.

'Of course,' she replied bravely. 'But you'd better go. Once they know I'm safe they won't be so worried, so you should be able to get away.'

'Thank you, Sara.'

'Will I ever see you again?' she asked.

'I don't know.'

She nodded, accepting his honesty for what it was, then stood up and offered him her hand to pull him to his feet. He rose, but before he released her hand, he leant forward and kissed her gently on the cheek. Finding himself unable to form the words to say goodbye, he ran off into the forest, heading away from the farm.

Sarafia watched him go until he was out of sight, then drew herself up to her full height and began to walk in the opposite direction.

Much later, when he was far enough from the farm to be sure that he was not being pursued, Terrel at last found some time for reflection. That he had been forced to resume the comfortless life of a vagabond was dispiriting, but at least he felt a little better prepared for it this time – and he had several reasons for feeling a lot happier than he had when he'd left the haven.

The first was the relief of Alyssa's reassurances about her safety. He did not understand how she was being protected, but it was abundantly clear that her life was touched with magic, and Terrel felt certain that she would be able to keep her promise. The second was that some of the guilt he felt over Elam's death had been lifted by the revelation that his friend had been going to die anyway. The sadness and grief were still there, but he hadn't been responsible for Elam's fall, and this meant that he did not need to blame himself so much for what had happened afterwards. And then there was the proof that Elam's spirit had survived. Alyssa had been right all along. Ghosts *were* real! But the best thing of all was that Alyssa had given her word that she would see him again. This thought alone was enough to keep him going.

After foraging for the next four days, Terrel was feeling lonely and discouraged. He was hungry and tired, and his earlier feelings of optimism were fading. He had been travelling aimlessly, wondering what he was supposed to do now.

After another cold night in the open, he awoke from a dream that had been as vivid and unsettling as any he had ever experienced. What was more, his entire body was burning with shame.

CHAPTER TWENTY

Chief Seer Kamin read the letter for perhaps the twentieth time. He still didn't know what to do about it. Nor did he know who had written it, although he had his suspicions – but he was sure that those involved were now very frightened men. They had signed themselves only with the cryptic name 'Alakor', which meant 'the disaffected' in the old tongue, and nothing had been heard from them since the letter had been delivered to Mirival's home. It was not hard to work out why. Mirival had been the only one who knew where Jax's twin had been sent – and therefore where he might be now if he was still alive – and Shahan had been the only one who'd been actively looking for the boy. Now they had both met untimely ends. It did not take a genius to work out that interest in the missing twin might not be good for one's health.

Mirival had been dead now for exactly two median months, but the letter had only come into Kamin's possession a few days ago. When the other leading candidates decided not to put themselves forward, it had been a foregone conclusion that he would be elected the new Chief Seer.

As Mirival's deputy, Kamin had already been the forerunner, but when Fauria withdrew his name from consideration – for reasons he chose not to divulge – and Lathan made it clear that he had other things on his mind, the succession was more or less guaranteed. For the sake of appearances, two other seers were persuaded to allow their names to be entered for the ballot, but they had no realistic chance of winning and they knew it. Nevertheless, the wheels of protocol turned with frustrating slowness in such matters, and no one had dared try to speed up the long-drawn-out process for fear of being branded as a constitutional heretic. As a result, Kamin found – when he was officially sworn in at last – that the backlog of paperwork had built up alarmingly. It was some time before he was able to make any headway and was free to examine the rest of his late master's effects. It was then that he had found the letter.

Although he could not be certain, Kamin believed it had probably been delivered on the actual night of Mirival's death, which made it doubly ominous. The Chief Seer had been working late, having dismissed all his servants, and his chamberlain had not found him until the next morning. Mirival had been poisoned. The subsequent investigation, carried out by no less a person than Castellan Deltoro, the commander of the palace garrison of the Imperial Guard, had established that a deadly toxin had been mixed with Mirival's wine. However, despite exhaustive enquiries – which included the questioning of everyone in the palace, from the lowest scullery maid to the Emperor himself – no evidence could be found to determine whether his death had been murder or suicide. In his final report, Deltoro had carefully left his conclusions open. Privately, Kamin was certain that his former superior had not been the type of man to take his own life, but no one could be found who had both the motive and the opportunity to kill him.

It was not the way Kamin would have wished to attain the role of Chief Seer. He was a man of ambition, but – even though he knew himself to be innocent of any involvement – the fact that he had benefited directly from the tragedy was bound to make others suspicious. More-over, assuming the mantle of leadership at a time when all the Empire was in turmoil was a challenge few men would have relished. He still had much to decide before the council met later that morning.

For a start, he had to decide whether to make public the letter he still held in his hands. Doing so could be dan-gerous – for himself and for 'Alakor' – but it might also bring the true feelings of the council to the surface. Even Kamin had occasional doubts about the way Jax's twin had been treated. And if they had missed something important in the prophecy . . .

With an effort, he shrugged the misgivings aside. The child had almost certainly died in infancy, so there was no point in pursuing the matter. He would begin the day anew, with a clear mind.

Glancing over at the window, he saw the first glow of dawn in the northern sky – in itself a reminder that he lived in a time of great upheaval. He had already been up and about for some hours, having hardly slept at all, and he had wasted too much of that time. He deliberately set the corner of the letter into the flame of a candle burning on his desk, and watched as it flared up and then crum-pled into ash.

Lathan's dreams were filled with huge waves that threat-ened to overwhelm him, racing currents of boiling white water that swept him towards gaping whirlpools. He went down into darkness, spinning and spinning . . .

He woke to find himself slumped over his desk. Even

though he was stiff and sore from his cramped and awkward position, it was a relief to know that he was back in
Makhaya, many miles from the coast. Then he saw the
vast array of tabulated readings and meticulously recorded
observations littering the desktop, and knew that there
was still work to be done. He had been toiling long into
the night before exhaustion had finally overtaken him, and
the calculations were almost complete. Instinct had already
told him what the results would show, but he was not a
man to leave anything to chance.

The last two months had been the most hectic of his
life. There had been times when he thought he was only
retaining his grip on sanity by devoting himself to the task
set by Mirival, and not even the Chief Seer's death had
diverted him from it. Earlier in his career Lathan might
have considered himself a suitable candidate to lead the
council – and many others would have agreed with him –
but now that no longer interested him. He had work to do.

He had personally travelled to every important coastal
settlement, and had dispatched his chosen deputies to the
more remote parts of Vadanis as well as to some of
the larger outlying isles. He'd watched and measured the
Empire's journey through the ocean, and had seen the
heavens rotate above. He had talked to the few men
whose boats still braved the roaring currents and
treacherous straits around the shore, and had seen for
himself the floods and raging seas caused by the recent
changes. There were no tides as such – all the connected
islands rose and fell with the ocean – but the direction in
which they were travelling produced the same effects as if
the entire mass was one gigantic ship. In normal times,
one part of the coastline – the bows – would be assailed by
slow but mountainous waves, while the opposite side – the
stern – would see a massive wake trailing away into the

distance. But now, with the islands rotating – no matter how slowly – even that could not be relied upon, and the alongshore races were alarmingly unpredictable. By the time of his more recent visits, all but the dullest minds had grasped the fact that the islands were revolving. The laws of nature that had maintained their orientation for centuries past were failing – or were being countered by even more powerful forces. Lathan could not explain this, any more than he could explain the anomalous behaviour of the Dark Moon. But he could measure the effects, and he had done so in thorough fashion – in spite of the fact that every new reading brought him closer to predicting the unthinkable.

He had done everything he could, in time for the council meeting, and all he had to do now was complete the final calculation. Taking his pen in hand, Lathan prepared to confront destiny.

Jax also woke early that morning, but he came to in the comfort of his bed and in a state of smug elation – almost exultation. The girl who lay beside him had proved as pliant in body as she had been in mind. Even though she was older than him, she'd had only a little more experience in the ways of men and women, and the dream that had called her to Jax had been enough to make her do whatever he wanted. He had discovered that his pleasure was not dependent upon hers, although it had filled him with a self-admiring pride when she'd responded with passion of her own. The night had left him sated and contentedly weary – and the best of it was, it had been so easy!

The girl – Jax couldn't remember her name – was one of Adina's chambermaids. He smiled at the thought of his mother's reaction, were she ever to find out how he was taking advantage of what she had taught him about the manipulation of other people's minds. She never *would* find out, of course, because – once the girl left his chamber – she would remember nothing of where she had been or who she had been with. Those details would slip from her mind like the images of a fading dream.

This was only one of the improvements the prince had made to his mother's technique, and he was now presented with the beguiling prospect of being able to repeat this enterprise at any time he chose. He already knew that there were other girls who would be susceptible, should he decide to share a night with them. One of the most intriguing of these was a daughter of Dheran's by an earlier marriage, who was particularly beautiful, and the fact that she was forbidden to him only made her more attractive.

Dawn was breaking over the city when Jax woke the girl and told her to leave. He watched complacently as she dressed, thinking back on an aspect of their lovemaking that he had found especially amusing. He had shared his dream unwittingly, but the watching eyes had been both horrified and envious – and when the prince had become aware of the unseen presence, he had gloried in his triumph.

Once the girl had left, Jax wondered how long it would be before he was summoned to the presence of his tutor – if anything, Kamin was even more boring than Mirival had been – but then he remembered that there would be no lessons that day. The Seers' Council was due to meet, and so he was free to do as he pleased. What could be more perfect?

Jax smiled to himself, and went back to sleep.

'In conclusion, gentlemen,' Kamin said, looking round the circular chamber at the solemn faces of his peers, 'the

Dark Moon has not only changed in size and velocity, it is *still* changing. The day-to-day alterations are very small, but measurable. We need therefore to constantly recalculate our forecasts and, if possible, to predict the course of future changes. If we can do that, we may eventually discover what unknown force is causing these anomalies. In the meantime, what we can and must do is determine the effects of the changes on the Floating Islands, and decide what measures we can take to counteract them if necessary.'

The council had already been in session for almost two hours, and much of that time had been spent discussing the now universally acknowledged facts concerning the Dark Moon and the movements of the islands. Many theories had been put forward, including some that were patently ludicrous. Batou, always one to introduce a note of anarchy into any debate, had even claimed that the impact of so-called 'meteors' could have been enough to knock the Empire off course. This was dismissed by the majority as laughable, on the grounds that anything large enough to effect such a change could not possibly fall from the sky – and even if it did, it could not have done so without someone noticing. Others had speculated on the recent abnormal weather conditions and, of course, the Dark Moon's malign influence was also blamed, even though no one could demonstrate how it could have caused such a major disruption. A few men had even quoted from apocalyptic sections of the Tindaya Code, alleging that mankind's own evil had brought the misfortunes upon themselves. That sort of hysterical invective was greeted with derision by most of the seers, but the fact that such feelings had surfaced at all showed how close they were to panic. Kamin had stepped in at this point, hoping to restore an air of calm and rationality to the proceedings. His summary of recent findings had at least put the matter into perspective.

'As you all know,' he went on, realizing that this was a crucial moment and hoping that Lathan would not let him down, 'our colleague here has been conducting a detailed study of the islands' movements, and he is now in a position to report his findings.'

Lathan rose to his feet as Kamin sat down on his ceremonial throne, and the chamber grew silent in anticipation. As Lathan cleared his throat, he thought he saw a flicker of movement by one of the doors, but when he looked again there was nobody there, and he decided it must have been a trick of the light.

'I shall keep this brief and to the point,' he began. 'If any of you wish to study the data I have collected, or to check my calculations, you are welcome to do so, but I am confident that they will withstand any test.

'Firstly, as is common knowledge, the Empire is now rotating. The rate of turn is currently equivalent to one complete revolution every two hundred and ninety-six days, but although the rate has recently stabilized, we have no way of knowing if and when it will increase again, or indeed reverse itself. I can find no explanation to account for the failure of the lodestone principle, but it surely cannot be a coincidence that it has occurred at the same time as the phenomena associated with the Dark Moon.'

There were nods of approval around the chamber.

'Be that as it may,' Lathan continued, 'I *can* tell you one curious fact. I had postulated that the axis for the rotation would be the islands' accepted centre of mass, and the first indications were that this was correct. However, more detailed analysis has revealed that the centre of rotation is not at Mount Pajara, but some twenty-five miles south of there. This puts it exactly in the centre of the mining district at Betancuria.'

'Must be the monster's doing, then,' one of the seers commented. He had meant it as a joke, and indeed this rare moment of light-heartedness did provoke a good deal of laughter, but – to Kamin's dismay – there were also many who seemed to take the idea seriously, glancing at each other and whispering.

'It is more likely,' Lathan said, unsmiling, 'that earlier estimates of the mass of the Empire below sea level were inaccurate, and that Betancuria is the actual centre of mass.' He paused to take a deep breath, and his expression became even more grim. 'However, it appears that in another matter the rumour-mongers may have got it right. Unless something changes soon, there is a possibility – in fact, a near certainty – that the Floating Islands will eventually collide with one of the mainland continents.'

This statement created an instant uproar, as everyone knew that such a collision would be a catastrophe of unimaginable proportions. For a time it seemed that everyone in the chamber was speaking at once, but eventually Kamin's appeals for quiet were heeded.

'Can you tell us when this is likely to happen?' he asked.

'Our speed relative to the fixed land masses has already increased by more than a fifth,' Lathan replied, 'and it seems to be rising still, albeit erratically. It's impossible to be precise, but my best estimate is in approximately three median months, possibly four.'

This time the reaction of the seers was one of stunned silence. Each man had heard his own death sentence spelt out in Lathan's words.

CHAPTER TWENTY-ONE

The piglet came trotting through the forest with a bright, purposeful air. Terrel heard its rapid footsteps before he saw it, and wondered what it could be. When the small pink creature emerged from the twilight gloom, his first thought was that it might be the young of a wild boar – a species that still roamed some of Vadanis's more remote woodland regions. If it was, he had no wish to meet its parents; their reputation for violence was well known. However, as the piglet came closer, heading straight for him, he guessed from its colouring and demeanour that it was more likely to have escaped from a domestic sty. Even so, its actions seemed a little odd and as it drew nearer still, Terrel began to harbour a new suspicion – and a new hope.

Expectation turned to near certainty when the animal stopped no more than two paces from where he sat, lowered itself onto its haunches and impaled him with a direct, questioning stare.

'Alyssa?'

You're learning.

Terrel had seen the ring now, looped around one of the piglet's delicate ears. He had been longing for this moment ever since the owl had flown away, but now he found himself tongue-tied. He had spent the day trying to forget the nature of the dream that had engulfed his mind and body the night before, but he'd been unable to do so – not least because a part of him had found the experience fascinating. He had felt the same sense of dislocation as he had when he'd 'witnessed' Shahan's death – as if he had been looking through another's eyes – and near the end he had heard mocking laughter that left him feeling humiliated as well as sickened. But his thoughts kept returning to some of the other images. Even though he had known that what he was doing was wrong, the pleasure of it had been very real. And now, faced with Alyssa, he was hoping desperately that the last vestiges of those images had dissipated. This was one dream he did not want her to see.

How do you like my outfit? Her voice betrayed no sign that she had noticed anything untoward, and Terrel began to relax.

'It suits you.'

Legs aren't as good as wings, but having four of them is fun once you remember what order to move them in.

'I still wish . . .' Terrel began, then pushed the thought aside. Alyssa could only come to him in her own form if she was a ghost – and he did not want that. 'How does the ring get . . . ?' he asked instead, pointing at her ear, '. . . on there?'

It comes with me, she replied simply.

'I know that, but how . . . ?'

Some things are more important than their physical size and shape. When that's true, where they are isn't important either.

Terrel didn't really understand any of this, but he knew it was the only answer he was going to get.

'I'm glad you're here,' he said. 'Just hearing your voice is wonderful.'

And you're lonely.

Terrel nodded.

'I don't know what to do, where to go,' he said.

I think we may be able to help you with that.

At her words the forest air shivered, and her retinue of ghosts appeared. Elam was lying on his back on the ground, with his hands beneath his head and his legs crossed at the ankles. He looked completely at ease. The other two were further away, walking slowly, deep in conversation. They weren't taking any notice of their surroundings. In fact, as Terrel watched, Muzeni walked straight *through* the trunk of a beech tree, only reacting to it with a look of mild puzzlement when he had come out the other side.

Elam roused himself from whatever quiet contemplation had been occupying him, sat up and looked around.

I didn't think it was possible, he said, *but your accommodations have actually got worse.*

'I don't have much choice,' Terrel responded.

We'll have to see about that, his friend declared, then looked over at the other ghosts. *Moons! Are those two still arguing?*

Shahan and Muzeni were closer now, glowing gently in the fading light. They were still intent on their discussion, to the exclusion of everything else.

'What are they arguing about?'

I'm not sure you want to know, Elam replied.

Listen, Alyssa advised. *You can hear them if you want.*

Terrel did as he was told, concentrating his attention on the two old men, and found that it was true.

If I didn't know you better, I'd say you were actually pleased *that the Dark Moon is misbehaving*, Shahan stated accusingly.

I'm just glad to be vindicated, Muzeni replied. His voice, like his image, was a little fuzzy round the edges. *If you or any of your precious council had had your wits about you, you'd have been able to predict it too. But nothing ever changes at court, does it? They only ever let dullards inside the palace walls.*

Yes, all right. We all know you're a genius, Shahan retorted, brushing aside the insult, *but that doesn't help us now, does it? In any case, the Dark Moon's not the only thing affecting the islands. Even we* dullards *have worked that out.*

I don't think I've ever had a more frustrating experience than being in that chamber and not being able to intervene, the heretic said. *I mean, it was all very well intentioned, but they're getting absolutely nowhere. Whenever they came close to something important, they just passed over it or dismissed it out of hand. And nobody so much as mentioned the boy.*

He's in the minds of many, Shahan said, *but they're afraid to speak.*

Politics! Muzeni spat disgustedly. *The illusion of power that turns all men into cowards.*

Not all, the seer contended. *Besides, can you blame them? I was the only one who expressed any interest in the boy, the only one who went looking for him – and look what happened to me.*

It had only just occurred to Terrel that he might be the boy they were talking about, but the reference to Shahan's fate had reminded him that he was supposed to have been instrumental in the seer's death – and this made him feel distinctly awkward.

What do you want? Muzeni grumbled peevishly. *A medal? There's no point being a martyr unless your sacrifice inspires others to follow in your footsteps. I don't see much sign of that.*

Whereas you inspired thousands, of course, Shahan replied, sarcastic in his turn.

I would have done, if anyone had been allowed to study my work, the heretic claimed angrily.

'Are they always like this?' Terrel whispered.

This is quite polite, for them, Elam replied. *Half the time I don't even know what they're talking about, but they're always insulting each other.*

'Do I have to listen to this?' Terrel asked.

I think you're meant to, Alyssa told him.

It's all right for you, Elam added. *You're only here for a short while. I'm stuck with these two old bores all the time.*

Why am I meant to listen? Terrel wondered. What's going on here? Are these ghosts – and Alyssa? – supposed to be helping one another? They seemed a hopelessly mismatched group.

Let's get back to what's important, Shahan said. The two old men were either unaware of the others' presence or were ignoring them completely.

All right, Muzeni agreed belligerently. *You found the boy. Why didn't you sort the matter out then?*

It wouldn't have been fair on him—

Fair? the heretic exclaimed. *What would have been fair? Turning back time to the night of his birth, so you could all start again?*

Terrel could stand no more of this.

'I wish you'd stop talking about me as if I wasn't here,' he said loudly.

The elderly ghosts turned to stare at him in surprise, as if aware of his existence for the first time. They were silent for a few moments, regarding him curiously.

'You *were* talking about me, weren't you?' Terrel asked, suddenly nervous.

Yes, Muzeni replied eventually, *but whether you are*

actually here *or not is an interesting question. Or whether* we *are here, come to that.*

Oh, don't get them started on comparative modes of existence, Elam groaned. *My brain still hurts from the last time.*

I'm not sure such an organ exists, Muzeni informed him, *comparatively or otherwise.*

See what I mean? Elam said. *They're hopeless.*

So you can hear us? Shahan asked, looking at Terrel.

'Yes.'

Then it's time.

'Time for what?'

The ghosts ignored his question and looked at each other again.

Can he do it? Muzeni asked.

I don't see why not, Shahan replied. *You know the story.*

All right, the heretic went on. *Are you sure we ought to do this? It's interfering in another world, after all.*

We're meant *to interfere*, the seer stated firmly. *All we've been arguing about is how.*

Muzeni nodded, considering.

And the collision gives us the necessary time scale, he said thoughtfully. *Do you think Lathan's right?*

I see no reason to doubt his findings, Shahan replied. *He's one of the more capable dullards.*

My feelings exactly. Perhaps—

'What are you talking about?' Terrel shouted, finally losing his temper.

Once again the strange pair turned to look at him in surprise.

He has some spirit, I see, Muzeni remarked.

And more education than we'd any right to expect, given his history, Shahan added.

'It's time! Talk to me,' Terrel demanded. 'Or go away. What's this collision you mentioned?' He thought he knew, but it was only when Shahan replied that his terrible premonition was confirmed.

The Floating Islands are on course to run into one of the fixed land masses.

'So you mean we'll run aground? The islands won't move any more?' Terrel was horrified by this prospect. Only barbaric lands remained in one place.

It's worse than that, Muzeni told him. *The Empire's speed through the water is only ponderous by human standards. But the vast momentum involved will make the impact catastrophic. The entire structure of the islands will buckle and probably break up.*

It'll be like a continuous earthquake for days on end, Shahan explained. *There won't be a building left standing.*

Fighting hard to take in this appalling imagery, Terrel could only think of Havenmoon – and of Alyssa lying beneath its fragile bulk.

Mountains will crumble and others rise, Muzeni went on. *Huge crevasses will open up, vegetation will be decimated. Vadanis will be completely devastated, and almost all its people will die.*

For a while no one spoke. There didn't seem to be anything to say.

'When will this happen?' Terrel asked eventually.

In three or four month's time, Shahan replied. *Unless we do something about it.*

'*We*? What can *we* do? Why are you telling me?'

Because you have a part to play in all this, Terrel, the seer answered. *An important part.*

The boy shook his head.

'I'm nobody. I—'

You were robbed of your birthright, Muzeni said.

I played a part in that, Shahan admitted. *It's something I've regretted for a long time now.*

'What birthright?' Terrel asked, bewildered still.

The Tindaya Code predicted a series of events between one four-moon conjunction and the next, Muzeni told him. *You were born on the night of one such confluence. Your destiny should have been part of the oracles.*

'This is crazy! Me? You're not suggesting I'm supposed to be some sort of hero?'

It's more complicated than that, Shahan said.

It's been made more complex by the fact that so many of the people who have taken it upon themselves to interpret the Code have had their wits addled by court propaganda, Muzeni added. *In the end, you're the only one who can understand your role.*

'I don't understand anything yet,' Terrel exclaimed. 'Am I supposed to *do* something?'

Yes, Muzeni replied. *That's one thing that has become clear to us. You have to go to Betancuria.*

'Betancuria? Why?'

Because that's where the monster is, Shahan replied.

CHAPTER TWENTY-TWO

Don't call it that! Alyssa cried, before Terrel had a chance to respond.

My colleague is just using the common parlance, my dear, Muzeni said, in a condescending tone that Terrel knew would only annoy Alyssa even more.

Well, you should both know better, she scolded them. *It's not a monster.*

'What is it, then?' Terrel asked.

Alyssa did not reply, and the piglet got up and began rooting round next to one of the tree trunks. At the same time the spectral images began to fade.

Come back! Muzeni ordered.

All right, young lady, Shahan added more calmly. *You've made your point.*

Elam just laughed.

The ghosts were almost invisible when the piglet finally lifted its head from a pile of leaf mould and snorted to clear the debris from its snout, then looked round at the others. Terrel, who had realized that the piglet had been just an animal again for a few moments, knew that Alyssa had returned – and his intuition was confirmed when she spoke.

Narrow minds lead to narrow sight.

This statement seemed rather obtuse, even for her, and Muzeni – who did not know her conversational foibles as well as Terrel or Elam – sought to challenge her.

My dear, I hope you're not implying—

Tunnel vision means there aren't any corners, Alyssa went on, overriding the old man easily. *We all need to see round corners. And what if there's only darkness at the end of the tunnel? What then?*

No one was brave enough to venture a reply to this vaguely ominous question. Terrel remembered her saying that, for him, ghosts would always be around the next corner, and he knew that unless she was there to guide them to him, he would not be able to see or hear them. But he could make neither head nor tail of her talk of darkness and tunnels.

Even as a pig you're still barmy, Elam declared eventually. *We'd be better off turning you into sausages.*

His companions all glanced at him in horror, then at Alyssa to see what her reaction would be.

Or perhaps we should stick an apple in your mouth and roast you whole, Elam went on, warming to his theme.

The piglet squealed. It was impossible to tell whether this was in rage or amusement, but then Terrel realized that he could hear Alyssa's laughter in his head.

I don't know why I'm bothering with you, she told Elam. *Even if they're rude, at least the other two have some brains and know a thing or two.*

I know. All I'm good for is pointing out the absurdities of life – or death – whatever you want to call it, Elam agreed amiably. *I've no idea what I'm doing here either.*

'You were – you *are* – my friend,' Terrel pointed out. 'We're going to have some adventures, remember?'

That must be it. Wake me up when these two have stopped waffling and the adventures are about to begin. Elam lay back and closed his eyes.

Terrel smiled, but he knew that what the old men had been telling him was important.

'Well, what is it about this . . . this . . .' he began.

It's not a monster, Alyssa repeated.

Of course it's not, Muzeni said placatingly. *Even assuming the rumours are exaggerated, no mere creature could be responsible for what has happened.*

The miners have clearly disturbed some kind of elemental force, Shahan added. *I'm sorry if my flippant remark upset you.* The seer did not sound very sorry, and the piglet continued to glare at him balefully.

Gossips always look for the worst in everything, Muzeni went on. *And, given the circumstances, it's not surprising that some tall tales are being bandied about. After all, you may feel some connection with this force, but you've no more idea than we have about what it really is.*

Shahan seemed about to argue with this statement, but Terrel – who had been bewildered by their exchange – grasped the one idea he could readily understand, and interrupted.

'You have a link with this force?' he asked Alyssa.

Yes. That's why . . . I can't explain it properly. She sounded frustrated now. *But I don't think it's evil.*

But it's easy to see why people believe it is, Shahan pointed out. *It has killed people.*

So do bears and wolves, she countered. *That doesn't make them evil.*

'Yes, but I wouldn't particularly want to come face to face with a bear or a pack of wolves,' Terrel said. 'Why do you want me to go there?'

First of all, because it might be more important than anyone in your world recognizes, Shahan told him. *So far they've only been paying it any attention because it's disrupted the mining operations – and all they've thought about is how to counteract it.*

Destroy it, you mean, Alyssa amended bitterly.

Whereas we want you to study it, learn from it, Muzeni said, ignoring the interruption.

Great, Terrel thought. I get to be taught by a man-eating bear! The piglet glared at him, and he wondered if Alyssa could 'hear' his private thoughts.

'What makes it so important?' he asked aloud.

It emerged at the same time as the Dark Moon's first aberration, Shahan replied. *That might just be a coincidence, of course.*

'But you doubt it?'

I do. No one knows where it sprang from, and subsequent events have confirmed that it's no ordinary force of nature.

'I thought it was just a rumour,' Terrel said. 'Something the miners made up.'

Oh no. It's real enough, Muzeni told him. *And if only a fraction of the things that are supposed to have happened are true, then this is power beyond our imagining.*

'You mean making people disappear?' Terrel asked, remembering Jehar's report of marketplace gossip.

That sort of thing, the heretic agreed. *But there's something else too. The axis around which the islands are now spinning is at Betancuria.*

'Are you saying this force is *responsible* for that?' Terrel exclaimed, unable to hide his astonishment.

It might be.

There are many unseen forces that control the worlds we live in, Terrel, Shahan said, taking up the story. *It's possible this is one that's unknown to our science, one that has lain dormant until something . . . roused it – whether it was the mining operations or the Dark Moon. We don't know what it is, but we can measure its effects. Apart from being at the centre of the rotation, Betancuria has also been the epicentre of several recent earthquakes. That's one too many coincidences for me.*

'But why do I have to study it? Why don't you go and see what it is for yourselves?'

They can't, Alyssa replied flatly. *The force is affecting their world too. Do you remember how Sevin and the other ghosts at the haven felt an earthquake that one time? That made no sense till I realized what had caused it. None of us understands it, but no ghost can get within twenty miles of Betancuria.*

We tried, believe me, Muzeni assured Terrel.

It seems you need some . . . well, substance, Shahan added.

And we don't have much of that here, Elam completed for him.

I thought you were asleep, Alyssa remarked.

Someone has to keep you lot in order, he replied, his eyes still closed.

I'd really like to see this phenomenon for myself, Muzeni said, *but for us it's like trying to walk into a hurricane that gets stronger all the time. It's simply impossible.*

'So I'm going to have to do the last part alone,' Terrel said. The task already sounded daunting enough, but this made it seem much worse. There would be no one to tell him what to do.

Not necessarily, Alyssa replied. *I should be able to come with you – as long as I'm in an animal's body.*

That's the theory, at least, Shahan added. *We haven't tested it yet.*

Terrel felt a great weight lift from his shoulders at the thought that he would not be alone. But then something else occurred to him.

'What happens if the animal you're in gets injured, or is

trapped in the mines?' he asked. Or is killed? he added to himself. 'Would you be able to get away . . . back to your own body?'

I don't know, Alyssa replied. *Possibly not.*

'But what would happen to you then?'

No one answered.

'It could happen to me too, couldn't it?' Terrel went on. 'If the force kills me, it might destroy my spirit too. I wouldn't even get the chance to go to your world, to be a ghost.'

Their silence told him all he needed to know. The prospect of complete annihilation was terrifying. He had only just learnt that death need not be final, and now that reassurance was being taken from him.

It won't come to that, Alyssa said eventually.

'Is that prophecy, or are you just hoping?'

It's not evil, she repeated. *We just have to make sure we don't repeat any of the mistakes the miners made.*

'And how do we do that?'

We don't know yet. But you're the only one who might be able to understand. She glanced at Shahan and Muzeni, hoping for support, and they came to her aid.

It all comes back to the Code, Terrel, the seer explained.

That's right, Muzeni confirmed. *You've read my journals. They should have made things clearer.*

'I only read one, and not all of that.'

And it was impossible to understand half of what he did read, Elam remarked.

Only one? the heretic queried, sounding disappointed. *Where are the rest?*

Terrel told him. To his surprise, Muzeni burst out laughing.

In a tomb, eh? Apt enough, I suppose. Not my own grave, I assume?

Terrel felt awkward, remembering the sad pile of bones.

Don't worry, the old man said, still smiling. *I know where my bones lie. It's as good a resting place as any. I must say I miss my pipe though.*

Terrel reached inside the pocket of his tattered tunic. The clay pipe had travelled with him ever since he'd left the haven, more or less forgotten until now.

'I'm sorry. I took it.' He offered it to the old man, who stretched out a hand, then laughed at Terrel's nervous astonishment when his spectral fingers passed clean through the boy's own and the pipe.

Keep it for me, Muzeni said. *Leave it with my skeleton when you're next at the observatory.*

'I will,' Terrel promised.

Can we get back to the matter in hand? Shahan enquired. *The prophecy—*

'Tell me another time,' Terrel cut in. 'I'll go to Betancuria.'

Good. The seer looked relieved. *I know it's a lot to ask of you, but—*

'But I don't want Alyssa to come with me,' the boy added, interrupting him again. 'There's no reason to risk both our lives.'

I'm coming, Alyssa stated determinedly. *Whether you like it or not. Whatever's there is protecting me.*

By putting you in a coma? Elam asked sceptically.

It's just like sleeping, she replied. *Besides, how would I be able to travel if my spirit hadn't been set free that way? How would I be able to act as your guide?*

The ghosts had no answer to that – and Terrel knew better than to try to argue with Alyssa when she was in such a mood. And in his heart, he was glad. Having her at his side – in whatever form – would give him strength and courage.

You've a long journey ahead of you, Shahan said.

'I know,' Terrel replied. He knew that Betancuria lay in one of the mountainous central provinces of Vadanis and – judging from what he remembered of the maps in Havenmoon's library – it was probably around three hundred miles south of where he was now. 'That's why I need to rest now. I'll start at first light.'

If you want a decent night's sleep, let us find you a better place than this, Elam offered. *The piglet's farm isn't so far away, and one of the few advantages of being a ghost is that we can scare anyone off if we put our minds to it. You might even get a proper bed.*

'I'll be fine here.' Terrel had no wish to see an innocent pig farmer terrified out of his wits for his benefit.

Suit yourself, his friend responded, sounding disappointed.

As before, the ghosts vanished simultaneously and without warning. The night seemed darker without them. Back around the corner, Terrel thought.

'Do you have to go too?' he asked.

Hedges look different from the inside, Alyssa remarked, as if this were a perfectly sensible answer to his question, and then the piglet got up and trotted away into the darkness. Although this parting was not quite as wrenching as the last, it was bad enough. Terrel lay down and hoped that sleep would come soon, so that the aching would stop.

CHAPTER TWENTY-THREE

Three days later, Terrel met the man who would change the way he looked at the world – and the way the world looked at him.

After the meeting with Alyssa's piglet and the ghosts, Terrel had blithely assumed that they would visit him again soon, to guide his path, explain the nature of his mission, and help him on his way. Every time he saw an animal he waited hopefully, but when none of them spoke to him or even paid him any more attention than normal, he eventually set aside such wishful thinking. Alyssa would announce her presence when she arrived.

After a while, he realized that – for whatever reasons – he had been left to his own devices. Perhaps his friends thought he had no need of further aid or advice, or perhaps something was preventing them from making the journey between worlds. In either case, all Terrel could do was make his own way as best he could, and hope to see them again before too long. He had no real plan in mind, and just hoped to travel in the general direction of

Betancuria and obtain further instructions when he was closer to the mining district.

Terrel was not sure exactly how much progress he had made so far. He had been heading in what he still thought of as a southerly course – even though this was now where the sun set – but he knew his walking pace was slow by normal standards. And because the islands were rotating, he could not even be certain of his bearings. He also had the constant problem of having to find somewhere relatively safe to sleep each night, and of scavenging enough food to keep himself alive and capable of motion. His life was once more that of an outcast, and there were times when he came close to despair. Only the fact that he had given his word – and Alyssa's reassurance that he would see her again – kept him going.

He was crossing an area of open heathland when the trail he was using came to a fork. His choice, unless he meant to force his way over rough ground, was between veering either to the southwest or the southeast. Both options would mean progress towards his destination, but not by the direct route he had been hoping for – and now that he believed he had left Saefir Province behind, his knowledge of the roads and byways of Vadanis was almost non-existent. All he had left was instinct and, on this occasion, even that had deserted him.

While deliberating, Terrel became aware of a cart rumbling up the track behind him. He turned, and saw that it was being drawn by an ancient-looking donkey and driven by a small man who was hunched over the reins. Used to being spurned and even being forced to hide from fellow travellers at times, Terrel hesitated about standing his ground, but there seemed no immediate threat and he was in need of advice. The cart came on steadily, then halted at the fork, a few paces from where Terrel stood.

Man and boy looked at each other. Terrel saw a
wizened and stooped figure of indeterminate age, with lus-
trous black hair tied back in a ponytail. The skin on the
man's sharp-featured face and surprisingly delicate hands
was naturally swarthy, but its colour was obviously deepened by an outdoor life, and his clothes were old and
worn but of good quality. He seemed quite at ease and
Terrel saw none of the usual revulsion in his dark eyes,
only a little surprise followed by a swift moment of calculation.

'Where are you going, stranger?' The voice was deep
and resonant, contrasting oddly with the man's appearance.

'South,' Terrel replied. 'To Betancuria.'

'Not a pilgrim, then?'

Terrel shook his head, not sure what the question
meant.

'That's a long way to travel on foot,' the carter observed.
'You look leg-weary already.'

'I'm used to it.'

'A wanderer like me!' The sudden smile transformed the
man's face, and made him seem much younger, more
handsome. Even the curve of his back and the droop of his
shoulders had gone now, so that he appeared taller. Terrel
stared in amazement, wondering what had sparked such a
change.

'My name is Babak,' the traveller said. 'It means—'

'The king,' Terrel completed for him.

Babak was obviously impressed.

'So you're familiar with the old tongue.'

'Is that your real name?'

The other man laughed.

'My parents were obviously prescient,' he said. 'I am
king of my trade.'

'I am called Terrel.'

'Ah.' Babak nodded as if this meant something significant to him. 'No wonder you've taken up the life of a wayfarer.'

Terrel wanted to ask what he meant, but he had more pressing needs.

'I am a traveller, but not from choice,' he admitted, 'and I have no experience of this country. Which way should I go for Betancuria?'

'That depends on whether you want the shortest or the fastest route.'

'They're not the same?'

'That way,' Babak replied, nodding towards the left-hand fork, 'will take you almost directly towards Betancuria, but it leads through the mountains and it's harsh country, even for a seasoned traveller. This road, on the other hand, takes you out of your way, but it's an easier route and there will be more opportunities to make the journey a little more comfortable as you go. Best of all, if your feet are sore, you can ride with me.' He patted the other side of the wooden bench on which he sat.

'You would take me with you?' Terrel asked, unused to such generosity.

'Why not? It costs me nothing, and any man familiar with the old tongue must be worth talking to. I'm usually alone, as you can see, and conversation is welcome. What do you say?'

'You don't find me . . . off-putting?'

'Eyes in themselves aren't important,' Babak replied. 'It's how we see the world that matters.'

'Most of our countrymen would not agree,' Terrel said. The carter laughed.

'Superstition can be dangerous,' he conceded. 'The trick is to turn it to your own advantage. I can show you how, if you like.'

This sounded too good to be true, but Babak seemed genuine enough, and Terrel's suspicions were fading.

'Is conversation all you want of me in return?' He could not think of any ulterior motive for the offer.

'Oh, we'll find a way for you to earn your keep,' Babak said breezily. 'From the look of you, I'd wager you could do with a decent meal or two and a proper bed to sleep in tonight.'

Terrel could not deny the truth of that. Just the thought of it was filling him with longing – and brought the doubts back. How could he possibly earn such rewards?

'Accept a little kindness from a fellow wanderer,' the other man went on, smiling again. 'You can always walk away, whenever you want.'

Terrel made up his mind at last, telling himself that it would be stupid to reject such an offer, even if he could not fathom the motives behind it. He climbed up and sat beside Babak, who flicked the reins at once. The donkey, who had remained perfectly still – as if it were a matter of supreme indifference whether it stood or moved – began to trudge down the right-hand fork.

Now that Terrel was alongside him, Babak seemed to shrink once more, to become the bent and weather-beaten figure the boy had first seen. It was a peculiar and unnerving transformation. They rode in silence for a while, and when the carter finally spoke, even his voice seemed a pale imitation of the one he had used to greet Terrel.

'There are more people leaving Betancuria than going to it,' he remarked. 'You've heard the rumours, of course?'

'Some of them.'

'So the monster doesn't bother you?'

'I doubt it's as bad as the gossips would have us believe,' Terrel replied, thinking back to his conversation with the ghosts.

'You're probably right,' Babak said, chuckling, 'but when you hear that one of the miners who got too close vanished completely, right in front of his companions, and another . . . well, all they found of him was a few smears of blood and grease on the tunnel walls . . . it makes you wonder. I've heard it said it can turn a man's blood to stone or boil it into steam. Even if the tales are exaggerated, it sounds like they've got something pretty nasty down there. I wouldn't want to meet it.'

'Me neither,' Terrel said heavily, horrified by these more specific accounts of the supposed atrocities. He could only hope they *were* exaggerated, and that Alyssa was a better judge than the rumour-mongers.

'So why are you heading that way?' Babak asked.

'There's someone there I have to talk to.'

The traveller glanced at him curiously.

'That doesn't sound like much of a reason.'

'It's important,' Terrel replied awkwardly.

'Suit yourself. I can be a nosy old bastard, I know that. You don't have to tell me anything if you don't want to.' He paused, obviously hoping that the boy would volunteer something more. When he didn't, Babak altered his approach. 'Most people who are running away just want to leave somewhere behind,' he remarked ingenuously. 'They don't usually have somewhere in mind to run to.'

'What makes you think I'm running away?'

'Free men don't usually have tattoos like that.'

Terrel glanced at his hand, seeing that the circles hardly showed through the dirt. Since he had left the immediate vicinity of Havenmoon, no one had even commented on it – and he had begun to think it was unimportant.

'I don't miss much,' Babak added, grinning. 'I've only ever seen something like that on slaves, lunatics and criminals – and you don't strike me as the criminal type. You

wouldn't be worth much as a slave, and there are more
sane people in the madhouses now than there are loonies.
So it doesn't matter much to me which it is. I'm just nosy,
like I said.'

'I was in a madhouse,' Terrel admitted.

'You seem sane enough to me.'

'I am. At least I think I am. It was probably because of
the way I look.'

'Probably,' Babak agreed. 'Were you released, or did you
escape?'

Terrel hesitated for a few moments, but saw no point in
lying.

'I escaped.'

'Resourceful as well as bright,' the carter commented
approvingly. 'I'm glad I stopped for you.'

Terrel had had enough of this discussion, and sought to
change the subject.

'What is your trade . . . Your Majesty?'

Babak laughed.

'A sense of humour too,' he said delightedly. 'We must
try to persuade this one to stay with us a while, eh, Luci?'
This remark was directed to the donkey, who pricked up
her ears at the sound of her name, but did not look round
or alter her steady pace.

'You don't mind *me* being nosy?' Terrel asked.

'Not at all. Seems only fair. I prefer to think of myself
as an apothecary – and one of rare talents at that – but
most of my customers would call me a pedlar, and I
wouldn't disown the name. It's an honourable profession.'

'What do you sell?' Terrel wasn't sure what an apothecary was.

'Whatever is to hand,' Babak replied, 'but mainly elixirs,
potions, ointments and tinctures. There's hardly a human
ailment I don't have a remedy for.'

'So you're a physician?'

'Of sorts.'

'Do you make your medicines yourself?'

'Mostly. I purchase some from other reputable sources.' This was said with a sly grin that Terrel could not interpret.

'What's in them?'

'You *are* nosy, aren't you,' the pedlar said, but then went on to answer the question anyway. 'Various essences, herbs, roots, honey and other natural ingredients. The exact recipes are secret, of course.'

'And these things can really cure people?'

Babak glanced at his passenger again, trying to see if he was really as serious as he sounded.

'Look, Terrel. Most people want to believe that they're beautiful, that they're intelligent, that they'll never grow old, and that their illnesses will be cured. All I do is encourage those beliefs. Understand?'

Terrel took some time to consider this statement.

'So you're a—' he began eventually.

'An apothecary,' Babak cut in. 'I told you what my potions are made from, but the most important ingredient is faith. If my patients *believe* they're going to get well, then they do. The human mind is a wonderful physician. I just help it to work. And if by any chance it doesn't, then the other essential part of my medicines comes into play.'

'What's that?'

'Alcohol. If the cure isn't effective, at least they're too happy to notice until I'm well on my way.' Babak grinned again, while Terrel stared at him.

'No wonder you stay on the move,' the boy said.

The pedlar laughed.

'I travel because I wouldn't want to live any other way,' he said. 'And I'm welcome anywhere.'

'Even somewhere you've been before and—'

'Everywhere,' Babak confirmed. 'You'll see. Whatever you think of me now, I do more good than harm – and how many people can say that?'

Terrel thought about this for a while. Part of him could not believe that people were so gullible, but then if Babak's cure-alls really did some good, what was the harm in that? He was also thinking about his own naiveté, and realized that if he'd known more about the world, the pedlar's cynicism would have seemed less shocking. And the strange thing was that Terrel's feelings towards Babak had not changed. He liked him, even if he was a swindler.

'Are all your potions back there?' he asked curiously, glancing round at the cart. Its contents were covered with canvas sheeting, neatly secured with ropes.

'Yes. That and my bed roll and a few essentials for the wanderer's life.'

'Aren't you afraid of thieves, travelling alone like this?'

'No one would be stupid enough to rob an apothecary,' Babak replied confidently. 'They all know I can make them worse as well as better. The curse of a pedlar is not to be taken lightly. Besides, I'm handy with a knife if I need to be – but the best way to combat trouble is to avoid it in the first place. That's my speciality. That, and ridding the world of evils such as warts, impotence, hair loss, the pox and such like.'

'Do you have anything that'll cure my eyes?' Terrel asked, laughing now, amused by Babak's supreme confidence.

'As it happens, I do,' Babak said merrily, 'but it doesn't come from any of my bottles. You have a gift for it, lad, just like me. I knew that the moment I saw you.'

'A gift for what?' Terrel asked.

'The glamour,' Babak replied, then turned to gaze at his passenger.

As Terrel watched, the pedlar's eyes turned from dark brown to a bright pale blue.

CHAPTER TWENTY-FOUR

'How did you do that?' Terrel gasped.

'Do what?' Babak replied, grinning. He turned away again, but Terrel could see that his eyes had returned to their normal colour.

'Your eyes were blue! Just for a moment. I saw—'

'Are you sure?'

Terrel hesitated. What *had* he seen? An illusion? A reflection of the sky? Or had he simply imagined the whole thing? It seemed unreal now, like the memory of a fading dream.

'The glamour?' he hazarded.

Babak nodded.

'My eyes didn't change colour, but you *thought* they did, because you wanted to. I just helped the process along.'

'How?'

'With suggestion and belief. My suggestion and your belief. I put the idea in your head, and you persuaded yourself it was true.'

'But—'

'Don't you sometimes know something's true, without knowing how or why?' the pedlar asked.

'Intuition, you mean?'

'Exactly. In this case, *I* am your intuition. In the old tongue it was called "psinoma", which means "invisible words". A transfer of thoughts directly between minds, without the need of verbal communication – and sometimes without the person on the receiving end even being aware of what's happening.'

'So you control their minds?' Terrel asked. All his instincts were rebelling at the idea, insisting that it was wrong, but he was fascinated nonetheless.

'Not exactly,' Babak replied. 'I can't make anyone believe something they don't want to believe. In effect, all I said to you was "You're right. My eyes are changing colour."'

'And I saw what I wanted to be true?'

'That's right. Of course I don't usually waste the glamour on something like the colour of my eyes. There'd be no point in that. But it might be different for you.'

'You really think I could do it too?' Terrel asked.

'I'm sure of it.'

'But how? Can you teach me? I've no idea how to even begin.'

'Oh, you began long before you even met me,' Babak said. 'If you think about it, you'll realize that.'

Terrel thought about it. The first, and most obvious, thing that came to mind was his ability to converse with Alyssa and the ghosts. During those exchanges he had always spoken aloud, but now he was wondering if that had really been necessary. He had sometimes felt that Alyssa might be aware of his unspoken thoughts. But, up until that moment, he had assumed that he was able to converse with them because of *their* skills. Now he was not so sure. The second, and far more surprising, idea concerned his premonitions about earth tremors. That was a form of intuition he could not explain, but it seemed to be felt by his entire being, rather than just his mind. And if that were a form of psinoma, he could not imagine who the other mind might be.

'Well?' Babak prompted.

'I may well have been on the receiving end of something,' Terrel conceded vaguely. He had no wish to elaborate further at that moment. 'But I still don't see how I can use it for myself.'

'All right,' the pedlar said. 'Let's try an experiment. Picture something in your mind as clearly as you can, and then imagine you're telling me all about it — but don't say anything. Can you do that? Make sure it's something I couldn't have seen.'

Terrel nodded his agreement. He concentrated as hard as he could, closing his eyes to picture the scene, then 'heard' himself telling Babak all about it. The pedlar laughed.

'A piglet with an earring?' he exclaimed. 'By the stars, but you do keep some peculiar company!'

Although that night did not bring the proper bed Babak had promised, it was still a lot more comfortable than Terrel had been used to. The pedlar decided they would camp by the roadside in open country and, once Luci had pulled the cart onto a convenient patch of grass, he showed Terrel how his mode of transport became his living quarters. An ingenious system of levers and pulleys converted the canvas covering into a tent, and while the contents were usually laid out to fit only one bed roll, it took only minor adjustments to make space for a second. Terrel got the feeling that Babak had done this before. The tent would be a little cramped when they were both inside, surrounded by the chests and boxes that presumably held the pedlar's merchandise, but to the young wanderer it seemed like absolute luxury.

Babak did provide the decent meal he had mentioned earlier, lighting a fire and producing a remarkably succulent vegetable stew that they ate with hard biscuits flavoured with salt and herbs. Only when they had finished the last of the food did the pedlar allow his guest to continue their conversation from earlier in the day.

It had taken Terrel quite some time to recover from his astonishment at the success of their experiment – and when he had, the list of questions he'd wanted to ask had been almost endless. He could not deny that an exchange of thoughts had taken place, but he believed that this had only been possible because of Babak's own talent. The pedlar had denied this and told Terrel he would give him further proof the next day, when they would meet other people. 'You could disguise your eyes now, if you wanted to,' he had said. 'But I realize you wouldn't accept that, because I'd know what you were trying to do. We'll have to wait until we meet someone who doesn't know you.' Terrel had been both frightened and excited by this idea, and they had talked a great deal about how he should go about it, before Babak decided that he had had enough of the subject for the time being and left the boy to his own reflections. Now, as he cleared away their bowls, the pedlar seemed amenable again.

'You used the glamour on me earlier, didn't you?' Terrel began. 'To change your appearance and your voice. Why did you bother to do that? You had no need to impress me.'

'Habit, I suppose – at first, at least,' Babak answered. 'But then, like I said, you looked like someone interesting.'

'And someone who could earn his keep?' Terrel prompted.

'I could see ways you might be able to help me make a sale or two,' the pedlar admitted.

'By lying to people? Pretending you can cure this?' Terrel waved his withered right arm.

'You disapprove.' It was a statement rather than a question.

'I don't like the idea of cheating people.'

'I never promise the impossible,' Babak claimed. 'If people infer miracles from what they see and hear, that's another matter. Besides, as I said, they'll only believe what they want to believe.'

'That's another thing,' Terrel said. 'You told me your curses are effective too. Why would anyone want to believe a curse?'

'Because, deep in their hearts, they know I wouldn't curse them unless it was just, unless they deserved punishment.'

'So, in effect, they bring the curse on themselves?'

'You could look at it that way.'

Terrel shook his head. He found such ideas disturbing, and he did not know how his mentor had come to terms with them.

'Doesn't it frighten you?' he asked. 'The power you have?'

'Why should it?' Babak replied. 'Some people are beautiful, or phenomenally strong, others are talented musicians or artists, and some have an aptitude for healing or prophecy. We all take advantage of the gifts we've been given in life.'

'But isn't this rather more than that?' Terrel persisted. 'I mean, you could make people believe *anything*.'

'You mean I lack the ambition to go with my evil sorcery?' the pedlar responded, a humorous glint in his eyes. 'Why don't I go to Makhaya and make the Emperor do what I want?'

'Well, why don't you?' Terrel challenged.

'Firstly, because even *my* powers are limited,' Babak said, still smiling, 'and secondly, because even if I could do it, I've no wish for the sort of life and status you'd find at court.'

'You'd rather separate peasants from their hard-earned coins?'

'What can I say? They're my audience.'

'You . . . are a rogue,' Terrel declared, but he could not help smiling even as he said it.

'A rogue?' Babak gasped, fluttering a hand over his heart. 'Such language from the lips of one so young and innocent! Forgive me, I have to recover my breath.'

Terrel was glad the fire had died down and the evening was drawing in, so that the blush on his face was less noticeable, but he was laughing too, unable to summon up the righteous anger that he knew he should be feeling.

'I can be generous too,' the pedlar said, when they had both quietened down.

'I know. And I'm grateful.'

'I don't mean helping you on your way, or the bed and the meal,' Babak told him. 'I want you to fulfil your potential. You're my apprentice now, Terrel, whether you like it or not. And tomorrow we'll put what you've already learnt into practice.'

'Where are we going?' the boy asked, trying not to think about his own possible use of the glamour.

'By evening we'll be in Tiscamanita.'

'Isn't that on the coast?' Terrel had not realized that his wanderings had taken him so far to the west of the island.

'It is indeed,' the pedlar replied. 'And the day after tomorrow will be the Moon Festival there.'

'The Red Moon will be full,' Terrel said, but his thoughts were elsewhere. He had only ever seen the ocean in his dreams. Now he was close to seeing the real thing.

'And the fires of love will burn bright,' Babak intoned.
'What?'
'You'll see,' the pedlar promised.

The ruin dominated the landscape for miles around. Luci
had been pulling them along at her unchanging pace for
some time when Terrel first saw it, but it had taken
another two hours to reach the foot of the hill. From that
earliest glimpse, the boy's gaze had been drawn to the
jagged outline of dark stone, caught as much by its position – atop a single bare hill in the middle of the wide
coastal plain – as by the stark shapes above.

'According to legend, even the hill itself is man-made,'
Babak remarked, 'though I don't see how anyone could
know that.'

'Because it's symmetrical,' Terrel said, 'and it's so different from the rest of the landscape round here.'

'Even so, that's a lot of trouble to go to,' the pedlar went
on. 'Unless they were giants, it would've taken years to
move all that earth, and then they'd have had to make sure
it was solid enough to build on. Makes no sense.'

'They must have had their reasons. Doesn't anyone
know who built it?'

'No. It's supposed to be even older than the temple at
Tindaya, but the funny thing is that some of its construction was apparently very sophisticated. Someone estimated
from the thickness of the lower walls that the central tower
might have been five or six storeys high, and the masonry
was perfectly crafted. I don't know how they can tell that
from this pile of rubble, but that's what they say.' He
shrugged. 'There was stained glass in some of the windows
too, apparently. It's gone now, of course, but there were
lots of fragments left. The only place you come across such
things these days is in the best temples and houses of

Makhaya, not some primitive castle in the middle of nowhere.'

'So whoever built this place must have been part of a highly developed civilization,' Terrel concluded.

'Seems like it,' Babak agreed, 'but there's no record of them anywhere else. It's as if they just vanished – and the only thing they left was this ruin.'

'Can we go up and take a closer look?' The road curved round the base of the hill.

'You go,' the pedlar replied. 'I've seen it all before. I'll pick you up again on the far side.'

By the time Terrel reached the castle he was breathing heavily, because the slope was steep and the day was warm and humid, but he soon forgot about this and about his aching legs as he walked among the ruins. It was obvious that it had once been a monumental construction. Some of the blocks of stone were massive and, even though they'd been eroded by time and the weather, the precise nature of their cutting was clear. Terrel could make out the remnants of graceful arches, columns, and great walls amid the general clutter of rock, but he was most fascinated by a pattern incised upon what must once have been the floor of a great hall. The paving was partly obscured by debris, and was broken in places, but the original design was still clear. It had been a floor maze, leading via an almost impossibly convoluted route to the centre of the circular pattern. Terrel imagined people making the slow, symbolic journey to the heart of the maze, and wished it was possible for him to do the same. The place had a strangely peaceful atmosphere, and had surely once been the site of ritual and worship. This thought made him glance up at the sky, but none of the moons was visible – and he could only guess at what the stars might look like from where he stood, their light mirrored by candles below.

Coming back down to earth, he went to look at the centre of the maze. The mosaic there was also partly hidden by fallen masonry, but he could see enough to realize that it looked like a great black star, each of its five points extended in wavy lines – like tentacles reaching out into the labyrinth that surrounded it. For the first time Terrel felt a momentary unease, a small chill of foreboding that made him glad of the noonday heat.

As he made his way down the far side of the hill, he found himself thinking about the purpose of his journey. Like the dark star here, his destination also lay at the heart of a man-made labyrinth.

CHAPTER TWENTY-FIVE

'You can't hide for ever.' Babak sounded disappointed, but impatient too.

Terrel knew this was true, but part of him wished that it wasn't. The nearer they got to Tiscamanita, the more people they met on the road. Some contact was inevitable, but Terrel had chosen to look down, or to raise his hand as if shading himself from the sun, in order to hide his eyes.

'Listen,' Babak went on. 'Even if you fail, nothing's going to happen. You may get a few strange looks, but that's all. You're with me.'

Terrel had already seen that the pedlar commanded respect – even a little awe – from most of their fellow travellers, and being under his protection did indeed make the boy feel safer in the midst of so many strangers. Even so, his earlier experiences had made him wary – and Babak's reassurances had done nothing to rid Terrel of his own distrust of the glamour, his conviction that somehow it was wrong.

'Besides, you're not going to fail,' his companion added.

'You think I don't know when someone has the gift? Look. I know him.' He pointed ahead, to where a merchant had pulled his wagon over to the side of the road in order to talk to a man on horseback. 'We'll stop for a chat. You can try with them.'

'No, please,' Terrel whispered. The horseman was in uniform and, even though it was not one he recognized, the idea of confronting someone in authority made the prospect even more daunting.

'Just remember what I told you,' Babak said, cheerfully relentless. 'Concentrate on one thing. Don't try to hide your arm or your leg. Use them to distract attention if necessary. Most people won't even notice your eyes if you do that – and if they do, they'll think they're a perfectly ordinary blue – as long as you convince them. And they'll be happier believing that than seeing the eyes of an enchanter!' Babak had been told of the harvesters' accusations. 'Now just relax and do it.'

Having drawn alongside the wagon, the pedlar brought Luci to a halt with a casual flick of the reins, while Terrel tried to make himself as small and inconspicuous as possible.

'Greetings, Phailas,' Babak said.

'Hello, Babak,' the merchant replied coolly, then glanced reluctantly at his companion. 'You know Seneschal Cadrez, of course.'

The pedlar transferred his gaze to the imposing figure who sat stiffly erect on his mount.

'Only by reputation,' he replied. 'I am honoured to make your acquaintance, sir.'

The seneschal nodded, but did not speak.

'Don't waste your time on him, Babak,' Phailas advised. 'He has too much sense to be taken in by your cozenage.'

Babak pretended to be shocked and offended, then smiled.

'I'm sure the seneschal is capable of making up his own mind in such matters,' he said. 'And *I* shan't lack for customers at the fair. People prefer a little entertainment to being overcharged for your trinkets.'

'Hadn't you better move along?' the merchant responded. 'You're blocking the road.'

Throughout this pointed but not unfriendly exchange, Terrel had kept his head down. However, Babak was determined not to allow him to hide any longer and pulled him forward.

'This is my new apprentice,' the pedlar announced. 'Greet our distinguished friends, Terrel.'

I have blue eyes, Terrel recited softly. Perfectly ordinary. Blue eyes.

He looked up, forcing himself not to squint.

'Good afternoon, gentlemen,' he said quietly. The horrified reaction he was expecting did not come. He held his breath, waiting.

'He has better manners than the last one, at least,' Phailas remarked.

'And he is a most able student,' Babak said, in a self-satisfied tone.

'Then he deserves a better master than you,' the merchant responded.

'I doubt I could do better than the one I have,' Terrel stated with more conviction, aghast at his own daring.

The merchant gave the boy a second, measuring glance, as if he thought he had spoken out of turn, but once again he saw nothing untoward. Terrel held his gaze in triumph, before looking at the seneschal. Cadrez was paying him no attention, watching the road behind the cart.

'Farewell, gentlemen,' Babak said as he set Luci in motion again. 'Enjoy the festival.'

Once they were out of earshot, Terrel expected his

mentor to make some comment, but the smug grin on the pedlar's face said it all. He had been proved right – and they both knew it. Terrel was able to use the glamour.

He was still dwelling on the implications this could have for his life when they reached the outskirts of Tiscamanita. Until now this had only been a name on a map, but Terrel soon realized that it was by far the largest town he had ever seen. Even the outlying districts seemed opulent, and further towards the centre he could see several tall buildings – including one lofty tower that seemed to him like a gigantic finger pointing towards the heavens. There were people everywhere but, emboldened by his recent success, Terrel stared about him openly, still keeping up the silent litany within his head. I have blue eyes. Blue . . .

The last part of their journey had been alongside a wide, meandering river that flowed sluggishly over the plain, but Terrel realized – with a rush of disappointment – that he had not yet caught so much as a glimpse of the sea. And it was clear that he would have to wait for that when Babak steered the cart into the yard of a prosperous looking tavern. Stableboys appeared as if by magic to tend to Luci and to stow the cart in one of the guarded sheds, and the innkeeper himself – who obviously knew Babak of old – took them up to a room on the first floor. Nobody gave Terrel more than a second glance.

'Will this suit you?' the pedlar enquired, when they were alone.

Terrel lay back on the smaller of the two beds in the room, and sighed. It was softer than anything he had ever imagined. He felt a wave of contentment wash over him, allowing himself to revel in the moment and to forget about the storm clouds gathering over his future. At that moment, it was hard to believe they were real.

'It's wonderful,' he said, looking up at his companion. Babak smiled.

'It's becoming instinctive already, isn't it?' he said. 'After a while you won't even have to think about it. Unless you want to, of course. There might be times when your real eyes could be useful.'

Terrel couldn't imagine such a situation, but he didn't really care. He was still lost in amazement at his own achievement – and gratitude towards Babak for forcing him to recognize it.

'Thank you. You were right.'

'Of course!' the pedlar responded. 'Now let's go down and get some dinner.'

'Can we go and see the occan first?' Terrel asked eagerly.

'Anyone would think you've never seen the sea before.'

'I haven't,' the boy admitted.

Babak looked surprised, obviously thinking that Terrel's life as a wanderer did not seem to have led him very far.

'It's still quite a walk from here,' he said, clearly reluctant, then brightened as another possibility occurred to him. 'However . . . Come on.'

A little while later, they approached the tower Terrel had first seen from a distance. From close to, the soaring circular construction was even more breathtaking, reaching up to the clouds. However, the door at its base was guarded by two men. Their very size was intimidating, and they gave off an unmistakable air of menace.

'There's an entrance fee for the viewing platform,' one of them announced as the visitors arrived.

'Save it for the pilgrims,' Babak advised him dismissively. 'This tower's public property, and we both know it. What would Seneschal Cadrez think of you duping innocents like this, I wonder?'

The big man scowled, but neither he nor his partner showed any sign of giving in.

'Two phinars each,' he stated flatly. 'Any argument and the price goes up.'

'Oh, I don't intend to argue,' Babak replied, 'but my colleague here might. He needs to take a look around from up there. And he has just the eyes to do it.'

The pedlar nudged Terrel gently, and the boy realized with a start what he was meant to do. He stopped the internal monologue that he'd resumed since leaving their room in the tavern. The effect was both instantaneous and remarkable. Neither of the guards had paid him any attention until that moment, but now they stared at him in open-mouthed horror. Without thinking, Terrel smiled – and this seemed to complete their terror. Both men stepped aside and allowed the travellers to enter.

'I told you that might come in useful,' Babak said, as they began to climb the long spiral staircase, and his laughter chimed softly in the echoing spaces of the tower.

When they finally reached the viewing platform they were both out of breath, but the view from the parapet was worth the effort. They were so high that Terrel felt momentarily dizzy, as if he were flying. The entire town was laid out below them, like a map, and he could see for many miles over the surrounding plain. But he was transfixed by his first sight of the ocean. Nothing in his imagination could have prepared him for the immensity of it, a shimmering blue-grey expanse that stretched away to the far horizon. Even from a distance he was awed by its restless energy, its elemental grandeur – and was left speechless. Babak, who had seen such sights many times before, was not so inhibited.

'Ordinarily we'd be facing northwest,' he said, when he'd got his breath back, 'but now it's nearer northeast.

That means we'll all be able to see the moons rise over the ocean, rather than watching them set. The festival will officially start in the early evening tomorrow, when the Red Moon rises, but there'll be plenty going on before then.'

Terrel continued to gaze at the ocean in silence. He was wondering what Alyssa's reaction would be on seeing such an unimaginably vast expanse of water. Compared to this, the lake at Havenmoon was nothing more than a single raindrop.

'See over there,' Babak said, pointing to their left. 'That's Vaka, the most northerly of the western islands – or it would be if we were still pointing the right way.'

Terrel stared at the low-lying shape in the ocean.

'If you look clearly, you can see the edge of the underwater bridge,' the pedlar went on. 'That curve where the sea changes colour.'

As soon as it had been pointed out, the division was obvious. A line of white water marked the rim of the submerged link and, beyond it, the relatively shallow sea was a much brighter blue.

'Navigation's hard enough in those waters at the best of times,' Babak added. 'It's even worse now, I'll wager. I doubt there'll be as many pilgrims as usual from Vaka.'

'What's so special about Tiscamanita?' Terrel asked. 'Why do people come here to celebrate the full moon? They could do that anywhere.'

'Because of Kativa's Shrine,' the pedlar answered.

'What's that?'

'You've never heard of it? I could tell you the story, but it would be better if we wait till tomorrow, when you can see it for yourself.'

'More dramatic that way?' Terrel queried, disappointed by the delay, but knowing that Babak was an actor at heart, and that he wanted to set the scene.

'Exactly,' the pedlar replied, aware that he was being teased, but choosing to ignore the fact. 'Right now I need to eat.'

Their meal at the tavern came in vast portions and was much richer fare than Terrel was used to, so that eventually he was forced to restrain his appetite or risk making himself ill. Babak ate like a trencherman, washing down the roast meats, cheeses and potatoes with quantities of beer, then calling for cake and a jug of wine. Terrel had drunk only water until then, but he was persuaded to try some of the wine. At first it tasted metallic and sour, but after a few tentative sips he began to appreciate the more subtle aspects of its flavour. The only alcohol he had ever drunk before had been a little of Ahmeza's cider, but that had been watery stuff by comparison, and he had not really liked it much. The warm feeling that was now flowing through him was unlike anything he had ever experienced. It made him feel optimistic, invincible.

Babak raised his cup, and smiled to see his companion's flushed cheeks.

'"Give me chastity and sobriety . . ."' he quoted. '"But not now."'

Terrel joined in the toast, without considering what it meant, then frowned as a stray thought popped into his head.

'You didn't use the glamour on Phailas and the seneschal. Why not?'

'Keep your voice down, boy,' the pedlar hissed. 'Walls have ears.'

It took Terrel a few moments to work out what Babak meant, and when he had, he repeated the question more quietly.

'I'd still like to know why you didn't.'

'Because it pays to have people like that underestimate you.'

Terrel nodded, though he was not sure he understood.

'I've never drunk wine before,' he remarked, his mind flitting from one thought to the next.

'You truly are an innocent,' Babak commented. 'You'll be telling me next you've never kissed a girl.'

Terrel felt his face grow hot and knew, to his shame, that he was blushing furiously.

'I have a girlfriend,' he claimed defensively.

'In Betancuria?' the pedlar guessed.

'No.' Terrel thought of Alyssa lying in her cell, abandoned and alone, her spirit wandering. He longed to see her again, preferably in her own shape, but as an animal if necessary. He needed to talk to her, to tell her how he felt. Why wasn't she there? He was the one who had been abandoned now. And then the import of their most recent meeting came back to him in a rush, and all the terrible things he had learnt then left him sobered and afraid.

Babak watched the changes come over him with interest, wondering what secrets his apprentice was hiding.

'Ordinarily, I'd say that most worries are soluble in wine,' he said, 'but in your case I think that would be a mistake.'

Terrel nodded, pushing his half-empty cup away. He no longer wanted any part of its falsehood.

'It's been a long day,' the pedlar observed. 'You should get some rest.'

The boy nodded again, his eyes downcast, but made no move to rise from his seat.

'Is there something you want to talk about?' Babak asked.

What can I say? Terrel thought. His companion's generosity deserved the truth, but that was impossible. Better to say nothing. He looked up and shook his head.

'Remember your eyes,' the pedlar said quietly.

In his distraction, Terrel's eyes had returned to their genuine colouring, and although no one in the tavern seemed to have noticed, they were bound to do so as he walked from the hall.

Terrel blinked, and his eyes were blue again.

'Good lad,' Babak said, with some relief. Whatever was ailing the boy, he was still able to control his talent. 'I'll see you later. And tomorrow we'll have some fun, eh?'

Terrel stood up and left without a word, threading his way between the tables with his awkward, lopsided gait. Babak watched him go, feeling a disquiet of his own.

Some time later, when all the wine was gone, the pedlar went out into the street. He had a 'girlfriend' of his own in Tiscamanita – one of several in various places around Vadanis – and after his conversation with Terrel, he felt in need of the comfort she would provide.

CHAPTER TWENTY-SIX

On his first morning in Tiscamanita, Terrel woke to the sound of snoring. Even though he had lain awake for some time the night before, he had eventually succumbed to the comfort of the soft bed, and had not been aware of Babak's return. He was there now all right, making a sound that shook the walls.

For a while Terrel was content to rest in unaccustomed luxury, but as he listened to the noises of the tavern and the town beyond coming to life, he grew restless. He guessed that the sun had only just risen, but had no idea when the pedlar would wake up. The temptation to get up and explore on his own became too great, and he slipped out of bed and dressed quietly.

There was a cool breeze blowing down the street outside, and Terrel instinctively turned to walk into it, realizing that it must be coming from the sea. The air carried with it a tang of salt, and another, unidentifiable, odour that made him feel strangely invigorated. The lure of the ocean was strong, and he wanted to view it from close to, but he was not destined to reach the shore that day.

After walking for a while, Terrel reached an enormous paved square, clearly the hub of the town's activity. Near each corner piles of wood and other dry material were stacked in such a way that Terrel assumed they were bonfires waiting to be lit. He recalled Babak's remark about the 'fires of love' burning brightly, and decided they must be part of the festival. In between these piles, keeping a respectful distance, a number of merchants were already setting up their stalls in readiness for the fair. Terrel paid them little attention, because he had seen what must be Kativa's Shrine.

It stood at the exact centre of the market place but, as if by unspoken agreement, none of the traders had set up for business within fifty paces of the extraordinary structure. The shrine rose in a twisted, sinuous curve, like an unruly flame that had been frozen in time, reaching further into the sky than the two-storey buildings that lined the perimeter of the arena. There was something alive about it, as if it had grown to that height rather than being built.

As Terrel drew closer, he could see that it was made entirely of wood, intricately carved to resemble a vast, distorted trellis, entwined with thousands of roses – all of them painted red. It should have been ugly, the most unnatural of sculptures, but its perverse, obsessive patterns were strangely beautiful – and Terrel wished that he had waited for Babak after all, so that the pedlar could have told him its story. He was far from alone in his absorption. Several other people were staring at the shrine, all apparently caught in its spell.

'They used to be real roses once.'

Terrel glanced round to see who had spoken, and saw a young woman, not much older than himself. Her gaze was fixed on the shrine, and her voice was quiet and respectful.

'And all of them the colour of the lovers' moon,' she added. 'Wonderful, isn't it?'

'Yes, it is,' he replied. 'Do you know when it was built?'

'You don't know the story?' she exclaimed, looking at him in surprise. 'I thought everybody . . .'

Her voice died away, and Terrel mentally checked to see that his eyes were still 'blue'.

'I've never been in this part of Vadanis before,' he explained. 'Will you tell me?'

'Of course.' She was obviously delighted at the chance to display her knowledge. 'Kativa lived here over two hundred years ago. She was the only daughter of the foremost noble family of the province, and she was very beautiful. Her fame spread as far as Makhaya, and the Emperor sent for her to be his fourth bride, but she'd already fallen in love with one of her household, a squire named Siverio. Knowing that their love would be forbidden, they planned to elope on the night when the Red Moon was full, but they were betrayed. Kativa's father held her prisoner, while some of his men went to meet Siverio in this square and murdered him.' The young woman paused. 'When Kativa found out what had happened,' she went on in a wistful tone, 'she took poison rather than submit to an unwanted betrothal, but she didn't die. Instead she fell into a coma, still alive, but unable to do anything except breathe and dream.'

Terrel had been engrossed in the tale, but at this mention of a coma his thoughts flew to Alyssa. Was *she* dreaming as her spirit wandered?

'Kativa lay, unmoving, for almost three years,' the storyteller continued, 'but then, when almost all hope was gone, she revived. She came here, to see where her true love had died. Siverio's blood had stained the paving stones and, no matter how hard anyone scrubbed at it, the mark could not be removed. When Kativa saw this she wept, and her tears made his blood shine red again.

'By then, of course, the Emperor had lost interest in her, and so she was free to stay in Tiscamanita. She commissioned the best craftsmen of the town to build a monument to love, and this is what it became. Every day for the rest of her life, Kativa brought a single red rose and placed it on the monument. Even in the depths of winter, when no other flowers grew, she still came, faithful to the last. And as each rose faded and decayed, the woodcarvers replaced it with one of their own making, so that her love would never die.'

Terrel found himself looking at the shrine with a new reverence. He was close to tears.

'Is there someone *you* love?' his companion asked kindly.

Terrel hesitated before replying, then simply nodded, not trusting his voice.

'Then you must come back tonight,' she told him, 'and place a flower on the shrine. A rose would be best, of course, but they're always expensive, so anything will do – as long as it's red. The flower sellers will be here soon. That's why I came early, so I could get one of the best.'

Terrel did not like to tell her that he had no money at all, and could not afford to buy a flower of any kind.

'Does leaving a flower bring good luck?' he asked.

'For lovers, yes,' his informant replied happily. 'Jari and me are getting married soon, so I had to come this year.'

'The festival is only held once a year?' He had been assuming it was every long month, whenever the Red Moon was full.

'Every year at the full moon closest to the autumnal equinox,' she confirmed, 'but it only starts when the moon has risen and the fires have been lit. I can hardly wait!'

Terrel saw the excitement shining in her eyes and smiled, then looked back at the shrine, wondering whether Babak would give him some money so that he could leave a rose for Alyssa.

Terrel watched Babak from a distance. The contrast between the stooped figure he had first encountered and the charismatic salesman who was now standing on his cart, regaling his eager audience with his irrepressible patter, was startling. Although Terrel could put a name to the difference, that did not make it any less astounding. In one sense, nothing he was seeing was real; in another it was all as real as the paving stones beneath his feet.

The afternoon was some hours old now, and as the time of moon-rise drew nearer, the atmosphere in the crowded square had reached fever pitch. What had once been a sober, almost religious festival, was now simply an excuse for riotous celebrations — and this year, because of the inexplicable events in the heavens — there was an almost hysterical note to the proceedings.

As well as the stalls selling all sorts of goods, platforms had been set up in various parts of the square on which entertainments were performed and couples publicly announced their betrothals. Mock battles were staged too, depicting the third of the Red Moon's major influences. Violence, even in a strictly symbolic form, took its accepted place alongside fire and love. Musicians, jugglers, beggars and pickpockets roamed the streets, plying their various trades, and both food and wine were in plentiful supply. A riot of smells assaulted every nose, with the heavy perfume of flowers the most prominent element in the intoxicating medley.

Terrel found the spectacle both bewildering and fascinating. He had never seen anything like it. Having already spotted a good deal of drunkenness and a few genuine fights, he could not help wondering whether the entire gathering might not spiral out of control once dusk came and the bonfires were lit. He had seen only a few soldiers – hardly enough to ensure law and order – but the air of imminent danger just seemed to add to the general atmosphere.

Unlike Terrel, Babak was in his element in the midst of this colourful chaos, and was already doing a brisk trade – but he was getting close to the moment when, with Terrel's unwilling help, he would reveal his masterstroke. The boy fidgeted, despising himself for having agreed to play his part in the deception, but knowing he would have to go through with it now. He owed Babak that much at least.

When the signal came, he adjusted his sling and tucked the crutch beneath his twisted arm, then lurched over towards the pedlar's cart, exaggerating his limp. Most people made way for him to pass, but some regarded him contemptuously and forced him to wait or go around them – while a few made callous remarks about cripples being allowed to spoil the festive mood. When he judged he was close enough, he stopped and joined Babak's audience.

'This precious elixir,' the self-styled apothecary cried, holding up a small stone phial, 'is distilled from over a hundred essences, and has been mixed to a recipe that's been in my family for many generations. It can restore vigour to every part of a man's body.'

'Every part?' a woman's voice called out, provoking a round of laughter.

'Indisputably!' Babak replied, winking at the heckler. '*Every* part. Even one that has atrophied and gone soft from lack of use. Tonight of all nights a lover should be fervent and tireless – and this will make him so. But that is not all,' he went on, overriding the crowd's buzz of speculation. 'It can effect marvels upon the limbs of those afflicted by the palsy, or who have not recovered their agility and strength after breaking a bone.'

Babak looked around his audience, ignoring their cries of disbelief, until his gaze fell – apparently by chance – on Terrel.

'You, sir!' he called, pointing. 'How long has it been since you walked without a stick?'

Terrel made a pantomime of surprise at being so addressed, then replied in a deliberately hoarse voice.

'Many years.'

'Then drink this,' the pedlar cried, tossing the phial in the boy's direction.

As he had been instructed, Terrel lunged awkwardly at the bottle, missed hopelessly, then staggered and almost fell. The phial clattered to the ground, where it was picked up by another onlooker. The man unstoppered it, took a sniff, then recoiled as if the smell was vile.

'You look healthy enough to me, sir!' Babak called. 'Give the elixir to one who needs it.'

'Gladly,' the man said, passing it over.

Terrel took the bottle and emptied it into his mouth. It did indeed smell – and taste – vile, and it scorched his throat as he swallowed convulsively. He gagged, his eyes watering, but then, as the spectators watched, an extraordinary change came over the cripple. His crutch fell to the ground unheeded, his back straightened so that he stood taller, and even his withered leg seemed less deformed. He tore off the sling that held his right arm and threw that away too, flexing his twisted fingers as though this was the first time he had been able to move them. Then he performed a stuttering, lopsided jig on the spot. His face was a mask of astonishment and joy – and his eyes glittered in the strangest fashion.

After that Babak could hardly take the money in fast enough. Terrel wandered away, aware that people were still watching him, and wanting to put the entire episode behind him. During his performance he had dreaded being recognized by someone who had seen him at the tavern, or on his early morning walk, but there'd been so many people milling about that the chances of this happening had been very small. Now, feeling ashamed and humiliated, he almost wished that the fraud had been exposed. And yet another small but insistent voice inside his head was exclaiming with pride at his success. He had done it! At least his debt to the pedlar was paid now. And the funny thing was, the elixir *had* seemed to give him more energy.

What was more, knowing that Terrel would have to fend for himself for most of the day, Babak had given him some money, and he was now free to spend it any way he chose. He found one of the flower sellers – who regarded him suspiciously until he saw the coins in his hand – and spent some time picking out the right bloom. A rose was beyond his means, but he was able to buy a fiery-red snapdragon.

Having completed his transaction – the merchant seemed surprised when the boy paid without haggling – Terrel became aware that many people in the square were now looking up expectantly at the roof of one of the surrounding buildings. The time of the festival was approaching, and a lookout was stationed there, ready to give the signal for the fires to be lit as soon as the Red Moon was clear of the horizon. Terrel wished he could see for himself as it rose above the ocean, but there was no chance of that. He had to bide his time, like everyone else.

They did not have to wait long. A great cheer went up when the signal came, and moments later flames were rippling through the piles of wood. As night drew in, the square was lit by the fires of love, and a procession of pilgrims began to make their way towards Kativa's Shrine. Terrel went with them, not hurrying or pushing forward like some, knowing that this should be a solemn moment. When he finally reached the towering sculpture, the Red Moon was visible to all in the sky above, and the lower parts of the shrine were already festooned with a blanket of red flowers of all shapes and sizes. The scent was overwhelming.

Terrel had been feeling light-headed ever since drinking the elixir and now, as he laid his delicate offering among all the others, and whispered Alyssa's name, he began to feel a kind of detachment — as if there was some kind of invisible barrier between himself and the rest of the world. It was disorientating for a while, but then he got used to it and began to enjoy floating through the crowds, observing everything in minute detail: the way a couple's fingers intertwined as they held hands; the twisting pattern of sparks as they rose into the sky within swirls of smoke; flames reflected in a child's eyes; a drunken kiss; a single shoe lying discarded on the ground. He was fascinated by all these things and many more, before finding himself outside an inn that was doing a roaring trade. Several trestle tables had been set up in the open air and, while all the benches were occupied, Terrel returned from purchasing a jug of wine to discover that a seat was readily available amid a group of revellers. Sharing his wine gained him acceptance, and he in turn had his cup filled several times from other flagons and jugs. The conversation around the table was good-natured and ribald, and Terrel only took in about half of what was said. But that did not seem to matter. He was euphoric now, laughing with all the rest, just aware enough to realize that he was drunk for the first time in his life.

The bonfires had died down to a glowing mass of embers by the time he finally rose from his seat, intending to make his way back to the tavern where he and Babak were staying. Time had ceased to mean very much, but the night was growing colder, so Terrel made his way closer to the dying fires and warmed himself, before looking round for familiar landmarks. Somewhat to his surprise, he couldn't find any. All four corners of the square now looked exactly the same. He spent some time wandering aimlessly, even as the revels continued about him. His head was spinning, from wine or tiredness or both, and in the end he had to sit down on the ground, leaning his back against the cool stone of one of the buildings. And there, without feeling more than a moment's alarm, he slowly toppled over to one side and fell asleep.

On his second morning in Tiscamanita, Terrel woke to the sound of snoring. But this time the noise was muffled and faraway, and when he opened his eyes, he saw not the tavern room but bare stone walls, with the only light coming from a tiny barred window set in a door. And he was not lying in a soft bed but on a hard, unforgiving floor. His entire body felt bruised and stiff, and his clothes reeked of smoke. Memories of fantastical dreams assailed him, but those were forgotten as soon as he tried to move and his head threatened to implode. The pain and the immediate wave of nausea that accompanied it made him gasp for breath and then groan aloud. He had never felt so ill in his life. There was a dull pounding in his ears, someone seemed to be sticking needles in the back of his eyes, and his tongue felt too big for his mouth.

The fact that he had no idea where he was was a secondary problem. There was no way he could call out or even speak, and movement was clearly impossible. He would just have to lie there and wait.

Time passed with agonizing slowness, and in the end Terrel managed to overcome his body's reluctance and sit up. Every movement made him wince, but after a while he felt a bit better, and when he heard footsteps on the far side of the door he forced himself to shout. Nothing more than a croak emerged from his ravaged throat, but the noise served its purpose, and a face appeared in the window.

'So you're awake, are you?'

'Where am I?' Terrel grated.

'You're in prison. And likely to be here for a while.'

'Prison? What for?' He was afraid now, as well as bewildered. 'I can't stay here.'

'You're lucky the seneschal locked you up in here, my lad,' the man replied. 'After you burnt down Kativa's Shrine, most people wanted to string you up.'

CHAPTER TWENTY-SEVEN

'You really are an innocent, aren't you?'

Terrel shook his head, looking up at his inquisitor.

'I'm not *an* innocent. I *am* innocent. I didn't do it!'

'Then why do I have more than a dozen witnesses ready to swear that you did?' Seneschal Cadrez appeared calm, and his tone was mild, but he was an imposing figure nonetheless. He had had to stoop under the doorway of the cell.

'I don't know,' Terrel replied helplessly. 'It must have been someone else they saw.'

'You're a pretty distinctive figure,' Cadrez pointed out.

'But hardly unique.' He knew this was a feeble argument – and yet he could not explain what had happened. Claiming to have been asleep wasn't much of a defence but, much to the seneschal's scorn, Terrel hadn't been able to come up with anything better. 'Besides,' he added, 'most of the people in the square were drunk. They're hardly going to be the most reliable witnesses.'

Cadrez nodded thoughtfully.

'Some of them did come up with one or two rather

fanciful tales,' he conceded. 'A few even claimed to have seen you breathing fire from your mouth – like a dragon!'

Terrel felt a glimmer of hope. Even if he had little in the way of an alibi, no one could possibly give much credence to such obvious nonsense. And, for all his stern countenance, the boy instinctively believed that Cadrez was a fair man.

'Of course,' the seneschal went on, 'you could have been using liquid spirit, like the circus fire-eaters, but we found no evidence of that.'

'Then how can you believe anything these witnesses say?' Terrel persisted.

'They also said that the fire might have been coming from your eyes, that they were shining like stars,' Cadrez added, his measuring gaze fixed upon his prisoner. 'But your eyes are blue, aren't they?'

Terrel looked back at him as boldly as he was able, grateful for the fact that the glamour still seemed to be working for him. If the citizens of Tiscamanita ever found out he had the eyes of an enchanter, his fate would be sealed. Even so, he had caught the note of doubt in the seneschal's final words, and felt he should respond.

'Don't you trust your *own* eyes?'

'Where you're concerned,' Cadrez replied, 'I'm not sure I do.'

'Then you must be drunk too.' Terrel regretted the words as soon as they were out of his mouth, but his interrogator seemed unmoved by the insult. 'I mean . . .' the boy stammered. 'I mean . . .'

'Unfortunately for you,' the seneschal went on, ignoring the interruption, 'some of the witnesses were soldiers. Most of my men are chosen because they're sober characters by nature.' A slight smile touched his wide mouth. 'And they were under strict orders not to touch a drop of liquor last night. So they *are* reliable, and they are just as adamant as the other witnesses that you were responsible for the fire.'

This was bad news for Terrel, and his face must have shown his dismay, but Cadrez's expression remained merely curious. He was evidently not a man to jump to conclusions, nor to dispense instant 'justice'. Terrel shuddered as he remembered how Captain Aylor's very different approach to guilt and punishment had led to Elam's death – and was glad that his present captor at least seemed intrigued enough to want to discover the truth before he acted.

'You don't think the atmosphere of the festival might have made people see something that wasn't there?' Terrel asked. 'Drink wasn't the only influence last night.' He was grasping at straws now, and they both knew it.

'Hallucinations? Because of the enchantment of the Red Moon?'

'And the smoke and the scents in the air, the light of the bonfires . . .'

'The apparently contradictory claims of love and violence,' Cadrez finished for him.

Terrel knew that the seneschal was toying with him now, as a cat plays with a half-dead mouse. It was not a comforting analogy.

'I'm only surprised that it hasn't happened before,' the seneschal admitted unexpectedly. 'The festival always threatens to get out of hand, and what with all the fires, and the drunken pilgrims, accidents are almost inevitable. You just happened to be the one—'

'It wasn't me!' Terrel cut in desperately.

Cadrez remained silent for a while after this outburst, and it was only then that the boy realized he had been offered the word 'accident' as a possible way out. He had ignored the opportunity – and avoided the trap.

'Tell me again what happened,' his inquisitor demanded eventually.

Terrel groaned. They had been over his story twice already, and his headache was threatening to crush his skull. Even so, he decided this time to begin at an earlier point, to set the scene properly.

'I came to the square in the early afternoon, and spent some time looking around. Then I had some work to do for Babak, the apothecary.'

'Yes, I heard about that,' Cadrez remarked. 'Quite a performance, I gather.'

Terrel hung his head for a moment, fighting against his need to justify his part in the pedlar's scam. However much shame he felt, he told himself, that was the least of his worries now.

'When that was over,' he went on doggedly, 'it was almost dusk. I bought a flower – a snapdragon – to lay on the shrine. Why would I have done that, if I meant to burn it down?'

'Perhaps the object of your affections did not return your love, so you decided on revenge instead.'

This was the first time anyone had mentioned a possible motive for Terrel's supposed crime, and he sought to undermine it at once. The unanswered question of why he should have wanted to destroy the shrine was one of the strongest arguments for his defence.

'She wouldn't even have known,' he said. 'She's many miles away from here.'

'Where, exactly?'

'Cotillo. It's a village in Saefir Province.' Terrel was sure that Cadrez would not have heard of it – or know that it was the nearest settlement to a madhouse. He suspected that the seneschal had not really been interested in the answer, only in judging whether his prisoner was lying.

Terrel's answer had been as close to the truth as he could make it – and he could only hope it had been convincing.

'Go on,' Cadrez prompted.

'After the festival proper was under way, I left my flower, then went to an inn and bought some wine.'

'Where did you get the money to buy these things?'

'From Babak. I was his apprentice. Why don't you check with him?'

'I would, but the good apothecary appears to have left town in rather a hurry. As far as we can judge, he left in the early hours of this morning.'

Terrel felt a sense of betrayal, but realized that he was not really surprised. Babak made a habit of vanishing soon after his business was complete – and, on this occasion, he would not have welcomed any association with his former apprentice.

'I sent some men after him,' Cadrez went on, 'but there are dozens of trails he could have taken. He won't be found unless he wants to be, and that doesn't seem very likely. So, what happened when you'd drunk your wine?'

'I told you,' Terrel replied wearily. 'I shared my jug with several people at one of the tables outside.'

'But you can't remember any of their names?'

'No.'

'No matter. We've located enough of them to confirm that part of your story.'

Then why are you making me repeat it? Terrel thought angrily.

'When did you leave the inn?' Cadrez asked.

'I don't know exactly. The bonfires had burnt down by then, and it was getting cold.'

'Had the midnight bells rung?'

'I don't remember hearing any bells. I tried to find my

way back to the tavern where Babak and I were staying, but I got lost.'

'Lost? I thought you said you never left the square.'

'I didn't. I must've been drunk, because I couldn't remember where to go, and in the end I had to sit down.'

'Where?'

'Near one of the corners of the square. I leant against the wall, then passed out. The next thing I knew I woke up in here.'

'And that's it?' Cadrez queried. 'You're leaving nothing out?'

Terrel shook his head.

'Nothing.'

There was another silence then, and Terrel felt worse than ever, imagining all sorts of unspoken accusations.

'Tell me something,' Cadrez said eventually. 'When the guard first spoke to you this morning, why did you yell at him about a dream?'

'I didn't . . .' Terrel claimed, recalling his horrified reaction. 'I . . .'

'Your exact words were "No! It was just a dream!",' his interrogator said calmly, and waited.

Terrel had no intention of telling Cadrez about the dream – or the little he could remember of it now. He had been enveloped in flame, and there had been running. And laughter . . . But none of that was real! It couldn't be.

'I'd just woken up,' he said. 'I didn't know where I was, and I was scared. I didn't know what I was saying.'

'You don't think it was possible that you were confusing dreams with reality?'

'No,' Terrel replied adamantly, stubborn now, even as his own treacherous doubts began to nag at him.

'What's that on your hand?'

The question took the boy completely by surprise. With

a sinking feeling he realized that Cadrez didn't miss much – and that his own reaction had already given him away.

'I was a slave once,' he said. 'That was my master's brand.'

'But you're a free man now?' the seneschal asked, apparently unaware of any irony.

'Yes. He said I wasn't worth feeding any more, because of this,' Terrel replied, raising his withered arm. 'So he threw me out.' The lies sat uneasily on his conscience, but he knew he had no choice.

Cadrez nodded, appearing to find the story plausible enough.

'What will happen now?' Terrel asked quietly, unable to bear another silence.

'Arson is a serious crime,' the seneschal replied. 'And choosing such a target was unwise, to say the least. But you'll get a fair trial.'

In that moment, Terrel knew that – for all his curiosity – Cadrez believed him to be guilty, and that the verdict of any trial was a foregone conclusion. The entire town was convinced of his guilt. The supreme irony was that, even though he could use the glamour to persuade them that his eyes were blue – something he knew to be untrue – he was completely unable to make them accept his innocence – which was genuine. The difference, he realized, was that they did not *want* to believe him.

'When will the trial take place?' he asked, as the reality of his predicament slowly sank in.

'Not for a while. The way people are feeling right now, they'd probably vote to burn you at the stake. Either way, you're not going anywhere for a long time.'

'But you don't understand,' Terrel pleaded. 'I can't stay here. I've—'

'You should have thought of that before you decided to burn down our shrine,' the seneschal told him.

The cell door clanged shut, leaving his prisoner alone with his misery.

As the day passed, Terrel's body recovered slowly, so that he no longer felt sick all the time. The pain diminished to a dull ache that – although it seemed to affect every bone in his body – was preferable to the pounding headache he had woken to. His physical improvement was not matched by a mental revival, however, as his doubts, fears and bouts of self-recrimination gave him no respite. Even the earlier certainty of his innocence was being eroded as he began to wonder if somehow he *had* done the things he was accused of. At first this idea seemed ridiculous, but then he remembered how his dream of Shahan's death had mirrored reality – and how Alyssa had thought that he had in some way been responsible for the violence. Then again, that had been a remote occurrence, whereas here he was supposed to have been involved in person. Was it possible that his body could have done those things while his mind was asleep, leaving no memory of them afterwards? This idea was frightening enough, but the only alternative – assuming that the witnesses were right – was even worse.

Am I mad?

If he really *was* going insane he would not even be able to trust his own senses. Life would become meaningless. The whole world would be his madhouse. Perhaps his meetings with Alyssa and the ghosts had simply been illusions conjured up by his lunatic mind – a mind that had run amok at the full of the Red Moon.

'No!' he declared aloud. 'No.' He was *not* mad. The very fact that he was able to pose the question meant that he must be sane. Didn't it?

As a satisfactory explanation of the night's events continued to elude him, Terrel's thoughts returned to their consequences. Sane or not, guilty or not, he was a prisoner, friendless and alone, with no prospect of ever being released. Which meant that he would be unable to continue his journey, to complete the task he had been given. He still found it hard to believe that his efforts might actually affect the great events engulfing Vadanis, but he had given his word that he would try – and there was no way he could do that while he was locked up. Somehow, he would have to escape.

Easier said than done, was his own immediate response. The door to his cell was kept locked and, even if he were to get out, he had no idea how to escape from whatever building he was in, or how many guards he might have to confront. Beyond that he would have to make his way through a town where everyone knew of him – and hated him for what he had done. Even with the help of the glamour, that would be no easy task. His situation seemed hopeless, and compounded his crushing sense of failure.

His one consoling thought was the notion that, even here, it might be possible for Alyssa and the ghosts to visit him. He couldn't see how they could help him, but at least it would mean he would not feel so alone. On the other hand, he had seen nothing of them for six days and – even though he felt sure they would not abandon him intentionally – his former concern that something was preventing them from finding him again was even stronger now. Closing his eyes, he pleaded silently for them to hear him, to heed his cry for help. But there was no response.

'I can't do this on my own,' he whispered. 'I don't know what to do.'

'They say talking to yourself is the first sign of madness.'

Terrel opened his eyes with a start, and saw a guard peering in through the barred window. The smile on his face was full of malice.

'I'm not mad!' he shouted back, but that night he had a dream that made him doubt his own denial.

It began in a world that was entirely grey, all colour leached away by the swirling banks of fog that blotted out the sun and made blue sky a distant memory. Grey trees dripped with constant dew, and people moved silently, like shadows in the mist. A brief gust of damp breeze pushed the curtain aside for a moment, and he saw a large house, built – impossibly – upon the surface of a lake. He had just glimpsed a dozen or so grey faces, looking back at him from its windows, when the fog returned and he was blind again.

The nature of the darkness changed then, became hot and dry and stifling, clogging his throat and nose and scratching his eyes. When it cleared, he looked out onto a barren landscape that could only exist in his imagination. For mile upon mile there was nothing but sand and bare rock, shimmering in the heat, all of it the arid colour of sun-bleached clay. In its way it was even more oppressive than the greyness that had preceded it. Superimposed on this wasteland he saw the tattooed face of a woman, whose staring eyes shone white in her dark-skinned face. Her lips were moving, but he could hear nothing of what she said – and then she was gone, replaced by a ludicrous, ungainly creature with long, crooked legs and flat feet. It looked like the biggest, ugliest horse ever born – and it had a massive hump on its back. Its voice *was* audible, an absurd, grumbling roar that sounded much too fierce for its comical appearance.

The roar became an ominous muttering from below his

feet, and Terrel looked down to see that he was now standing on solid ice. The contrast to the previous landscape could not have been more extreme. As far as the eye could see, all the world was coated in ice, shining white in the pale sunlight, except where the crevices that marked the surface were shadowed with pale blue. It reminded him of the crystal city of an earlier dream, but this was much more solid – even though it could only be another creation of his wayward imagination. Surely nothing like this frozen sea could actually exist?

You're good at this, aren't you?

The voice broke into his subconscious without warning.

Good at what? he thought.

Seeing stuff. Remembering.

Once again he recalled the crystal city, the one that had encased Alyssa – but he pushed those images away instinctively. He didn't want the intruder to see that.

Too late, the voice said, laughing. *You can't hide from your own dreams. You never could.*

Who are you? Terrel demanded, but got no answer.

The pain caught him unprepared, and he gasped, unable to breathe. Even then he knew better than to fight back. He surrendered to the blindness, to the hatred, to the deep, echoing rhythms of the invisible sea. The familiar mocking laughter followed him into the void.

CHAPTER TWENTY-EIGHT

When Terrel woke after his third night in prison he was greeted by absolute silence. The drunk in the next cell, whose snoring had so confused him, had dried out and been released. As far as Terrel knew, he was now the only captive in the entire building. For the past two days his only visitors had been the guards who brought his frugal meals, and he had no idea when his trial would begin. Nor had he made any progress towards finding any possible means of escape. The isolation and the waiting were making him feel angry and depressed, and he longed for something — anything — to happen. So when he heard footsteps in the corridor outside his cell, he was instantly alert, ready to grasp whatever chances were offered.

A guard peered through the bars, told the prisoner to retreat to the far wall and sit down on his pallet, and only unlocked the door when Terrel had obeyed. A man he had not seen before opened the door and came in, watching the prisoner with a mixture of curiosity and suspicion. He left the door wide open, but beyond it Terrel could see two soldiers, their eyes fixed on him, waiting for any unexpected move. If he tried to make a run for it, he would not get far.

'I am Uzellin, Chief Underseer of Tiscamanita,' the visitor announced grandly.

Terrel nodded in acknowledgement, but said nothing, wondering what an underseer could want with him. This was clearly not the reaction Uzellin had been expecting, and for a moment he seemed nonplussed. Then he recovered his composure, and stared at the prisoner.

'Have you no faith, boy?'

'I honour the moons and stars,' Terrel responded formally.

'And their prophets?'

Terrel got to his feet and bowed, hoping that this would be enough to satisfy the man's pride. There seemed little chance of his being an ally, but in his present predicament the boy could not afford to ignore any possibility, no matter how remote. His actions seemed to placate the underseer, who relaxed a little.

'I have been discussing your case with Seneschal Cadrez,' he stated, full of his own self-importance. 'The legal ramifications are naturally complex, but the one fact that seems crystal clear is that you did indeed start the fire that destroyed Kativa's Shrine.'

Terrel shook his head, but before he could speak Uzellin continued.

'And yet you claim to have been asleep, to remember nothing of those events. Cadrez is as good a judge of character as I have ever known in such matters, and he believes you are telling the truth.'

This was remarkably good news, and Terrel's face lit up with sudden hope.

'Which leads me to the obvious conclusion,' the underseer added.

'And that is?' Terrel prompted.

'That you must have been possessed by a demon while you slept.'

'What? Don't be ridiculous!'

'Have you any other explanation for what happened?' Uzellin asked.

Terrel thought about this for a while. What the underseer was suggesting was something from the myths of a distant, superstitious past. Surely no one believed in such things any more? And yet Terrel hesitated, his instinctive scepticism warring against the small voice that insisted that Uzellin might prove useful – even though his theory was utterly ludicrous.

'No, I haven't,' he replied eventually.

'Then we are agreed,' the underseer stated. 'I will begin preparations for a ritual of exorcism.'

'What, here?' Terrel exclaimed in disbelief. 'Now?'

'Of course not,' Uzellin said. 'When the demon is expelled it must be in a public place, so that the people can witness the truth.'

It was Terrel's turn to be struck dumb. He could not believe what he was hearing, but if Uzellin was serious – and he gave every indication of being in deadly earnest – then it would at least get him out of this confinement, perhaps even give him the chance of escaping once he was in the open.

'Don't worry,' the underseer said, mistaking the reason for the boy's silence. 'My skills are more than a match for any demon. This rite is ancient, but the tradition is well-established. Nothing will go wrong.'

'And what will happen when it's over?' Terrel asked.

'Then you'll be free of this evil,' Uzellin replied, his eyes gleaming with excitement.

'And will they let me go?'

'Once the real culprit has been exposed for all to see, Cadrez will have no choice but to pronounce you innocent. You will be released.'

Even though Terrel could not prevent a surge of hope, this sounded too good to be true.

'What if no demon comes out?' he asked.

'It will,' the underseer replied confidently. 'It will be helpless against my conjuration.'

'And if there's nothing there?' Terrel persisted. 'If I'm *not* possessed?'

'Do not concern yourself with irrelevancies. This will be a triumph.' Uzellin's face was pink now, shining with anticipatory fervour, but he would not meet the boy's gaze.

'When's it going to be?' Terrel asked.

'The ceremony will take place this afternoon, an hour before sunset. Prepare yourself.'

With that the underseer turned and strode from the cell, leaving the guards to close and lock the door.

Who was that pompous ass?

Terrel spun round, and his heart leapt as he saw Elam's ghost sitting casually in the corner of the room.

'How long have you been there?'

Long enough to know he wasn't telling you the whole truth.

Terrel had assumed the same thing, and he was about to speak again when they were interrupted by a guard, who was peering in through the window.

'You talking to your demon, boy?' The soldier rolled his eyes and walked off, laughing.

Terrel knew that his reputation as a lunatic would be confirmed if he was seen holding conversations with invisible people, so he decided to try an experiment.

Can you hear me like this? he asked silently, deliberately forming the question in his mind and trying to project it to his friend.

Of course, Elam replied. *You're learning.*

Is Alyssa here too? Terrel asked, eager now that he knew that psinoma worked with the ghosts.

She's somewhere around, trying to work out how best to get to you. It's not easy getting into these dungeons if you have to lug a body round with you. I'm a sort of advance guard.

The news buoyed Terrel up even more. She was close.

The others'll be with you soon, I'm sure, Elam added, *but right now I'm going to follow your exorcist and see what he's up to.*

Don't go! Terrel cried, but Elam was already on the move. He walked through the locked door, leaving his companion alone again, and wishing that he could do the same.

Terrel knew, even before she spoke, that the sparrow was Alyssa, for no bird would willingly enter such a dark and unattractive place. Then he saw the 'ring', entwined round one of her legs, like the laces of a boot. The bird was small enough to slip between the bars in the window, but she came no further than the sill, evidently wanting to keep an eye out for the guards. She could move fast, but her size made her vulnerable, especially in such a confined space.

Did you really burn down their shrine?

It was not the greeting Terrel had been expecting – or hoping for – but he could not blame her for being preoccupied with the reason for his incarceration.

Yes, it looks as though I did, he admitted reluctantly, accepting the truth of it for the first time.

What were you thinking?

I wasn't thinking. That's the whole point. I wasn't even awake!

You dreamt it? Alyssa exclaimed. *Then why can't I see it? It was three days ago.*

That silenced her for a while, and Terrel got the impression that for some reason she was confused about the time scale.

The dream I had last night was quite different, he began, wanting to tell her about the fantastic visions he had seen, and about the mysterious voice at the end, but she evidently had more important things on her mind.

You can't stay here, she said. *You still have a long way to go, and time's getting short.*

I know, Terrel agreed. *I've been trying to think of a way to escape, but it's hopeless.*

I could try to get the keys for you, but I'd have to come back as something bigger, and then—

That wouldn't be any good, he cut in. *There's no keyhole on this side of the lock and anyway, I'm going to be taken out of here this afternoon.*

Where to?

I'm not sure. Somewhere public. The square, probably. After the exorcism I should be released.

After the what?

Terrel explained Uzellin's theory about demonic possession, and about his plans to counteract it. When he had finished, Alyssa regarded him steadily with the bird's tiny, jewelled eyes.

You're not possessed, she stated bluntly.

Are you sure? he countered. *Something happened – and I can't come up with a better explanation. Don't you think it's possible that some sort of spirit might have used me?*

It doesn't work like that. Only a few spirits are able to return to this world – or even want to – and when they do it's for a reason, good or bad. Even making themselves visible to the living takes enormous effort – and they certainly don't go around taking people over just for the fun of it. And why would any ghost want to destroy a shrine to love?

Terrel could think of several possible answers to that, but once again he did not get the chance to respond.

What are you doing to your eyes? Alyssa demanded, her tone suddenly fierce.

Terrel told her about Babak, and about how the glamour allowed him to move among people more easily. He expected her to be impressed and gladdened by this development, but her reaction was much more sobering.

Be careful of such things, Terrel, she warned. *All magic exacts a price.*

What do you mean?

Can you shut the door again?

Terrel frowned. The door to his cell was already closed, and locked.

I live in a vast palace, Alyssa went on, confusing him even more. *Parts of it are very fine, while others are in ruins. There are more rooms than even I can imagine. None of the doors are locked, but few men choose to open them. At most they peer through the cracks in the walls, and find it hard to believe what they see. But if you do open one of the doors, it's sometimes impossible to close it again. Is that what you want?*

I . . . I . . . Terrel had no idea what she was talking about.

Better to find a window to look through, Alyssa added enigmatically, before the tone of her voice changed abruptly, becoming businesslike once more. *Where's Elam?*

'You really believe the boy is possessed?' Cadrez asked.

'I believe he *was*,' Uzellin replied. 'It's possible he may still be.'

'And you think this exorcism will satisfy people?'

'I do. More than that, it will restore some of their faith. I don't need to tell you that recent events have undermined their confidence in the seers and in our governance.

As the spiritual leader of this community, it is my duty to redress that balance, to re-establish the authority of law. The destruction of the shrine was only the culmination of a series of events that have signalled the disintegration of our society. You, of all people, will be aware of the omens.'

The seneschal could not deny the truth of that. The number of crimes committed in Tiscamanita over the last few months had been much higher than usual. But he did not see how this grotesque exercise could change that for the better. Like most citizens of the town, Cadrez had always regarded the underseers as more or less irrelevant to the normal course of their lives, but in such a time of general uncertainty he was beginning to think that perhaps he should embrace them as allies.

'Tell me about the ceremony.'

'It's a very ancient rite,' Uzellin replied eagerly, 'and all the elements are clearly defined. First of all, the time must be chosen so that the Amber Moon is at its weakest, because that is the indicator of the spirit realm.'

'And tonight is the dark of the Amber Moon,' Cadrez said. Like all educated men – as well as many ignorant peasants – he was constantly aware of the phases of all the moons.

'Exactly!' the underseer exclaimed. 'My calculations reveal that the ideal time will be one hour before sunset this afternoon.'

'Can you have everything ready so soon?'

'I can,' Uzellin answered confidently. 'All I ask is that you detail some of your men to erect a platform in the main square. The best place would be among the ashes of the shrine, don't you think?'

Cadrez nodded, approving of the symbolism.

'That won't be a problem,' he said. 'What will the ritual entail?'

'The subject must be cleansed thoroughly, and then the demon driven from his body by fire and pain.'

'You intend to torture him?'

'I would not call it that,' the underseer said, defensive in the face of the seneschal's disapproval. 'He will be flogged and branded, as the ritual demands, but that is the only way to drive away such evil and ensure it does not return. It is a small price to pay for such a blessing.'

It did not sound like much of a blessing to Cadrez, but he knew the good citizens of Tiscamanita would approve. He did not share their vengeful blood lust, but he was aware that it would have to be appeased somehow.

'Once the ritual is complete,' Uzellin went on, 'I intend to use the opportunity to speak out for a new beginning, a renewal of faith, under the rule of the skies. With luck I can inspire the people to rebuild the shrine, so that the town regains its pride.'

Cadrez nodded. Such a project might help bring the community together again – and it would also give the pilgrims a reason to return, bringing their trade with them. Even so, the seneschal was aware of his own secular responsibilities.

'There are other legal considerations,' he pointed out.

'The charge of arson can still be answered,' the underseer reassured him quickly. 'When my work is done, the boy will become your prisoner again, to await trial and punishment as you see fit. His worldly crime may have been instigated by otherworldly forces, but he must have been in part responsible for allowing the demon to possess him in the first place. Such creatures do not choose their victims at random.'

'You saw the mark on his hand?' Cadrez asked.

'I did. It could have been the sign of the demon or, more likely, of his own depraved invitation to the spirit world. The boy's guilt in this matter is not in doubt, whichever way you look at it.'

In the corner of the seneschal's chamber, unnoticed by either man, the air quivered briefly, then grew still. Elam had heard all he needed to hear.

CHAPTER TWENTY-NINE

Uzellin's nervousness was affecting his acolytes, who were all treading softly, and speaking in low voices. The Chief Underseer's anxiety had been growing steadily throughout the day, mainly because he could not shake the conviction that he was being watched. Even when he had been in his own library – a private sanctuary that not even his deputies were allowed to enter – the feeling had persisted, in spite of the fact that it should have been impossible for anyone to spy on him there. And now, as the appointed time for the ceremony drew near, he was even more on edge, fussing incessantly over details he'd already checked a dozen times.

'The brands are all prepared?'

'They are, master,' his deputy, Hacon, replied, indicating the coals in the large brazier. Four irons had been placed in the red-hot fire, each in the shape of one of the sacred symbols of the rite: the snake, the many-pointed sun, the crescent, and the circle that represented the full of the moons.

'And the birch has been properly doused and purified?'

'I saw to it myself, master,' Hacon assured him. 'And the cleansing materials have also been prepared,' he added, anticipating the Chief Underseer's next question. 'Everything is ready.'

The two men were standing on the wooden stage that had been built amid the charred ruins of the shrine, and which was already surrounded by a large crowd. Criers had announced the exorcism to the town earlier in the day, and it seemed that most of the population was intent on cramming themselves into the square in order to witness the spectacle. Uzellin knew that this was the greatest opportunity – as well as the greatest risk – of his career, and he was determined to leave little to chance. His own doubts about whether the prisoner was still possessed by a demon – if indeed he ever had been – had been pushed aside. The audience would be expecting a show – and, one way or another, he was going to make sure they got one.

'The salves and ointments?' he queried.

'The apothecary is here,' Hacon confirmed. 'He has everything that will be needed.'

'Good,' Uzellin responded, with a nervous smile. 'Once the ceremony is over and the boy's flesh is innocent once more, we must do all we can to heal his wounds. Justice must be merciful as well as unbending.'

His deputy bowed his head in acknowledgement, then opened the bulky tome he was carrying and consulted it again.

'Master, may I clarify a point?'

Uzellin nodded, but he was not looking at the other man. His gaze was moving distractedly from the brazier to the lashing pole to the crowd, and back again.

'It says here,' Hacon said, tracing a line of text with his finger, 'that the subject of the ritual has the right to make a public statement once his purification is complete, so that he may either deny or confess his possession.'

The Chief Underseer looked annoyed. He had noted the same thing earlier.

'Yes, well, I think we may safely dispense with such a pointless interlude, don't you?' he muttered. 'It says the subject may make a statement *if* he requests the opportunity to do so. Otherwise, he is assumed to have waived his right. Given his background, it seems unlikely that this boy will even be aware of such a privilege.'

'Then should we not inform him of it?' Hacon asked doubtfully.

'What purpose would that serve?' Uzellin snapped. 'There's no necessity for it. He will not ask to speak, so there is no need for him to do so.'

'But—'

'That is the end of the matter, Hacon.'

Uzellin turned away, only to find Keran, his second deputy, approaching, an agitated expression on his face.

'Master, I have grave news.'

'Keep your voice down,' the Chief Underseer whispered urgently, glancing at the nearest faces in the crowd. 'What is it?'

'I checked the calculations, as you instructed,' Keran replied. 'And . . .'

'I was in a hurry,' Uzellin said, as his deputy hesitated. 'A minor inaccuracy is of little consequence.'

'But the true dark of the Amber Moon is not until five hours *after* sunset tonight,' Keran said.

Uzellin frowned. His deputies were both fully trained underseers in their own right, and Keran was not likely to have made a mistake. His mathematical skills were excellent. And yet the Underseer could not believe that his own estimate had been out by a full six hours.

'I checked the figures three times,' the deputy added, proffering his workings. 'I used the tables that came with the latest proclamation from Makhaya. The Dark Moon's new orbit has affected the others. That's why—'

'I see,' Uzellin said, cutting him off, even as he cursed the Dark Moon and its mystifying changes. He hadn't even thought to incorporate that into his own calculation. 'Your exactitude does you credit, Keran, but we can't possibly wait that long.' He waved a hand at the assembled throng. 'We'd have a riot on our hands.'

'As you wish, master,' his deputy replied, looking relieved. His duty was done; it was someone else's responsibility now.

'We proceed on schedule as announced,' Uzellin stated firmly, taking a last look around. 'Tell Cadrez to bring the prisoner to us now.'

Terrel walked slowly over the timeworn stones of the square. He was limping badly, even though his captors had allowed him to keep his fitted boot, and his twisted leg threatened to buckle at every step. But he did not notice the stabbing pains that racked his body. Nor was he aware of the coolness of the day, even though he was wearing only a pair of short breeches. In fact he was perspiring, and his trembling – which he was doing his best to hide – was because he was desperately nervous. Thanks to Elam, he was aware of the ordeal he faced, unless their hastily laid – and recently amended – plans came off. Terrel had been accustomed to pain from the first day of his life, but the prospect of being branded with hot irons filled him with terror.

Ahead of him, Cadrez rode upon his regal stallion, flanked by foot soldiers who forced a corridor through the closely packed crowd. Terrel kept his eyes fixed ahead, avoiding the stares of the onlookers, most of whom fell silent as he passed by. When the procession reached the stage, the seneschal turned the prisoner over to Uzellin's acolytes, then retreated a short distance, keeping a watchful eye on all around him. Terrel's escorts joined the other soldiers guarding the perimeter of the ruined shrine, as the boy was guided up onto the platform. He could now be seen by almost everyone in the throng, and a low murmuring spread through the square.

Uzellin stepped forward and, in a loud, strident voice, asked the skies for their blessing, and then told his audience that the first stage of the ceremony would be the ritual cleansing of the subject. Terrel submitted to this without protest, knowing that he had to bide his time. He was first scrubbed with a mixture of sand and oil, then doused with buckets of water, and finally scoured with smooth heart-stones. By the end of this his skin was pink and sore, but the discomfort only served to sharpen his wits. As Uzellin's deputies took hold of his arms and led him towards the stake at the centre of the stage, Terrel heard several dogs howling in the distance – and the sound gave him the courage to grasp the moment. He knew that if he allowed himself to be tied up, the chances of his escaping would be greatly reduced. As it was, there were any number of things that could go wrong. He pretended to stumble, then straightened up sharply.

'Wait!' With an effort he pulled his arms free from his startled captors, and held them high. The sudden outcry had disconcerted Hacon and Keran, but as Terrel made no effort to flee or fight, they hesitated, giving him the chance he wanted. 'I wish to make a statement, a confession!' he shouted. 'It is my right!'

The deputies glanced quickly at their master, who stood behind them, next to the brazier. Uzellin's face was burning almost as brightly as the fire. However, he controlled his temper with some difficulty, and nodded his assent.

'Go ahead,' Hacon said quietly.

Terrel let out a sigh of relief, took a single step forward, then stopped, gazing out over the heads of the crowds. The silence in the square became absolute.

Summoning the glamour, Terrel fed its power into his voice. He had never tried this before, but he'd listened to Babak perform the same trick, and instinctively knew what was needed. Make them believe, he told himself, before he opened his mouth. They want to believe.

'Uzellin is no match for me.'

The voice that emerged from his lips surprised even Terrel. It was deep and resonant, burning with contempt and filled with cruel humour. Combined with his provocative words, it created just the impact he'd been hoping for. The three underseers were frozen where they stood, while the crowd muttered and stared.

'He could not even calculate the correct time for this mockery,' Terrel went on in his new voice. 'The dark of the Amber Moon will not take place for another six hours. Look at the skies for yourselves if you don't believe me.'

A thousand pairs of eyes glanced up to the heavens, where the merest pale sliver of golden orange had just risen above the northern horizon. Fingers pointed, and the whispering grew to a sibilant wind that swirled round the arena.

'Shut him up!' Uzellin hissed desperately, but Terrel was ready for him now.

He raised his good arm in a dramatic gesture, and as the air around him glittered and flashed, Hacon and Keran hesitated. Terrel was aware of the sparkling display only in the corner of his eye – but everyone else in the square was awed by the sight. Far away, the dogs howled in unison again.

'Uzellin just wanted to put on a show, a meaningless charade,' Terrel went on quickly. 'He never really believed that I was possessed . . . But I am, and I am too strong for him!' As he spoke, the boy released the glamour from his eyes so that their true colours were revealed.

The nearest onlookers gasped. Then some of the crowd screamed as the news of the appearance of the 'demon' spread like wildfire through the square. Terrel smiled, knowing that this would increase the impact of his gaze, and thinking that Uzellin was not the only one who could put on a show. Behind him, the underseers could not understand what was happening, because the boy had not yet turned round to confront his captors.

'This exorcism is a farce!' the demon voice declared. 'I can leave this pathetic shell of a body any time I choose, and return whenever I want, regardless of what is done to it. Pain cannot touch me.'

This time, as he spoke, Terrel sensed someone else listening and watching, someone familiar and yet remote – but he had no time to wonder about this. Elam's warning sounded urgently inside his head, and he knew that the crisis point was almost upon them.

'Stay where you are, Uzellin!' he commanded, still keeping his back to the Chief Underseer. 'You see,' he told the crowd, 'I know what he is planning to do even before he does. Right now, he's standing there with a stupid look on his face, holding a brand in the shape of a snake.'

When the spectators saw that this was indeed true, their exclamations of surprise were mixed with a smattering of laughter, and Terrel knew that he was close to achieving his first objective – discrediting Uzellin. He had also convinced many of the onlookers that he was indeed possessed by a powerful demon. All that was left was to use his 'power' to escape.

For the first time, he glanced to his side, wondering where Alyssa had got to. Unless she arrived soon, he was going to run out of rhetoric.

'If he's not careful, he could do himself a nasty injury,' he remarked, provoking further amusement in the crowd. 'In fact—'

Terrel faltered, suddenly finding himself quite out of his depth. He had done nothing, but suddenly everything had changed, and he was no longer in control of his own actions. It was as though he really *was* possessed!

'Is this how you honour my memory?'

Although the words came from Terrel, the voice was not his own, nor was it the 'demon's'. It was just as strong and passionate, but its timbre and pitch were indisputably female.

'First you destroy my shrine, and now you desecrate the ruins with this vile shadow play.'

Terrel knew who was speaking then, even as the astonished onlookers began to whisper her name. Looking down, he saw not his own twisted hand, but pale, soft fingers clutching the stem of a deep red rose. He was now as lost in wonder as any of the spectators, and he knew that his own image was no longer on the stage. Everyone in the square was now staring, awe-struck, at Kativa.

At the same time he sensed her anguish – undiminished even after two centuries – as it pervaded every nerve and fibre of his being. Her grief was overwhelming, and he was filled with pity for her. Not even Kativa's own death, nor all the time since, had reunited her with her love, nor had it reconciled her to her family. The yawning chasm of loss and the bitterness of betrayal lived on in her ghost, a spirit that was now tied to the wrong world. As he realized this, Terrel was determined not to remain idle. Somehow he must go to her aid, even though he had no idea what to do. Elam had been responsible for the shifting lights in the air around him, but this spectral presence was quite different. She was somehow *inside* him, looking out through his eyes, but he didn't know if he could even talk to her.

Elam? Terrel queried tentatively, hoping for some guidance, but he received no answer — because Alyssa had arrived.

The disturbance in the crowd had rippled across the square, as if a great fish were swimming beneath the surface of the human sea. But when it reached the platform its real nature was immediately apparent. The first of the dogs to leap up onto the stage was a huge, brindled wolfhound, which snarled at the underseers and then barked in an apparent frenzy. The rest of the motley pack soon joined their leader, adding their voices to the cacophony. However, the voice Terrel heard inside his head was much more familiar.

You don't look much like a demon to me, Alyssa declared. *What's going on? And who's she?*

Even as she spoke, the wolfhound, whose tail bore the telltale ring, bounded across the stage and deliberately knocked the brazier over. The fire toppled onto the wooden boards, scattering the glowing irons and bright coals in all directions. This increased the panic among the acolytes and the closest spectators, and a number of soldiers were forced to leap for safety. Smoke rose as the wood began to scorch.

Terrel could see Kativa now. She had stepped away from his body, becoming a separate entity, a normal ghost. She was looking at him with a mixture of horror and bewilderment, tears coursing down her cheeks. The sight –

which he now knew could not be seen by anyone else alive — tore at his heart. But Alyssa was demanding his attention.

Are you ready? I'll be back soon.

Left to its own devices, the hound shuddered, silent now, as it looked around, wondering how it had come to be in the midst of so many people. Its comrades were still prowling over the stage, keeping well clear of Terrel, but menacing anyone else who came close.

Kativa?

Who are you? she asked.

That's not important. I—

He got no further, because he was distracted by yet another disturbance. For no apparent reason, Cadrez's mount had reared up without warning, unseating the seneschal and dumping him on the ground. Then, its hooves flailing, the horse began to force its way towards the stage.

You're a demon, remember, Alyssa told him urgently. *Look like one! Or we'll* never *get out of here.*

A war was being waged inside Terrel's mind. One part of him wanted to flee, to complete the plan he had put together with his spectral friends, but another part told him that there was something he had to do first.

Come on! Alyssa shouted, as the horse she now controlled reached the edge of the platform.

Wait a moment, Terrel replied.

Don't be stupid. We've got to go!

Cadrez was on his feet now, shouting orders to the milling soldiers.

It's Kativa, Alyssa, Elam explained. *Let him do this.*

His friend's unexpected intervention allowed Terrel the respite he needed. Stretching out, he took Kativa's hands in his own, feeling them like the gentlest of breezes across his fingertips. He knew that she had entered the arena through him; she could only leave that way too.

It's time to move on, he said. *Forgive them. All of them. But most of all, forgive yourself. If you do that, then you'll find him.*

Ancient, red-rimmed eyes stared back at him, disbelief countering hope. Terrel let his intuition take over.

There's no need for this pain any more, he added gently. *You can heal yourself. Like this.*

The stallion was stamping and fretting behind him, but he was hardly aware of it, nor of the guards who were slowly pressing closer. For a moment he felt a touch of warmth from Kativa's hands, and glimpsed the beauty of her youth.

She began to fade then, disappearing slowly before his gaze, but before she vanished entirely, Kativa smiled – for the first time in two hundred years.

Terrel felt a spark of joy flare up inside, but also experienced a wave of exhaustion that nearly brought him to his knees. It took another furious exhortation from Alyssa to bring his thoughts back to his own predicament.

It's now or never, Terrel. Move!

Hobbling to the edge of the platform, he clambered into the saddle, almost overbalancing completely before hanging on for grim death as Alyssa galloped away through the crowd. The multitude parted before her thunderous charge as if the crowds were no more than dry leaves blown aside by a sudden wind. Above Terrel's head, Elam made the most of his flagging energies to add a little demonic sparkle to the scene, and the fugitive himself remembered to let his true eyes range over the terrified throng, his smile now set in a gargoyle-like grimace.

CHAPTER THIRTY

Marshal Karuna gazed out over the devastated landscape, and did his best to suppress a shudder. He was not usually a man of much imagination, and prided himself on his hard, practical mind, but the view in front of him was testing his composure to the limit. It was as though some vengeful god had decided to smash a mountain range into rubble, and then set fire to what was left by inundating the entire area with flaming thunderbolts. No one believed in gods any more, of course – the seers and their astrological certainties had seen to that – but as a child, Karuna had listened to his grandmother as she brought the old pagan myths and legends to life, and now he could hear her rasping whisper again.

'Chaosu, the god of war, walked the land in fire and blood, destroying all before him.'

'I beg your pardon.'

Karuna came back to the present with a rush. He had not realized that he'd spoken out loud.

'It's nothing,' he said, embarrassed. 'I hadn't realized the mine workings were so extensive.'

The marshal's companion allowed himself a quiet smile. He had seen this reaction in newcomers many times. The sheer scale of the operation, and the desolate nature of the terrain it had produced, often shocked them. But to Commissioner Hoban it was a scene not of devastation, but of grandeur.

'Betancuria has been a centre of mining operations for more than two hundred years,' he explained. 'What you see here is only the visible legacy of the exploration that's been going on below ground.'

The two men were standing atop a hill that was itself man-made, one part of the legacy Hoban had mentioned. From there they could see for miles over the jagged, pock-marked expanse of barren rock. Karuna still found it hard to believe that such havoc could have been wrought by man alone. Parts of the land had been torn away, robbing it of any connection to the living world, and exposing Nydus's bones in those great gaping wounds. Other areas were riddled with black holes, as if some giant worm had been eating them from within. Vast piles of waste rock and slag littered this inhuman battlefield, and the whole area was wreathed in swirls of bitter smoke from the smelting furnaces. Even from their remote vantage point, the air smelt poisonous.

'There's another world beneath our feet,' Hoban added.

The marshal nodded, recognizing the pride with which his companion had spoken, even though he did not understand it, and sought to bring their conversation back to more immediate concerns. Chief Seer Kamin had dispatched his senior army officer to Betancuria – somewhat reluctantly, Karuna suspected – because a cool head was required to assess the situation there, and to provide an accurate report. The rumours that had been spreading from the mining community had become increasingly far-fetched, and Karuna had been prepared to discount most of them. But now he was not so sure. Who knew what mysteries might lurk beneath this ravaged earth?

'The phenomenon,' he began. 'Have you seen it for yourself?'

'I have,' Hoban replied, his expression serious now.

Karuna believed him. The marshal had gained the impression that Hoban was not one of the usual self-serving functionaries who preferred to oversee operations from afar. The commissioner had been an engineer himself once, and had evidently earned the respect of the men who worked for him. Such a man would certainly have investigated the so-called monster for himself.

'Can you describe it?'

'Not really. The thing is . . .' Hoban's hesitation betrayed his unease. 'There just isn't anything *to* describe. All I can say is that it's a swirling sort of darkness, that you feel it as much as see it – like a shadow that should not be there.'

Karuna had heard similar reports before, but coming from Hoban it sounded somewhat more believable.

'So it's not real? It's not . . .' The marshal hesitated.

'A monster? No, nothing so simple.' Hoban paused, apparently considering his next words carefully. 'I've seen a few things in my time. Rocks so hot that pouring water on them makes them explode, pressure releases that can break every bone in a man's body, gas pockets that can fill an entire shaft with flame in moments if you take a light too close . . . but I've never seen anything like this. I don't know what's causing it. But it's real, I can tell you that much. All too real.'

The pain and anger were obvious in his tone, and Karuna guessed the reason for it.

'How many men have you lost?'

'Six dead and three more unaccounted for,' the commissioner replied. 'We're assuming they're dead too, but we haven't been able to find a single trace of any of them. And after seeing what happened to the ones we *did* find, I'm not prepared to risk any more men in the search.'

From the sensational gossip he had heard, Karuna had thought that the casualties would have been much higher, but he noted the distress in Hoban's voice and knew that he felt even the loss of nine men keenly.

'Where did you see the darkness, exactly?'

'Directly beneath that mound,' Hoban replied, pointing to a hillock in the middle distance. 'No one's been close enough to check for the last few days, but as far as we know that's still the area being affected. About half a mile down.'

'Half a mile!'

'Oh, we go much deeper than that in places. The trouble is, we think its present position is at the hub of the main workings – an underground crossroads, if you like – so it's not just the immediate area that's been cut off. Half the lower seams can't be reached at all now. That's why we've been falling behind in our quotas,' he added defensively.

Karuna was not particularly concerned about the loss of production from the mines, and was disappointed that Hoban should think he was. That was for someone else to worry about.

'You said "its present position". Am I to assume that this . . . this freak of nature moves about?'

'Yes. Its effects have been felt in many different places.'

'But always underground?'

'Yes.' Hoban shuddered, imagining the effect the

swirling darkness might have in the world *above* ground. 'I've seen reports from almost every section of the mines. Whatever these forces are they're not constant, but we can't see any pattern to them.'

'You've checked for lunar influences?'

'Of course. That was the first thing we looked for, but there's no correlation as far as we can tell.'

'Do the forces vary in strength as well as location?'

The commissioner spread his hands in a gesture of bewilderment.

'There's no way of knowing,' he said. 'All I *do* know is that there's enough power there to frighten any sane man.'

Karuna was not a man who frightened easily, but even he was beginning to feel out of his depth now. The two men stood silently for a while, each lost in his own thoughts.

'None of your attempts to counteract these forces have been effective, I gather,' the marshal said eventually.

'We've run out of ideas,' Hoban admitted. 'Not that we had many to start with. Short of collapsing the entire mine, we've tried everything.'

'Let's hope it doesn't come to that.'

The commissioner looked aghast at the suggestion that this idea might be taken seriously.

'Indeed not,' he said quietly.

'I am told that this phenomenon is not the only thing disrupting your operations here,' Karuna remarked. 'Tell me about that.'

'You know about the tremors, of course,' Hoban began. 'They're a problem everywhere now, I know, but they take on an even greater significance when you're working underground. It wasn't too bad when the seers were able to predict them accurately, but now . . .'

'Do you think these forces could be producing the earthquakes?' the marshal asked.

'No. Of course not,' the commissioner replied, though he did not sound entirely convinced. 'They've been far too widespread, all over Vadanis. But there have been several related events that seem to be unique to this region.'

'Such as?'

'Some very localized effects of the quakes. One relatively minor tremor set off an avalanche in the hills which was out of all proportion to the scale of the disturbance, and because of that, the Roynin River was diverted miles from its normal course. Another time it was a whole ridge that sank, so that Lake Tomarr overflowed its banks. Until then the hills had acted as a natural dam. There was massive flooding, and a lot of people died. There was even a report from further to the west that one of the Roynin's tributaries had begun to flow backwards! I don't put much store in that, of course, but most of this is beyond me. The point is, it means that all the wells in Betancuria are drying up, and with the river gone, the town's already running short of water. We'll be facing a serious drought soon if this goes on. Even some of the underground streams in the mines have vanished – including one that's been running continuously for decades.'

'And you don't think it's a coincidence?' Karuna said.

'I don't know what to think,' Hoban answered honestly. 'If whatever's going on underground *does* have something to do with any of this, I can't think why it should be turning the whole region into a desert. More to the point, I don't see *how* it could be responsible for any of this.'

'But the whole thing does seem to have been deliberate?'

The commissioner nodded.

'The weather hasn't helped, of course,' he added. 'The

summer here was unusually dry – and the moons know what's going on now.'

'What do you mean?'

'You won't have been here long enough to notice it,' Hoban replied, glancing up at the sky, 'but if you watch the clouds, you'll see they're all moving in different directions.'

Karuna looked up, and saw that it was true.

'It's almost as if they're circling round Betancuria,' he said after a while.

'They are,' Hoban confirmed. 'And guess where the centre of the rotation is.'

'The mound?'

'Exactly.'

'Another coincidence,' the marshal said heavily. The more he heard about this situation, the less he liked it. 'You know the seers have decided that this place is now the axis around which the Empire is turning?'

'I'd heard that,' Hoban replied. 'It doesn't surprise me.'

'Maybe that's what's creating the peculiar weather conditions,' Karuna suggested.

'Perhaps.'

They were silent for a while, each now aware of the breeze, wondering what forces had brought it into life.

'There's one more thing,' Hoban said eventually.

The tone of his voice made it clear that he was reluctant to go on, but Karuna couldn't see how anything he was told now could make matters any worse.

'Tell me.'

'The whole province has been plagued by whirlwinds in recent months, sometimes several in a single day. They haven't done much damage yet, but you can imagine how frightening they are. It's disrupted our work even more – as if we didn't have enough to deal with already! – but it's affected the town and the nearby farms too. And the worst of it is, they're coming more often, and getting more powerful all the time.'

'There've been reports of tornadoes in the southern provinces,' Karuna said. 'You think that could happen here?'

'Unless something changes, it *will* happen here,' Hoban replied. 'And sooner rather than later.'

'And?' the marshal prompted, knowing there was more to come.

The commissioner took a deep breath.

'We realized a few days ago where they were coming from.'

Karuna turned to look across the mine workings again, his eyes drawn instinctively to the hillock at the centre of the plain.

'You think the force is responsible for the whirlwinds too?' he asked.

'I'd like to say no,' Hoban replied. 'It's a preposterous idea, after all. But I can't deny the evidence of my own eyes – and whatever's producing them can't be natural. Stand here long enough and you'll see what I mean. In fact . . .' He pointed, but Karuna had no need of the indication.

It began as no more than a slight wavering in the air, like a column of heat haze, but it quickly grew in size and strength. Dust and smoke were drawn into its funnel, swirling round at dizzying speeds. Small offshoots – like the unruly children of this wild sprite – skimmed away across the ground, raising their own eddying dust trails before blowing themselves out. In contrast, the core of the disturbance grew taller and wider, reaching up in the sky and out into the surrounding atmosphere.

'Moons!' Hoban breathed, his tone a mixture of awe and horror. 'This is the biggest yet. We'd better get to shelter.'

Neither man moved, each still transfixed by the expanding cone of violence. They could hear it now; an eerie, rushing howl that sucked all other sounds into its smothering embrace.

The lower tip of the vortex was still anchored to the mound, but further up the funnel bulged and swayed, as if it were a drunk who wasn't sure which way to go. And all the time it drew more and more debris from the land about it, so that it grew dark with dust and sand. Several large objects were hurled into the air, and Karuna saw what looked like a wooden shed plucked from its foundations and torn apart, its planking tossed aside as if it was no heavier than dry leaves.

'It'll break free soon!' Hoban yelled over the tumultuous roar. 'If it heads this way . . .'

He had no need to finish the sentence. There would be no escape for the two men, and they knew it. What was worse, if the tornado *did* turn in their direction, it would soon pass them and move on into the town of Betancuria itself. The possible death toll there did not bear thinking about.

A few moments later, with a sudden convulsive effort, the whirlwind tore itself free of the land and began to fly. Then, after spiralling outwards for a while, it moved off – accelerating not towards the mesmerized spectators, but in a southeasterly direction.

Hoban and Karuna watched it go without speaking, stunned by what they had seen, as the outer limits of its influence buffeted the air about them. When the sinister dark shape was several miles away, and the noise had reduced to a level where they could speak normally, Hoban let out a long breath.

'At least it missed the town,' he said.

'That's the good news,' Karuna replied.

Hoban glanced at him.

'What's the bad news?' he asked.

'If it stays on that course, there's going to be a lot of trouble,' the marshal replied, still staring into the distance. 'It's heading directly towards Makhaya.'

CHAPTER THIRTY-ONE

Kamin finally allowed his exasperation to get the better of him.

'I don't see any point in continuing.'

'At last!' Jax responded scornfully. 'Something we can agree on.'

The prince had been even less attentive than usual during that afternoon's tutorial, and his insolence was becoming unbearable.

'Don't you ever think of the future?' Kamin snapped. 'Doesn't it ever occur to you that you've got an important part to play in the fate of the Empire?' The Chief Seer's anger had boiled over now, and he went on without giving his pupil the chance to respond. 'The gravest crisis for a thousand years is facing us, and all you can do is make facetious remarks! The collision could be less than three months away.'

'What do you want me to do?' Jax asked. 'Get out and paddle?' He had been taken aback by Kamin's uncharacteristic vehemence, but soon recovered his self-confidence.

'You're impossible,' the seer exclaimed, with a dismissive gesture. 'That's exactly the sort of flippant comment I was talking about. Don't you realize, we could all be dead before the end of the year?'

'Not me,' the prince replied complacently. 'I'm the Guardian, remember? Even if we *do* collide, I'm going to survive. It's in the prophecy.'

This casual display of double standards took Kamin's breath away. Ever since he had become the prince's tutor, he'd been labouring – as Mirival had done before him – to teach Jax not only the content but also the spirit of the Tindaya Code. In recent days the seer had even been foolish enough to hope that the boy – as one of the principal figures in the prophecy – might allow him to gain some insight into the present situation. Throughout, Jax had remained completely disinterested – and yet now he was claiming his destiny, as outlined in the augury, as the reason for his apathy. It was too incredible for words.

'Are you mad?' Kamin shouted, when he had finally recovered his wits.

'Remember who you're talking to,' Jax retorted, growing angry himself now.

'Oh, I do. How could I forget?' the seer replied, sarcastic in his turn. 'Has it ever occurred to you that even if you do survive the collision, there'll be no Empire left for you to rule?'

'So what? It's not doing me much good at the moment, is it?'

'And of course it doesn't bother you that thousands of people will die, that this city and all the others will be destroyed, that—'

'If you're so concerned about it, *you* do something!' Jax yelled.

'I'm trying. So are we all,' Kamin shot back. 'Except you!'

'Tell me what to do and I'll do it,' the prince countered. 'All you've done so far is drone on about theories. This section of the Code, and that section, and the moons' orbits, and angles of rotation, and on and on. It doesn't mean anything. So until you have something I can act on, I've better things to do with my time. Now get out!'

The Chief Seer left with as much dignity as he could muster, too frustrated to even try to have the last word. When the door had closed behind him, Jax smiled, knowing that Kamin had recognized the truth of his final words – and had had no answer to them. He was just like all the other seers – feeble sheep, bleating on about impending doom but doing nothing about it. And they were ignoring the obvious fact that their own prophecies made it clear the Empire was not going to end. They were probably exaggerating the likely effects of the collision. There would be some destruction, of course, but it could not be as bad as they were predicting. The islands only moved slowly, after all, and Makhaya had already withstood many earthquakes. In any case, that was still months away. In the meantime, the prince had other things on his mind.

It was true that he had been even more preoccupied than usual this afternoon, but there had been good reason for that. He had not thought his twin capable of surprising him, but his escape, first from prison and then from the crowd, had shown a hitherto unsuspected degree of initiative. Jax had viewed the whole thing from afar, in a fragmented daydream, and would not have been able to intervene in those remote events even if he'd wanted to. This was in marked contrast to one of their most recent contacts, when Terrel – the prince even knew his name now – had been much more vulnerable. Today had been the first time they'd both been awake, and it had been a most curious sensation. Jax had sat opposite Kamin, who had been rambling on as usual, while the adventure played out in his head. Not all of it had been clear. His twin had obviously had some help, but Jax had not been able to see his allies, and he didn't know who they were. He would try to find out next time.

He was sure there would be a next time. Their link was well-established now and, even though his contempt for his twin remained, Jax enjoyed the chance to play with the other boy's life. Terrel didn't even know that he had a brother, which made the whole thing more amusing. And he had some talents that were intriguing. He was doing something now – the prince couldn't be sure what it was, though he suspected it had something to do with Terrel's physical appearance – which allowed Jax to see some way into his twin's waking mind. That was interesting, because the only times the contact had been strong before this had been during their shared dreams. And the one that had taken place a few nights ago had been the most revealing yet.

When the dream had begun, Jax had realized that – even asleep – the mental gateway between them was still open. And, even more significantly, his twin's brain had been in a muddled, euphoric state that made it particularly defenceless. It had taken the prince some time to work out why this was so, but as their sleeping thoughts merged, he'd realized that Terrel was hopelessly drunk. This knowledge had encouraged him to pry deeper than he ever had before, and in the process he found, to his astonished glee, that he could take control of his brother's mind – and of his body. Making him burn down that ridiculous rose-thing had been hilarious, and ever since then Jax had been wondering when Terrel would give him the chance to take over again. Even the echoes of their shared hangover, which he had felt the following morning, had been worth it.

The link had been there again the very next night, but Terrel had been sober by then, and the prince had had to content himself with tormenting his twin as he had done before. That had been a fascinating dream too, but on that occasion he had merely been an observer.

Then there had been nothing until this afternoon's much fainter contact. The fact that this had coincided with Kamin's tutorial had been unfortunate in one way, because the prince had been unable to concentrate on those distant events properly, but at least it had hastened the end of the lesson. Jax was pleased by this, because he had plans for the rest of the day – and for the night.

Kamin had only just got back to his own quarters when one of his servants announced that Seer Lathan was requesting an audience. Torn between duty and the need to calm his temper with a cup or two of wine, the Chief Seer decided to combine the two, and asked for a second goblet to be sent in with his visitor.

Lathan was clearly agitated when he entered the room – which was the last thing Kamin needed – and both men drank their first measure of wine in a single gulp.

'You have something you wish to discuss?' Kamin asked as he refilled their cups.

'Two things,' Lathan replied, then fell silent, staring into his wine.

'And they are?' Kamin prompted, schooling himself to patience even though he felt like slapping his fellow seer.

'Betancuria. It's important. For . . .' Once again, Lathan ran out of words.

'I think so too. Karuna is there now. We should have his report—'

'The Guardian should be there,' Lathan cut in.

'Jax? I doubt he'd be much use,' Kamin said with feeling.

'That's the second thing. No.'

The conversation was becoming more disjointed by the moment. This was unusual for Lathan, who was normally both articulate and cogent.

'Sit down,' Kamin instructed his colleague. 'Have another drink. Calm down. Then tell me what's on your mind.'

Lathan did as he was told, composing himself with obvious difficulty.

'I'm sorry. I'm just on edge.'

'We all are.'

'Have you ever wondered if Jax really *is* the Guardian?'

So that's it, Kamin thought.

'It's crossed my mind,' he admitted with some reluctance. 'Why?'

Lathan took a deep breath.

'It's clear now that unless we can do something about it, the Empire won't survive until the next lunar conjunction – whenever that is – and so the prophecy must be wrong. Even if Jax lives until then, there'd be no point in his being a hero if the islands have already been destroyed.'

'I've been trying to make the same point to the prince,' Kamin said bitterly, 'but he's no help. He doesn't seem to understand what's going on.'

'Whereas if he really *were* the Guardian, we'd expect him to know what he had to do, wouldn't we?' Lathan responded eagerly.

'Wait a moment. You're losing me. What makes you think the Guardian should be able to resolve this crisis?'

'Because *nothing* in the Code makes sense unless he does,' Lathan replied, sure of his ground now. 'And I've found a section that could be a direct reference.'

'Where?'

'In Gaylor's Adjunct,' Lathan answered, naming an obscure codicil to one of the least known passages in the Tindaya Code. 'I only came across it by chance.'

Kamin had already risen to his feet and was searching along the shelves of reference books, looking for the appropriate volume. Every part of the Code had been transcribed over the years, so that it was no longer necessary to refer to the original inscribed stones. This was fortunate, because some of them were so large that it had proved impossible to transport them down from the mountains.

'Ah, here it is,' he said, taking down one of the tomes and laying it on his desk. By the time he had found the relevant page, Lathan was at his side.

'Look there,' his visitor said, pointing. 'That symbol's always been translated as "orbit" or "cycle", and in some places that's obviously correct, but on this occasion I think it means "rotation".'

'Which would mean that this isn't "midpoint", but "centre",' Kamin added, indicating another of the signs on the page.

'Exactly,' Lathan concurred. 'The centre of rotation, the axis. And this – which we always thought was some sort of unfinished genealogical tree – I think it's a diagram of mine workings, the shafts and tunnels. Do you see?'

'And this?' Kamin asked, touching a curious, star-shaped symbol at the centre of the diagram.

'There's never been a proper explanation for that.'

Kamin nodded. The possible connection to the rumours that had spread from Betancuria was obvious. Then he looked up, frowning.

'But there's no mention of the Guardian anywhere here,' he pointed out.

'No, but this codicil is connected to the Intempest Stone,' Lathan replied, 'which some scholars believe refers to the Guardian's childhood.'

'That's stretching it a bit far, isn't it?' the Chief Seer said, after a moment's thought. 'And even if you're right, there's nothing here about the rotation being connected to the islands going off course.'

'The two things go together. Stop one and you stop the other, I'm sure of it.'

'But—'

'Do you have any other suggestion as to how we prevent the collision?'

Kamin had no answer to that.

'All right,' he said. 'Supposing you're right, and Jax isn't the Guardian. Then who is?'

'His twin.'

It was the answer Kamin had both expected and feared.

'I know it's considered treasonous even to think such a thing,' Lathan added, 'but it makes a kind of sense.'

'This is dangerous talk,' the Chief Seer muttered. 'Have you spoken to anyone else about this?'

Lathan shook his head.

'Not yet. But I'm going to. Someone's got to speak out. I was hoping you'd support me. That way, if any of the others feel like we do, it would give them the courage to join us. To investigate the possibility, at least.'

Kamin almost told his colleague about the Alakor conspiracy then, but he was feeling nervous about the speed they were travelling, and decided to slow the process down a bit.

'We need more facts before we can go to the council.'

'*You* do,' Lathan corrected him. '*I* don't. I don't have to consider the responsibilities of my position. And once it's out in the open, no one can lock the secret away again.'

'You're not afraid you might meet the same fate as Mirival and Shahan?'

'I'm prepared to take the risk, if it means saving the Empire,' Lathan declared boldly. 'The fact that they were murdered only reinforces my argument.'

'How so?'

'What would have been the point in killing them if Jax's twin were not still alive?'

'You're assuming the deaths are connected.'

'So were you,' Lathan replied. 'Everyone does. And the only link is the twin. We've just been looking for the motive in the wrong places. Who benefited from their deaths?'

'Apart from me?' Kamin asked sourly.

'Jax and Adina!' Lathan exclaimed. 'If the twin is alive, he represents a threat to their ambitions. Only Mirival knew where he might be, and only Shahan was looking for him.'

'Now that definitely *is* treason,' Kamin responded, but he was considering the idea nonetheless. 'Even hinting at such a notion would be dangerous.'

'I know,' Lathan agreed. 'I'm not a complete fool. There's no proof, and there's never likely to be. All I want to do is renew the search for the twin, so that he can go to Betancuria before it's too late. I may make enemies in the process, but if I already know who they are I should be able to cope. And if we succeed, it'll be worth it.'

The seer's conviction was obvious, and – at the very least – he had given Kamin several new ideas to consider.

'All right. Let me think about this. We mustn't do anything too precipitate.'

'Fair enough,' Lathan conceded. 'But remember, we haven't got much time.'

'I'm well aware of that,' the Chief Seer replied testily.

In another part of the palace, a second council of war was in progress.

'So you think it's time to make a public announcement?' Adina said, her amber eyes aglow.

'I see no point in delaying any further,' Fauria replied. 'We have all the evidence we're ever going to get.' Without his really being aware of it, most of the seer's researches into the Tindaya Code over the past few years had been dedicated to selecting appropriate passages, and redefining their exact meanings to suit the Empress's purpose.

'You don't think the imminence of this possible collision might make such a gesture meaningless?' Remi asked.

'Of course not!' Adina exclaimed angrily.

'If disaster is averted,' Fauria replied calmly, 'then it's essential to have staked the Empress's claim before it happens. That way she can assert that her official acceptance as Mentor was fully justified.' And if it's not averted, he thought, this is all academic.

'When, then?' Adina demanded.

'There's a full council meeting in three days' time,' Fauria replied. 'Women are not normally allowed into the chamber, but—'

'But they'll make an exception for me,' Adina completed for him, smiling at the thought.

'All will be ready,' the seer confirmed. There had been a time when he had harboured vague ambitions to be hailed as the Mentor himself – and the Empress had encouraged him to think of this as a possibility – but he had no wish for the job now, and he knew he was no match for Adina.

After letting the seer out, Remi returned to the Empress.

'When are you going to tell your son about this?'

'I haven't decided yet. Why?'

'Jax has inherited many of your talents,' the chamberlain replied. 'He may even have the makings of an enchanter.'

Adina laughed. She had indeed taught her son to manipulate people, but she found it hard to believe that he would ever match her expertise.

'Have you ever wondered whether he might have been responsible for the deaths of Mirival and Shahan?' Remi asked.

'What?' Her shocked expression answered his question. 'Don't be ridiculous. He was nowhere near either of them.'

'I don't mean by his own hand,' the chamberlain explained. 'But it is possible he could have influenced the actual killers.'

'I don't want to hear any more of this,' Adina hissed. 'Leave me.'

Remi bowed and left without another word, leaving the Empress seething. When she had calmed down a little, she could not get the chamberlain's words out of her mind. Could it be true? Or was Remi scheming on his own behalf? Her servant had always proved loyal in the past, and he was normally the most astute observer of court affairs, but why then should he harbour such foul suspicions about Jax? One way or another, Adina decided grimly, she would have to talk to her son.

Jax's sense of triumph was fading fast as the night wore on. He was alone again now, but Mela's perfume still lingered in the air, a telltale reminder of an encounter that had promised so much and delivered so little. It had not been easy to arrange for a princess, albeit a minor one, to come to his chambers unobserved, but he had managed that perfectly. The dream that had led her to him would also ensure that she would remember nothing afterwards, but even though it had made her willing enough, she had been stiff and awkward in bed. She was undoubtedly beautiful – the sight of her naked had been delightful – but she was clearly even less experienced than he was, and even the fact that he was enjoying forbidden pleasures had not made their embraces any more memorable. All in all, the rewards had simply not been worth the risk.

Jax was about to go back to bed, to sleep this time, when he sensed a distant howling. It was not so much a sound as a vibration, a quivering that reached inside him and made his heart race. He felt it coming closer with a growing excitement, knowing that another of his wishes had been granted.

Striding over to the window, he threw open the shutters and looked out over the city at a sky that was full of stars. But one part of the night, over to the northwest, was wreathed in a greater darkness – and it was this that caught the prince's eye. The howling grew louder, even more insistent, and Jax knew that this was no ordinary storm.

He could see the shape of the tornado now, as it reached the outskirts of the city. He was elated by its ferocity and sheer size, and he shouted aloud above the roaring of the wind that tore at his clothes and hair. He welcomed its elemental fury, glorying in its primeval violence, its indiscriminate power – and he sensed its connection to himself.

With a single thought he nudged it to one side, altering its path by a fraction so that it tore the roof off a nearby mansion. Tiles and timbers fizzed through the air, scattered by the tornado's whim and the prince's malice.

The enchanter smiled, ready for more. He would need no dreams this night.

CHAPTER THIRTY-TWO

You ride with all the grace of a sack of rocks, Alyssa grumbled.

Well, you're not helping, Terrel replied. *I feel as if I'm being split in half with all this bouncing up and down.*

That's how horses move, she informed him tartly. *I can't help it.*

After their rapid departure from Tiscamanita, the two friends had ridden through the night at a steadier pace. Their route had been chosen at random, each decision reached on the spur of the moment, and their progress had been erratic. Terrel had no idea where they were now, except that they were somewhere inland, on the other side of the coastal plain. The fear of capture had driven them on, but they had seen no sign of any pursuit and, having reached some wooded country that offered plenty of cover in which to hide, Terrel was beginning to believe that they really had made a clean escape.

I need to rest, Alyssa said.

Me too, he replied. *We can stop anywhere you like now.*

At first, Terrel had been sustained by his own excitement

and fear, and this had given him the strength to cling to the great horse. Those internal fires had also kept him warm for a time, but now he was cold, sore and very, very tired.

I don't mean I need to stop, Alyssa said. *I mean I've got to rest. I've got to get out of the animal.*

Oh. That meant he would lose her and, even though they'd exchanged only a few words in the last hour or so, Terrel had still been comforted by her presence.

It gets uncomfortable, Alyssa told him.

I thought you liked horses, he said.

I do, she replied. *But not from the inside.*

Why the difference?

Horses' minds are very peculiar, she explained. *If I stay too long—*

It'll drive you mad? he suggested.

Very funny. Just be glad I put up with it for this long.

I am, he said, feeling properly chastised. He was perfectly aware that he could never have escaped without her help. *Thank you.*

There's just something odd about a wild spirit that allows another creature to bend it to its will, Alyssa went on, apparently unaware of the irony in her statement. *I suppose that's why men have to 'break' horses before they can ride them.* She sounded rather sad now, as well as weary.

I hadn't thought of it like that, Terrel responded.

Do you think you can handle him on your own?

No! he replied quickly. *Not at the moment.* He knew that he was a terrible horseman. Even knowing that Alyssa would do nothing to harm him, he'd been very nervous, and had been in constant danger of falling off. During their ride he had often gripped not only the reins but also the stallion's mane, twisting the coarse hair in his fingers to give himself some extra security. It was on one of these occasions that he had felt the 'ring', knotted into the mane, and when he realized what it was, he had stared at it frequently – rather than at the ground, which seemed a long way down.

All right, Alyssa said. *You'll have to stop, then. I doubt anyone's going to find you now, and you ought to get some sleep. If you nod off in the saddle even I wouldn't be able to stop you falling.*

Dawn was breaking as they threaded their way deeper into the forest, eventually reaching a small glade that was lush with tall grass and flowers. There had been no sign of any habitation for some miles, and Terrel was confident that no one was likely to stumble upon him here.

His dismount was awkward and painful. Long hours in the saddle had left all his muscles stiff, and he did not have the benefit of a platform to help him as he'd had in Tiscamanita. In the end he managed it, but then stumbled and fell heavily. Alyssa turned her equine head to look at him, but mercifully made no comment on his ineptitude. When he'd picked himself up, Terrel loosened the reins and looped them over a low branch, leaving enough slack to allow the horse to graze on the nearby grass.

I'll bet Cadrez is the butt of a few jokes now, don't you think? Alyssa remarked, whinnying with laughter. *To have a prisoner escape is bad enough, but on his own horse? Honestly!*

Terrel grinned, knowing she was introducing an element of humour in order to try to make their parting easier. When she'd visited him before, it had always been the animal that had left him, physically moving away, which had made it seem more natural somehow. This time would be different.

You'd better go, he said quietly.

Yes. She was grateful for his acceptance. *I'll be back as soon as I can.*

Goodbye, Alyssa.

We own this palace, Terrel, she replied. *Never forget that.*

He was about to ask what she meant when he realized she was no longer there. There had been no visible sign of her departure; he was simply alone again. The stallion blinked, looked around at his unfamiliar surroundings, and then began to eat placidly, as if nothing had happened. Terrel did not need to inspect his mane to know that the ring was no longer in place, but he did it anyway, feeling chilled inside as well as out.

He shivered, telling himself that he'd have to get some new clothes soon. The nights were getting colder, and a traveller wearing only boots and breeches would attract unwanted attention. He supposed he'd be forced to steal some new garments. The idea didn't please him, but he couldn't think of any alternative. As it was, he was glad that at least he still had his specially made boots. Replacing them would have been next to impossible. Uzellin had wanted him to go barefoot – 'as a proper penitent', he had said – but he'd relented when Terrel pointed out that he would hardly be able to walk at all like that.

Setting aside the problem of his clothing, Terrel began to look for a soft place to sleep, knowing this was an even more urgent necessity. He made a mattress of grass, then lay down, still cold but thankful for the growing warmth of the newly-risen sun.

Before he fell asleep, his last thoughts were of Kativa. He had acted instinctively with her, and even though he knew the effort had cost him much of his strength, he was glad he had helped her. He was pleased that her long ordeal was over, but he wished he knew how she had been able to speak through him. Was she a different type of ghost from Elam and the others? He remembered her tears, the gentle touch of her hands and – at the last – her smile. Was she with Siverio now? Would the citizens of Tiscamanita rebuild her shrine? And would it matter if they didn't?

No dreams came to answer his questions, or to disturb his rest.

When Terrel awoke, he was instantly alert. The sun was past its zenith, and the sky — which had been clear at first light — was now grey with fast-moving clouds. The wind was rustling the trees all around him, but that was not what had disturbed him. He was no longer alone.

His first thought was that Alyssa had returned, but some sixth sense told him that she was nowhere near, and he felt a premonition of danger. Sitting up slowly, he saw two men at the edge of the clearing, staring at the horse. The stallion was looking back at them, standing quite still, and there was a degree of menace in its gaze. The strangers were talking quietly, so that Terrel was unable to hear what they were saying, but they were clearly nervous. One of the men, obviously younger than his companion, kept glancing around. He didn't see the boy, who was still concealed behind tall grass.

As Terrel watched, the men clearly came to a decision, and cautiously began to advance upon the horse. The boy knew that he had to act, and he scrambled to his feet.

'Hey!'

The intruders were startled, and they tensed, ready to flee, their faces showing their alarm. Then, much to Terrel's dismay, one of the men — clearly the bolder of the pair — began to laugh. His companion soon joined in, and Terrel realized how absurd he must look. He stood where he was, not knowing what to do next, watching their hilarity — and noting that a knife had appeared in the braver man's left hand.

For a moment he was tempted to use the glamour and try to scare them away, but even the thought of it made him feel exhausted. Instinct told him to keep his eyes blue, although even that had become something of an effort. Without realizing it, his disguise had reasserted itself when he woke, in what was becoming a natural process for him now – and it was worth the effort to maintain it. He had the feeling that, with these two, the true appearance of his eyes might get him killed. They were clearly up to no good, and if they meant to steal the horse there was nothing he could do to stop them. He wished now that he'd remained hidden and left them to it.

The laughter eventually subsided, but both men were still smiling. Terrel was relieved to see that the knife had been sheathed again.

'This is *your* horse?' the bolder man asked.

'Yes,' Terrel replied, then hesitated, wondering if he might bluff his way out of this. 'Well, no, it's my master's, really. He'll be back soon.'

The younger man glanced round again, obviously uncomfortable.

'I don't like this, Gegan,' he said. 'Let's get out of here.'

His companion merely grinned.

'Where'd he go, then?' he asked the boy.

'To relieve himself.'

'You're lying,' Gegan stated confidently. 'Why would he need to wander off to take a piss? One tree's as good as another. And where's your master's baggage, eh? The owner of a grand beast like this wouldn't normally travel light. Where are his clothes? Or yours, for that matter?'

Terrel didn't answer.

'And why are you undressed in the middle of the day?' the man went on. 'You got a girl there in the long grass?'

His companion sniggered.

'My clothes were stolen,' Terrel claimed.

'Really? Thieves took the clothes off your back, but left you with this valuable horse? Pretty stupid of them, wasn't it?'

Once again Terrel remained silent.

'Shall I tell you what I think?' Gegan asked, then went on without waiting for an answer. 'I think *you* stole the horse.'

Terrel was about to deny it, then changed his mind.

'What if I did?'

'Ah, now we're getting somewhere. You're a fugitive from justice – though what crime requires you to dress in your underpants is a mystery to me. Get caught seducing a rich man's wife, did you?'

The younger man guffawed at this witticism, then looked at his partner and grinned idiotically.

'If he stole it, we can take it off him, can't we,' he declared triumphantly. 'He won't be able to do a thing about it.'

'I'll *give* him to you in exchange for some clothes,' Terrel offered.

Gegan smiled.

'How generous!' he exclaimed sarcastically. 'You're an odd one, boy. You can nick a beast like that, but you can't keep hold of your own trousers. You going to tell us what really happened?'

'No.' Terrel made his tone as belligerent as he dared.

'Fair enough,' Gegan said, laughing. 'Then we have a deal.'

'What?' the other man shouted in disbelief. 'We can just take it. Why should—'

'Come on, Kaz. It's a good deal,' his partner cut in. 'The saddle alone's worth more than everything we've got

on. And there should be *some* honour among thieves, don't
you think?'

'You're crazy!' Kaz exclaimed.

'Let's just say I've got a feeling about this boy,' Gegan
replied calmly. 'I don't think we should annoy him. Come
on. He's nearer your size than mine. It doesn't have to be
any of your good stuff.'

'What good stuff?' his companion muttered. 'I never get
any of the good stuff.' But he went over to his discarded
backpack and rummaged around in it nonetheless.

'Where'd you steal the horse from?' Gegan asked.

'Why do you want to know?'

'Because if I'm going to deal in stolen goods, I don't
want to offer them back to the rightful owner, do I?'

The last thing Terrel wanted was for the two men to try
to sell the horse back to Cadrez, and possibly give the
seneschal news of his prisoner's whereabouts. And he
could see no point in lying now.

'Tiscamanita.'

Gegan nodded.

'You're a long way from home already, then,' he commented.

Further than you know, Terrel thought.

A little while later, he was dressed in drab but service-
able clothes that fitted reasonably well once he'd made
some adjustments. Kaz was still annoyed at having to give
up his possessions, and he was even more incredulous
when Gegan invited Terrel to share some food with them.
The boy ate gladly, not sure why he was being granted this
extra hospitality, but grateful for it nonetheless. However,
he refused a drink because all they had was wine.

'Pretty joyless life if you're teetotal,' Gegan said amiably.

'It doesn't agree with me,' Terrel replied.

After the meal, the two men went to inspect the stallion.

'You want to ride?' the older man asked. 'He looks a bit fierce for me.'

'No,' Kaz answered. 'I'll lead him.' He was clearly in awe of the animal.

Gegan left his partner to untether the horse, and came back to Terrel.

'Which way are you headed?'

'South.'

'There's a village about three miles away. You'll find the track easily enough. There's a tavern there called the Rocking Stone, run by a man called Drake. Tell him I said to give you a room for the night.'

'But I've no money,' Terrel said doubtfully.

'You'll find some way of paying him back,' Gegan replied. 'And if you don't, it won't matter. The old bastard owes me a favour or two.'

'Thank you.' Terrel was not sure he trusted the man's apparent kindness, and he had no idea what his motives were, but finding the village would at least be better than wandering around the forest.

Kaz was leading the horse away now and, even though this was going to make his own journey longer and harder, Terrel was not sorry to see the animal go. His back and legs were still aching from the ride.

'Get some more rest tonight,' Gegan advised. 'You need your strength. I've used a touch of the glamour myself on occasion, so I know the signs. And yours is starting to slip a little. You've been overdoing it, boy.' He tapped his own temple with the fingers of his left hand, then turned and walked after his partner, whistling a jaunty tune as he went.

CHAPTER THIRTY-THREE

Finding the tavern was not as easy as Gegan had predicted, and it was early evening by the time Terrel finally reached the outskirts of the village. The Rocking Stone stood beside a well-used road and – judging by its size and by the stables that had been built next to the inn – it catered for travellers as well as locals. As far as Terrel was concerned, that was a good sign. He might be able to join up with others who were heading south.

The village streets were deserted, but lamplight shone through the tavern's slatted shutters, and as he drew closer Terrel could hear the rumble of several conversations from within. There was a painted sign above the door that creaked in the wind, which was rising still and held the promise of rain. This was not going to be a night to spend in the open, but Terrel hesitated even so, uncertain of his welcome. It was possible that Gegan had played a cruel trick on him, and that he would be better off sneaking into the stables without approaching the landlord – and after Gegan's parting comment, Terrel was no longer sure of his ability to disguise his eyes. In the end, he decided to take the chance. My eyes are blue, he told himself, as he pushed open the door. Believe it.

Conversations died away for a moment as everyone inside the tavern turned to look at the newcomer. There was a surprisingly large number of people in the cavernous room, but none of them gave the boy more than a passing glance, and their chatter soon resumed. They were clearly used to strangers here, and even Terrel's obvious deformities did not mark him out as worthy of much attention. Fortunately, no one looked twice at his eyes, so he knew the glamour must be working. Gaining confidence, he approached the counter at the back of the room, where the barman stood among the barrels that contained his wares. He was a big man, and even though his beard was streaked with grey, he looked more than capable of dealing with any troublemakers.

'Are you Drake?' Terrel asked.

'I am. Who's asking?'

'My name's Terrel. Gegan said you'd give me a bed for the night.'

'Did he now?' Although the landlord sounded surprised, he seemed friendly enough, and Terrel began to feel more hopeful.

'I can work for my keep,' he added hurriedly.

Drake smiled, revealing a set of discoloured, uneven teeth.

'What do you think, lads?' he called to the bar in general. 'Shall we make him sing for his supper?' The question was greeted with a chorus of approval and some laughter.

Terrel was wondering what the landlord meant when the ugliest cat he had ever seen sauntered into the room from a back door. It was a dirty grey, with splodges of brown and black on its neck and flanks, and there was an evil expression on its face. Its nose seemed to have been flattened, giving it a pugnacious look, and this impression was reinforced by the fact that half of one ear was missing and there were several rips in the other. One of its eyes was green and the other yellow, but both regarded their surroundings with a malicious indifference. The cat's tail was bent, where it had once been broken, and its fangs, when it yawned lazily, were revealed as stained brown but horribly sharp. This was a creature from a child's nightmare, but Terrel was delighted.

Hello, Alyssa. I'm glad—

Moons! she interrupted. *This is worse than the horse.*

Terrel didn't get the chance to ask her what she meant because, unaware of the silent conversation, Drake was growing impatient.

'Come on, boy. We could do with some fresh entertainment. What can you offer us? A song at least, eh?'

Terrel remembered what Gegan had said about finding a way to pay Drake. It seemed that the price of a room might be ritual humiliation.

'I can't sing,' he told the landlord nervously.

'Neither can this lot,' Drake replied, nodding towards his patrons, most of whom were now listening to the conversation with interest. 'Never stops them after a few beers, though.'

'It'd take more than a few of your beers!' someone shouted. 'Weak as pond water, this.'

'Then I shan't serve you any more,' Drake replied, untroubled by the jovial insult. 'What about it, boy?'

Terrel had been wondering whether he could somehow use the glamour to enhance his voice, but the mere thought made him feel exhausted. Then he had a flash of inspiration.

'I've never been able to carry a tune,' he said, 'but I can make that cat sing for you.'

This claim was greeted with uproarious laughter.

What are you doing? Alyssa enquired indignantly, but Terrel ignored the silent interruption.

'Will you give me a meal and a bed for the night if I do?' he asked Drake.

'That's the meanest, most selfish animal you'll ever meet,' the barman told him. 'Get too close and she'll bite your fingers off. She's a great ratter, I'll give her that, but she don't sing for no one but herself.'

'She will for me.' *Help me, Alyssa.*

'Prove that, and you can have food and a bed – and all the beer you can drink,' Drake told him, winking at his customers. 'This ought to be good for a laugh.'

Terrel squatted down and beckoned to the cat, holding out his good hand.

'Here, kitty.'

Don't push your luck, Alyssa advised him, as the onlookers roared with laughter and waited for the bloodshed to begin.

The cat stalked up to Terrel, sniffed his outstretched fingers, then sat down, her crooked tail waving crossly. This unusually placid behaviour surprised and amused the spectators, who were all intrigued now.

'They won't hear you properly down there,' Terrel told her. 'Jump up on the counter.' *Please, Alyssa!*

The cat hissed, then tensed and sprang up onto her stage, her claws skidding for a moment on the stained wood. Drake took a step back, keeping himself at a safe distance. His face was a picture of astonishment.

Alyssa turned to face Terrel and the rest of her audience.

I'm going to remember this, she vowed, glaring at him with mismatched eyes.

Terrel was enjoying himself, and couldn't resist putting

out a hand to stroke her. Ignoring the cries of warning from all around, he ruffled her surprisingly soft fur and even tickled her under the chin.

'Well, I'll be!' Drake breathed.

I suppose you'd like me to purr now? There was a dangerous tone to Alyssa's voice, and Terrel wondered whether she might decide to bite him after all.

No, he replied. *I want you to sing. Do your best. Please.* Aloud, he said, 'Sing for us, kitty.'

Alyssa remained perfectly still for a moment or two, then she threw her head back, opened her murderous jaws, and let out the most appalling yowl. Her display was greeted with a fresh wave of laughter and incredulity. Terrel smiled and bowed to the audience, accepting their applause.

You can stop now.

Oh, no! Alyssa replied. *I haven't finished yet.*

The cat's fur was standing on end now, making her seem even bigger and more ferocious, and as the nerve-grating wail continued, Terrel saw that many of the audience had put their hands over their ears.

'Shut her up!' Drake shouted.

'I only said I could get her to sing,' Terrel replied over the unearthly howling. 'I never said I could make her stop.'

The song went on and on, part battle cry, part mating call. After a while, honour satisfied, the cat fell silent. As she stalked along the bar, she was purring for her own pleasure. She jumped down to the floor and, with one last defiant miaow, made a dignified exit.

Much later, Terrel was finally able to get away to his allotted room. After Alyssa's bravura performance, Drake had been as good as his word. The meal had been substantial,

and Terrel had been forced to wash it down with beer —
discovering in the process that it was not at all watery. He'd
drunk as little as he could get away with, remembering with
horror the last time he'd been drunk, but he had still felt
rather light-headed.

Eventually, pleading exhaustion, he had managed to
escape, anxious now not only to sleep, but also to have the
chance to be alone with Alyssa. He knew she would not
take long to find him again.

His room was small, and its few furnishings were
threadbare, but it was clean — and the prospect of a real
bed was wonderful. Terrel lay down, and although he had
every intention of staying awake until Alyssa arrived, he
fell asleep almost at once. He was just beginning to
dream when he was disturbed by a scratching noise, and
woke up with a start. The scrabbling sound was coming
from the door and when he got up and opened it, the cat
walked in.

*I can't stand being in this creature much longer, so we'd
better talk fast*, Alyssa told him. *What happened to the horse?*

Terrel told her the story. He was getting used to organ-
izing his thoughts for a conversation without the need of
speech.

Oh, well, she remarked when he had finished. *We can
always get another one.*

Do we have to? Terrel asked. *Neither of us like horses.
And we'd have to steal one.*

They were both aware that horses were valuable animals,
especially for those whose livelihoods depended on them,
and there would be little chance of them being able to
return it to its owner.

All right, Alyssa replied, sounding rather relieved. *But
time's getting on. We may have to think again if you don't
make good progress. Have you got any other ideas?*

Not at the moment. During his time in the bar, Terrel had tried to find out what he could about ways of travelling south, but he hadn't learnt much. *Travellers do pass through here, though, so I may be able to tag along with them.*

Let's hope someone comes soon, then, Alyssa commented.

Is this soon enough? Elam asked, as his glimmering form appeared at the foot of the bed.

We weren't talking about you, Alyssa informed him.

Well, I'm here now, even if I am knackered. You've no idea how hard it is to make yourself seen by people living in your world, he told Terrel. *You should count yourself lucky.*

I do. Thanks for your help. Are the others here too?

Somewhere, Elam replied vaguely. *They're arguing, as usual.*

Do you know what happened to Kativa? Terrel asked. Her fate had been on his mind ever since he'd left Tiscamanita.

She's moved on, his friend told him. *You did well there.*

I still don't know where she came from, Alyssa added. *She was as real as you are, Elam, but she was on a different . . .* She paused, evidently searching for a way to explain what she meant.

In a different room of the palace? Terrel suggested.

Alyssa turned and gave him a curious feline stare.

You could put it that way, she agreed eventually.

I suppose you two know what you're talking about, Elam remarked. *I've a feeling Muzeni and Shahan might have had something to do with Kativa's turning up like that.*

On cue, the two elderly ghosts walked through the wall of the room. They stopped when they saw the others.

Was someone taking our names in vain? Muzeni enquired, looking at the small group. When his gaze fell on the cat, he smiled. *You're looking particularly lovely this evening, my dear.*

Alyssa hissed at him.

Tut, tut. Such language. What have you been talking about?

Kativa, Terrel said.

Ah. A satisfactory conclusion, don't you think? There was an elaborately innocent expression on the heretic's face.

Did you bring her there? Terrel asked.

The two ghosts exchanged glances.

We were partly responsible, yes, Shahan replied.

We pulled some strings, Muzeni added self-importantly.

Why?

We thought you could use some help, the seer told him.

How did that help me? Terrel thought to himself. If anything, Kativa had been an unwanted distraction. His own impersonation of a demon would have been enough to impress the crowd.

Can ghosts lie? he asked, looking at Elam.

Do squirrels climb trees? his friend answered. *But we're good at evading questions too, if we don't want to answer them. We can just walk through walls or simply vanish.*

Terrel realized that he would get no further explanation.

We have something more important to discuss with you, Muzeni said. *It's possible that you will have to make a detour on your way to Betancuria.*

We don't know that, Shahan objected, before Terrel had a chance to ask where he was supposed to go.

How else can you explain the ambiguities we've uncovered in the text of the Intempest Stone? Muzeni responded impatiently.

There are many possible interpretations— the seer began.

Yes, and only one makes any sense! the heretic cut in.

You can't ever accept the possibility that you might be wrong, can you? What if—

Enough! Alyssa exclaimed forcefully. *Unless you two are going to tell us something useful, you can keep quiet.*

Her outburst earnt her two indignant glares, and a smile from Elam.

Do you know where Terrel's supposed to go? she asked.

Not yet, Muzeni replied, *but we're working on it, and making good progress.*

Not good enough, obviously, Alyssa stated bluntly. *Unless you can give us some practical advice, you'd better get back to work.*

This time her vehemence startled them into silence.

Well, what are you waiting for? she demanded, then had second thoughts. *No. Wait. Don't go yet. Just listen for a few moments.*

The ghosts stayed where they were, and remained obediently silent.

I wish you'd teach me how to do that, Elam commented enviously. *Sometimes it takes me hours to shut them up.*

I'm not in a good mood, Elam, Alyssa warned him. *This creature keeps trying to throw me out. She's too independent for her own good. Quite different from that idiot stallion, but just as difficult — so I'm not going to be able to stay much longer.* Her tail was twitching violently as she spoke. *Before I go, I just wanted to tell you all something. Some of the forces beneath Betancuria are starting to leak into the outside world.*

As what? Elam asked.

The weather's changing, she replied. *It's only gradual, but there've already been some tornadoes. And it's only going to get worse unless we can do something to calm it down. If we don't, there may not be much of Vadanis left to collide with the mainland!*

There was a horrified pause.

So there's another reason for us to get Terrel to Betancuria as soon as possible, Shahan concluded.

Exactly, Alyssa said. *So let's all get on with it, shall we?*

Slave-driver, Elam muttered.

How do you know all this? Muzeni asked.

I have to go now, Alyssa said, ignoring the question.

'It was a test, wasn't it,' Terrel said aloud.

What was?

'To see what I would do,' he went on, looking at Muzeni and Shahan. 'That's why you brought Kativa to the square. You were testing me!'

No one denied it.

CHAPTER THIRTY-FOUR

Terrel had not expected to sleep well that night, but in the event he had the best rest he'd had for some time. The knowledge that the ghosts – whom he had come to regard as allies – had felt the need to test him in some way was unsettling. What they were expecting him to do was bad enough, but his task would seem even more daunting if he could not count on his friends. He had not even been able to work out *why* they had tested him – and they had given him no explanation. Even Alyssa's cat had left without offering him any reason. However, further reflection had lessened his feelings of surprise and indignation. Why *should* the ghosts trust him, after all? The two old men hardly knew him, and only had their own vague interpretation of the prophecy to go on. Terrel himself was not sure that this was the most reliable recommendation. He had mulled it all over for some time, but then exhaustion had overcome his worries, and he had fallen into a deep and dreamless sleep.

The gathering bustle of the Rocking Stone as it came to life about him did not disturb his slumber, and he didn't wake until late morning, when the sound of music came drifting through the shutters. As he roused himself and went to look out of the window, the music stopped, but he saw at once that the open space next to the tavern was now a hive of activity. Two carts, whose once bright colours had faded with time, had been drawn together to form a makeshift stage and, as Terrel watched, a man in a gaudy costume climbed up and turned to address the small crowd of curious villagers.

'Tonight, for one night only, the Great Laevo's Theatrical Company will perform my latest dramatic masterpiece for your delectation!' he announced in ringing tones. 'Together with dance and song, mirth and magic, this will be an evening to remember. Come one, come all. The best seats are only two phinars. The curtain rises one hour before sunset for the greatest show on Vadanis!'

Terrel smiled to himself, amused by the Great Laevo's confident introduction. He watched for a while, but nothing much happened. These were evidently some of the travelling players whose way of life had seemed so attractive to Sarafia. Terrel wondered if she had ever seen this very troupe. Only their leader seemed at all out of the ordinary. Most of the others wore drab clothes, and seemed rather bored as they went about their task of setting up camp, apparently less than enchanted by their situation. Even the musicians looked indifferent as they began to play again. Even so, Terrel would have liked to stay and see their performance, but he knew he ought to resume his journey south as soon as possible.

He dressed and went downstairs, hoping that Drake's hospitality might extend to some breakfast. He found the landlord leaning on the counter, in conversation with the Great Laevo himself, over a mug of beer. No other sort of sustenance seemed to be on offer.

'Now here's a lad you could put in your show,' Drake announced when he spotted Terrel in the doorway. 'Last night he charmed old Mograt and made her sing on cue. Never seen anything like it.'

Laevo was not impressed.

'I don't deal in freaks,' he said dismissively, after glancing at the boy.

'Hey, there's no call for that. Terrel's a friend of mine.'

Terrel was not offended by the actor's attitude. He'd been called much worse in his time. Even so, he was grateful to the landlord for defending him and claiming him as a friend.

Laevo waved an apologetic hand and mumbled something into his beer.

'Yes, well, we've all got our troubles,' Drake told him. 'Yours only seem worse because they're your own.'

'But Parga was the only one of us who could read!' the actor exclaimed. 'Apart from me, of course. How am I supposed to replace him, when there's a new play to rehearse? I'll have to do everything myself – and even then half those bumbleheads'll forget their lines without a prompter.'

'Then you'll just have to bedazzle us country bumpkins with your own quick wit, won't you,' the landlord replied unsympathetically.

'It wouldn't be for the first time,' Laevo said. 'Without me, this lot . . .' He threw up his hands in a gesture of despair.

'I can read,' Terrel ventured.

The two men turned to look at him, and he sensed their scepticism.

'I can,' he repeated.

'Then come here and prove it,' Laevo commanded, pulling a battered manuscript from the inside pocket of his jacket and slapping it down on the counter. As Terrel limped over to him, he opened it and pointed. 'Read from there.'

'"Enter Empress, laughing,"' Terrel read. '"How fares my hackle-hounded son?"'

'"I am well, mother,"' Laevo responded, taking up the part of the prince.

'"So, like the moons, he turns his face to suit the day, and waxes or wanes, dependent upon shadows,"' Terrel continued.

The actor looked up, glanced at Drake with raised eyebrows, then turned to the boy.

'A scholar as well as an animal charmer,' he remarked. His opinion of Terrel had obviously been revised. 'Do you want a job?'

'That depends on the pay,' Terrel replied.

Drake laughed.

'I told you he's no fool, this one,' he commented.

'We each get a share of the takings,' Laevo told the boy. 'Parga's was a twentieth, but you're a rookie, so you'll get half that until you earn your spurs.'

Terrel glanced at Drake for guidance.

'That's fair,' the landlord decreed. 'But make sure you get your twentieth if you stay with this scapejack for more than a few days.'

The idea that he might continue his journey with the troupe had not occurred to the boy until then.

'Which way do you go from here?' he asked.

'South,' Laevo replied. 'To Rigel, then—'

'Can I come with you?' Terrel cut in, having heard all he needed.

'If you do all right tonight, why not?' The actor held out his right hand, then switched to his left when he saw the boy's hesitation. Terrel had never had occasion to shake hands before, but did so now with a sense of excitement.

'Welcome to the company,' Laevo said.

'Thank you.'

They grinned at one another.

'What does "hackle-hounded" mean?' Terrel asked.

'Who cares?' Laevo replied. 'It sounds good, and that's all I care about.'

The rehearsal took place in the early afternoon, in an empty barn behind the stables, well away from prying eyes. Two members of the troupe, who would not be performing that night, were posted as guards, to deter the village children from coming too close.

Terrel's job was to sit to one side and read out stage directions. Most of these were hardly necessary; the play was not new, as Laevo had claimed, but a variation on one they had obviously performed many times before. The company's leader had added some extra jokes and comments, which had been scribbled onto the manuscript, and which he passed on to the rest of the cast before the run-through began. As prompter, Terrel was also responsible for feeding the actors their lines if any of them faltered.

The play itself was a satire, set in an imperial court which, although never named, was clearly based on Makhaya – and Terrel was surprised that such a deliberately insulting burlesque was thought suitable for public performance. He hoped that no Imperial Guards would see the play. They would not be amused.

The action, such as it was, revolved around the Emperor Drone-on, played by Laevo himself, whose long-winded speeches invariably descended from pompous philosophizing into downright idiocy, while at the same time managing to ridicule all those around him. His chief targets were the Empress Hyena, who always laughed raucously before she spoke, and Prince Wax, who was played by the youngest of the troupe, an eighteen-year-old called Sill. Wax was portrayed as two-faced — literally so, because the actor's head was encased in a circular double mask. This could be swivelled round to change Sill's appearance from that of a drooling imbecile to the face of a handsome, bright-eyed hero. The other two main characters were both seers, Merry-Al, who wore an absurd velvet hat studded with tiny mirrors, and Creep-in, who was the villain of the piece. In the first act, the seers were presented as buffoons who never understood what was going on about them. However, in the second, Creep-in was revealed as a scheming wizard, who murdered Merry-Al in order to steal his magic hat and thus gain the power to take control of the Empire. It was his maniacal folly that set the islands spinning, released monsters from the earth, and caused the moons to behave unnaturally. Only when Wax changed from dunce to hero and killed the usurper was the world saved.

The rest of the cast played various lackeys and hangers-on, and the narrative was interspersed with music and dancing — which did not need rehearsing as these elements had not been changed. The script was full of comic asides and innuendo, as well as a number of references to recent events. This made Terrel feel rather uncomfortable. The mention of monsters inevitably made him think of his own intimidating journey to Betancuria, but the general tone of the play was so nonsensical that he was soon able to dismiss any serious considerations.

Terrel managed his duties well enough. He had thought that a newcomer might face some resentment from the actors, but they seemed to accept him readily enough. Even when he made mistakes — prompting someone too soon when they were merely pausing for dramatic effect, or stumbling over an obscure phrase — they took it in their stride. He repaid their faith by concentrating hard, and keeping his errors to a minimum.

Laevo was a hard taskmaster, wanting everything to be played precisely as he had written it, but he had a sense of humour too — and, even though Terrel did not find the play particularly funny, the boy often had a smile on his face as any problems with the new text were ironed out. Laevo was easily the most talented of the group, and some of his monologues were the best things in the play. He was the only actor who was allowed to improvise, and he did so frequently — which sometimes confused his new prompter. The fact that Terrel always managed to catch up quickly clearly pleased the troupe's leader, and when he at last called a halt to the rehearsal, he made a point of clapping the boy on the back.

'You'll do,' he pronounced. 'Come on, let's go and see if Drake can spare some of that dishwater he calls beer.'

A little while later, they were settled at a table in the tavern, with the landlord sharing not only some of his ale but also a platter of bread and cheese. Terrel refused the drink, but was very glad of the food.

'He'll need to earn his keep if he's going to eat like that,' Drake remarked.

'The boy has impeccable thespian instincts,' Laevo informed him, in Drone-on's most imperious tone. 'Such things are above price.'

'If you say so,' the landlord replied, laughing.

Terrel found that he was enjoying the actor's company — and that he was actually looking forward to the evening's performance. Then he wondered about the fate of his predecessor.

'What happened to Parga?' he asked, between mouthfuls.

'Drank himself to death,' Laevo replied. 'Literally.'

'Not on my beer,' Drake added hurriedly. 'I may have been responsible for a few headaches in my time, but no one's dropped dead on me yet.'

'True enough,' the actor agreed, hefting his mug. 'As poison goes, this isn't bad. The stuff Parga had taken to drinking must have pickled him from the inside. Towards the end he was half asleep all day, but give him his due, he never missed a prompt in the evening.'

'The show must go on,' Drake quoted.

'Exactly,' Laevo said, nodding. 'But unless his ghost turns up tonight, it'll be going on without him. Think you can live up to his heritage, boy?'

'I'll try,' Terrel replied.

As it turned out, Terrel had no time to become nervous about stepping into a dead man's shoes. The news of his ability to read and write had spread through the village, and a number of people came to him with requests for his talents. The function of scribe was usually fulfilled by the local underseer, but – as one of the villagers put it – this particular man was 'too full of himself to help the likes of us nowadays'. Terrel, on the other hand, was glad to help.

The reading came easily to him and, even though some of the letters were barely literate, he was able to decipher all but the most illegible. His writing – left-handed – was much more laborious, but the requests were usually for something short and simple, concerning mundane matters, and he coped well enough. Most of those who came to see him were surprised that he did not charge for his services, and when Drake learnt of this, he took the boy aside and insisted that he demand *something* in return. As a result Terrel received an assortment of gifts – mostly items of food – and even a few small coins. These represented the first wages he had earnt since his ill-fated alliance with Babak, and this time he felt good about it.

There was only one awkward moment during these transactions, and this was when Mograt made her way into the bar. Terrel knew instantly that Alyssa's spirit was not inside the cat, and was glad that no one suggested he repeat his trick of getting her to sing. The animal seemed to regard all humankind with a lofty disdain, and Terrel was sure that he'd be risking serious injury if he tried to coerce her into doing anything.

Terrel watched the audience arrive from his place behind decorated boards at the side of the stage. The 'best seats' Laevo had mentioned turned out to be those spaces on the open ground with the most direct view, while many of the villagers stood further back, hoping to avoid the collectors who moved purposefully among them.

Behind the carts, the actors were making final adjustments to their costumes, which transformed them from ordinary people into gaudy peacocks. The stage itself had now been enhanced by the addition of a large circular backdrop, which was mounted on a pivot so that it could be rotated by one of the actors or their assistants. The board had been painted with a vivid depiction of the night sky, and as it revolved the three visible moons could be seen in various phases – reflecting either the passage of time or the prevailing astrological influences.

The first half of the performance went smoothly, and Terrel only had to intervene twice – once when Sill missed a cue and had to be reminded to make his entrance, and later, when the Empress overdid her increasingly hysterical laughter and almost choked. Terrel was on hand to pass her his own cup of water, so that she could continue, thereby earning the gratitude of the actress and the approval of the entire cast.

'Quick thinking, lad,' Laevo commented as he came off stage at the interval. 'Well done.'

The play had been very successful so far, eliciting much laughter and only a little heckling — which Laevo dealt with easily enough. Terrel was surprised by how readily the villagers accepted the chance to mock their country's leaders. It seemed that the more grotesque the parodies became, the more popular they were.

After a short musical introduction, the second act began with one of Emperor Drone-on's soliloquies. Laevo, draped in a tattered robe and wearing a painted wooden crown, strode out onto the stage, pretended to trip and almost fell, making quite a performance of recovering his balance. By the time he'd finished, the audience were roaring with laughter. The Emperor's crown was now tipped sideways, so that it almost covered one of his eyes and this, together with the fact that his false beard had also been pulled to one side, made him look even more ridiculous.

'As Emperor, one must always be conscious of one's dignity,' he declared solemnly, staring out at his subjects. 'No, please, this is no laughing matter.'

This obvious contradiction of the truth provoked even more hilarity, and Laevo had to wait until the noise died down a little before continuing.

'Just think of all the things that weigh heavy on my shoulders.' He paused to pat the upper part of his robe, raising a cloud of carefully prepared dust. Looking surprised, he sneezed loudly before resuming his theme. 'There's the fate of the Empire, the future of an entire people, the leadership of all these clucking seers.'

That drew another round of applause.

'Why else would I have agreed to all the demands of my destiny?' the actor went on plaintively. 'Do you think I *wanted* to live in a luxurious palace, to eat only the finest foods? When I was forced to marry seven beautiful women, one after the other, to bed them all and produce children, did I complain? And let me remind you, this means I have seven mothers-in-law — which is no small consideration, I can tell you. It's enough to drive a man to drink.'

'Di' someone menshun drink?' Merry-Al asked in a drunken slur as he lurched onto the stage, his mirrored hat swaying dangerously. 'I never usually touch more 'an a drop meself, but . . .'

This was Creep-in's cue to enter with goblets of wine – into one of which he was to drop his poison, before handing it to his fellow seer – but before he could do so, a voice from the back of the audience interrupted the proceedings.

'This has gone far enough. I will not allow such vile slander to continue.'

Everyone turned to see who had spoken, then looked back at Laevo, waiting for his response. He did not disappoint them.

'Do I hear clucking?' he asked, cupping one hand to an ear.

'I am the duly appointed underseer of this village,' the heckler retorted angrily. 'I'll thank you to—'

'I'll not thank you,' Laevo cut in. 'Ill manners deserve no thanks.'

'*You* are the one with no manners,' the underseer claimed, stepping forward from the shadows. 'This play is a travesty!'

'Not true,' the actor replied innocently. 'It's a comedy. And, unless I am very much mistaken, a very fine one.' He spread his hands, imploring the audience to support him. This they did, with whistles, applause and cries of agreement – much to the underseer's disgust. He tried to speak again, but most of his words were drowned out by the spectators, with the aid of the musicians who had struck up again.

All Terrel had been able to hear was a promise that the authorities would learn of this outrage. This sounded ominous, but the actors were clearly used to such threats, and as soon as the underseer had departed in high dudgeon, they took up their parts again as if nothing had happened.

The audience, their appetites whetted by the interruption, were even more vociferous in their approval of the second act.

CHAPTER THIRTY-FIVE

Terrel found himself living in an uneasy balance between bouts of happiness and dread. Being on the road with the troupe was proving to be one of the most enjoyable experiences of his life, and it gave him a sense of belonging which not even his time on Ferrand's farm had been able to match. His peculiarities had made him an outsider there, even when he'd tried to think of himself as part of the family, and he had not been well suited to the work. With the actors, he was merely one eccentric among several others, and he took pleasure in becoming proficient in his job. If it had not been for the constant thought of what he was to do in Betancuria, he would have been content.

There were times when he could not help marvelling at the extraordinary changes in his life. So much had happened in such a short time, and he had experienced things he could not even have imagined when he was confined in the haven. His horizons had broadened, both literally and metaphorically – and it was hard to believe that he was to face even more drastic changes soon.

Whenever he talked to Alyssa and the ghosts, the threat

that hung over his entire world seemed plausible, as well as frightening. But when they were absent – and Terrel hadn't seen any of them for six days now – it all seemed so unlikely. There was no denying that the Floating Islands were rotating, but was it really possible that they were going to collide with the mainland after so many centuries of safely navigating the Movaghassi Ocean? It made no sense.

The idea that some force that had emerged inside the mines of Betancuria was responsible for all this also seemed far-fetched now. And the idea that Terrel could do anything about it was even more ludicrous. He was no hero. His bungled exploits over the past few months proved that – and no one had explained what he was supposed to do if and when he actually reached his goal. All in all, he found it easier not to think about it, to pretend he was just a member of a theatrical company – and the fact that they were travelling south meant nothing more than a different venue for their performance each night.

Although their progress was leisurely enough, Terrel knew that he could never have travelled so far if he had been left to his own devices. Laevo had not headed towards the coast, but had chosen instead the more arduous inland route. Terrel was grateful for this – in spite of Babak's earlier advice – not only because every day took him closer to Betancuria, but also because he had not wanted to risk the possibility of capture by the authorities in Tiscamanita. As it was, it seemed that he had got clean away. He had begun to feel safe – especially as the threats of the village underseer had come to nothing, just as Laevo had predicted. Only the future suggested danger now, and Terrel was more than happy to live in the present, and to let the possible demands of fate remain vague and remote.

*

The troupe's latest campsite was – as all the others had been – next to a tavern. Most of the actors liked a drink or two, and Laevo seemed to spend most of his spare time with a mug of beer in his hand. However, unlike the others, he always appeared to remain perfectly sober.

Apart from the obvious preferences of the actors, setting up next to a hostelry had advantages for both the company and the landlords. The inns were natural gathering places for the locals and for travellers, so news of the troupe's arrival always spread quickly – and the crowds they drew also needed refreshment. Laevo appeared to be on good terms with all the proprietors, and made the most of these financially beneficial arrangements. Terrel was often tempted to join in when he saw his companions enjoying a lively drinking session after a performance, but his resistance was stiffened not only by his own memories of what had happened in Tiscamanita, but also by the knowledge of what too much alcohol could do. Given the troupe's habits, it was easy to see how Parga had been able to drink himself to death.

The scream froze everyone on and around the stage. A moment later, everyone seemed to be moving at once. Terrel, who had been spreading grease on the backdrop's axle, limped round from behind the carts and found Sill lying on the ground. The young actor was white-faced and groaning, his right forearm clutched in his left hand.

'What happened?' Laevo demanded, striding into the midst of the gathering knot of players.

'He tripped on a loose board and fell off the stage,' one of them told him. 'He landed awkwardly.'

'I think I heard something snap,' someone else added anxiously.

Laevo knelt beside his colleague.

'Can you move your fingers?'

Sill tried, then grimaced in agony, beads of sweat standing out on his forehead.

'No,' he whispered. He was obviously frightened and in a lot of pain.

'It's all right,' Laevo reassured him. 'It's probably broken, but it doesn't look too bad. Do what you can for him, Lisa,' he added, looking up at the actress who nursed her colleagues' minor injuries and illnesses. 'Bric, go and fetch the local physician. Quick!'

The troupe's leader stood up and moved away, his expression changing from one of concern to a frown. Then his gaze fell on Terrel, and he beckoned the boy over to join him.

'Will he be all right?' Terrel asked, once they were out of earshot.

'I think so,' Laevo said. 'There's a good chance it's just a simple fracture. Sill's young. He'll mend quickly enough if it's set properly. Our more immediate problem is what to do about tonight's performance. There's no way he can go on, and none of the others know enough of the part.'

Terrel was not taken aback by this apparently callous attitude. He had been with the company long enough to have learnt – and accepted – that no matter what the circumstances were, the show must go on.

'I can prompt—' he began.

'No,' Laevo cut in. 'They'd still make a hash of it.'

'What if we went through the script and cut as much of the part as possible?' Terrel suggested. 'It'd be easier then.'

The actor shook his head.

'No,' he said. 'Wax is too important a character. I've got a better idea,' he went on. '*You* can take the part.'

'Me?' Terrel laughed nervously, not sure whether Laevo was joking or not.

'Why not? My guess is you're pretty much word perfect on the whole play by now, and you know Sill's cues and moves better than he does.'

'But—'

'We won't have time for a full run-through,' Laevo continued remorselessly, 'but you can adjust some of his marks if you need to. And between us we can handle the prompting on stage if necessary.' He was taking Terrel's agreement for granted, not even looking at the boy, and his inexhaustible self-confidence had reasserted itself. 'Let's go and see about getting the costume altered.'

Terrel followed helplessly in his wake.

Performances were always timed to begin about an hour before sunset, so that the second half was enhanced by the torches and coloured lamps set about the stage. This day was overcast, the sun no more than a pale disc behind clouds, and the afternoon was darker than usual.

Terrel stood at the side of the stage, shaking with nerves. It had been one thing to prompt actors from his hidden location; it was quite another to be out in public view. His hastily fitted costume was hot and uncomfortable, and even though he was glad the mask would hide his face, it made him feel claustrophobic, so he had left putting it on until the last moment. The extra complexities presented by its dual nature increased his anxiety. He had only had a short time to get used to the mechanism, and he knew that if he somehow managed to get it stuck halfway round, he would be trapped between the sets of eyeholes and would leave himself blind. Laevo had tried to convince the boy that this could not happen, but Terrel was not so sure. By comparison, the rest of his role seemed easy enough. He had convinced himself that he knew the script. Now all he had to do was remember it on stage.

There would be no unseen prompter to help him out if he failed.

As the time for 'curtain up' drew near – the stage had no curtain, but that was how the actors all referred to the start of their performance – Terrel glanced up at the sky. It seemed to him that dusk had come too soon, and now he saw the reason why. The sun, its normal brilliance dulled by the clouds, was no longer a perfect circle. He could see a 'bite' taken out of the orange disc, and knew that an eclipse was in progress.

A moment's thought established that it could only be the Dark Moon, and though he had seen similar sights many times before, Terrel could not escape a sense of foreboding. Even the clouds above seemed full of ominous patterns, dark ridges and shadowed steps that appeared unnatural. A slight breeze sprang up out of nowhere, and Terrel shivered.

'Drink this.'

Laevo had arrived at his side unnoticed, and now put a small glass of amber-coloured liquid into the boy's hand.

'It'll do you a power of good,' the actor added forcefully.

Terrel obediently swallowed the contents of the glass in one gulp, almost choking as the neat spirit exploded in his throat. Laevo laughed and slapped him on the back.

'If I tell you to break a leg, please don't take it literally,' he said, then glanced up at the sky. 'And don't worry about the eclipse. It'll just add an extra touch of drama to the play. Come on. You're going to be great.' He paused, watching his protégé's face. 'Not so nervous now, eh?'

Terrel nodded, astonished to find that it was true. He had immediately regretted his impulsive action, but as the drink warmed him from within, he felt his confidence grow.

'I'll do my best,' he said, surprised to find that his throat had recovered from the onslaught.

'Just follow your instincts,' Laevo advised. 'That way you can't go far wrong. Ready?'

'As ready as I'll ever be.'

The next few moments were agonizing. Now that the play had begun, and he had donned and adjusted his helmet-like mask, Terrel just wanted to get his first entrance over and done with. There was no going back now, and waiting for his cue was almost unbearable. He ran over his initial lines again, trying out different phrasing, and hoping his tongue wouldn't stumble over the words. It was only at the last moment, as he prepared to step on to the stage at last, that he thought of using the glamour to augment his natural voice. That way he could differentiate between the two sides of his character's nature by speaking their words in contrasting styles. Once the idea was born, instinct took over.

It was not long before Terrel forgot his nervousness and began to enjoy himself. He was feeling strangely light-headed now, but managed to remember all of his lines and moves – and coped with the mask as well. After a while, buoyed up by his colleagues' obvious appreciation of what he was doing, he became positively inspired, varying more than his voice when he switched from one persona to the other. As he changed his mask, he contrived to turn his body round too, making use of his own skewed physique to emphasize the dual nature of his role. When he was the hero, he presented his left side, the good one; when he was the dunce he displayed his deformed limbs. Laevo and the other actors soon caught on to what he was doing, and altered their own movements to facilitate his.

Off stage between scenes, Terrel found himself standing next to the Empress. He was intoxicated with success, anticipating his next entry eagerly, drinking in every murmur, every peal of laughter, every round of applause from the audience.

'You're a natural,' the actress whispered, smiling. 'Keep it up.'

Several lamps had been lit now, earlier than usual, because although the cloud cover appeared to be thinning, the Dark Moon was covering more and more of the sun as they sank together towards the southeastern horizon. When Terrel saw this, through the holes that gave him his restricted view of the world, he felt another twinge of foreboding – and the light-headedness, which he had assumed to be a consequence of the spirit he had drunk, became more marked. As he stepped on stage again he almost stumbled, and had to be given his cue twice before he spoke his next lines.

Don't get overconfident, he told himself, fighting to keep his concentration – but the earlier enjoyment had gone, and his anxiety returned.

From that moment on, things went from bad to worse. It was as though he were having to fight an internal battle, knowing what the script required of him and yet always tempted to do or say something else entirely. Anger bubbled up inside him for reasons he could not explain, and he kept seeing flashes of inexplicable colour, as if a second stage set and a second group of actors were being superimposed upon the real ones, one court upon another. It took all Terrel's resolve to fix his mind upon the play – and even then he knew that his performance had lost its earlier panache. Even his increasingly desperate attempts to use the glamour were less effective now.

His fellow actors were obviously aware of his difficulties and, even though they were confused about why the change had come about, they tried to help him as best they could. Even so, the audience grew restless, intensifying Terrel's sense of doom.

They were about three quarters of the way through the first act when the script called for the prince to turn from hero to idiot, and Terrel managed to swivel the mask successfully only to overbalance and fall to the boards. As he struggled to get up, his restricted view fell upon the stage backdrop, which was spinning round. This disorientated him further, especially when, as it finally came to rest, it showed the four-moon confluence – something that was not supposed to happen until the climax of the second act, when Wax became a hero for the final time and slew the traitorous Creep-in.

Then, as helping hands pulled him to his feet, Terrel saw two ghosts in the middle of the stage. Behind them, perched on one of the side boards, was a raven, its black eyes glittering.

'Come on, lad,' Laevo hissed in his ear, but the boy hardly heard him. Muzeni and Shahan were also speaking, unheard by anyone except Terrel, and he wanted to know what they were talking about.

What purpose would that serve? Muzeni asked. *He has enough to cope with already.*

I only thought— Shahan replied.

What purpose would what serve? Terrel asked silently, prompting the ghosts to look in his direction for the first time.

There you are! the seer exclaimed, looking relieved.

We've no time to explain, his companion added. *We know where you must go before you get to Betancuria. And you've got to go right now.*

But I'm in the middle of a performance! Terrel objected. He was already aware of strange looks from his fellow actors, and of murmurings of unrest in the audience. *I can't just*—

Just let go, Terrel! Shahan snapped. *You don't have any choice.*

I don't understand. What are you talking about?

There's no time to travel by conventional means, the raven told him. *You have to sleep, like me.*

Terrel felt his vision fading, slipping into a pit of darkness and fear.

But where are we going? he asked helplessly.

It was Shahan who answered, giving his answer in almost reverential tones.

We're going to Tindaya, he said.

CHAPTER THIRTY-SIX

The Empress Adina gazed at Jax with a mixture of admiration and puzzlement. Ever since Remi had put certain thoughts into her head, she had begun to wonder whether she actually understood her son. In all his fourteen years he had rarely done anything to surprise her, and yet now he seemed capable of almost any unexpected act. His mind, once so clear to her, had become an enigma.

Remi's accusations – mere suggestions, really – that the prince might have been responsible for the deaths of Shahan and Mirival, had preyed on Adina's mind during the last few days. She had longed to confront her son with the idea, to demand the truth, but had not been able to bring herself to do it. Instead she had skirted round the issue several times, hoping that he would volunteer the answer, or at least give her some clues. But he had proved evasive, using words with disconcerting skill and leaving her none the wiser.

The uncertainty annoyed the Empress. If Jax *had* commissioned the murders, it showed a commendable ruthlessness that Adina had previously had no reason to suspect.

But she could not quite believe it yet. On the other hand, if he was innocent, then who was responsible for having removed their foremost enemies? And would they strike again now that Lathan had declared his own treasonous views? Adina's own anger at the seer's treachery boiled up again, but she quelled it, telling herself that Lathan was unimportant, that he had no support – and that there were other, far more important issues to be decided. Now that her own claim to the title of Mentor was out in the open and was being discussed by the Seers' Council, she had to keep her mind clear – and, in particular, she had to be certain of her son.

That thought brought her back to another mystery, her pretext for visiting Jax this afternoon.

'Have you injured yourself recently?' she asked, her voice full of maternal concern.

The prince glanced up at her, but his expression remained impassive.

'No. Why?'

'There were bloodstains found on some of your sheets. Naturally I—'

'It's nothing,' Jax told her shortly. 'A scratch. I'm quite well.'

Adina nodded and smiled, but she had seen the flicker of fear in her son's eyes, the instantly quashed doubt. He might be an accomplished liar, but she had not been fooled.

'That's good,' she commented.

The rumour had reached her from the servants' quarters – where she had several spies – having originated in the palace laundry. She had suspected – and Jax's guilty reaction had confirmed – that it had not been her son's blood on the bed linen. The Empress did not know who the girl was, but she was confident she would find out in due course. In the meantime, it was yet another indication that the prince was capable of more subtlety and discretion than she had supposed. It was natural for one of his age and position to be curious about sex, but there were unwritten rules in such matters. The fact that Jax had managed to hide his conquest from even his own mother was evidence that he was aware of the most important of these rules, but Adina felt it was time to demonstrate that she was not to be trifled with.

'You will be careful of such *scratches*, won't you,' she said. 'Sometimes they can have unfortunate consequences.'

'What are you talking about?' He had tried to sound indifferent, but she caught the edge in his voice and knew that he understood her meaning.

'You are a prince,' she told him, discarding all pretence. 'In due course you will be Emperor. Your marriages will be carefully selected. When the auguries are complete, the next Emperor will be chosen from among your children. At that time it would be best if there are no *complications* in your past that might confuse the prophecy.'

The prince's face had darkened as she spoke, but he was not yet willing to admit defeat.

'If the recent auguries are right,' he remarked defiantly, 'there won't even *be* an Empire soon, so we won't need any more Emperors, will we?'

'That's nonsense, and you know it,' she retorted angrily. 'Do not think to deny your destiny. You are the Guardian, and together we—'

The Empress broke off abruptly, aware that her son was no longer paying her the slightest attention. After a few moments his blank expression changed to a frown, then to a snarl of rage. And then, without offering any explanation for his insolence, Jax leapt to his feet and stormed out of the chamber.

Taken aback by this flagrant display of disrespect, Adina could only stare at the empty doorway. She stood quite still, until – as her shock turned to fury – she sensed a change in the room. The light was growing dim with unnatural haste.

The Empress strode over to the open window and looked out. And saw a great darkness rushing towards her.

Kamin was usually among the most active of men, but today an almost debilitating lethargy had overtaken him, making even the smallest task seem like an enormous effort. For the past hour he had been sitting motionless at his desk, staring – unseeing – at a letter held in his hand. But his thoughts were not still. They had ranged over recent events, over ancient history, over the suffocating intricacies of court politics and the various perils now facing the Empire. His problems all seemed insoluble, and it was as much as he could do to stop himself from falling into a bottomless well of self-pity.

It had been the latest meeting of the Seers' Council that had brought so many matters to a head. The gathering had taken place a few days ago, but the repercussions of what had happened there were resounding still. It had been a complete fiasco from the start.

The first item on the agenda had been the report from Marshal Karuna, on his return from Betancuria. Kamin had chosen to relay this to his fellow seers himself, but had not been prepared for the violent reaction it had provoked. It was true that the commander's description of the situation had painted a bleak and frightening picture, even though it had been couched in deliberately unemotional language, but Kamin did not think it had warranted such an extreme response. The faction – which had once been composed only of the most eccentric elements in the council – who wanted to do something about the 'monster' had now grown in size and vehemence. The news of the recent tornadoes that had afflicted Vadanis – including the one that had done so much damage in Makhaya itself a few days earlier – had only increased the pressure for action. Colleagues whom Kamin had previously regarded as both sane and reasonable were now demanding that steps be taken – and they were making outrageous claims about the consequences should these attempts fail. Specific suggestions as to *how* to counteract such bizarre and elusive forces were not so plentiful, but Kamin knew that unless he did *something*, he would soon face a wholesale revolt. The army had been put on stand-by, with some units already sent to the mining district – even though no one knew what they were supposed to do when they got there – and Commissioner Huban had been instructed to keep Makhaya informed of any developments. Kamin had wondered whether to take Jax to Betancuria, but the prince still showed little interest in or understanding of their predicament, and only seemed concerned with his own selfish desires. If he really *was* the Guardian – and Kamin had begun to doubt even that recently – he was showing no sign of living up to his supposed destiny.

That thought had brought the Chief Seer back to the next disaster at the council. Ignoring all the advice he had been given, Lathan had spoken up about his theory concerning Jax's twin. His outburst had stunned the assembly, but Kamin had seen signs of both outright disagreement and surreptitious support on the faces of various colleagues. However, no one had had the opportunity to express their views because, almost as soon as Lathan had concluded his impassioned plea, the council had been distracted by the late arrival of Fauria – with the Empress.

The outrage Kamin had felt at this monstrous intrusion had been mirrored by most of the seers, but Adina had been immune to their antagonism. It didn't matter to her that she was the first woman ever to set foot inside the venerable chamber, and she had stared about defiantly as Fauria, his true colours revealed, had listed her claims to the title of Mentor. Many of his arguments were spurious, but some points had won grudging acceptance, and at the end of this second sensational development, the council had been in uproar. It had taken the determined intervention of Kamin himself to restore order, and in the face of an impossible situation, his only solution had been to delay any decision. The Empress had accepted – ungraciously – that the council needed time to debate her claim, but now time was rapidly running out, and they were no nearer a conclusion. Kamin no longer coveted the title she sought, and could not understand Adina's motives, but he was in no doubt that she was *not* the true Mentor. His problem – and that of those who agreed with him – was deciding how to break this news to the Empress.

There was only one aspect of Adina's invasion of the council chamber that gave Kamin any reason to be thankful. Because of the timing of her entrance, both she and Fauria had not heard about Lathan's announcement until much later. The consequences of a confrontation between the Empress and the seer did not bear thinking about, and that at least had been avoided. As it was, when Adina did finally learn of Lathan's arguments, she had predictably denounced him as a traitor. However, by that time Lathan had vanished from sight – and had not been seen since. Not even his chamberlain had any idea where he was. There were even some rumours circulating that he was dead, that he had met the same fate as Shahan and Mirival – and even though he did not want to believe this,

Kamin could not help wondering if the gossipmongers had got it right for once.

The Chief Seer shook his head, as if trying to clear it, and made himself focus on the letter he still held in his hand. Compared to his other problems, the matter reported by the writer – a village underseer from the Tetico Province – seemed trivial. That a group of travelling players sought to mock the Imperial Court hardly seemed surprising in such troubled times – and even the information that Kamin himself had been depicted in a distinctly unflattering light gave him no great cause for concern. Human nature being what it was, he imagined that such things were probably quite common.

Kamin crushed the letter in his hand, and was about to throw it into a wastebasket when the door of his study was thrown open and Jax thundered into the room. There was a wild look in his eyes that alarmed the seer.

'You'd better do something about this!' the prince declared.

'About what?' Kamin responded calmly, trying to moderate the intruder's bluster.

'There's a bunch of actors mocking me,' the boy exclaimed. 'And you, and my mother, even the Emperor. It's treason!'

The seer glanced at the crumpled letter in his fist, wondering what strange quirk of fate had brought the prince to him at that precise moment. He knew that coincidences were a fact of life – but he had learnt not to trust them.

'Slander, perhaps,' he replied mildly. 'But hardly treason.'

'It's got to be stopped!' Jax shouted. 'I want them arrested and punished. I *order* you to do it.'

Kamin ignored this latest outburst.

'How do you know of these players?' he asked.

That stopped the prince in his tracks. For the first time he appeared to think before he spoke, and Kamin could not help wondering what was going on inside that hot head.

In fact, Jax was reliving the first moments of his latest encounter with his twin – an encounter that was still going on. The link had been established suddenly, for reasons Jax could not fathom, but as soon as he had realized what was happening he'd tried to intervene. He had been furious at the mockery of himself, unable to believe that it was anything other than a deliberate insult on Terrel's part, but he was calmer now. His rage had lessened his ability to influence his twin – whose brain was not nearly as responsive as it had been when he'd been hopelessly drunk – and Terrel had managed to escape from the enchanter's grip. After that, Jax had only been able to watch impotently as ignorant peasants laughed at the vile depiction of the imperial prince. Eventually, unable to stomach it any more, he had decided to appeal to other, more worldly powers for help – without waiting to consider the questions he was bound to be asked.

'I have my sources,' he replied. 'That's not the point. What are you going to do about it?'

'Do your sources know where these actors are?' Kamin asked.

'No,' Jax admitted, sullen now. He would not look at the seer, and Kamin got the feeling that the prince's attention was elsewhere.

'We're all public figures. Ridicule, however unpleasant, is simply—' He fell silent, aware that the boy was no longer listening to him. The prince's eyes were blank, their pupils dilated to such an extent that they were like twin reflections of the Dark Moon. 'Are you all right, Jax?'

There was no response.

The silence around them grew eerie, and Kamin realized that the room had become unnaturally dark. That triggered another unwelcome memory, about a recent discussion with a group of his colleagues. Some of them were claiming that a 'total' eclipse of the sun was imminent. This prediction was controversial, because such a thing had never before been seen on Nydus. Each of the four moons was too small to blot out the sun entirely, given the relative distances between them and the planet. But now, so the renegade secrs claimed, the Dark Moon's increase in size would make the phenomenon possible – if only within a narrow band stretching across the planet's surface. What was more, it was predicted that this band would fall upon Vadanis – and over Makhaya itself. Kamin had not had time to check the calculations himself, but the prospect had raised in him – as it had done for all the astrologers – a mixture of scientific excitement and superstitious awe. Partial eclipses were common, and most went almost unnoticed, but the idea that total darkness could fall during daytime, even for a few short moments, was incredible. That it should happen in Makhaya defied belief. It was yet another sinister coincidence. Even so, it was a measure of Kamin's preoccupation that he should have forgotten it was supposed to happen that very afternoon.

Jax had still not moved or spoken, but he did not seem to be in any distress, so Kamin allowed himself to indulge his curiosity. He went to the window, pushed the shutters further back – and saw the last diamond-bright remnant of the sun flicker out. The city below him became a black wilderness, without substance or depth. The sky went dark, blossoming with stars, and the Dark Moon was surrounded by a beautiful, shifting halo of light. The silence was total. No voice broke the spell, no bird sang. Even the wind had died away to nothing as the world held its breath.

And then, as quickly as it had arrived, the shadow withdrew. The sun edged back into view, blinding even in its first re-emergence, and Kamin felt his heart thumping inside his chest. He had been amazed – and strangely moved – by what he had just witnessed. He could explain it rationally in terms of subtended angles and elliptical orbits, but there had been something primitive, almost supernatural, about those few moments of darkness that went beyond mere science.

Belatedly remembering his visitor, Kamin turned back, wondering if it had been the eclipse that had affected Jax, and expecting to see that he had recovered.

But the prince had not moved, and was still caught in his strange trance.

CHAPTER THIRTY-SEVEN

Terrel had experienced a strange premonition when the ghosts had told him where he was going – and the unnatural darkness that followed only intensified his dread.

He could see nothing, feel nothing, within the void that had claimed him, but there were voices – distorted and weak, but still familiar.

Go to the centre.

The Code speaks of a talisman, an amulet. You must find it.

He wanted to ask how he would recognize this talisman, but he had no tongue, no voice.

Not much time . . .

He wondered why no one else had ever found the amulet. Every fragment of the ancient temple, every particle of the sacred mountain itself, had been examined, catalogued. Surely such an important artefact could not have been missed.

This is your only chance. It's been hidden until now.

Go to the centre.

Don't . . .

The voices faded, and he was left with his own silence, still blind, and utterly alone.

Lathan had been ill-prepared for his abrupt departure from Makhaya – and even less ready for a trip into the mountains. Even so, he knew that the journey was necessary, and had pressed ahead regardless. As a result, he was tired, cold and hungry by the time he reached the summit of Tindaya and made his way among the familiar ruins. He also had no idea what would happen next, but knew that he had arrived just in time. When the eclipse had begun, his decision had seemed justified. At least part of his revised interpretation of the Intempest Stone made sense now.

He climbed to the highest point of the scattered ruins, ignoring the keen wind that sliced through his thin city clothes, and sat down to wait. From his perch he could see almost all that was left of the 'dark star' mosaic, the curious emblem that had once been surrounded by a floor maze of staggering complexity. It was broken and partly hidden by debris now, but in his mind's eye Lathan could see the design, imagining pilgrims processing towards the heart of the five-pointed star. He would have given anything to have known the temple in its heyday. He was sure there was nothing in Vadanis now that could stand comparison with the glory of that lost time, but whatever disaster had reduced it to rubble had also swept away any chance of knowing what it had really been like. All that was left were fragments of stone and the enigmatic clues hidden within the Code. And now it seemed almost certain that the islands would suffer another catastrophe before many of these had even been deciphered.

Lathan waited, hugging himself to preserve the last

shreds of his body's warmth, as the Dark Moon slid across the falling sun.

As the world reassembled itself around Terrel, he saw that he was no longer on stage, but on the top of a great mountain that could only be Tindaya. The wind whispered in the ruins as the false dusk deepened the shadows of the place.

Terrel looked around, unable to believe his eyes and yet unable to doubt them either. This was real – and he *was* there. He had no idea how long the journey had taken – it had seemed no more than a few moments – but somehow in that time he had travelled over a hundred miles. During the voyage his mask had vanished, so that he was able to see clearly now, but the fading light made it difficult for him to make out many details. There was no sign of the ghosts, or the raven, and he was wondering about the instructions they had given him when he was distracted by a sudden cry.

'Aieee! Are you demon or guide?'

Terrel glanced round, and saw a man getting to his feet at the uppermost point of the ruins, only a few paces away. As the boy looked at him, the stranger gasped again.

'You! I knew it!'

There was a crazed excitement on the man's face now. He had obviously recognized Terrel, even though the boy was sure they'd never met before. He began to wonder if his fellow mountaineer was a lunatic, and was about to speak when the stranger's expression changed again.

'Am I too late?' he cried. 'Are you really dead?'

Terrel was about to deny this mad accusation when he caught a glimpse of his own hand. It was transparent and faintly luminous – just like a ghost's. He stared at his fingers in horror, unable to think logically, panic clawing at his chest.

Eventually he became aware that his companion was speaking again, but only caught the last part of what he said.

'. . . not much time. Look! It's coming.'

The echo of the ghosts' words brought Terrel back to some degree of sanity as he turned to see what the stranger was pointing at. A great shadow was rushing across the land below him, beginning to climb the slopes of Mount Tindaya itself. In the sky above, the eclipse was almost complete – and Terrel knew that this marked the crucial time. The Dark Moon was going to devour the sun, leaving the world below in darkness, and whether he was dead, whether he was a ghost, or whether this was just a waking dream, did not matter. He was there for a reason.

The clouds that had masked the heavens all afternoon finally cleared, and gave him a sudden glimpse of the drama unfolding above. The sun was almost totally obscured now, and it appeared briefly as a necklace of fiery beads that quickly died away until the last bead was swallowed by the moon. The wings of night swept over the sky, and Terrel recalled the ominous words from Muzeni's journal. *Black wings stooped in a hunter's silent flight, black eyes fixed upon her target, talons outstretched* . . . The Dark Moon was indeed like a giant bird of prey – and on this occasion her quarry had been the sun itself. And the hunt was over.

The vast shadow had engulfed the entire mountain now, moving with mind-numbing speed, and it seemed as though the air itself had turned black. The temperature dropped even more, and the strange gusts of wind that had preceded the shadow's approach died away. Tindaya became as silent as the grave.

Terrel stared in awe at the pearly-white halo that now spread out in graceful curves around the invisible mass of the Dark Moon. He had never seen anything quite so beautiful. The rest of the sky was not black, as he had first thought, but deep purple, and sprinkled with stars. Along the far horizon there were streaks of orange and grey among the clouds, but from where Terrel stood the darkness was unchallenged. He knew, beyond any doubt, that there had never been an eclipse like this before.

A moment later he caught his breath at the sight of a new wonder. Far away, across the darkened valley below him, an earthbound star sprang into life. And then another. Turning round, he saw that there were five in all, equally spaced, each shining like a beacon atop one of the lesser mountains that surrounded Tindaya. Their silvery light added another element of magic to the scene – and then reality shifted again. Terrel blinked, unable to take in what was happening.

Just as there had seemed to be two overlapping courts when he'd been on stage, now there was a second nether-realm covering the mountain. In what his mind still insisted was the real world, the eclipse held sway, mimicking night. In the second, it was already true night. And in this second world another Dark Moon was rising, from the opposite horizon to its twin, blotting out stars and heading towards the other three moons – and towards the conjunction. It was the same scene Terrel had seen painted on the stage backdrop, and he felt as though he was travelling back in time to the night of his birth. He was suddenly haunted by the past, but the present gave him no chance to dwell on what was gone.

Five beams of light sped towards him from the beacons, converging in unison until they met at a point only a few paces from where he stood. They collided in a silent explosion, shattering into a million firefly points of radiance, each glittering like the facet of some impossible jewel as they spread out into a shifting, sinuous pattern. It was a beautiful and entrancing sight, but Terrel had no idea what it meant. He was aware now of time passing, of the priceless moments of this double night slipping away – and knew that he was no closer to his goal.

In desperation, he turned to look at the stranger, hoping for some advice, but the man was rooted to the spot, spellbound by the whirling tracery of sparks – and Terrel knew he would get no help there. He glanced back at the mesmerizing lights – then gasped as he saw that in the second world there were other people on the mountaintop.

Two young men, one thin and twisted, the other pale but solidly built, were confronting each other on the far side of the ruins. They seemed to be arguing, but Terrel could not hear what they said. Above them, a grey bird swooped and circled.

Straining his eyes against the gloom and the distraction of the intervening sparks, Terrel saw that the newcomers were – like him – transparent, shadow-ghosts in a shadow world. The smaller of the pair was obviously crippled and – as Terrel continued to study him – he realized with a shudder of unease that the man's right arm and leg were deformed. He was taller and much older than Terrel, but otherwise the resemblance was uncanny. The bulkier of the two had a perfectly sound body. Although Terrel had no idea who he was, he could not look at him without feeling a sense of cold fear. A venomous malevolence seemed to emanate from him, and when Terrel saw the sword in his hand he tried to shout out a warning. His words came out in a half-strangled yelp, and the two adversaries paid no attention. The boy forced himself into action, stumbling forward towards the ill-matched pair, knowing that

he ought to intervene. However, before he had gone more
than a few paces, he was knocked to the ground by the
loudest noise he had ever heard.

The vast wordless rumbling filled the sky, shook the
mountain, and threatened to crush the boy's puny frame.
He had no idea where the sound was coming from, nor
what it presaged. In some ways it was more of a vibration
than a noise, felt rather than heard, but it left him deafened and breathless nonetheless. A second, less cavernous
note had now been added to the roar, as if in answer to the
first, and the monumental dialogue ground every thought
into dust. Contradictory emotions, inexplicable in both
their meaning and their intensity, flooded through Terrel.
He was held captive by that great avalanche of sound, but
inside he trembled and cried, laughed and raged, without
knowing why.

And then, as suddenly as it had begun, it stopped. The
silence sang in his ears and he gulped the cold mountain
air, hoping to restore some tiny portion of his equilib-
rium. A short distance away, the stranger who had been
there when Terrel arrived now lay on the ground. The
boy's first thought was that he was dead, but then he saw
the man's chest rise and fall, and assumed that he had
fainted.

The next thing he noticed, as his wits slowly recovered
and he got to his feet, was that the shimmering lights had
frozen into a single convoluted pattern in the air above the
ruins. At its centre, a tiny new star, brighter than all the
rest, had begun to glow. He was still staring at this latest
marvel when he saw that the two young men were gazing
at him.

Go to the centre.

The thought leapt into Terrel's mind, and he cursed his
own stupidity. The star was the amulet he sought – but it

would not be there for long. Unless he reached the talisman in the next few moments . . .

He hurled himself forward over the tumbled stones, heedless of his own safety, until he reached the edge of the pattern of light. There he felt the air shiver, and he was thrown backwards. So violent was the repulsing force that he fell and landed heavily on his back, but he picked himself up again quickly, knowing that he had no option but to try again. As he rose, he glimpsed a fragment of mosaic beneath his feet, and felt a tug of memory. A moment later he remembered another ruin – and the design he had seen there upon that ancient floor.

He knew now what he had to do, but was also aware that time was running out. He found the entrance easily enough, now that he knew what to look for, and stepped into the maze, glancing first at the floor, then at the walls of light. He forced himself to walk, not run, because the ceremony demanded a certain reverence and haste would be counterproductive. Even so, as he limped on and on, and seemed to get no closer to his target, he began to grow fearful. The total eclipse must end soon, and his chance – his only chance – would be gone. He could already sense the light returning to some of the distant mountains.

His route had doubled back on itself so many times that he began to despair of ever reaching the centre, suspecting that he would soon come to a dead end and have to retrace his steps and start again. But then, just as all seemed to be lost, he sensed that he was almost there. Two more turns, two more thankful steps – and the star was within his reach.

It floated in the air before him, an amulet of pure energy, and yet he hesitated, unable to touch such dazzling beauty.

Take it!

The instruction formed in Terrel's head, not heard but understood. There was no denying that demand.

Trembling, he leant forward to obey, stretching out his good arm until he was able to enfold the miniature sun in his fingers. A shudder ran through him as his hand shone blood red, lit from within, but he felt no pain. He had his prize.

Looking up, he saw the crippled young man smiling at him with diamond bright eyes. Behind him his malevolent companion was approaching, his face contorted with fury, his sword raised in readiness. Terrel cried out a warning as the death blow was about to fall, but his voice was lost in the void. Then the shadow of the Dark Moon passed by. As the darkness departed, so too did the second world – taking with it the two young men, the pattern of stars and the four illusory moons.

Terrel cried out again, even though he knew it would do no good.

It was more than a premonition now. The dread was all too real. Terrel was sure he had just witnessed his own death.

CHAPTER THIRTY-EIGHT

Terrel woke, remembering. His experience on Tindaya already had the elusive unreality of a dream, and his mind, unable to cope, tried to reject it as a phantasm, an hallucination. All that was left, all that was true and substantial, was the certainty inside him. That had come just before the dream had ended — and it shook him still. An earthquake was coming, an earthquake more violent and powerful than any he had known before.

He opened his eyes to darkness, aware only of the fear around him, of the silence. Finding his voice, he tried to shout a warning.

'Take cover. There's an earthquake coming.' The words emerged as a croak, rasping in his throat. He felt the terror shift around him, but no one responded to his cry. The trembling within him receded a little, and his conviction wavered.

'An earthquake,' he repeated, but the urgency was gone from his voice.

The darkness lifted as the first incandescent bead peered round the edge of the Dark Moon, shining on the frightened faces of the people below. In a day that was suddenly bright, Terrel realized that he was back on the stage, lying on the boards. His discarded mask lay beside him. He was surrounded by his fellow actors, but none of them was paying him any attention. Further away, the audience was still there, although they were not concerned with the abandoned play. Almost every face was turned towards the sky.

As the sun grew to a blinding brilliance once more, people began to look down again. There was nervous laughter as conversations resumed; words of relief, of released tension. The sun was returning, and they had all survived. The earthquake did not come, and Terrel returned to his dream memories.

Looking at his left hand, he saw the knuckles white with tension, the skin taut over his still clenched fist. He slowly uncurled his cramped fingers and stared, his heart sinking. His hand was empty. There was nothing to show where the star had been, not even any mark to show that he had clasped its fragile radiance. All that was left were four red curves where his nails had dug into the skin of his palm. The talisman was lost.

A scream broke his dismal train of thought.

'Look at his eyes!' The Empress, her face pale under the make-up, was staring at him in horror, and others turned to follow her gaze. The air filled with gasps and muttered oaths.

Terrel blinked, realizing that with all that had happened he had let the glamour slip. He tried to use it now, but found the effort almost too much for his waning spirit and gave up. It was too late. They had all seen the true colour of his eyes.

'An enchanter!' one of the other actresses whispered. 'We've had an enchanter among us.' There was anger in her voice as well as fear.

'No,' Terrel protested. 'I'm not the enchanter. He – '
He broke off, knowing it would be impossible to explain –
not sure that he understood it himself.

'An evil one is twice . . .' someone hissed, leaving the
proverb unfinished.

'Did *he* do this?' another actor asked, waving a hand at
the sky. 'We should—'

'Enough!' Laevo commanded, as he came to kneel beside
the boy.

Their leader's decree silenced the company, though the
air of menace remained. The expression on Laevo's face
was calm, but Terrel could sense that he too was afraid.

'What happened?' the actor asked quietly.

'It was an eclipse—'

'Not that,' Laevo cut in. 'With you, I mean.'

'I don't know,' Terrel answered truthfully. He had no
intention of trying to describe his fantastical exploits.

'You fainted,' the actor told him. 'We managed to get
your mask off, but then everything went dark and . . . The
next thing I know, you're raving about an earthquake.' He
spread his hands in an eloquent gesture of bewilderment.
'Are you ill?'

'No.'

'But you hold your own secrets? Your eyes . . .'

They're the least of it, Terrel thought, wondering
what – if anything – to tell his friend.

'I'm sorry,' he said eventually. 'I'm not an enchanter,
but people jump to conclusions, so I usually keep them
hidden. I didn't mean to deceive you.'

Laevo considered this. He did not appear unsympa-
thetic, but Terrel knew that the troupe's leader had no
choice. One way or another, the boy's time with the company was over.

'I'll go,' he said, swamped by a wave of sadness.

'That would be best,' Laevo replied. He sounded relieved. 'I'll be sorry to lose your talents.'

'But not my secrets,' Terrel responded quietly.

Terrel trudged along the moonlit track, trying to make sense of this latest episode in his increasingly chaotic life. Somewhere at the back of his mind, he knew that he ought to be on the lookout for somewhere to sleep, but for the moment such practical matters seemed unimportant. He was still trying to fathom the meaning of his fleeting visit to Tindaya. Had he actually been there? Had what he'd witnessed been real? Or had the whole experience been some kind of insane hallucination, the product of his delusions? And if it *had* been real, what did it all mean? Had he seen into the past, or the future? What would be the consequences of his failure to capture the amulet? Who were the strangers he had seen, and where had the overwhelming burst of noise come from? The list of questions was endless, and he wished that Alyssa and the ghosts would come to him so that he could at least discuss it with them.

It had taken Terrel only a short time to gather his few belongings together, and he had slipped away as quietly as possible. He had restored the glamour that disguised his eyes, and – once he had escaped from the suspicious and resentful glances of his former colleagues – the rest had been easy. The entire village had still been in turmoil following the terror of the unprecedented eclipse, and none of the locals had paid him any heed. By the time the sun had set – in a conventional manner, this time – Terrel was out in open countryside, alone again.

He walked on long into the night, ignoring the weariness of his limbs, wanting only to be on the move. Part of him wished he could reach Betancuria immediately and face what was to come, no matter what the consequences might be. He just wanted to get it over with. Yet such fatalism sat uneasily beside his other thoughts. He was no longer sure that it was actually worth trying to get to the mining district. Could he achieve anything without the talisman – which was presumably the reason why the ghosts had insisted that he go to Tindaya first? He was still puzzling over this latest unanswered question when something black and menacing flew past his head. Terrel flinched, thinking of the Dark Moon's other incarnation, but then realized that this visitor was not a bird of prey.

Will you please stop! Alyssa snapped irritably. *This creature isn't equipped for flying at night, and it's all I can do to stop myself crashing into things or falling asleep in midair.*

Terrel came to a halt and sat down on the ground, suddenly very tired. The raven landed nearby and strutted closer.

Have you got it?

No, Terrel answered. Alyssa's arrival had lifted his spirits briefly, but her question plunged him into misery once more. *I thought I had, but it's gone.*

The feathers on the bird's throat bristled, but she said nothing.

I don't know what went wrong, he added, feeling the need to justify his failure.

Tell me everything that happened, from the beginning.

Terrel did as he was told. Because he had no idea what Alyssa might find significant, he tried to remember every detail. She was particularly interested in the thunderous noise, and he told her everything he could about it, including the emotions he had felt. And then, when he told her that he didn't know what else to say, she persisted.

What were the dominant feelings?

Calm, he replied after a few moments' thought. *An immense calm on one side. Rage and fear on the other.*

There were two sides? Alyssa queried. *Do you mean like a conversation?*

I suppose so, he replied doubtfully.

Can you put what the two sides were saying into words?

Terrel shook his head. He didn't even know where to begin.

Try.

It's impossible.

Let your mind hear it again, Alyssa suggested. *Tell me what you feel. Don't think. Just let yourself react instinctively.*

Terrel was exhausted now, but he knew he'd get no peace until he at least tried to do as she asked. He let his mind slip back, reliving the moment when the gigantic sound had stopped him in his tracks.

It's all to do with time, he ventured at last. *Patience and waiting on one side, haste and denial on the other. But it's all mixed up. It doesn't make any sense.*

He could tell that Alyssa was not satisfied, but she apparently realized that he could not tell her any more, and moved on. She wanted to know about the appearance of the shadow-ghosts, the two young men whose conflict had come to a head just as the eclipse ended. Remembering that moment shook Terrel to the core.

I think one of them was me, he said, putting his suspicion into words at last.

It sounds as though they were made-up, Alyssa remarked thoughtfully.

Made-up? You mean they weren't real?

No ghosts are real in this world, she replied.

But what was the point? What were they supposed to mean?

I've no idea.

His hopes dashed, Terrel was silent for a while.

Do you think Muzeni or Shahan might be able to tell us? he asked eventually.

Perhaps, Alyssa replied, *but I don't think we'll be seeing them for a while.*

Why not?

It was Alyssa's turn to hesitate.

The effort involved in transporting your spirit was considerable, she said finally. *I think, in some sense, they had to break their own rules in order to do it.*

That gave Terrel pause for thought. If the ghosts had believed his visit to Tindaya was so important that they were prepared to ignore the laws of their own world to get him there, then the fact that he had not achieved his objective was even more damning.

They'll help us as soon as they're able, Alyssa added. *In the meantime, we'd better make sure you get to Betancuria as quickly as possible. But right now I need to sleep, and so do you.*

'Don't go,' Terrel implored out loud, but it was already too late. The raven had taken wing, and was soon no more than a darker speck in the shadows of the night.

Too downcast even to look for a more comfortable bed, Terrel curled up where he was and fell asleep.

Alone now in his moonlit eyrie, Lathan also slept.

Terrel dreamt of the crystal city. This time it was surrounded by glowing lines of light, billions of tiny stars weaving patterns in the abyss. Guided by unseen forces, they formed a glowing shield, a protective maze around the labyrinth. The raven, the bird that so many people considered a creature of ill omen, was inside, trapped and waiting. Helpless. Terrel wondered why, even in his dreams, he never saw Alyssa's own face.

He went underground, into the darkness of the permanent eclipse of stone — where there was no light, no warmth, but where the invisible patterns still held sway. He walked, unwilling, to the heart of the dark star, felt it drain him of all hope, all purpose.

Patience or haste? Calm or rage?

Time passed, and he could not tell whether it was the silence or the thunder of his own heartbeat that roared in his ears.

The crimson sea came next, of course, as full of hate and pain as always, but for once he was able to ignore it. It could not touch him, even with fear. His course was set, and in that decision came peace — of a sort.

When Terrel awoke, he rose and set his feet towards the south again. Each step took him closer to Betancuria.

PART THREE

BETANCURIA

CHAPTER THIRTY-NINE

'The alignments are not a matter for debate, Captain,' Kamin said. 'They must be precise.'

'I told him this, Seer,' the acolyte said, his exasperation evident.

'But we've reached solid rock,' the soldier protested. 'There's no way of telling how big a boulder is down there. All I know is we can't drive the stake any lower without excavating the entire area.'

All three men knew that this was impossible, given the project's time constraints. Conflict was inevitable when seers tried to work with the military, and this argument was only the latest sign of tensions running high. It was an uneasy partnership. Because Marshal Karuna had ordered his men to defer to the Chief Seer in this matter, Kamin – like it or not – was the ultimate arbitrator of all disputes.

'Very well. Saw the top from the pole until it's the exact height required,' Kamin decreed.

Under any other circumstances, such a desecration of the intricately carved collimation rods would have been unthinkable. As it was, the acolyte was obviously still shocked by Kamin's decision.

'Yes, Seer.' The soldier strode away to carry out his orders, a look of relief on his face.

Thinking better of trying to argue with his superior, the acolyte turned and hurried after him, intent on making sure that the job was done properly. Kamin watched them go, wondering whether they'd make it through the day without one of these petty squabbles turning to violence.

There had been times during the last few days when Kamin had found it hard to believe what was happening. The crisis they faced was indeed both incredible and terrifying, but the suspicion that he had allowed the court's response to spiral out of control was something that made him feel distinctly uneasy. The very fact that he was now ensconced in Betancuria, together with almost all of his fellow seers and most of the Imperial Court, was remarkable in itself; the circumstances that had brought them there were even more bizarre. However, now that the crucial time was almost upon them, Kamin was surprised to find that he was beginning to feel almost hopeful. He had initially been reluctant to involve himself in what he privately regarded as a harebrained scheme, but he had gradually been convinced of its political necessity. From that moment on, his own role had been central to the whole exercise, until – with just one day to go – he was so busy that he barely had time to dwell on the possible consequences of what they were doing. He reflected ruefully that this was probably for the best.

In a rare moment of respite between consultations, it occurred to the Chief Seer that exactly one median month had passed since the total eclipse had spread its sinister pall across the land. That had been the last astronomical event of any significance; the next would take place tomorrow. Not only would the Amber and Red Moons be full then – which was enough to mark the night as special for most people – but the Dark Moon would also be at its time of maximum influence. There would be no visible evidence of this, of course; the Dark Moon looked exactly the same whether it was full, new, or anything in between. However, although only the initiated and the most astute observers would realize it, the fact that the sky shadow would be the third moon to reach its point of greatest potency made the chosen date far and away the most propitious moment possible. The only drawback was the relative weakness of the White Moon, which would be waning and only three days from being new. Two of its spheres of influence were destiny – which was obviously all too relevant – and logic. If the people of the Empire had ever had the need of logic it was now! They would just have to try and work around the waning influence.

Kamin surveyed the site – which had itself been chosen only after lengthy astrological consultations – for perhaps the hundredth time. It was a shambles, and looked more like a building site than a ceremonial arena. It was hard to believe that by the next evening all would be ready, but he knew that everyone would work through the night if necessary. At such times, sleep was a minor consideration.

Most of the current activity was taking place in a kind of man-made amphitheatre which lay at the edge of the mine workings. The land had not been deliberately sculpted for this purpose – it was a chance configuration of waste materials from some of the older excavations – but its design was convenient. Kamin wanted as many people as possible to witness the ritual, and the size of the arena meant that several hundred spectators would get a good view. Part of the audience would be made up of travellers and specially invited guests from all over Vadanis – people who would carry reports of the event back to their homes. This was important, because the ceremony itself was really only for the benefit of the population at large. All these elaborate preparations were not strictly necessary. The astrological readings and subsequent prophecy could have been done quietly by a few seers, but on this occasion it was essential to put on a show.

The reasons for this lay in the events of the previous month. It had been a time marked by unprecedented civil unrest in the Empire, and as the rumours generated by the rotation of the islands — rumours which the total eclipse had intensified — had grown to epidemic proportions, the people of Vadanis had been assailed by confusion and mutual suspicion. Underseers everywhere had found themselves held in contempt. The rule of law was beginning to break down, and there had even been demonstrations and riots in some towns. Army resources were stretched as never before, as the commanders tried to cope with the various demands being made on their time. It was as though the entire country was in the grip of a collective nightmare.

In Makhaya, the court had been close to panic. Kamin and his fellow seers had done their best to keep the knowledge of the impending collision a secret, but it had proved impossible to stop some gossip leaking out. As the harbingers of doom grew more and more vociferous, the official denials had had less and less effect. The mood of the city became tense and feverish, and Kamin had been able to do little about it. After all, he was one of those who knew that the nightmare was all too real.

The latest estimate of the timing of the collision with the mainland had come not from Lathan — there was still no sign of him — but from several other members of the council. Their calculations varied slightly, but all put the time of the catastrophe at no more than two months away – unless something happened to alter their course. The most recent date when the Floating Islands would normally have changed direction – something which a few optimists had still hoped might happen – was long past now, and every day brought them closer to the coastline of the barbarian land known as Macul.

As in the earlier debates, many theories had been put forward to try to explain the anomalous behaviour of the islands. Some theories were more ludicrous than others, but none of them made much sense to Kamin. However, the one faction within the council whose support had grown in strength day by day had been that which claimed the anomalous forces in the mines of Betancuria were responsible for the impending disaster. Kamin had initially thought that this was utter madness, but the lack of any plausible alternative explanation had forced him to think again. And on examining the facts, he had become aware that something strange *was* happening at Betancuria.

There had been another earthquake, centred on the mining district, more tornadoes had been born there, and the entire region was facing a freak drought. Further analysis had confirmed that it was definitely the axis around which the islands were now rotating. A number of seers were even claiming that it was because of this rotation that the Empire was drifting off course, and – incredibly – evidence was growing to support their theories. Kamin had eventually decided to lend his support to this idea, because it was the only one that allowed him to *act*. All the other possibilities involved forces that were quite beyond human control, and yet the council had to do something – and had to be seen to be doing something.

His first step had been to send several army detachments to Betancuria, in the hope of bringing some order to the area. In retrospect, that had probably done more harm than good, because their passage had led to some wild rumours – including one about a possible invasion from Macul. It was ironic, Kamin thought, that seafaring was not one of the traditions of the Empire. They were an island people, after all. But the perilous nature of navigation in coastal waters where not only the ocean but also the land moved, had made them wary of longer journeys. Because of this, relations with other countries were nonexistent. Over the centuries of this self-imposed isolation, it had become axiomatic to the people of Vadanis that land *ought* to move, and therefore any land that did not must be uncivilized and inferior to their own. Horrific tales of remote barbarian tribes, who would jump at the chance to invade the Floating Islands, had become ingrained in the collective mind of the population, and the unusual military movements had caused considerable alarm. Although Kamin knew the rumours to be false, he could understand the revulsion felt at the thought of foreigners setting foot on his homeland.

Proclamations broadcasting the real reason for the army's marching had been sent out as soon as possible, but this had only added another layer of uncertainty to the gossip, and Kamin had quickly realized that something more was needed. He had reluctantly put forward the suggestion that he and Jax, as the Guardian, ought to travel to Betancuria too – and from that moment on, the entire operation had snowballed. First, the Empress demanded that because she was the Mentor, she should accompany her son. The fact that no official decision had been reached about her claim – Kamin had managed to delay any announcement – did nothing to lessen her presumption. That in turn led to the Emperor himself deciding that he ought to go too, 'to demonstrate our unity'. After that it had only been a matter of time before the court and the Seers' Council had agreed that they *all* ought to go.

The ritual at the mine had seemed to be the next logical step, and Kamin hoped that it would not only provide the answers they needed but also restore the people's faith in their leaders. To that end, teams of seers, acolytes and scribes had been working out the details of the ceremony for some days now. Their preparations had been meticulous, but now that the Chief Seer was there in person to oversee the final practical arrangements, he could see that the amount of work still to be done was daunting. If it had not been for an almost unlimited supply of military manpower, the whole thing would have been impossible.

Kamin was aware that he had staked his personal future on the enterprise. He had many loyal supporters among the council and at court, but he had enemies too, waiting to pounce if he faltered. Tomorrow would see his first appearance as Chief Seer at a major public occasion, and he knew only too well that it might also be his last.

When Kamin was finally able to retire to his temporary lodgings that night, he believed that sufficient progress had been made. In due course, order *would* emerge out of chaos.

He called for some wine, and allowed his mind to wander from his immediate concerns and dwell instead on some issues that were less important, but intriguing nonetheless. He thought about Lathan, and wondered what had happened to him. The longer he was missing, the more likely it seemed that he had fallen foul of the same curse that had caused the downfall of Mirival and Shahan. If that *was* the case, then the obvious suspects were the Empress and her son, but – just as with the earlier deaths – there was no evidence that might indicate their involvement. In fact, Adina had demanded on several occasions that the traitor be found and punished. Although this could have been a bluff on her part, her anger had been convincing. Whatever the truth of the matter – and Kamin secretly hoped that Lathan was still alive and in hiding somewhere – his disappearance had at least solved one of the Chief Seer's problems. After Lathan's intemperate speech to the council, it had been obvious that a number of his colleagues had shared his views, but – understandably – no one had come forward to support him publicly. It had therefore been possible to let the matter of Jax's discarded twin slide back into obscurity, and the Chief Seer was relieved by this. He did not need the extra complication.

Kamin's chamberlain brought his wine, and with it the news that Prince Jax was on his way. Kamin suppressed a groan; this was something else he did not need. He took solace in his first mouthful of wine.

When Jax entered the room, he seemed to be in an uncharacteristically sombre mood. He greeted Kamin quietly, refused the offer of wine, and waited until the chamberlain had left them before speaking again. This came as something of a relief to the seer. He was not sure he would have been able to cope with the prince's usual bombastic manner. And then he realized that Jax had generally been more subdued of late. Ever since the day of the total eclipse, and his strange blackout, the prince had often seemed withdrawn and thoughtful. Although such moods did not last for long, they were so out of character that they were noticeable. Was it possible that he was actually beginning to grow up at last?

'Have there been any reports about the travelling players yet?' the prince asked.

This was an oft-repeated question, and Kamin still had no idea why Jax found it so important.

'Not that I'm aware of,' he replied. Nor were there likely to be, he thought. With all the extra duties that had been thrust upon the army recently, arresting a few ill-mannered actors was not much of a priority. 'I'll inform you the moment I hear anything.'

Jax nodded, but he still seemed distracted, and Kamin was sure that this was not what the prince had come to see him about.

'Do you have any questions about your role in the ceremony tomorrow?' he asked, picking on his visitor's most likely concern. 'If you like, I can run through—'

'No,' the boy cut in. 'That doesn't bother me.'

Then what *is* worrying you? Kamin wondered. Could the possible results of the forthcoming augury be causing the prince's anxiety? Was it possible that the trip to Betancuria, and the strange things that were happening there, had brought home the responsibilities that Jax might eventually have to bear? One of the specific aims of the ritual was to discover what action they should take underground, and it was possible that the prince might have a role to play in that action. For the very first time, it might be dawning on him that being the Guardian might not be a guarantee of safety. Knowing that the prophecy could demand that he face unknown dangers – and actually attempt to become the hero his assumed title claimed him to be – might well be enough to explain the prince's current unease. Since Marshal Karuna's initial report had reached Makhaya, several more miners had been killed, and when a scout team from one of the best units of the Imperial Guard had ventured underground they had simply vanished without trace. Following in their footsteps would be a daunting task indeed. Kamin was wondering how he could raise this possibility in a sufficiently tactful manner when Jax spoke again.

'Is it possible to see the future?'

'Prophecy is not an exact science,' Kamin began, believing that the prince was referring to the augury that would follow the ceremony. 'But with—'

'I don't mean that,' Jax interrupted. 'I mean actually *see* it, as if you were there.'

The Chief Seer was taken aback by this question, and even as he answered he was speculating on the possible reasons for it.

'It is said that, under the right conditions, especially talented seers have been granted visions,' he replied carefully. 'There are several well-known historical examples, but it's very rare.'

Jax nodded, but said nothing.

'Have you experienced anything like that?' Kamin asked tentatively. A wild hope had sprung up inside him. Was it possible that the prince's destiny was driving him at last, that the instincts of a hero might be waking up within him at the crucial moment? If so, the seer wanted to hear more.

However, Jax ignored the question and his next words were almost as surprising as his earlier query.

'I've never been to Tindaya,' he said. 'When we're finished here, I should like to visit the temple.'

CHAPTER FORTY

The silence in the amphitheatre was profound, and Kamin found it hard to believe that over a thousand people were looking on from the surrounding slopes. The solemnity of the occasion even seemed to have affected the weather. The wind had dropped to no more than a whisper and, as if in answer to the seers' fervent prayers, the sky above was perfectly clear.

Almost everything had been in place by sunset and now, an hour and a half later, the only light came from the multitude of glittering stars. No lamps or torches burned, the nearby smelting fires and furnaces had been shut down, and the lights of the town were hidden by the intervening hill. As the Chief Seer surveyed the arena, he was grateful for the fact that there had not been so much as a hint of restlessness among the spectators, even though they had had to wait a long time as the darkness drew in.

Soon now, Kamin promised silently, his eyes on the horizon. Your patience will be rewarded soon.

*

It had been important for the audience to take their places while there was still daylight left. Kamin had wanted them to see the impressive nature of the astrological observatory that had been set up in the amphitheatre. The collimation rods had been driven into the ground in an alignment that mimicked the ancient stone circles and rows found in various remote areas of Vadanis. It was believed that these had been temples, left by their ancient ancestors, but when it was found that they could be used to predict the time and location of significant astronomical events – sunrises, moonrises, even eclipses and conjunctions – the remains had been studied in great detail. Before long it became apparent that those early temple-builders had studied the movements of the heavens closely.

Of course, in designing this particular replica the seers had had to adapt the layout for the chosen time and location, and had taken into account the islands' unexpected position in the ocean and the recent alterations to the orbit of the Dark Moon. These calculations had been fearfully complicated, and had occupied many of their best mathematical brains for many hours. So far, from observations of the visible constellations, it appeared as though they had got it right, although the real test would come only when all the moons had risen. More than a hundred rods now stood awaiting their arrival, each with a black-robed acolyte nearby, ready to take the necessary shadow-readings.

However, the most impressive artefact within the area – a precisely sculpted block of dark rock, set upon a low altar – had been set at its centre. Above the altar and to one side, set on metal tripods, were four large spheres of solid, clear glass. Few of those present had ever seen these sacred items before. In his welcoming address, Kamin had told the spectators that the stone was known as 'The Well of the Moons', and that it had once been part of the temple at Tindaya. That such an important relic should have been transported to Betancuria for use in this ceremony had made a deep impression on the onlookers, although Kamin had been deliberately vague about the exact role it would play in the ritual.

The only clue had come after the Chief Seer's speech, during the penultimate task in the lengthy preparations. This had been carried out – with a calm dignity that was as surprising as it was admirable – by Jax. Kamin had been delighted by his reluctant pupil's performance, but had wondered cynically whether the boy's behaviour might have been influenced by the fact that he'd been accompanied by the lunar paranymph – who just happened to be a very attractive girl the same age as the prince. She had been carefully chosen from among the citizens of Betancuria to play a largely symbolic role, and wore a dress fashioned from material whose colours matched those of the four moons. According to ritual lore, her character represented the virgin bridesmaid at the wedding of the sun and his four lunar wives, a union that represented mankind's plea for fertility – for women, animals and crops – on the land below. In the distant past she would have been sacrificed to ensure that these prayers were answered, but those barbaric times were long gone.

The prince, who was dressed in a shining white robe that echoed the light of the sun, played the girl's male counterpart. Part of their ceremonial task had been to pour water into the hollow carved in the flat upper surface of the black rock. Their double-handed ewer held exactly the right amount, measured to the last drop, so that when they had finished pouring, the liquid came precisely to the brim of the pool. Only those who had had the opportunity to examine the Well of the Moons closely knew that four shallow channels led from the main hollow to four much smaller holes. Each of these channels led directly away from their respective glass spheres.

It was appropriate that water was a major element in the ceremony, because one of the reasons for staging the performance had been to publicly obtain the heavens' seal of approval for the project – already underway – that was aimed at restoring the water supply of the drought-stricken town. This was to be done by diverting the river back to its original course. The complex procedure – which was taking place under military supervision – obviously met with the wholehearted approval of the local population, and Kamin wanted to ensure that the Seers' Council received at least some of the credit for its implementation. People would then be more likely to accept the other parts of the augury – and the government of the country would regain some of the respect it had lost.

Once the water was in place and the level had been checked by one of the seers, all that remained was the formal blessing of the temple. This too had been performed by Jax and his companion. They had walked slowly, hand in hand, around the perimeter, repeating words from one of the best known passages in the Tindaya Code.

'As we revere the skies, grant us knowledge.

Red Queen bequeath us the fires of conflict and of love.

White Queen grant us precision, logic and a reckoning of fate.

Amber Queen lead us into the spirit realm, into dreams and second sight.

Dark Queen mould the invisible forces, the mysteries, and the paths of life and death.

Now that the King sleeps, we have need of your wisdom.'

The prince had excelled in this duty, his surprisingly deep and resonant voice contrasting nicely with the girl's lighter tone. There had been no intimation of his habitual sarcasm or flippancy, and Kamin had wondered whether this was because Jax was finally beginning to mature, or simply because he had been playing to an unusually large audience. Either way, the seer could only be pleased at the outcome.

Once the blessing had been completed, all that had been left to do was to douse the remaining torches. And wait.

The Amber Moon was the first to rise that night. Watching as it spread its warm glow over the scene, Kamin saw it for a moment not as one of the rulers of his science but as a simple object of beauty, a celestial work of art. His heart was filled with joy – until he remembered the night's true purpose and became a professional observer once more. He was not normally prey to such bouts of romanticism, and he was glad that no one could have seen the brief glint of childlike wonder in his eyes.

When the light from the moon reached the lower levels of the amphitheatre, the acolytes became busy, recording arcs, angles and the stately progression of the subtly coloured moon-shadows that crept around the carefully placed rods. Although such things were predictable, they made an impressive spectacle for the uninitiated – and the patterns from the moon-dials could later be compared to the paths that had been forecast, just in case there were any discrepancies.

However, the sight that drew everyone's attention once the Amber Moon had risen a little higher in the sky was the remarkable transformation of the central altar. A second moon appeared, reflected in the mirror surface of the water, and this image was in turn captured by the crystal sphere aligned with it on the opposite side. It seemed to the spectators as though the moon itself was contained

within the ball of glass. Lesser images were caught round
the edges of the other spheres, but there was no doubting
which one corresponded to the real moon. It was an entrancing, almost magical sight that drew murmurs of awe
from the crowd. But the last and most impressive effect
was yet to come.

The sharpest-eyed of the onlookers noticed a glittering
trail of gold that moved down the channel orientated in the
direction of the Amber Moon. As they alerted their neighbours, pointing and whispering, a few drops of the sacred
water trickled towards the smaller hollow, drawn there by
the remote power of the moon itself.

Kamin smiled in triumph, hoping that the other alignments would prove to be as accurate.

The Red Moon came next, and the spectacle was repeated in another hue. Although it did not have the same
impact as the first, it was spellbinding nonetheless – and this
time everyone was watching and ready. The murmuring
grew in volume, and there was even a muted round of
applause when the water – now the colour of blood – ran
down the second channel.

Some people were expecting the White Moon to appear
next, but those with more acute astrological sensibilities
were aware that its influence on the ritual would be minimal – and that, in fact, its slim crescent would not even be
visible during the ceremony. The realization that what
they were now waiting for was the entrance of the Dark
Moon spread slowly through the crowd.

Kamin had expected that the last of the quartet would
be something of an anticlimax. After all, there would be
nothing to see when the Dark Moon rose. But, for the first
time that night, he was proved wrong.

It might have been his imagination, but when the
moment arrived, a chill seemed to sweep over the arena.

The only way to tell that the fourth moon was rising was to watch for the distant stars to be blotted out, but because almost everyone was looking for this in the correct part of the sky, the Dark Moon's passage was – for once – clearly observed. And everyone, no matter how poor their eyesight, *felt* its arrival.

There were no shadows for the scribes to follow, of course, but with the other moons now quite high it was possible to watch for any movement of water by their light. No one expected to see anything within the last glass – and when they did, they could not be sure they weren't hallucinating. For an instant, the sphere – which until then had merely been glowing gently in the refracted light of the Red and Amber Moons – flickered with a swirling rainbow-hued fire. And then, just as swiftly, the heart of the crystal became black.

In the deathly silence that attended this inexplicable vision, the sound of trickling water was heard by those nearby. A moment later, the darkness became invisible once more and the spell released them.

Even though Kamin had been as shaken as anyone else by this ominous development, he was the first to react. To all intents and purposes the rite was over now, and he got up from his seat among the other dignitaries and strode towards the centre of the arena.

As he walked, he signalled to the acolytes to light torches so that he could be seen clearly. He had always felt rather self-conscious in his ceremonial robes – especially in the mirrored hat that denoted his rank as Chief Seer – but he knew that such considerations were unimportant. He had to try to dispel the doom-laden aura that had fallen over the gathering, and restore the earlier sense of awe and expectation. As the torches flared into life, and the night retreated, he composed himself, ready to speak.

He was about to tell the audience that this vision was a
sign that they had been favoured by the skies – and that
the augury they sought would be determined by the relative amounts of water in each of the small hollows in the
Well of the Moons – when he heard something that made
him hesitate. A moment later, he knew that his destiny was
no longer in his own hands.

The rumbling grew much louder, and the earth beneath
Kamin's feet began to shake. Panic was averted only by the
fact that the tremor lasted no more than two or three
heartbeats, but in that time the damage had been done.

Although the tripods had miraculously remained
upright, and the glass spheres were undamaged, a sharp
crack rang loudly in the air. When Kamin looked round,
he saw to his dismay that the precious relic from Tindaya
had split from end to end, so that the two halves had actually fallen away from each other. The fracture ran directly
across the pool, so that the water gushed away, then continued down the Dark Moon's channel until its smaller
hollow had also been emptied.

In a single moment the Well of the Moons had been
destroyed, and the augury was ruined.

CHAPTER FORTY-ONE

What do you think is going on down there?

I don't know, Alyssa replied.

The stonechat that currently housed her spirit was perched on Terrel's shoulder. Although he liked this it also made him nervous, because the bird seemed so fragile. He enjoyed being so close to Alyssa, but was afraid of making any sudden movement. The tiny creature weighed almost nothing, and he could only just feel the touch of her claws through the material of his shirt.

Should we go and find out? he asked.

Alyssa jerked her tail and wings in what had become a familiar gesture of irritation.

I'm used to seeing things that aren't there, she remarked enigmatically. *Why should this be any different?*

Terrel turned his head slightly, trying to look at her, but of course he could tell nothing from the stonechat's appearance. Alyssa's mysterious comments had become more frequent recently, and this concerned him.

Are you all right? he asked.

I'm tired of flying.

Terrel was about to tell his friend to find somewhere to sleep for the rest of the night, but then realized it was not the physical act of taking wing that was affecting Alyssa. She had inhabited the bird's tiny but surprisingly robust frame for two days now, and the continuous occupation was obviously taking its toll on her mental wellbeing. Unfortunately, there would be no respite for some time.

Can I do anything to help? The thought that she might be forced to leave him was terrifying.

I can smell water, she said. She had either not heard his question or was ignoring it.

Down there?

Terrel looked again at the strange gathering, and wished he could see what was going on. His position on the hill between the town and the amphitheatre allowed him a clear but distant view of the vale and of the crowds around it. There was something happening in the shadows near the centre of the arena, some odd flickers of light, but he was too far away to see what it was.

There's movement, Alyssa said.

Terrel strained his eyes, and saw that a man was walking out into the open space with a purposeful air. But then the boy suddenly lost interest in what was happening in the amphitheatre. His internal trembling began just as, down below him, torches flared into life.

Terrel and his winged companion had arrived in Betancuria late that afternoon, and had found the town all but deserted. Their month-long journey had been uneventful, and Alyssa had been with him for most of the time, taking on a variety of guises. At one point she had overcome her dislike of being inside a horse's brain, and they had stolen a mare that was being badly treated by her owner. Terrel had been able to ride for two days, and had been grateful for the fact that this had speeded up their progress considerably. But then a couple of falls convinced them both to let the creature go free. More often Alyssa just chose whichever animal was close to hand, providing Terrel with company rather than help along the way. She generally preferred birds, finding in their comparatively simple minds an ease that more complex creatures lacked, and the advantages of being able to fly also outweighed the limitations of avian form. Terrel was amused by her preference, remembering that he had always thought his friend was rather bird-like. However, even in this form she had had to escape regularly, to free herself from the shape she had adopted and — so Terrel presumed — return to the haven to rest within her own body. But when they'd got to within twenty miles of Betancuria, this had become impossible. He did not understand the reasons for this, but knew it had something to do with the same force that had prevented the ghosts from getting any closer to the mines. As a result, Alyssa was now stuck within the stonechat, and would not be able to return to her own body until they were far enough away again. Trying to 'rest' while any closer would, it seemed, prove fatal. Terrel could not feel the malign force that was causing this problem, but he did not doubt its existence.

Overall their journey had been an exercise in endurance, slogging onwards in the hope that Terrel's presence in Betancuria would solve at least some of the mysteries that surrounded him. Their path had crossed increasingly rugged terrain. At one point they had been no more than five miles from Mount Tindaya, and Terrel had glanced at its towering summit many times as they passed by. The weather had become cold and damp, which added to his discomfort, but at last they had reached the mining district. The town's apparent desertion had confused Terrel

until he had learned the reason for it – and then he had
hurriedly climbed the hill, his weariness forgotten.

There's going to be an earthquake.

Are you sure? Alyssa asked. They had talked at length
about Tindaya, and about the quake that Terrel had felt
approaching there, but which had never arrived.

I think so, he replied, wondering whether his strange
instinct had deserted him.

A moment later there was no more room for doubt. The
ground beneath his feet was vibrating.

The scene below them froze, on the edge of panic. Only
the light of the torches moved, wavering as though the
flames themselves were being shaken by the tremor. A
loud crack sounded from the arena, and then it was over.
The ground became solid again.

Did it come from the mines? Alyssa asked.

I don't know, Terrel admitted. *Did you feel it coming?*

I'm not a ghost, she replied, sounding aggrieved. *I'm not
sure there's any connection when I'm in this shape.*

You still think it's protecting you?

I know it is, she told him. *I've been sleeping for more than
four months now. How do you think I'd have survived otherwise?*

Terrel had no answer to that, and he took comfort from
the fact that – in some sense he could not understand –
Alyssa and the force were allies. It made the thought of his
forthcoming encounter just a bit less terrifying. Then
again, he thought anxiously, if it didn't recognize her as
the stonechat, would their alliance count for anything?

You worry too much, she informed him, and Terrel wondered if his private thoughts were leaking out again. *What's
going on now?*

There seemed to be some sort of commotion near the

centre of the amphitheatre, but even with the light of the torches Terrel could not see what the sudden gathering of robed figures was doing.

I've no idea, he said.

Then don't you think we should go and find out? Alyssa commented tartly.

She flew off into the night and was soon lost to view. Wrapping his stolen cloak around him, Terrel began to walk down the hill to join the rest of the milling crowds.

Later that night Terrel was trudging wearily through the streets of Betancuria, looking for somewhere to sleep. The money he'd earned during his time with Laevo's troupe was long gone and, in any case, he was fairly sure that the hostelries had already been filled by the influx of visitors. He decided that this was probably just as well. Keeping to himself had become a habit now. After all, he was an escaped lunatic, a runaway criminal and a fugitive suspected of being an enchanter. Although he knew he was unlikely to run into anyone who would denounce him on any of these charges, he preferred not to take any chances. He was also nervous about being in a large town again.

He was surprised to find the streets so busy. With all the horror stories about the so-called monster, the shortage of water and the constant danger from tornadoes, he had expected more people to have fled from the area. That they had not done so was either testament to the obstinacy of the residents, or to the fact that rendering themselves voluntarily homeless was something most people would only contemplate as a last resort. Even here, life went on.

Eventually, in one of the quieter backstreets, Terrel came across a house that had obviously been damaged by a whirlwind and subsequently abandoned. The roof had vanished, and most of the walls had been reduced to rubble. Only one ground floor room offered anything in the way of shelter, but that was enough. He crawled inside and made himself as comfortable as possible, clearing a space on the bare floor and then waiting, hoping that Alyssa would find him soon. She duly arrived a little while later, but although Terrel was delighted to see her, he noticed from the constant twitching of her small, square head that she was agitated. He was about to ask what the matter was when she spoke first, dispelling his anxiety with her unexpectedly jaunty tone.

It's a good job Elam's not here.

It took Terrel a moment to work out what she meant, but then he smiled.

Not the most luxurious accommodations, are they? he agreed, grateful for her attempt to lighten the mood before they got down to serious business.

Did you learn anything? she asked.

Nothing useful. In the confusion following the tremor, the crowd had been alive with all sorts of rumours, but Terrel had not been able to distinguish fact from fiction.

There was an announcement, Alyssa said. *The seers are going to tell everyone the results of their augury in the morning.*

I heard that too, Terrel said. It had taken a while to silence the clamour of the throng, and the confident tone of the man who had made the announcement had seemed a little forced to Terrel.

I got the feeling it was supposed to have happened straight away, Alyssa added, echoing his thoughts. *I think something went wrong.*

Either way, we'd better go and hear what they have to say, Terrel said.

Agreed. It might give us a better idea about what we should do next.

Terrel nodded, dread knotting in his stomach. Now that they were actually in Betancuria, the prospect of going down into the darkness of the mines horrified him.

Sleep now, Alyssa advised. *Think of this place as another room in the palace.*

Terrel grinned in spite of himself.

I'm not sure my imagination's that good.

You'd be surprised, she replied. *Goodnight, Terrel. I need to rest too.*

Goodnight, Alyssa.

Slumber came to the bird almost instantly and Terrel watched her for a few moments, trying to convince himself that he really did worry too much about her. He did not succeed. Even in her sleep, Alyssa twitched constantly.

CHAPTER FORTY-TWO

'I didn't ask you if you *liked* the idea, Commissioner,' Kamin stated bluntly. 'I asked you if it was possible.'

'Yes, I suppose so,' Hoban replied, with obvious reluctance, 'but—'

'Thank you. I shall expect detailed plans for its implementation by midday.'

The miners' leader was clearly horrified by the idea of such haste.

'There must be some other way,' he pleaded.

'The augury was quite clear,' Kamin told him. This was a lie, but one he felt quite justified in using. In many respects the results of the ceremony had surpassed all his expectations – especially given the unexpected difficulties they'd encountered – but the course of action he was now demanding had been only one of several possible interpretations of the data they had obtained. In fact, the arguments among the seers had only been settled when one of Hoban's engineers had told them of his own, earlier observations.

'I have no reason to doubt your augury,' Hoban said,

wishing that he could claim otherwise, 'but I'm not sure you realize the consequences for this region. If we flood the mine, it will be many years before we can begin operations again. Much of the damage will be irreparable. Hundreds of people will lose their jobs, but that won't be the end of it. The metals we produce are necessary for life on Vadanis. Without them—'

'Commissioner,' Kamin cut in sharply, his patience beginning to wear thin. 'I appreciate your concerns, but I'm not sure you realize what the consequences for the Empire will be if we don't take action. I'm fully aware that what I'm proposing will cause widespread hardship. But unless we can stop the islands rotating and put them back on their proper course, Vadanis will soon collide with the coast of Macul. That will not only destroy your mine workings, it will devastate every town, every building, the land itself!'

The colour drained from Hoban's face, and for a few moments he was unable to speak. His horror was echoed in the expressions of most of the other men in the room, but they too remained silent. Kamin's fellow seers had known the true situation for a while, but this was the first time Hoban's staff and most of Marshal Karuna's officers had been given confirmation of the disaster that faced them.

'You mean the rumours are true?' Hoban breathed eventually. 'I thought . . .'

'According to our latest calculations, the islands are actually accelerating towards the collision,' Kamin told him, relentless now. 'We may have little more than a month left, and unless we reverse the current changes during the next few days it'll be too late to do anything about it. Our momentum will be irreversible.'

Now that the Chief Seer was finally convinced that the

forces affecting the mines were responsible for the crisis, he was filled with the single-mindedness of a convert. He had no room for doubt.

'I'm sure I don't need to tell you,' he went on, calmer now, 'that this information is not to be made public. Rumours are unavoidable, but we don't want the entire population to panic.'

Hoban nodded his agreement, still trying to come to terms with what he had heard.

'Much of the work has already been done,' Kamin added. 'All we have to do now is divert the river again to suit our new purpose. Once that's been achieved, the town's water supply can be restored.'

'Are you sure it'll work?' the commissioner asked, admitting defeat. 'It still seems a drastic solution to me.'

'It'll work,' Kamin replied. 'Even if it had not been for the augury, it was one of your own engineers who pointed out that the phenomenon seems to have been absent from those tunnels or caverns which are anywhere near underground streams or lakes. I think that's significant, don't you?' He was anxious now to move on – the time for his public announcement was drawing near – and he continued his argument without giving Hoban a chance to reply. 'We have every reason to believe that the water will either block out these anomalous forces, or possibly even destroy their source altogether. Either way, it's our one chance of resolving this crisis.'

The Chief Seer glanced around the room, and saw the strain reflected on the faces of the soldiers and engineers.

'It's not all bad news,' he reassured them. 'In many respects the outcome of the ritual was favourable, confirming theories that until now had been nothing more than supposition. It's given us a way out of our dilemma. I'll be saying more in my address to the townspeople, but right now you all have a vital role to play in our salvation. And there's no time to waste.'

As Hoban and Karuna led their men from the room, and the seers also began to disperse, Kamin was already thinking about the public announcement. It would be his chance to repair the damage done the previous night. He had salvaged what he could at the time, but the tremor – its unfortunate timing still seemed like deliberate sabotage – and the breaking of the Well of the Moons had been a fiasco as far as the public perception of the ritual was concerned. His only choice had been to delay the release of any of the results until he and his fellow seers had been able to gauge the impact of the disruption. They had worked through the night, meticulously studying each detail of the ceremony, and arguing over their meaning until a consensus had emerged. It had been with a feeling of great relief that they had concluded that the incomplete augury was still valid. Given that, it was true that many of the results had been unexpectedly positive, but it was only when they had put their findings together with those of the percipient engineer that the last piece of the puzzle had slotted into place. Now all Kamin had to do was convince the inhabitants of Betancuria that the course of action he was proposing was not only the right thing to do, but also their only hope. At least now he had something definite to tell them.

He was about to make his way towards the town's central market square when the sound of raised voices from the corridor outside the meeting room made him hesitate. His heart sank when he realized who it was, but he knew there was no escape. A moment later the Empress burst in through the door, her son close behind her. Adina's face was pink with indignation as she glared at the seer.

'Good morning, Your Majesty.'

The Empress ignored his greeting. Swinging round, she grabbed Jax by the arm and pulled him forward.

'Do you know who this is?' she demanded. 'Do you know who *I* am?'

Kamin knew better than to interrupt her tirade by actually answering these rhetorical questions.

'This is the Guardian. I am the Mentor,' Adina went on. 'And yet you don't seem to think it necessary to consult us, or even inform us that important decisions are being made.' She paused, and when Kamin remained silent, added, 'Well? What do you have to say for yourself?'

'My apologies, Your Majesty,' the seer replied formally. 'The repercussions of last night's unexpected events have necessitated lengthy discussions among the council.'

'I see. And you chose not to include us in these discussions?'

'They were somewhat technical in nature, ma'am. We did not seek to exclude you, but I thought it better that you and the prince should sleep and reserve your strength for the tasks ahead.'

Adina did not seem to be placated by this explanation, but she was thrown off her stride when Jax pulled his arm from her grasp. If the prince was intimidated by his mother, he gave no sign of it. The look on his face was one of sullen arrogance.

'When were you intending to tell me of the outcome of your deliberations?' the Empress enquired. 'Or was I supposed to hear the news with the common rabble in the market square?'

'I was just on my way to inform you of our plans, and to ask for your approval,' Kamin lied.

Adina favoured him with a baleful stare, obviously wondering whether to take his words at face value.

'Good,' she said eventually. 'You can do so now.'

Summoning the last reserves of his patience, the seer submitted to the inevitable.

'As you know, the purpose of the ritual was to use the readings to answer some specific questions. And in spite of the unfortunate accident that delayed our findings, the augury has proved to be almost entirely successful. Apart from the matter of restoring the water supply to this region – which is of relatively minor importance – our concerns were obvious. The first thing we can now say with absolute certainty is that the anomaly in the mines is responsible for the rotation of the islands.'

'I thought we knew that already,' Jax remarked.

'We *suspected* it,' Kamin conceded, 'but it was hard to believe that such a force could be so powerful. However, the augury was unequivocal in this matter. It also confirmed that the rotation and the alteration in the islands' course are linked. We're still not sure which is the cause and which the effect, or whether the two were initiated together by some outside power, but we are certain now that if we can stop one we will stop the other.'

'So if we stop the rotation we won't collide with the mainland?' Jax asked.

'Exactly. The forces that have governed our movements for centuries will take over again, and we'll return to a safe path.' Kamin knew that it might not be quite as simple as this, but trying to explain all the possible ramifications of the changes that had already taken place would take hours. 'Which is why we now know that we have to deal with the situation here,' he added blandly.

'And how are we to do that?' Adina asked.

'The augury also revealed that there may be a way of counteracting these destructive forces.'

'Water,' Jax said.

Kamin glanced at the prince in surprise, and felt the beginnings of a grudging respect. The young man was starting to show signs of an intelligence no one had noticed in him before.

'Water,' the seer confirmed, then went on to describe the plan to flood the mine workings. He could see from the glint in the prince's eyes that Jax approved of the idea, and Kamin himself was beginning to feel more optimistic. The earlier arguments about the ambiguous nature of the prophecy were forgotten. Adina was not so easily satisfied.

'What is our role in this enterprise?' she asked. 'Surely, as Guardian, my son should be part of your plans.'

Jax glanced at her and frowned, but then looked to Kamin for an answer.

'The augury also indicated that both the Guardian and the Mentor were in Betancuria,' Kamin replied. When he'd been told this he had been greatly relieved. It was vindication – at last! – of their assumption that Jax was indeed the hero indicated by the Tindaya Code. He remained less convinced of Adina's claims, but it seemed that the Mentor's role would be less important anyway.

'We didn't need your augury to know that,' the Empress snapped. 'I asked you what we will actually be *doing*.'

'Our exact plans have yet to be finalized,' Kamin told her. 'As soon as they are, I'm sure your roles will become obvious.'

'I could be the one to open the sluices,' Jax suggested eagerly.

'That's one possibility,' the Chief Seer agreed.

'And me?' Adina said shortly.

'I think you should remain close to your son, Ma'am. Your advice will no doubt be invaluable at critical moments.'

The Empress nodded doubtfully and, unseen by his mother, Jax rolled his eyes in disgust. Kamin fought to hide a smile.

'At the very least I am sure your joint presence will serve as an inspiration for us all,' he added smoothly.

Kamin reached the market square later than expected, and immediately sensed that the crowd was growing restless. His appearance on the steps of the town's meeting hall brought a rumble of anticipation and a few shouts from the gathering, and he wasted no time in fulfilling his promise to reveal the outcome of the ritual. He gave them a full report, leaving out only the seriousness of the possible collision with the mainland. He spoke instead of the vital need to correct the islands' course and orientation, and his words met with general approval – especially when he said that the imperial government intended to do this by cancelling out the mysterious forces that had disrupted all their lives. However, when he came to the means by which they intended to do this, the reaction was quite different – as he had known it would be. His announcement caused an uproar, but Kamin stood his ground and was eventually able to explain the reasons for the council's decision. He ended by informing the crowd that all the mines were now under military jurisdiction, and that no unauthorized access to any of the shafts or tunnels would be allowed. Then he returned to his headquarters, leaving the townspeople to argue over what they'd been told.

I have a bad feeling about this, Alyssa said.

The stonechat was perched on a first floor windowsill, overlooking the market square. Terrel, who was leaning against the wall below her, had listened to the Chief Seer's speech with mixed feelings. Like Alyssa, his instinctive reaction to the proposed flooding was that it would be a mistake, but the idea that someone else might be dealing with the problem — and thereby relieving him of that onerous duty — had seemed attractive.

Me too, he replied. *But I don't see what we can do to stop them.*

You can deal with that sort of magic, Alyssa said. *I can't. And I don't think my link can either.*

Terrel knew he had missed some stage in her thought process, but as yet he could not work out what it was.

Magic? he queried.

It would be better if the sea wasn't underneath us. She ruffled her feathers and hopped from one end of the sill to the other.

Because we wouldn't be moving then? Terrel guessed.

No. Because it would feel safer.

All because of water? he said, catching on. *Then the seers' plan ought to work.*

Yes, it will, Alyssa agreed. *But I'm not sure we want it to.*

It had taken Kamin a long time to arrange a private meeting with Jax, but when he had he soon began to wonder why he'd bothered. The prince had reverted to type, displaying none of his new-found insightfulness, and was generally behaving in a surly and insolent manner. The hopes that had been raised in Kamin's mind were dashed, and this was especially disappointing because he was now as sure as he could be that Jax was the Guardian. As such, the prince would surely have a genuine role to play in their efforts to avert catastrophe, but he no longer seemed interested.

'What's the point?' Jax declared. 'You know what's going to happen.'

'Augury isn't—'

'An exact science,' the prince completed for him. 'Yes, I know. But the council and engineers have taken over now. Even the soldiers are just being used as labourers. There isn't going to be any fighting. How am I supposed to become a hero if we don't have some sort of battle?'

'Conflicts can often be settled by means other than fighting,' the seer responded.

'Such as?'

'Strategy. Instinct. Subterfuge. That's where you might be able to help. That's what your education has been leading up to.'

'You could've fooled me,' Jax commented derisively. 'Besides, aren't we supposed to get advice about stuff like that from my mother?'

'Perhaps.'

The prince laughed.

'You're a liar, Kamin. You don't believe she's the Mentor any more than I do.'

'Why do you say that?'

Jax did not get the chance to reply, because just at that moment the subject of their conversation entered the room.

'Any news?' Adina was clearly anxious not to miss any developments.

'Kamin has just been telling me how to win battles without fighting,' Jax announced facetiously.

'No news as yet, Ma'am,' the seer replied, through gritted teeth.

'Well, I have some,' the Empress remarked, her eyes alight with the joy of gossip. 'Princess Mela's had to go back to Makhaya. The stupid girl's managed to get herself pregnant. And laughable though it may seem, she claims not to know who the father is! Incredible. Still, her mother was a slut, so I suppose it's all in the breeding. It's a sign of the degenerate times we live in, Kamin.'

The seer could not think of anything to say. Even Jax had been silenced by the news, his face now a mask of contempt.

'Oy, you! Where d'you think you're going?'

Terrel stopped, knowing he couldn't match the sentry for pace, and waited until the soldier came up to him.

'I was just curious,' he said, pretending to be feeble-minded.

'Clear off,' the guard told him. 'You know this place is out of bounds now.'

'I only wanted to look.'

'Well you can't. Listen, son, what do you want to go in there for anyway? The place is deserted, and pretty soon half of it'll be under water. Go back to the town before one of my officers sees you and I get into trouble for letting you get this far.'

Terrel nodded, and did as he was told. Each of his four attempts to enter the mining district had taken place at a different location, but had ended with his being turned back. The whole area was cordoned off now, with patrols and guard posts set up at regular intervals around the perimeter. Marshal Karuna was evidently enforcing military rule with a vengeance, utilizing the considerable manpower now at his disposal.

It's hopeless, Terrel informed Alyssa, who was circling restlessly overhead. *There's no way I'll ever be able to get to one of the shafts, let alone find my way inside.*

We'll see about that, she replied. *At least they can't stop me. You go back to the town. I'll see if I can spot any weak links in their lines. And I'll try to have a look at the central area.*

Be careful. That's where the tornadoes start. He dreaded to think what would happen to the stonechat if she was caught near one of the violent whirlwinds.

It's not the nesting season, Alyssa said. Before Terrel

could ask her what she meant she flew off, her small wings
beating furiously, and was soon lost to sight.

Knowing that he'd be no use to anyone if he starved to
death, Terrel devoted the rest of the afternoon to earning
himself a meal. After several attempts, he managed to get
a job in the overworked kitchens of a tavern and, after several exhausting hours, was rewarded with a large dinner.
By the time he finished he was ready to go to sleep, and
made his way back to the ruined house, hoping that Alyssa
would already be there.

She greeted him as he crawled inside, and flitted to her
usual perch on his shoulder once he sat down.

What did you find out? he asked wearily.

Nothing much. I'm getting to like worms, though.

Terrel laughed. He hadn't considered the fact that the
bird needed to eat too.

So what are we going to do?

There must be a way, Alyssa said. *We can't just give up,
but if the soldiers keep catching you, they're bound to get suspicious sooner or later.* She paused, considering a new idea.
*Maybe we could wait for the next tornado and go in after
that. It's bound to disrupt the guards.*

Terrel did not like the sound of that, but the conversation ended there because they were distracted by a sudden
flapping nearby. They waited, wondering what was going
on, and eventually a kestrel flew into the room. Alyssa
twittered in alarm at the sight of a predator, and Terrel
tensed, ready to defend her if necessary. But the kestrel
made no move to attack. Instead it flopped down to the
floor and folded its wings, drooping with exhaustion.

Terrel stared at the bird, wondering what had prompted
such odd behaviour, while Alyssa twitched and hopped
nervously on his shoulder.

I won't let it hurt you, he reassured her.

The kestrel raised its head and looked directly at the boy.

I have a message for you, it said.

CHAPTER FORTY-THREE

For a few moments both Terrel and Alyssa were too astonished to speak. The kestrel too was silent, its head drooping again.

You're a sleeper! Alyssa exclaimed eventually.

To tell you the truth, I'm not sure what's happening to me, the newcomer replied, *but I am like you, yes.*

Who are you? Terrel asked. The voice sounded familiar to him, but he could not place it.

My name is Lathan. We met on top of Mount Tindaya, but you looked a little different then.

So did you, Terrel commented, remembering the stranger who had thought he was a ghost.

How are you hiding your real eyes? Lathan asked curiously.

You said you had a message, Alyssa reminded him, anxious to get to more important matters.

There are several, actually, he replied, *but first you've got to tell me something. Is it true they're planning to flood the mines?*

Yes.

Moons! Lathan breathed, a shrill scream escaping from the kestrel's beak. *I'd hoped that was only a rumour. You've got to stop them.*

How? Alyssa asked.

Why? Terrel said at the same time.

The kestrel looked from one to the other, as if trying to decide which question to answer.

Look, you'd better tell us everything, Terrel advised, sensing the stranger's confusion. *I don't suppose there's much we can do tonight, so you can take your time.*

There was a pause while Lathan collected his thoughts. Terrel sat still, but Alyssa fidgeted on his shoulder, her impatience obvious.

I don't remember much after that incredible noise, Lathan began. *There was a light . . . lights . . . then I collapsed. I've been dreaming ever since.* He hesitated again, and Terrel could tell that he was wondering if he was dreaming still.

At Tindaya?

That's where my body is. That's where they found me.

Who?

The ghosts.

From the way he said this, Terrel knew that Lathan was having to overcome his own instinctive doubts. He had obviously not believed in the existence of ghosts until he'd been forced to think otherwise.

I knew Shahan, of course, Lathan went on. *He was on the council with me until he was killed.*

You're a seer? Terrel exclaimed.

Yes. Muzeni claimed to be one too, but I'd never met him before. Or the boy.

Elam.

He was the one who showed me how to leave my body and take over this bird. He said he'd been studying the way you did it, Lathan added, glancing at Alyssa. *That was three days ago. They told me I'd been unconscious for a month.* He obviously found this hard to believe.

Terrel had seen nothing of the ghosts since they'd transported him to Tindaya, and wondered now why they should have gone to Lathan rather than come to him.

They were only able to return to our world then because of something they'd done, the seer said, answering Terrel's unspoken question. *I don't know why, exactly, but they were very frustrated about it. They seemed anxious to talk to you, but by then you were too close to Betancuria — which is why they needed me. They wanted to go to Makhaya too, to see what was going on there, but by the time they were able to do so the entire court had moved here. They kept arguing about it.*

That sounded like the ghosts Terrel had come to know.

And the messages are from the ghosts? he asked.

The kestrel dipped its head as if nodding.

The first thing they wanted me to tell you is that the elemental is definitely responsible for—

The what? Terrel cut in sharply.

The elemental, Lathan repeated. *That's what Muzeni and Shahan have started calling the creature. It's quite apt really when you consider—*

There's a creature down there? Terrel interrupted again.

Yes. The disembodied seer sounded confused now. They've known for some time that the problems were being caused by a sentient being. Didn't they tell you?

We haven't seen them for a long time. Terrel's mind was reeling. The rumours were right, he thought. There *is* a monster in the mines — and I'm supposed to go and meet it! *I thought . . .*

Maybe it is the nesting season, Alyssa commented enigmatically. She did not seem very surprised by the news, and Terrel wondered if — on some level — she had known all along. The link that she felt made a little more sense if it was with another living creature.

Are you sure about this? he asked.

I found it hard to believe at first, Lathan replied, *but I've seen their latest interpretations. It makes much more sense now.*

There wasn't much that made sense to Terrel at that moment. Fear threatened to overwhelm him completely, and it was only when Alyssa pecked his ear that he realized their visitor was speaking again. He struggled to overcome his sudden disorientation.

. . . not like any other life form we've ever come across before, but the elemental's power is undeniable. And what is certain is that it's responsible for both the rotation of the islands, and for the fact that they've drifted off course. Some of the forces that caused these things also brought about the earthquakes. The point is that the ghosts felt them in their world too.

Alyssa chirruped softly at this, but if she had any thoughts on the matter Terrel could not hear them.

I don't really know why that was so significant, Lathan went on, *but they said you must go ahead with your original plan. You're the only one who can understand the creature. You have to learn from it, communicate with it — and get it to stop what it's doing.*

Why me? Terrel asked. *I—*

It's in the Code. Even I can see that now, but the council still won't admit it.

Yes, but why am I in the Code in the first place? Is it just because I was born at a specific time? There must be others who—

You have to find your own destiny. Lathan sounded embarrassed now, and Terrel suspected that there was something the sleeper could not or would not tell him.

There is some advice none of us is qualified to give, the seer added weakly.

Terrel recalled Shahan and Muzeni being similarly evasive, telling him only that he had been 'robbed of his birthright'. He felt a spurt of anger. What were they hiding from him? Why wouldn't anyone tell him the truth?

No one else could have done what you did at Tindaya, Lathan went on. *You can't deny fate, Terrel.*

The boy did not respond immediately. Something else was puzzling him.

How did you recognize me at Tindaya? he asked. *I'd never seen you before in my life.*

I can't tell you that.

Why not? Terrel demanded angrily. *If—*

He's telling the truth, Terrel, Alyssa interrupted. *Just listen to what he* can *say.* She turned back to the kestrel. *What else did they want you to tell us?*

They said you'd face opposition before you could get to the elemental, Lathan replied, clearly relieved by the change of subject.

I didn't need them to tell me that, Terrel muttered. *There are soldiers all over the mines.*

That's not what he means, Alyssa said.

There are forces . . . beyond the reach of normal life, Lathan added.

What does that *mean?*

I've no idea, the seer told him awkwardly, *but they said you'd know what they meant.*

The enchanter? Terrel whispered. He had told Alyssa about the malevolent being that had invaded his dreams and even, on occasion, his waking mind, but she had been as mystified as he was. They had no clue as to who it might be, but the possibility that this person had actually taken control of his body at Tiscamanita, when he'd set fire to the shrine, still haunted Terrel. He had tried to tell himself that it had only happened because he had been hopelessly drunk, but he was still not entirely convinced about this.

I don't know anything about an enchanter, Lathan said, sounding alarmed at the idea, *but Muzeni said you'd be protected now. You just have to keep your wits about you and be careful.*

At first Terrel didn't know what this meant, but then he realized – with a sinking feeling in the pit of his stomach – that the ghosts were assuming he'd taken the amulet. They wouldn't know that he hadn't been able to hang on to it when the eclipse ended and the star-maze had vanished. He was about to tell Lathan about this when he remembered that the seer had collapsed as the maze formed – and so he wouldn't know what Terrel was talking about. Even in the boy's own memories it seemed more like a dream. So he said nothing, and listened as Lathan passed on the rest of the ghosts' messages.

Knowing the council also felt that what was happening in the mines was central to the crisis nearly drove Shahan and Muzeni mad. I think they were furious that they couldn't find out what Kamin was going to do about it. When they finally heard the rumour that the authorities were planning to divert the river back to the town, they knew it would be a mistake. The creature was responsible for the drought in the first place, and bringing the water back was only likely to drive it into a rage. Now you tell me they're actually going to flood the mines. That would be appalling! His voice was rising in panic. *It'll go berserk. Trying to drown it won't save the Empire. It'll make things a hundred times worse!*

I told you it couldn't deal with that magic, Alyssa said.

You have to stop them. Lathan sounded almost desperate now.

Or we have to get to the elemental first, she went on, calm in the face of Lathan's hysteria. *If you can somehow get it to see sense, there won't be any need to flood the mines.*

But we can't even get close to it, Terrel pointed out. *So what are we supposed to do?*

There's something else, Lathan said reluctantly.

Terrel's heart sank. What more could there be?

There's a chance that your encounter with the elemental will also decide the fate of people like me and Alyssa. Shahan thinks it's probably responsible for the comas. He thinks you might be able to persuade it to end them.

Since leaving the haven, Terrel had often thought of Alyssa lying unconscious in her cell. It was hard to believe that she was not wasting away, in spite of her assurances to the contrary. The thought that by confronting the monster he might have the chance to free her restored a little of his wavering determination. That way he could go back to her . . . But if he failed she might remain in a coma for years, perhaps for ever. Or worse.

The sleeping is protecting us, Alyssa objected.

From what? Lathan asked. *I know we're surviving against all reason, but surviving isn't living, is it?*

This way I can be with Terrel, she argued. *That's important.*

The kestrel bobbed its head, the avian equivalent of a shrug.

If the water drives the elemental mad, he concluded heavily, *it might kill us.*

The chill of the night seemed to have turned Terrel's heart to ice. He was engulfed by a wave of hopelessness.

The kestrel had begun to seem uneasy now, shifting its feet and ruffling its feathers. Terrel knew that Lathan's newly acquired body was reflecting the seer's agitation and, given the news he had brought with him, that was hardly surprising. It was clear that he would not be able to stay with them for very much longer.

I'm sorry, Lathan whispered. *I'm sorry. I can't . . .*

Was there anything else? Terrel asked quickly, desperately hoping for some practical advice.

Yes, the seer replied. *From Elam. I'm not sure what it means. He told me to remind you that maybe not all rivers run downhill.*

Terrel didn't understand this either, but he caught the echo of something Alyssa had said in one of their conversations back at the haven. The three friends had been together then. Although it could only have been four or five months ago, it seemed like another lifetime, another world.

I can't stay in this creature any longer, Lathan muttered. The kestrel was trembling continuously now, its eyes darting about anxiously.

You can't leave the bird while you're here, Terrel said hurriedly. *You have to get away first or you'll die.*

The kestrel gave a feeble flap of its wings.

It'll drive me mad, Lathan groaned. *I think I'd rather die. I—*

If you do, you betray us all, Alyssa snapped.

Her anger seemed to stiffen the seer's resolve, and with a convulsive effort the kestrel lifted into the air. Without uttering another word, their visitor flew from the room.

In a sudden whirring of feathers, Alyssa left Terrel's shoulder and came to perch on a ledge atop one of the broken walls, from where she could follow Lathan's flight.

Will he make it? Terrel asked.

I hope so, she replied. *That's not an end I would wish on anyone.*

She spoke with feeling, and Terrel realized that she was thinking about the possibility of her own death. He wanted to promise to protect her, to promise that he wouldn't let anyone or anything harm her, but he knew he was dealing with forces beyond his control. Such a promise would be worthless.

What do we do now? he asked instead.

Look for the river that runs uphill, she replied quietly.

Terrel was about to ask Alyssa if she knew what Elam's message meant, but then he saw that he would get no answer. For one awful moment he thought her spirit might have left the stonechat, but then he realized that she was just sleeping. He didn't know whether her sudden descent into unconsciousness was because of her prolonged stay in a single creature, or whether the stonechat was simply unable to remain awake for long during the hours of darkness, but he felt an idiotic surge of resentment that she was able to rest at such a time. At that moment he felt as if he would never sleep again, and there was still so much for them to talk about, so much to decide.

Terrel brooded for a while, veering between bouts of self-pity and shame, and then berating himself for the opportunities he'd missed. It was only now, after Lathan had gone, that the boy thought of all the questions he should have asked. Had Lathan seen the other two men on the mountaintop? If he had, did he believe it could have been a vision from the future? What had the seer made of the deafening 'conversation' they had heard? And why had the same forces that had produced Terrel's ill-fated chance to grasp the talisman turned Lathan into a sleeper? Knowing that he'd get no answers to these puzzles, Terrel eventually made himself lie down and try to get some rest.

There had often been occasions recently when he'd been afraid of what his dreams might bring, but that wasn't the case tonight. It was hard to imagine anything worse than what was happening in the waking world.

CHAPTER FORTY-FOUR

When Fauria arrived at Kamin's temporary lodgings, he was in such a dishevelled and feverish state that the Chief Seer wondered at first if his visitor was drunk. Understandably, relations between the two men had been strained ever since Fauria had revealed his secret allegiance to the Empress, and that made his late-night appearance even more of a surprise. However, Fauria was an astrologer of considerable talent, and if – as seemed likely – he had some urgent news to pass on, Kamin was prepared to listen. He was about to offer his fellow seer some refreshment when Fauria pre-empted such courtesies with a bald statement that silenced his host.

'The rumour-mongers were right,' he stated soberly. 'There *is* a monster.'

For several moments Kamin could only stare in disbelief, his brain unable to shape his disordered thoughts into coherent speech. When he finally managed to find his voice, his visitor overrode his objections.

'Surely—'

'I've been studying the augury from the readings again.

Remember those slight discrepancies that we chose to ignore? Well, I can explain them now.'

'How?'

'They were brought about by *local* forces, not by the moons at all.'

'We surmised as much,' the Chief Seer said, recalling the lengthy discussions of the previous night. 'What's changed to make you think—'

'The source of the flux *moves*,' Fauria cut in. 'What's more, it moves in a random manner. No natural force could change so quickly, or so unpredictably.'

'No natural force that we're familiar with,' Kamin responded. 'We've known for some time that what's been happening in the mines defies ordinary logic.'

'Yes, but that could have been the result of a pattern so complex we were unable to recognize it for what it was.'

'But you don't believe that now?'

'No.'

'Why not?'

'Because even though some of the changes looked arbitrary, they're not.'

Kamin hesitated, feeling that the argument was going in circles.

'The forces that broke the Well of the Moons came into being at the precise moment necessary to combine with the natural flux and create such a disruption,' Fauria explained. 'I find it hard to believe in a coincidence that exact. It was an intelligent, *deliberate* act.'

Kamin remembered his own intuitive reaction to the destruction of the sacred stone. It had felt like an intentional act of sabotage then – and now that feeling had been reinforced by Fauria's explanation. The Chief Seer was beginning to consider the unthinkable.

'You can even see when it rested, drawing in its strength

before striking,' Fauria went on. 'No mere freak of nature could produce such actions.'

'Show me,' Kamin demanded.

An hour later, after poring over the mass of readings and calculations, the two seers were in agreement – and Kamin was beginning to readjust his thinking accordingly.

'So whatever's down there is a sentient being,' he concluded. 'Albeit one beyond our imagining.'

Fauria nodded wearily.

'And it was sending us a message when it destroyed the Well,' he said.

'But *what* message, that's the point.'

'I'd have thought it was obvious.'

Kamin glanced up at his companion, the unspoken question in his eyes.

'"Leave me alone,"' Fauria said.

For a time neither man spoke, then Kamin drew himself up and became deliberately businesslike.

'That's the one thing we *can't* do,' he stated. 'Even if this . . . *creature* was threatening us, what more can it do? If it's really responsible for the rotation of the islands, then there's nothing that could be any worse for the Empire. What we have to decide now is whether this changes the rest of the augury.'

'I don't think so,' Fauria ventured. 'Water is still the key.'

'I agree.' Kamin relaxed a little now that his course of action was clear once more. 'We go ahead as planned.'

'It can't be!' Hoban exclaimed. 'It's insane.'

The commissioner had not objected to being roused from his bed in the middle of the night, but now he wished that he was still asleep. From the moment he had arrived, together with a grim-faced Marshal Karuna, and joined the two seers, it had been obvious that the news was bad.

Kamin remained calm in the face of Hoban's incredulity.

'Insane or not, it's the truth,' he said quietly.

'I can't believe that. I'm the only one here who's seen it, remember? It has no substance, no features of any kind. It doesn't even need air to breathe! How can it be alive?'

'We're not saying it's an ordinary animal,' Kamin replied. 'Far from it. But if you think about it, this explains a lot about your observations.'

'The fact that it seems to move around, perhaps,' Hoban conceded, 'but the effects we've seen change as well. Sometimes they can fill a huge cavern – and yet, if you're right, it's been able to travel down narrow tunnels and even through solid rock. It's impervious to fire, and we know from experience that weapons don't touch it. Even when it's opaque it's not solid. It shifts, and . . . And sometimes we can see right through it! How can that be some sort of creature?'

For answer, Kamin opened a book that lay on the table between them and pointed to a diagram.

'Recognize anything?'

'It's a sectional plan of the central mine workings,' Hoban replied, frowning. 'Why?'

'This is taken from Gaylor's Adjunct, part of the Tindaya Code,' Kamin replied. 'It was carved in stone hundreds of years ago, long before any of your mines were excavated.' He had only been able to transport a tiny fraction of his library to Betancuria, but was glad now that this volume had been among those he had chosen in haste.

Hoban said nothing, merely shaking his head in disbelief.

'A colleague of mine discovered it,' the Chief Seer went

on, remembering Lathan's visit to his home in Makhaya. 'The one thing he could not explain was this.' He pointed to the star-shaped symbol at the centre of the diagram.

'You think that's the creature?'

'Its position is directly under the central mound,' Kamin pointed out.

'But that doesn't mean it's *alive*!' Hoban exclaimed.

'We didn't realize it at the time,' the seer went on, 'but this design appears elsewhere in the Code, in various forms. No one's come up with a satisfactory translation, but the various attempts have all been to do with flowers, seeds, in one case even a spring – which is what I thought this was until now. All of those things can be interpreted as symbolizing *life* in one form or another. And together with the evidence of the augury . . . the conclusion is obvious.'

As always, once he had been converted to a point of view, Kamin was its most ardent advocate. Hoban glanced at Karuna, hoping to find some support from another practically-minded man, but the marshal's expression was carefully neutral. In spite of the incredible nature of what they had been told, he had a soldier's natural obedience when dealing with a superior. Until someone proved the Chief Seer wrong, Karuna was prepared to take him at his word.

'So you're asking me to believe that all of this – the tremors, the drought, the whirlwinds, even the islands' rotation – is the result of the actions of one creature?' Hoban's last defiance was crumbling in spite of his words.

'A true monster,' Fauria replied. He had not spoken for some time and his voice was hoarse, but it carried the weight of conviction. 'If we can't imagine the form it takes, how can we be sure what forces it might control?'

'But if it's so powerful, how can we hope to defeat it?' Hoban cried.

'Everyone and everything has a weakness,' Karuna answered soberly. 'And we've already found the creature's.'

'Exactly,' Kamin agreed. 'Water may not just act to block the forces that have been plaguing us, it might be a way of ridding ourselves of the problem altogether. As the water level rises, the creature will either be trapped and drown, or it'll be driven to the surface – and I have every confidence that Marshal Karuna and his men will be able to deal with it then.'

Hoban raised his eyebrows at this, but the soldier's face remained impassive.

'That's the main reason I wanted to inform you both of this development,' Kamin went on. 'It seems we must be prepared for some fighting after all, even if our enemy is a rather unusual one. I don't want news of this to reach the general public yet if we can help it – there are enough rumours already – but you must each tell those of your men who need to be involved in the revised preparations. I rely upon your discretion, gentlemen.'

After they had gone and Kamin was alone again, he sat brooding, all possibility of sleep banished. He knew that the next people he would have to tell about the 'monster' were Jax – and Adina. It seemed that the Guardian of prophecy might yet be given the chance to become a hero by facing his country's foe in battle.

CHAPTER FORTY-FIVE

'Excellent,' Kamin commented. 'Excellent! You've done well, gentlemen.'

The Chief Seer was just completing his tour of inspection, and had been impressed by what he'd seen. As he had said at the meeting where the plans had first been hatched, much of the work had already been done, but a phenomenal amount had been achieved since then. The unexpectedly big lake they were standing beside was proof of that.

'We've been lucky with the weather,' Hoban remarked. He meant that there had been no tornadoes recently. The respite had allowed their work to go ahead unhindered by anything other than the normal constraints of the terrain. 'And even though there's been no rain here,' he added, 'the heavy falls further north mean there's more water in the rivers now.'

The commissioner was taking some satisfaction in a job well done, but both his grim expression and the tone of his voice made it clear that he did not share Kamin's enthusiasm for the project. Once it was set in motion, even if it did rid them of the creature, it would effectively destroy Hoban's life's work – and that of many generations before him.

'How long before there's enough in the reservoirs?' Kamin asked.

'At the current rate of fill, I'd say by tomorrow morning.'

'And when all the dams have been breached, how long will it be until the water in the mines reaches a level that would force the creature to the surface?'

'It's hard to say,' Hoban replied. 'We've no way of knowing how much the lower caverns and tunnels will absorb before the water rises to the main seams. And we don't know what the run-off rate will be.'

'What's your best guess?' Kamin persisted.

'Four hours. Maybe more. But I don't think we need worry about that too much. If we time it right, the central and upper levels will be inundated very quickly. That ought to be enough either to wash the creature away or drown it.'

'And in case it manages to avoid the deluge,' Marshal Karuna put in, 'we'll be stationed at all exit points. We'll get it one way or another.'

'We've arranged for some water to be siphoned off to fill temporary moats around the soldiers' positions,' Hoban explained. 'If the creature *does* reach the open air – and I'm hoping for all our sakes that it doesn't – that should at least give them some protection.'

Over the past three days, the commissioner had become used to the idea that they were dealing with a living entity, and had co-operated with Karuna in adjusting their plans.

'Once they can see what they're shooting at, my lads'll take care of it,' the marshal stated confidently.

'How many reservoirs are there in all?' Jax asked. The

prince had accompanied Kamin on the inspection, but until now had remained silent. He too had accepted the seers' conclusion and, while Kamin had seen occasional fear in the prince's eyes, Jax seemed to find the idea of a monster exciting.

'Six, Your Highness,' Hoban replied. 'Two main ones, including this one, and four more ranged around the site. The maximum flow will be directed to the main shafts directly above the creature. The others are to cover some of the outer entrances.'

'What about all the other tunnels? There must be more than that,' Jax said.

'Indeed there are, Sire. However, we've blocked the majority of them already, and the water will reach most of the others fairly quickly.'

'How did you block them?' Adina asked – obviously feeling that she ought to make some contribution to the discussion. While her son was clearly fascinated by the project – and by its destructive potential – the Empress had seemed bored by all the technical details. Kamin would have preferred it if neither of them had been there, but Jax had insisted on accompanying him, and – after the seer's own advice to the Empress – there had been no chance of getting rid of Adina.

'Arranging rock falls in a mine is relatively easy, Your Majesty,' Hoban replied. 'It's preventing them that requires skill. In fact, when our teams went in they found a lot of the work had already been done for them, probably by the recent quakes. As soon as the water starts flowing, it will bring several more tunnels down.'

'How are you going to breach the dams?' Jax asked.

'They've all been constructed in such a way that once a few critical supports are broken or removed, a section will collapse,' Hoban told him. 'The weight of water will do the rest. Of course we'll have to time each release carefully, depending on the size, gradient and length of the channel bringing the water to the point where it goes underground. Marshal Karuna has arranged a series of signal beacons to co-ordinate it all.'

'Where exactly *is* the monster?'

'The last sighting put it directly under that mound,' the commissioner replied, pointing into the distance. 'About half a mile below the surface.'

'And when *was* the last sighting?' the Empress enquired.

Hoban hesitated before answering, already anticipating the reaction his reply would provoke.

'Over a month ago, Ma'am,' he admitted.

'Then how do you know it's still there?' she asked.

'We can't be sure,' he conceded, 'but it seems to have been there for quite some time. And the tornadoes always form right over that spot.'

'But there haven't been any tornadoes for several days,' Adina pointed out. 'Perhaps it's moved.'

Although this thought had already occurred to both Hoban and Karuna, neither of them had been keen to send any of their men into the mine to check on the possibility.

'Shouldn't someone go and find out?' the Empress asked, her voice deceptively mild.

'I don't think that would be wise,' Kamin said, coming to the rescue of his colleagues. 'Even if the creature *has* shifted, our plan is to inundate the entire workings. It can't escape. And we don't want to give it any warning, do we? A patrol might alert it to the possibility of danger. We're better off catching it off guard.'

Adina's expression betrayed nothing. She was evidently deciding whether to pursue the matter when her son beat her to it.

'I could go,' he suggested. 'Perhaps that's what I'm here for. As Guardian, I mean.' He could not hide his grin when he saw the horrified expression on his mother's face. If she was to uphold her claim to be the Mentor, she would have to go with him – and he was sure that wasn't going to happen. His suggestion made him look like a hero, when in fact there was no chance of them actually letting him go.

'I'm sure that won't be necessary, Sire,' Kamin said on cue, giving the prince a measuring glance. Hoban and Karuna signalled their agreement. They both knew that the prince would be more trouble than he was worth.

'I should think not!' the Empress exclaimed, making it unanimous.

'Then we proceed as planned,' Kamin decreed. 'Until tomorrow morning, gentlemen. Ma'am.'

The tension that had been building in the town ever since Kamin's public announcement, and which had been fuelled by another round of rumours, finally erupted into violence that afternoon. Betancuria was now under military rule, with a curfew in place, and there had been little opportunity for the bitter locals to voice their grievances. So their anger had simmered beneath the surface instead – especially after the soldiers arrested a few young hot-headed troublemakers. The sense of injustice felt by the townspeople was intensified by the fact that even though large quantities of water were now available, very little had been released for their use. In the midst of plenty, their drought continued. That the water was to be used to destroy not only the cause of their recent troubles but also the mines on which almost all their livelihoods depended only made things worse. For every person who counselled patience, arguing that it was a fair price to pay to be rid of the problem and have the islands' position return to normal, there was another who claimed that there must be a different solution to the crisis, one that would not entail ruining their lives. Many felt that the army was evading its responsibilities, taking the easy option so that they wouldn't have to go into the mines themselves. Some of the engineers who had taken part in the planning of the operation had been subjected to threats and abuse, and all soldiers were now regarded as the enemy.

Marshal Karuna was fully aware that feelings were running high, and he had responded in the only way he understood – with a show of force. With almost all of the imperial army now in Betancuria, there was no problem about manpower. Patrols within the town watched for any signs of dissent, and all the dams, channels and reservoirs were heavily guarded in case anyone tried to sabotage the workings. Other units acted as personal bodyguards for the imperial family and other members of the court.

The situation came to a head when the women of Betancuria decided to take matters into their own hands. As if summoned by a clarion call, they came out onto the streets in ones and twos, then joined into small groups, each of which gravitated towards one of the larger thoroughfares. The small streams of women soon became a river, and then a torrent, pouring out of the town towards the nearest reservoir. Nearly all of them carried either a water jar, pots and pans, or a digging tool of some kind. As their numbers grew they banged these together, producing a frighteningly loud rhythmic clatter. Their actions were not planned; they had no specific goal in mind, other than to obtain some water for their families. But they knew they were going to do *something*.

At first the soldiers regarded the marchers as something

of a joke, but as the size of the gathering grew the patrol commanders began to get nervous. They could hardly take their swords to unarmed women. And yet if the protesters refused to obey orders and return to their homes, what was the army supposed to do? When the destination of the protest became obvious, some of the captains called for reinforcements and sent messages to their colleagues guarding the reservoir. By then, of course, the momentum of the demonstration had become unstoppable, and confrontation was inevitable.

Faced with such an unexpected and imposing force, the soldiers fell back until they lined the shore of the lake. As the women came on insults were exchanged and some weapons were drawn, but none of the guards was willing to attack female civilians. As the adversaries came closer still, some shoving matches turned into brawls, and a number of soldiers were pushed into the water. A few of the protesters then began to fill their containers with water, heedless of the mud that had been churned up in the shallows, and defying the guards to stop them. After that initial success, many more women pressed forward and helped themselves from the reservoir.

If it had been left at that, all might still have passed off without serious trouble – but when some of the women began digging at a stretch of the bank, intent on releasing the water into the old river bed, the nearest captain ordered his men to stop them. The fight that ensued was chaotic and, as the first blood was spilled, the scene degenerated into a riot.

By now the women had been joined by a fair number of their menfolk, and when they saw the soldiers attacking, there was no holding them back. By the time order was restored, six guards and more than a dozen locals were dead, many more were nursing injuries – and even though

the reservoir remained intact, there was some doubt about
the safety of the dam. It had sustained considerable damage from piecemeal attacks, but was still in place. None
of the mining engineers was willing to work on it after
what had happened, and so the military had to shore it up
as best they could and hope that it would continue to hold
as the water level rose overnight.

The air over the distant mound seemed to quiver, and
Terrel stared at it intently, willing it to be the start of
something more. Was it spinning? Or was it just a trick of
the light?

The disturbance, whatever it had been, dissolved, leaving the air clear again.

'There must be one soon!' he muttered to himself, then
sighed.

When he and Alyssa had devised their plan, it had
seemed logical enough. They would wait for the next tornado and then make their way into the mining area once
the whirlwind had cleared away a section of soldiers. The
two friends knew from watching the guards that they were
well practised in techniques for evading the tornadoes –
although there had apparently been some casualties earlier – but that it would take them some time to re-establish
their posts and patrols. In the confusion, Terrel and Alyssa
hoped to get past them and down into the mines. Terrel
was even prepared to try and use the glamour to a much
greater extent than ever before, should he need to do so in
order to avoid capture. Their plan wasn't perfect, but it
was the best they could think of.

They'd been waiting for a few days now, and were
becoming increasingly frustrated. They had begun to look
around for alternative strategies, but without success. The
cordon around the mines was as effective as ever, and

their attempts to penetrate the military lines had been even less successful than the earlier ones.

At the same time, as the days had passed, Terrel was growing more and more concerned about Alyssa. She was finding it hard to stay awake for more than half the hours of daylight now, and even when she wasn't sleeping, her once restless movements had given way to periods of lethargy. When she spoke, her words rarely made much sense. Although that had often been the case with Alyssa, her lucid times were growing less and less frequent now. It was as though she was not only having to guard her waning reserves of physical strength, but also her moments of sanity. Terrel could only hope that she'd be able to find both when the time came for action. He was exhausted too. He'd spent the last two nights in the open, only allowing himself brief spells of sleep for fear of missing the beginnings of a tornado. His body ached almost all the time now, and he had come close to madness himself as the time trickled away. But if the waiting had been hard for him, he knew it had been worse for Alyssa.

He had wanted to tell her to leave him, to fly away so that she could rest properly, but he hadn't been able to bring himself to do it. He told himself that she wouldn't have gone anyway, and hoped that this was true.

The bird was currently tucked inside the neck of his shirt, nestled against his chest. She felt warm and soft, and horribly vulnerable, and he had to keep reminding himself not to make any sudden moves. But she seemed to take comfort from their closeness – and that was all Terrel could offer her for now. She had not liked being confined initially, and when she had woken after sleeping next to his skin for the first time she had struggled, overcome by a wild creature's instinctive horror of being trapped. However, she had accepted the sanctuary after a while, and returned there whenever her senses began to fail her.

Terrel felt her feathers twitch minutely, and wondered what she was dreaming about. Were they the dreams of a stonechat, or of a girl whose mind was trapped here but whose body was far away?

A larger movement and the tiny prick of her claws on his skin told him that she was waking up. He reached in and took the bird gently in his hand, then placed her in her accustomed position on his shoulder.

Anything? Alyssa's voice sounded hoarse and sleepy, but she was evidently alert enough to want to know what was going on.

No, he replied. *A few false alarms, that's all.*

The sun was sinking towards the eastern horizon, on the far side of the mines. Night would come soon – and night was the most difficult time for them both.

We have to get in there soon, Alyssa said.

How long do you think we've got?

A day, she guessed. *Two at the most.* She had flown over the reservoirs several times, and had seen the construction of the channels from above.

There must *be a way*, Terrel said. *We can't get this close and not get in.*

There had been a time, not so long ago, when he would have given almost anything to avoid having to go underground. Now the idea that he might never get the chance appalled him.

There will be, Alyssa stated, staring across the man-made devastation.

They were sitting at the top of a hill, chosen because it was far enough away from the perimeter to avoid any patrols, but close enough to the mine entrance for them to get down to it fairly quickly. They had no idea which way a tornado would go, so one point had seemed as good as any other, but they had decided to move a mile or so away from the town to try to avoid the trouble they had sensed was brewing there.

Do you think the locals will have managed to hold up the work at all? Terrel asked.

Doesn't look like it, Alyssa replied.

I keep thinking we should've tried to do something, he said ruefully. *At least stir them up a little.*

And get you arrested again? she countered. *I don't think there was much we could've done.*

I suppose not. Just talking to his friend for a few moments had made him feel a little better.

A cuckoo's nest, Alyssa muttered. *Why isn't this the nesting season?*

Terrel did not know what to make of this, and so did not reply.

Everywhere's haunted, except here, she added. She seemed to find this idea amusing, although Terrel could not think why.

Ghosts can't come here, he said, hoping to prompt her into clarifying her enigmatic statement.

But Alyssa just took to the air, skimming down the hillside in a series of agile if erratic dives, heading for the nearest of the new lakes. Terrel watched her go, thinking that at least the soldiers would not be able to prevent *her* from drinking. His own water bottle was almost empty, and he was not likely to be able to fill it again any time soon.

Sunset brought with it a few sudden gusts of wind, but no embryonic tornadoes. Alyssa returned and, knowing that Terrel would not risk letting her sleep inside his shirt when night came, she settled on the topmost branch of a nearby bush. He wished her goodnight but got no reply, and returned to his vigil.

Some time later, in the amber moonlight, he closed his eyes, meaning to nap for a little while. The dream enveloped him like a tidal wave and swept him away.

CHAPTER FORTY-SIX

It was like a blend of every dream he'd ever had, a clutter of images that ranged from the mundane to the bizarre, from the personal to the wide-ranging. It was both welcoming and terrifying, full of noise and silence. There was nothing to hold on to, nothing solid, each quicksilver moment sliding into another, unrelated vision. Moons fell and stars danced; a dark bird spread its wings and filled the sky; smoke billowed from cornfields and a crystal city sank beneath grey waves. He was warmed by an unseen presence, and watched as a mirror splintered. Sun-scorched sand burnt his feet; a red rose burst into flame and a frozen sea cracked and shivered. He was assaulted by pain and joy; shame warred with curiosity; love shielded his heart when fear threatened to crush it. It was a journey with no beginning and no end, where every illusion, every image, was hurled into his path, and where every emotion tore at him in a frenzy.

But that was only the beginning.

His mind ranged further, beyond the realm of dreams, as if even that infinite landscape could no longer sustain his voyaging. He saw his life as a fragmented play upon an invisible stage – part tragedy, part comedy, part melodrama. It was as though his sleeping brain was filling itself with everything that had ever happened to him, cramming his entire existence into a smaller and smaller space. The dream had its own identity now, and it needed to remember *everything*.

There were the faces – more than he could ever hope to count – of his friends and enemies, those who had helped or betrayed him. They travelled with him, their expressions reflecting degrees of truth and deception beyond their smiles and frowns. Their eyes held his, or looked away.

The parade was endless. Elam, Ziolka, Ahmeza – the cook wielding a ladle like a sword. Old Timi – the toothless wolf – and all the other inmates. Ingo. Aylor – the blade of his dagger shining in his eyes. Shahan, Jon. Blind Efrin, young Rico, Gallia, Chenowith and their fellow villagers. Ferrand and his sons. Sarafia. Babak – the generous swindler. Seneschal Cadrez and Underseer Uzellin. Kativa. Gegan and Kaz, Drake, Laevo and Sill. Lathan. And many more whose names he could hardly remember.

The parade was endless, but one face – the only one he longed to see – was missing. Alyssa appeared in many guises, but never her own. She flew as an owl, a sparrow, a raven and a stonechat; she ran as a piglet, hound or horse, and sang as a cat with mismatched eyes. But her own face was always hidden behind the facade, out of reach.

There were voices too, sometimes matching the faces, sometimes disembodied. Their words filled the dream, overlapping and competing with each other to catch his sleeping ear. Whispers, shouts and conversations merged in an endless babble of noise, where meaning only rarely rose to the surface.

'That means you have to marry me now.'

He could not see Alyssa but he could hear her, easily picking out her voice from the multitude.

'Everywhere's haunted.'

'Like the moons, but different.'

She took her place among all the rest, and although he tried to listen only to her, other voices were demanding his attention now, rising like dolphins above the sea of sound.

'Fate didn't deal either of us a particularly good hand, did it.'

'You've got a visitor.'

'It was a test, wasn't it.'

If there was a message, an underlying meaning, in what he was hearing, there was no time for him to decipher it. There was just too much, and it was too diverse in both content and context. There were questions — some of them his own — but no answers.

'Why are you asking *me* these questions?'

'You're going to trust in a *dream*?'

'Can ghosts lie?'

'Does all this have anything to do with the Dark Moon?'

Time meant nothing here; each voice existed in its own frame of reference, its own self-contained world.

'I was going to die anyway.'

'Will I ever see you again?'

The litany went on even when he could not see any of their faces, when all he could see were the places his outward journey had led him to. Rivers ran past him; he flew over the restless ocean, and walked upon mountains . . .

'Mountains will crumble and others rise.'

He returned to the various villages and taverns, was trapped by the haven again, and clambered over the fallen stones of the distant past . . .

'And the only thing they left was this ruin.'

There were plains and roads, fields and forests, places of love and pain . . .

'Is this how you honour my memory?'

And above them all, the skies that ruled their world.

'Oh, you mean it bends light.'

'They're full of stars!'

How could there be so many words? So many – enough to drown his thoughts but still not enough to convey even a fraction of what each voice meant to him. He could not separate the warnings and advice, the puzzles and the messages, or control their flow. He could only let them pour over him and hope that he could remember what was important before he was washed away completely.

'All magic exacts a price.'

'It all comes back to the Code.'

'The most important ingredient is faith.'

'They used to be real roses once.'

'Just follow your instincts.'

'Why would a hero choose evil?'

'You're good at this, aren't you?'

The last voice sent a chill through him, a sudden wave of ice as he felt the change coming.

'You can't hide from your own dreams. You never could.'

Everything Terrel had seen, everything he'd heard, had come from within himself – until that moment. He had not surrendered willingly, but now the dream was shared.

I've been waiting for you.

Terrel did not reply. He held his breath, hoping he would not be found – like a child who closes his eyes and thinks that makes him invisible. The faces vanished and the voices fell silent as the dream changed. He was swallowed by darkness.

Oh, don't stop now, the voice mocked. *It was actually quite interesting for once. And it's been such a long time since I . . .*

The silence that followed this hesitation was full of speculation, the intruder's doubt turning to surprise and then to pleasure.

Where are you, exactly?

Terrel still refused to answer. He wanted no part of this.

You're close, aren't you? I can feel it. There was a touch of anger in the voice now. *That really was foolish, you know. I was bound to find you sooner or later. What are you doing here, anyway?*

Terrel had no intention of telling him anything.

You're meddling in matters that don't concern you, his inquisitor went on. *Just like you did at Tindaya. Oh, don't look so surprised! I know everything about you. You failed there, just as you'll fail here. And next time I'll be the one to collect the talisman.*

Terrel could stand it no longer.

Who are you? he cried.

You really don't know, do you? How can you be so stupid?

And then the connection was made, and Terrel was helpless. Not even his thoughts were safe now.

'The enchanter'? His antagonist's incredulity was replaced by amusement. *Is that how you think of me? How flattering! Apt too, of course.*

Within the nightmare, Terrel felt himself growing smaller. It was his only defence. But there was no escape.

Shall I give you a clue? the voice taunted him. *Something even your pathetic brain can work with? Remember this?*

The darkness became blood red, and pain and hatred leached away the last of Terrel's courage, leaving him blind and drenched with sweat. The crimson tide thundered in his ears, but even then the voice still sought him out, bringing with it memories of unreasoning terror.

Perhaps I should have crushed your skull instead of just an arm and a leg. That would have saved everyone a lot of trouble. This comment was followed by the mocking laughter that had haunted Terrel even when he was awake. He writhed in agony, willing himself to disappear, to become nothing.

Perhaps I was just too squeamish then. I was very young, after all. His tormentor laughed at a joke only he could understand. *I won't make that mistake again. Removing obstacles from my path is just a matter of will-power. And I've had some practice now.*

As the red sea dissolved, Terrel saw Shahan again, at the moment his life ended – and then found himself looking into the face of the man who had killed him.

That's Marik, the voice informed him. *Some people are easier to mould than others. Even you must have realized that. You have some puny talent of your own, don't you? Dreams are the easiest way of sending messages or orders, but then you already know that.*

The realization that it was the enchanter – and not himself – who had been responsible for the seer's death filled Terrel with a mixture of anger and relief, but he tried to keep his thoughts to himself.

Of course! You were part of that one, weren't you? the voice went on. *Seeing him with you led me to him, and then it was easy. Well, you saw what happened. I even managed to persuade you it had been your fault!* More laughter rubbed salt into the wounds inflicted by his heartless words.

Although Terrel wanted to scream, to vent his rage and fear, he kept silent, knowing that he had no choice but to listen until the torture ended. He was trapped by the dream turned nightmare, helpless and frustrated within its smothering embrace.

Then there was Mirival, of course, the enchanter went on. *Why didn't you see his end, I wonder? You'd never met him, I suppose, and his death was almost peaceful by comparison, but . . . Dreams can be so fickle, can't they? The maid who poisoned him never even knew she was doing anything wrong. And she never will. It was the perfect crime!*

Terrel thought back to Laevo's play and the murder of Merry-Al. It had been closer to the truth than he had believed at the time, but the identity of the killer had been wrong. Kamin had been the model for the play's villain, but having seen him in the market square Terrel knew that it was not the seer who invaded his dreams.

I was angry with you for taking part in that repulsive little show, his tormentor commented. *But it's not important now. Mirival was important, though. He was the only other person who knew about you. And his death should've solved the problem. But you just wouldn't keep away, would you? It was fun for a while, but you're in danger of becoming a nuisance now.*

The monologue had been wearing away at Terrel's nerves, and finally he snapped. For the second time he broke his self-imposed silence.

What do you want from me?

Want? What could I possibly want from you? You really should be paying more attention. 'Dreams are sometimes meant to show us things.' Isn't that what your little friend says?

At the mention of Alyssa Terrel instinctively shied away from confrontation again. He did not want her to become part of this horror. The crystal city floated into the darkness.

Oh, please! the enchanter exclaimed in disgust. *Is this the best you can do? I know all about her, and trying to protect her is pointless.*

Terrel knew now who had destroyed the city in an earlier dream, but he had rebuilt it with care and was determined that it would never be damaged again. And then he realized that the city had changed. Even though it was still flawed, it was now guarded by lines of fire and light. Terrel wondered where they'd come from, knowing they were not his creation.

This is ridiculous! the voice hissed. *You know what happened last time.*

But the crystal city remained intact and, for the first time, Terrel sensed a momentary lapse in his tormentor's confidence. Hope began to glimmer like the facets of Alyssa's shield.

Have you slept with her yet, by the way? the enchanter asked casually.

Terrel knew he was being baited, distracted from more important matters, but he could not help his response.

What a shame! the intruder mocked. *I don't suppose you'll ever get the chance now.*

She's my friend! Terrel cried. *I would never—*

But you wanted to, didn't you?

No!

Liar. I knew you were watching when I was in bed with that chambermaid. You enjoyed it, didn't you. You're a hypocrite, Terrel. If you had the chance—

Shut up! Terrel screamed, losing the last vestiges of his restraint. *Shut up!*

He felt, rather than saw, his tormentor smile, and knew he was beaten. His opponent's use of his name had revealed just how one-sided their contest was.

I really don't think you should talk to me like that. The voice was smug now. *You wouldn't want to annoy me, you know.* After a pause, he added, *Shall I show you what happens to people who annoy me?*

The nightmare shifted again, and Terrel found himself at the top of a high tower, looking out over the lights of a vast city. But this was not Tiscamanita. This was a place he had only ever seen in a dream. He had no idea where it was.

It's Makhaya, his guide informed him helpfully.

Terrel shuddered, realizing that this was no longer a dream. This was real, as his vision of Shahan's murder had been real.

And this is Mela.

The girl was standing beside the low, crenellated wall that surrounded the platform. She stood quite still, and an air of misery clung about her like a dark mist. There were tears in her eyes, but she made no sound.

The stupid girl's upset because she's got herself pregnant, the enchanter said contemptuously.

Terrel sensed another moment of unease – of guilt? – in his adversary, and tried to exploit it. His probing uncovered layers of doubt and suspicion, things that he ought not to have been able to see. There were cracks in the enchanter's defences after all.

She began to invade your dreams, didn't she! Terrel exclaimed. *She turned the tables on you.*

Of course not! She couldn't do anything, but it was annoying, the way she nagged on and on. I'll stick to servants in future. At least they know their place.

It was the most revealing thing the enchanter had said so far. He had made an error, though he seemed unaware of it. And then he spoke again, his voice filled with a vicious contempt.

She's become unstable, the stupid bitch, he said. *This will solve all the problems.*

Terrel watched, his skin crawling in horror, as Mela climbed slowly up onto the parapet.

Do you want to give her the final push? his tormentor enquired.

No! Terrel shouted. *Mela! Don't do this. You don't have to do this!*

The girl hesitated, looking round as though she might have heard a distant echo of his plea. She was weeping now, her face pale in the moonlight.

Terrel felt the invisible barrier crash down, and knew that she was beyond his help. Despair swept over him, matching the emotion he saw in the girl's eyes.

There's only one way this dream can end, the enchanter said.

There was only sadness in Mela's eyes now; the earlier confusion had gone. Her mind was made up – or had been made up for her. After one last glance up at the sky, she stepped out into the void.

She made no sound as she fell. All that was left was a distant vibration as her life, and that of her unborn child, was snuffed out.

The silence stretched until Terrel wondered if the dream was finally over. But the almost tangible presence of evil remained – quieter now, as though stunned by its own iniquity, but still there.

You killed your own child! Terrel whispered.

It doesn't matter, the murderer replied. *It would probably have been deformed anyway, like you.* He was striving to regain his earlier casual tone, but Terrel could tell that this was only a pretence.

What if she comes back to haunt you? he said.

Ghosts? The enchanter's disdain was genuine now. *I've no time for such fairy tales!*

In that moment, even in the midst of his revulsion, Terrel gained a tiny spark of encouragement. His enemy did *not* see everything, did not know everything. But the enchanter's next words filled him with dread.

She was just a nuisance, he said. *But not any more. And guess what, Terrel? You're next.*

Terrel woke, shivering. By the pale light of a newborn day he saw that the stonechat was staring, petrified, at the air above his head – but he had no time to ask what Alyssa could see of his dreams.

A fledgling tornado was struggling towards its full fury – and it was heading straight for them.

CHAPTER FORTY-SEVEN

Go, Alyssa! Terrel urged. *Get away!*

The stonechat did not move, her jewelled black eyes still fixed on the dream-clouds that floated over him.

'Get away!' he yelled aloud, above the growing roar of the wind. 'Alyssa!' He stood up and waved frantically with his good arm, hoping to catch her attention, and was rewarded when she looked at him at last.

I saw, she whispered. *I—*

There's no time for that now, Terrel cut in. *Look!* The tornado was closer now, and growing all the time. He knew he might not be able to escape from its path, but Alyssa could. She could move much faster than him – but she was also much more vulnerable. He was desperate for her to take to the air.

I should stay with you, she said anxiously, finally seeing the danger they were in.

No! We'll meet up again down there, he told her, pointing. *Please, Alyssa. Just go!*

She hesitated for a moment longer, then came to her senses, and in a sudden blur of feathers she was gone.

Terrel breathed a sigh of relief, then turned and began to run.

The ground was pitted with holes and gullies, and clumps of tangle-grass made the footing even more treacherous. Terrel headed downhill, running across the slope in the direction of the town, hoping to keep out of the path of the tornado. He went as fast as he could, heedless of the shooting pains in his weaker leg, but it was soon obvious that he could not outrun the whirlwind. Trying to go even faster, he tripped and fell, pulled himself to his feet and ran on, only to stumble and crash down again. Winded, he clung to the ground as the air around him howled. Glancing up, squinting into the gale, he saw that the tornado had almost reached the edge of the mining area. The cone twisted and bulged, writhing as though it were alive, a primeval creature of destruction.

Ahead of him, only a few paces away, Terrel saw the dry bed of a stream, and a slab of overhanging rock where the seasonal flow had gouged out the earth below. Although it might not offer much protection, it would be better than nothing. The wind was so strong now that he could not stand up, and it almost tore the clothes from his back as he crawled towards the shelter, dragging himself over the dirt and stones. By the time he wedged himself under the rock, he was almost deafened by the noise of the storm. He made himself as small as possible, and prayed for survival. He had been waiting for a tornado for so long; it would be ironic if his wish was granted only to be the cause of his downfall.

The air was full of flying dust and debris now, and Terrel could hardly open his eyes, but he sensed a slight shift in the tumult – and moments later a new element was added to the incredible buffeting. He didn't realize what it was at first, but then the thrumming sound, and a sudden drop in the temperature, told him that it must be raining. The whirlwind had swerved a little to the south, and had passed directly over one of the small reservoirs, siphoning its water into the sky and flinging it down again over a vast area. Even though he was partially sheltered from the onslaught, Terrel's clothes were soon soaked, and the gully bubbled and splashed with rivulets and small mud slides. He had no time to wonder how this sudden theft might affect the seers' plans, because he was now clinging on to his refuge with all his strength.

Having changed course, the tornado did not pass directly over him, but even on the edge of its vortex its power was incredible. Terrel was dragged along the ground, and he knew he would be killed if he was sucked out from beneath the rock. His only hope lay in staying where he was. But then he got caught in a narrow part of the crevice, and – as he was pummelled by a fresh gust of wind – his arms and shoulders were wedged tightly into the gap. He felt as though every part of his body was being beaten with iron hammers, his water bottle dug painfully into his side, and his chest was so constricted that it was becoming hard to breathe. Outlasting the storm was no longer a matter of courage or strength but of sheer determination. To have his life end in such a meaningless fashion was something Terrel refused to contemplate, and – even though he felt battered and half crushed – he realized as soon as the noise of the wind began to drop a fraction, that he was not going to die.

Relief turned to near panic when he realized that he was jammed so tightly into the crevice that he could not pull himself free. Struggle as he might, his shoulders just would not budge. As the tornado headed west, spreading a pall of shifting darkness over the newly-risen sun, Terrel was all too aware that this was the moment when he should be heading towards the mines. But he could not move. His left arm was trapped, and his right had little enough strength at the best of times. Only his legs were free, and he could not get enough purchase to drag his torso from the grip of stone.

Cursing under his breath, Terrel wriggled and squirmed to no avail, then told himself to calm down. He tried to relax, to make himself small. He was rewarded with a first tiny positive movement, and tried to repeat the process – only to be left gasping and spluttering as he was suddenly engulfed by a surge of water running down the gully. The deluge only lasted a few moments and, once he had overcome his fear of drowning, Terrel found that the extra dampness meant he could move a little more easily. Finally, with his left arm able to flex at last, he managed to pull himself out. His shirt was ripped, and there were cuts and grazes on his arms and shoulders, but he was free.

Racked by a coughing fit, and desperately trying to catch his breath, he got to his knees and looked out over the mines. Soldiers were already on the move, but the route taken by the tornado was still clear of any patrols. Necessity overcoming pain and exhaustion, Terrel staggered to his feet and set off down the hill.

'What happened?' Kamin asked as he joined Hoban, Karuna and their men at the observation post.

'There was another whirlwind,' the commissioner answered. 'It went right over the western reservoir,' he added, pointing.

'Any damage?'

'The dam held, but first reports indicate that almost all the water's gone.'

The Chief Seer frowned. He was aware of just how

olatile the situation in the town was, and wanted no more
delays.

'Are the other lakes intact?' he asked.

Hoban nodded.

'So we have enough water to go ahead as planned?'
Kamin queried.

'Yes.'

'I've already dispatched patrols to see if we can block the
tunnels that would've been filled by the water from the
western reservoir,' Karuna said. 'That should minimize
any disruption.'

'We should check the channels too,' Hoban added. 'In
case they were damaged.'

'Very well,' Kamin responded. 'How soon can we proceed?'

'Give us an hour,' Hoban replied.

Terrel crouched behind a pile of blackened stones, and
looked around anxiously. He'd been sure that Alyssa would
find him, but there was still no sign of her. He'd made
good progress, and had got past the perimeter and almost
halfway to the central mound, but although the way ahead
looked clear, he couldn't face the prospect of going underground without Alyssa.

Alyssa! he called silently. *Alyssa, where are you?* He
refused to believe that she might have been hurt – or even
killed – by the tornado, but the thought preyed at the back
of his mind nonetheless.

He was about to set off again when he was struck by
another horrible idea. What if the whirlwind had stripped
away the ring, which the stonechat wore twisted around
one of her thin legs? Would Alyssa still be able to find him?
Don't be stupid! he told himself. *How could that happen?*
Yet he could not dismiss it entirely, and wondered whether

he should show himself openly, rather than trying to hide
so that she'd have a better chance of spotting him.

In the end he compromised, moving forward with less
caution than before, reckoning that even if the soldiers saw
him now he'd be far enough inside their normal routes to
avoid being caught. He only realized his mistake when he
came across one of the main channels – built to guide the
water – and found that there were at least a dozen soldiers
walking along it. He ducked down again quickly, thankful
that the men were intent on inspecting the channel for any
possible leaks and so had their heads down. Even so, they
were moving towards his position, and if he stayed where
he was it was only a matter of time before he was discovered. On the other hand, if he tried to move there was also
a good chance that he would give himself away. He was
paralyzed by indecision. And then Alyssa's voice sounded
inside his head.

No circles of nature here. It's all spirals.

Terrel was greatly relieved to know that she was
unharmed, but the fact that she'd chosen to return at such
an inopportune moment – and that she'd announced herself with such a bizarre greeting – made him very nervous.

Be careful, he warned her. *There are soldiers close by.* He
knew that the men wouldn't pay any attention to a bird,
but he did not want her movements to alert them to his
own presence. He saw a flash of brown as the stonechat
shot into the sky only a few paces away.

Terrel? She sounded as though she wasn't sure who had
spoken to her.

It's me, he told her, hoping she had not entirely taken
leave of her senses.

The patrol was much closer now, and – for him – flight
was impossible. He only had one option left, and he didn't
really know if it would work. When he and Alyssa had

een alone on the hill, there had been no need for him to
disguise the true nature of his eyes, and so he had been
ble to harbour the internal energy he needed for the
lamour. Summoning that energy now, he tried to make
imself invisible, to convince the soldiers that there was no
ne there. I am just another rock, he thought, willing
hem to believe it. To his surprise he found that the effort
eeded to convey such a transformation was hardly more
han was needed to turn his eyes blue – but was only able
o believe that it was really working when one of the
uards walked up beside him, stopped, looked directly at
im, and then turned away to carry on his inspection. It
vas one of the most uncanny experiences of Terrel's life,
ut he forced himself to remain calm, reciting his illusion
ilently, and keeping perfectly still. The patrol was almost
ast him when his mounting sense of triumph was shat-
ered.

What are you doing now?

Terrel gasped, and his concentration faltered. His night-
aare had pursued him into the day.

Some of the guards glanced round suspiciously, but
'errel managed to hold onto enough of the glamour to
void detection. Quickly, knowing that he had no choice,
e reinforced his protective disguise.

'What was that noise?' one of the guards asked.

'I thought I saw something move,' another said.

'Probably a rat,' their captain decided. 'Anyway, there's
othing there now. Let's get moving.' He was keen to com-
lete their assignment and get out of the mining area as soon
s possible.

Clever, the enchanter remarked condescendingly. *You're
ore resourceful than I thought.*

Terrel was almost certain now that it was his use of the
lamour that had given his enemy access to his waking

mind, and he recalled Alyssa's warning. All magic exacts a price. On this occasion it was a price he had had to pay the soldiers were still only a few paces away, and represented a more immediate threat than the enchanter.

Where are you, Terrel? Alyssa asked, sounding bewil dered. *I can't see—*

Don't— he began, but it was already too late.

Who's this? the intruder crowed. *Well, if it isn't your littl friend. And as a bird! How sweet.*

Terrel cringed as his tormentor took what he wante from his newly defenceless mind.

I don't see any crystal around her now, the mocking voic went on. *There's nothing to protect her here, is there?*

What's going on, Terrel? Alyssa pleaded. *Why won't yo talk to me?*

Terrel realized that she could not hear the enchanter That link was for him alone. But he knew that by pro tecting himself he had betrayed her vulnerability. Th guards were still too close for comfort, but he almos released the glamour anyway. In the end, what was left o his common sense kept him hidden. The damage wa already done.

I could get them to arrest you, the enchanter declared *but I have a better idea. There's something I've been want ing to try for a long time, and you've given me the perfec excuse.* He was gloating now, delighting in his eviden superiority, and impatient to demonstrate his powers *Farewell, Terrel.*

'Out of my way!' Jax shouted, barging past the guards wh surrounded the viewing platform.

'What are you doing?' Adina cried breathlessly, as sh struggled to keep up with her son and retain her dignity a the same time. 'We're not due to break the dams yet.'

'That's not what I want to see,' the prince replied
shortly.

He reached the top of the bank and stared over towards
the mines, then shifted his gaze to the west. And smiled.

The soldiers saw it first.

'Moons!' one of them breathed, pointing.

Moments later the entire patrol began to run, trying to
head for safety.

Just before he released the glamour, knowing that he
could not be seen now, Terrel heard the enchanter's
malevolent laughter again – and heard his final message.

I told you you'd be next.

As the link was broken, and Alyssa flew down from the
sky to join him, Terrel turned to look at what had frightened the soldiers. At first he could not believe what he was
seeing, but his eyes – and then his ears – told him it was
true. The tornado had reversed its course and was heading
back to its starting point. For the second time that morning, Terrel and Alyssa were directly in its path.

CHAPTER FORTY-EIGHT

'You should take shelter, Ma'am,' Karuna said urgently.

The marshal had been summoned to the reservoir by one of his officers, after the unexpectedly early arrival of the Empress and her son. At first he'd simply been annoyed at having to nursemaid the imperial family once more, but now that the renegade whirlwind had switched course, he was beginning to get worried.

'As you wish,' Adina replied, feigning reluctance because she did not want to look like a coward in front of the guards. 'Come on, Jax.'

'I'm staying here,' the prince stated flatly. 'You do what you like.'

No one had ever seen him so determined before.

'Are you sure that's wise, Sire?' Karuna persisted.

Jax simply ignored him and, short of using physical force – which was unthinkable – the marshal could think of no way of resolving the impasse. He turned to watch the tornado as it crested the hills beyond the perimeter and began its descent towards the mines.

*

For a moment Terrel found himself staring not at the tornado but at a distant figure, one among a group who stood on a prominence outside the town. He was too far away to see what the stranger looked like, but the connection between them was such that there was no doubting his identity. What was more, Terrel knew that the enchanter was returning his gaze. For a few heartbeats he was back in the crimson sea, listening to the murmuring of the waves, and knew for the first time that it should have been a peaceful realm of warmth and protection. It had been his adversary's malign presence that had turned it into a place of hatred and pain.

Terrel?

Alyssa's voice brought him back to his senses, and he turned to face the advancing whirlwind. It was bigger than before, and was moving with terrifying speed. The noise of its approach was already deafening.

You have to get away, he told her.

I'm not leaving you again.

That's what he wants. Please, Alyssa, you must go!

What who *wants?* she asked, her confusion plain. *I won't leave.*

There was no time to explain, and Terrel realized that trying to overcome her stubborn determination would lose them valuable time.

There's only one chance then, he decided. *We've got to get underground. Where's the nearest shaft?*

At the centre.

That's too far. There must be something closer than that.

Most of the others have been blocked up, she told him.

But— He was close to despair, seeing no way out. *Come with me. We've got to find somewhere to hide.*

Alyssa flew onto his hand, and he tucked her inside the tattered material of his shirt before beginning to run. The

wind surged and bucked around them like a living creature and the noise rose to an unearthly howl, but Terrel
knew that this was nothing compared to the awesome
power of the tornado itself, which was still rushing towards them.

Just how powerful the storm was was illustrated in a
moment of pure horror. High above them, the flailing
shape of a man – presumably a soldier who'd been caught
by the vortex – was hurled through the air. His thin
screaming was soon lost in the tumult as he was blown
away, but Terrel knew that it was only a matter of time
before the man's unnatural flight would end with him
being smashed upon the rocks below. The boy began to
feel sick.

It's no good, he gasped, looking around in vain for a
viable shelter. *We'll never make it this way.*

He glanced back towards the town, but couldn't see
anything through all the dust and sand in the air. *There's
something I've been wanting to try . . .*

If the enchanter *was* responsible for reversing the
progress of the whirlwind, then there was only one way
Terrel could hope to survive. The idea appalled him, but
it was the only option left. He crouched down, his back
braced against a rock, and tried to concentrate.

What are you doing? Alyssa asked.

I have to try something.

It was hard to focus his mind sufficiently to invoke the
glamour, but he forced himself to concentrate.

You don't have to do this! he shouted into the void.

The initial response was a startled silence. The
enchanter had clearly not expected Terrel to renew their
contact – but he recovered quickly.

Enjoying yourself? he asked.

Terrel had already sensed the strain his opponent was

under, and knew the reason for it. Controlling the weather was powerful magic – and it too would exact a price.

I'm not drunk. You can't control me, Terrel claimed.

I don't need to, was the contemptuous reply. *You'll be dead soon.*

I can hurt you. There was a liberating effect in speaking out after hiding behind silence for so long. Terrel was filled with a feverish elation, brought on by the danger and by his own daring.

Don't be ridiculous, the enchanter replied, but Terrel caught the flicker of doubt behind the scorn.

Or I can heal you, he said.

The only response was mocking laughter, but once again the outward confidence masked another emotion.

That's it, isn't it, Terrel realized, and images flashed into his mind: his finger pressed to a cut on Elam's forehead; a calf struggling to its feet; Kativa smiling for the first time in two hundred years. His actions had all been instinctive, but now he was intent on *consciously* using whatever good was inside him. To heal the hatred.

But the moment he thought of it he knew it was beyond him. There was no antidote for such unreasoning malice, no way to melt that heart of ice. And yet his efforts did not go totally unrewarded. In fending off Terrel's attentions, the enchanter's own concentration had slipped. His magic – which was already fighting powers he did not understand – crumbled for a moment, and the tornado escaped his grasp. Returning to the forces that had controlled its movement earlier, it slowed to a halt, then turned its fury back towards the west again. Terrel felt the enchanter's enraged attempts to recapture the storm, but it was beyond his strength now. His earlier efforts had weakened him.

By now, Terrel's own strength was almost giving out,

but he had proved his point and had no need to speak to his enemy again. However, in the back of his mind the victory seemed somehow tainted, and he got little joy from it. He released the glamour and slumped to the ground, breathing heavily while about them the gale slowly relented.

Adina stared anxiously at her son. He was red-faced and sweating, and seemed unsteady on his feet. The expression on his face was a mixture of anger and disbelief.

'Karuna!' Jax rasped suddenly.

'Yes, Sire?'

'Send your men down to the mines. There's someone in there and I want him arrested.'

'But, Your Highness, the tornado—'

'It's going away now,' the prince informed him bitterly, and Karuna knew better than to ask how he could be certain.

'Covering the entire area will take a lot of men,' the marshal pointed out instead. 'Are you sure—'

'I don't care!' Jax snapped, his eyes blazing. 'Just do it! He's over there, near the centre.'

If the Chief Seer had been there, Karuna might have appealed to him, but as it was he had no choice but to obey. Calling his captains to him, he gave the necessary orders, then stepped back and watched as the patrols made their way into the wasteland.

Terrel. Terrel! Wake up!

He felt a sharp pricking at the side of his neck and realized, as he came to, that Alyssa was pecking him furiously.

The tornado's going away again, she told him, *but soldiers are coming. We've got to get moving.*

Feeling as though his limbs were full of lead weights,

nd exhausted both physically and mentally, Terrel strug-
led to respond to the urgency in her voice.

A lot of soldiers, Alyssa added forcefully. *Come on!*

As Terrel made himself get to his feet, he saw why she
vas so concerned. Patrols were converging on them from
hree sides, and the only way still clear lay directly towards
he central mound. As that was where they had planned to
o anyway, he set off, stumbling along as best he could.

Shouts indicated that he had been seen, and it was soon
lear that he was going to be cut off before he reached his
estination. As the cordon tightened around him and his
apture became certain, Terrel desperately tried to rein-
tate the glamour in one last attempt to avoid his pursuers.
Nothing happened, and he groaned aloud, knowing that
is magic was spent. To come so close and fail now was
nbearable.

When the trembling began inside him, he did not rec-
gnize it at first. He was close to tears, his emotions
hreatening to rip him apart. And then his unique sensi-
ivity offered him one last chance.

Standing up in full view of the advancing soldiers, he
aised his arm and shouted as loudly as he could.

'Get away from me! If you don't leave me alone, I'll
tart an earthquake!'

A few of the guards laughed at him, but then one of them
elled something about an enchanter, and Terrel realized
hat he must be close enough for them to see his undisguised
yes.

'It's coming!' he cried. 'I warned you!'

The tremor struck, sending him and all the soldiers
rashing to the ground. In the ensuing panic, none of the
uards had any thought except for their own safety. The
nearthly grinding noise and the shuddering went on,
haking pursuit unthinkable. In contrast, Terrel was

determined to make the most of his good fortune. Even as the quake rumbled on, he forced himself to get up and staggered towards the mound. He kept falling over – which made him glad that Alyssa had taken to the air again – but he would not be denied. No one paid him any attention, and by the time the tremor finally died away he was only a few paces from the entrance to the main shaft.

Although its effects had been less severe in the town, the quake had caused turmoil in Betancuria – especially coming so soon after the inexplicable behaviour of the tornado. Adina and Jax were quickly taken from the scene.

In all the confusion, no one noticed the trickle of water leaking from the dam that had been damaged in the earlier riot.

Alyssa had told Terrel that the miners had once been lowered to their work in baskets suspended from a huge pulley system at the head of the mine, but the tornadoes had wrecked the machinery and there was no way that he could do the same. The only way down was by the series of ladders set in the side of the shaft. It was a daunting prospect, and Terrel tried not to think about the consequences should he slip and fall.

With Alyssa trembling inside his shirt once more, he began his descent into the whispering darkness.

CHAPTER FORTY-NINE

The climb down into the mine seemed endless. As the light faded, Terrel was soon as good as blind, feeling his way in total darkness. Primeval fears rose up to claim him, and he began to wonder if he could even complete the journey, let alone confront a monster at the end of it.

Next to his chest, Alyssa felt his heart thumping, and – even though she shared the bird's instinctive terror of enclosed spaces – she sought to calm and encourage her friend.

You're doing fine, she told him as he rested for a while on one of the intermediate ledges. *Take your time. Nothing can stop us now.*

Terrel was grateful for her reassurance, but he had other things on his mind.

Do you feel it? he asked.

Feel what?

The wind. It's coming up the shaft, and circling round at the same time. Do you think this is where the tornadoes start?

It could be, she replied thoughtfully. *Spirals. Like a tree-creeper.*

Like a what?

They're the ones who follow ghosts.

Terrel realized that Alyssa's thoughts were drifting into areas he could not follow – and he hoped that she'd retain enough sanity to help him through the ordeal to come.

You're all the protection I need, she declared.

Although Terrel appreciated the sentiment, he was still unable to follow her train of thought.

I'm proud of you, she added, and the emotion in her voice only made him feel even more awkward.

I'm just doing what I can, he said.

I wish Elam was here, Alyssa went on. *This is one adventure I know he wouldn't want to miss.*

In spite of the danger of their situation, Terrel found that he could smile at the thought of his friend's frustration at not being able to join them.

He's here in our thoughts, he told her.

We'd better get on, she responded. *More spirals.*

The wind seemed to be getting stronger now, but Terrel wondered whether this might be just his imagination. Nonetheless, he decided that he didn't want to be in the shaft if it *was* the birthplace of the tornadoes and another one was on the way. He began to creep across the ledge, touching the wall with his hands and edging his feet carefully over the floor. He was constantly afraid of toppling over into the invisible abyss, but he was beginning to get used to the layout of the ladder system, and so far had not put a foot wrong. The whispering grew louder as they went down again.

Just as he was wondering how much deeper the shaft could possibly be, and whether he would ever reach the bottom, he saw a faint glimmer of yellow light below him. Comforted by the end of the complete darkness, he went on more quickly. When he eventually reached a solid stone floor he just stood there for a while, his legs shaking with the effort of the climb.

The source of light was obvious now. It came from a small cave a few paces away, where a large oil lamp hung from the ceiling, burning low. On further investigation, Terrel found that the cavern was a storeroom for mining equipment. The place was a shambles, with many of the tools strewn across the floor and several more lanterns smashed to pieces. Terrel assumed that the damage had been caused by earthquakes – which made it all the more remarkable that the big lamp had survived intact to guide him. He picked his way across the room with care, and was relieved to find that one of the smaller lamps was still in working order – and that there was also a taper with which to light it. He did so carefully, dreading to think what a fire down here would be like. He was delighted by his good fortune; the prospect of being able to carry a light with him was an enormous comfort. Somehow the inevitability of the confrontation to come seemed a little less menacing now.

Alyssa was wriggling around inside his shirt, and he took her out and set her on his shoulder.

Now what? he asked. *Which way should we go?*

Follow the spirals, she replied, and flew out of the cavern.

Don't go far! he cried nervously as he made his way after her. He did not want to let her out of his sight. He'd been worried that the darkness might send the bird to sleep, but now he was anxious in case she became too adventurous.

She was waiting for him a few paces away, standing guard on top of a spur of rock and darting glances at the various tunnels that led away from the bottom of the shaft. Hopping back and forth, and twitching her wings and tail, she would have made a comical sight if Terrel had been in the mood.

This one? he asked, pointing to the tunnel from which the spiral wind seemed to be blowing most strongly.

Yes.

Wedging the lamp's handle into his right hand, leaving his good arm free, Terrel set off. For a while the floor was fairly level and the going relatively easy, but after they'd reached another junction, and chosen to go down a small, sloping passage, he was forced to move more cautiously. Alyssa kept pace with him all the time, flitting ahead and then waiting for him to catch up. Once his lamp showed her the way ahead, she would go on again.

It was only after they'd been travelling in this fashion for some time that Terrel began to wonder whether he should have been marking their route in some way, so that he could find his way out again. Then he laughed out loud, realizing that this was the least of his worries. Paradoxically, he felt calmer from that moment on. Everything, including his chances of escaping from the mine, depended on his encounter with the elemental. If that went well, he had no doubt that he would survive somehow; if it didn't, any way out would be irrelevant.

The wind was strong in his face now, and there was a metallic tang in the air that seemed to grow sharper with every step he took. Eventually his whole body began to tingle, and his hair literally began to stand on end. With a growing sense of awe and anticipation, Terrel went on, certain now that he would soon come face to face with the monster.

'Very well,' Kamin conceded. 'We'll wait until midday. But no later.'

Hoban nodded.

'We'll have it all checked and ready by then,' he promised.

'Good.' Kamin turned to the marshal. 'Do you have everything under control?'

'The town is quiet,' Karuna replied. 'And we'll make sure it stays that way.'

'We can't allow anything or anyone to interfere with our progress today,' the Chief Seer told both men. 'The odds are we'll only get one chance at this. Unless we succeed now we'll probably be too late to prevent the collision. Nothing must be allowed to go wrong.'

When Terrel reached the entrance to a huge natural cavern, he knew at once that this was the elemental's lair – even though he couldn't actually *see* anything. The light from his lamp was thrown back and twisted, so that the air itself seemed to be distorted. The cave was filled with a writhing darkness that was beyond mere black, and brief flashes of all the colours of the spectrum were added to the mix – which made the irregular walls and jagged roof of the cavern flicker and gleam as though they too were in constant motion. It was hard to watch for more than a few moments without feeling dizzy – and Terrel found it impossible to make any sense of what he was seeing. Or not seeing. It was no wonder that the creature should have inspired so many fantastical rumours.

Terrel was stunned, sensing forces quite beyond his comprehension. The ghosts' suggestion that he communicate with and learn from such a being seemed utterly ludicrous now – especially when he remembered that he did not have the amulet, the talisman that was somehow crucial to this meeting. This sobering thought reminded him of what he'd heard about the elemental. That it had killed several men was beyond dispute – even if the ways in which they had supposedly met their deaths were open to doubt – but the possibility of it destroying not only Terrel's body but his spirit too was appalling, almost too awful to comprehend.

As the boy continued to stare, his eyes continually fooling themselves into thinking they could follow the convoluted patterns, he began to sense something other than unimaginable power. There were feelings here too, even if it was hard to match them to anything he had ever experienced. The nearest he could come was a kind of indifference, a monumental detachment, that he instinctively knew could only come from a creature that was very old. By human standards, the elemental must be incredibly ancient. However, this primal indifference was overlaid with a much more recent emotion – and Terrel was astonished to discover that this was fear. What could such a being possibly be afraid of?

Well, talk to it then, Alyssa demanded, startling him.

Terrel glanced over at her, and saw that her feathers were fluffed out to such an extent that she looked twice her normal size.

How? He still had no idea what he should do. If he was supposed to gain inspiration from actually encountering the elemental, it hadn't happened yet.

Just do it! she told him. *You know you're the one*— She broke off as one of the outer tendrils of the creature flicked out, seeming to come quite close to where she had perched but then disappearing like an illusion – leaving only the memory of darkness where there should have been light, movement where there should have been stillness.

It bends light, she said softly, but did not offer any more advice.

You've got to do something, he told himself. This is what you came here for.

The idea of talking aloud to such a being seemed absurd, but then Terrel remembered what Babak had taught him about psinoma, the 'invisible words' that could be transferred directly between minds, and which he now used automatically with Alyssa and the ghosts. It did not seem as if the creature had heard his exchange with Alyssa – unless the flickering was a reaction to it – but perhaps it was worth a try. Tentatively, he formed a word in his mind and tried to project it.

Hello?

Although he felt utterly foolish, he persevered.

Can I talk to you like this? Can you hear me?

The elemental did not respond in any way, and remained implacably remote. Terrel tried several more times, attempting to imbue his words with different emotions, and varying the tone of his voice, but all to no avail. Even if, as Babak had told him, the one on the receiving end need not necessarily be aware of what was happening, psinoma required *two* minds. The creature's mind – if indeed it *had* a mind – was too alien, too strange, for any contact to be made. Terrel wondered whether it was even aware of his presence.

What am I supposed to do now? he asked Alyssa, but then saw that he would get no more help from her. She seemed mesmerized, and would not even look at him. His mounting frustration boiled over into anger and, stooping, he picked up a small piece of rock and hurled it into the swirling vortex. To his astonishment the stone's flight was almost instantly reversed in midair. It came back much faster than he had thrown it, and narrowly missed both himself and Alyssa before it shattered into dust as it smashed into the cavern wall. The possible consequences for Alyssa should the bird have been hit made Terrel's blood run cold, and he regretted his impulsive action. And even though there had now been a reaction from the elemental, its total indifference to their presence remained unchanged.

'Why did you kill the miners, if you're just going to ignore me?' the boy shouted angrily. His voice echoed hollowly, coming back to him in distorted fragments of sound that were barely recognizable as human speech. For some reason this annoyed him even more. 'What have I got to do to make you *listen*?'

I'm the only one who's supposed to understand this, he thought to himself, remembering Alyssa's statement. It seemed like a cruel joke now.

And then, with a flash of intuition that he acted upon instantly, without giving himself a chance to reconsider, Terrel spat in the direction of the creature. It was a gesture born partly out of disgust, partly out of desperation – and to his amazement the patterns of darkness shifted violently, iridescent splinters whirling round as the walls seemed to slide and shiver. The cavern was suddenly full of a new watchfulness, a new layer of fear.

'Is that what you're afraid of? Water?' His suspicion had proved correct, but he had not expected such an extreme response.

Placing the lamp on the floor, Terrel unstoppered his battered water bottle, heedless of Alyssa's twittering alarm. Pouring a few drops onto his palm, he extended his hand towards the void.

'There's nothing to be afraid of. It's just water. Look. I can drink it.' He put the bottle to his lips and swallowed the last of the liquid, aware that he had the elemental's attention at last. Even the idea that he might be able to talk to it no longer seemed quite so far-fetched – assuming the creature didn't decide to kill him first.

The roar that suddenly deafened him, and which sent Alyssa fluttering up into the air in terror, was so loud that it left Terrel without a thought in his head. He felt as though all his bones had turned to jelly, and he fell to his knees, dropping the empty bottle as he clapped his hands over his ears. Even then there was no escape; the sound tore through every fibre of his being, shaking him until his teeth rattled. And the noise did not relent. It went on and on, crushing him with its immensity. All he could do was try to endure.

It took him a while to realize that the roaring was not constant, that there were subtle variations within its gigantic flow. But he couldn't work out what that might mean. He could scarcely breathe, let alone think logically. It was only when it dawned on him that this was something like the noise he'd heard at Tindaya that he began to think at all. This did not resemble the first earth-shaking vibration; there was nothing calm about this at all. It seemed closer to the second note, the one that had been the answering 'voice' in that colossal conversation. There were emotions hidden here too, just as there had been on the mountaintop, but other than the fact that these seemed more destructive in nature, he could make no sense of them at all. The inhuman torrent continued.

Terrel was in agony, trying to curl himself into as small a ball as possible, all his senses failing, when – as suddenly as it had begun – the assault stopped. The silence seemed as deafening as what had gone before, and he had to wait a few moments, intent only on breathing, before he was able to look up.

As he did so, the darkness reshaped itself again, reaching out towards him with unmistakable intent. Terrel screamed as shadows enveloped him and the world around him melted away. Solid rock flowed like oil, the lamplight warped and splintered, and Alyssa vanished from his sight. He floated, weightless and impotent.

Terror gripped him like a monstrous vice as he struggled to come to terms with what had happened. It was unbelievable but, in the end, undeniable. He was *inside* the elemental.

CHAPTER FIFTY

The terror was absolute. Trapped within the monster, and within his own fear, Terrel was powerless. But after a while, the realization that his fate was now entirely beyond his own control allowed his mind to start functioning again. Trying to move – he felt as though he was 'swimming' within the darkness – only made the unreality of his situation seem even more disorientating. The swirls of light simply rearranged themselves, and he went nowhere. But at least he was still alive – and unharmed. And then Terrel realized that his limbs had stopped aching and his head had cleared a little. The fact that nothing in his world remained still or seemed solid was disconcerting, but even more disturbing was the fact that he could not see Alyssa. Closing his eyes made the unsettling experience a little easier, but he soon opened them again, trying to make sense of the brief, distorted glimpses of the cavern and to locate the bird within the whirling eddies that surrounded him. He tried calling to her, but she did not respond, and not knowing where she was or what was happening to her was agonizing.

And then, as surely as if he had been able to talk to her himself, he knew that his friend was safe. The conviction that the creature would not harm her had arrived suddenly, and he could not explain it, but it was there – and he did not doubt the truth of it for one moment. What puzzled him was how he had arrived at this comforting conclusion in the first place. The obvious – if incredible – answer was that it must have come from the elemental itself, and after a few moments in which Terrel tried – and failed – to come to terms with this idea, he decided to put his theory to the test. There were so many questions he wanted to ask that he had no idea where to begin. But then the choice was made for him. Confirmation that the creature was indeed terrified of water – which it regarded as a dangerous, magical substance – came as no real surprise, but the manner in which this knowledge reached Terrel's mind was astonishing. He had not even formed the question, as he did when using psinoma, but the creature had evidently become aware of it anyway. Before the boy had had the chance to ask the question, he had known the answer.

The response had not come in words – such a concept was beyond the scope of its alien thought processes – but in the form of a spontaneous *understanding*. In a way that he could not even begin to comprehend, Terrel was communicating with the elemental. All he had to do was put the answer into his own words, to imagine the creature's response in human terms, and – even though he was aware that he could only manage an inadequate translation – it was enough for him to grasp its meaning. At the same time, Terrel learned that the elemental now regarded him as a sorcerer; the closest he could come to its name for him was 'container of magic'! His demonstration with the water bottle had obviously impressed it somehow.

The next unspoken question to be answered confirmed Terrel's instinctive belief that the creature was indeed incredibly ancient, thousands of years old. But he was amazed to discover that such an unimaginably vast period of time was the mere blink of an eye in the life span of such a being. By its own standards, the elemental was very young, a mere infant. In spite of this, Terrel began to think of it as the 'Ancient'.

The creature's relative youth piqued the boy's curiosity, and without conscious thought he wondered whether there were any others like it. The unprompted response was devastating in its simplicity, and because of that it took Terrel a while to recognize the feelings that were being transmitted to him. The overriding emotion was one of loneliness. If there *were* others of its kind, the Ancient did not know of them. For the first time in their exchange, Terrel sensed hesitation in the alien mind, a lack of certainty, and he found himself moved to pity. The creature was alone and friendless, a lost child, and its only contacts until now had been with men displaying enmity and violence. Adding to its fear was the fact that it was surrounded by what it regarded as a source of evil magic.

I could be your friend, Terrel offered, forming the words deliberately for once, but trying at the same time to *feel* what they meant.

The response was confusion, made visible by the increased agitation in the whirling chaos that surrounded him. Then it occurred to Terrel that the Ancient had not answered one of his earlier questions – one that he had spoken aloud – but he hesitated, wanting to avoid anything that might provoke the creature. It was clearly so powerful that it could easily crush him on a whim – or even by mistake. However, simply remembering his earlier question had brought it to the elemental's attention, and this time, although Terrel needed some time to work it all out, the answer was plain enough. He was apparently different from the miners in several ways. It had killed them – although it clearly had no understanding of the concept of death – because they had regarded it as an enemy, because they had tried to hurt it, and because they did not have the spiral inside them. This last reason made no sense to Terrel – the idea of a spiral was somehow connected to fire and light – but it was the closest he could come to putting it into words. He understood now that the Ancient had been frightened – just as Alyssa had surmised – and had simply wanted the miners to leave it alone. That its means of ensuring that they did so had led to their deaths was beyond its comprehension.

Do I have the spiral inside me? Terrel asked, hoping for some clarification.

On this occasion the reply took some time, and when it arrived it was not in the form of words, or thoughts, or knowledge. It took shape in Terrel's left hand.

The miniature star burned as brightly as it had done at Tindaya, and even amidst the swirling darkness Terrel saw it clearly and was astounded by its fragile beauty. He had captured the talisman after all. It was *inside* him, a part of him now, even though it was invisible in his own world. But the elemental could obviously see it – and had allowed Terrel to see it too. For the first time he began to believe that he might actually have a chance of succeeding in his task. Finding the amulet seemed like a good omen.

Even as he was thinking this, the nature of their exchange altered. Until then it had been Terrel who had asked the questions, sometimes unwittingly, and the creature who had responded. Now the boy felt a kind of emptiness all around him, a yearning, that he eventually interpreted as curiosity. It was his turn to answer a request, but the question being posed was so vague, its boundaries so wide, that he did not know where to begin. In the end, almost without realizing what he was doing, Terrel began to tell the story of his life. Before long, the recitation became effortless, without the need of conscious thought, and he found himself reliving a less muddled version of the dream that had taken possession of him the night before. That, he now knew, had simply been a rehearsal.

Of all the events and characters flashing through his mind, it seemed that the Ancient was most intrigued by the ghosts, and when Terrel reached the episode where he had met Kativa, he sensed a genuine feeling of approval from the elemental. He was not sure why this should be so, but he was left with the impression that the ghosts' world was somehow closer to that of the creature.

After that there was a period of quietness, in which he neither received nor sent any messages. He assumed that the Ancient was trying to absorb what it had learnt, just as Terrel was, and for the time being the boy was content to float within his extraordinary cocoon and wait to see what would happen next. It was only when he was almost overwhelmed by a new rush of impressions that he realized their contact had been resumed – and that its tone had changed for the worse.

After some initial confusion, Terrel realized that the Ancient was now giving him a glance of its own history. He learnt that, long ago, the Floating Islands had been fixed on the sea bed, unable to move, just like all the other land masses on the planet. His instinctive denial of this idea was swept aside as if it were of no consequence, and the tale moved on. With a growing sense of dread, Terrel discovered that since the creature had become aware that it was surrounded by seawater – below as well as on all sides – it had found a way to force the islands off course. It actually *wanted* the collision to take place, to regain its grip on solid ground – and the fact that this might destroy almost all the other life on the islands was of no concern at all.

This proof that the strange being was indeed responsible for the crisis facing his homeland brought Terrel back to his reason for being there in the first place. He was the only one who might have a chance of persuading the creature to relent – but he could not think of any way of doing so. Everyone who had so far come into contact with the Ancient had tried to destroy it, just as the soldiers were planning to do now by flooding the mines. Even as that thought crossed his mind, he realized his mistake. The elemental's reaction was one of alarm and anger, and Terrel realized that he had justified its determination to save itself at the expense of the islands' other inhabitants.

They don't understand, he explained desperately. *They're not really your enemy. They're just trying to protect themselves.* But the Ancient was not interested in his excuses.

I can be your friend, Terrel repeated. *Let me help you. Please—*

His words were drowned out by the return of the thunderous roar, but this time the volume had been tempered slightly as the elemental sought to find a voice that the boy could actually hear. Within the booming reverberation, the Ancient took its first faltering steps in the use of words.

Too late, it told him. *Magic comes.*

'Well, shore it up again!' Hoban demanded.

'We can't,' the engineer replied nervously. 'The whole

internal structure's saturated now. It's only a matter of time before the water breaks through.' The man was obviously terrified, and with good reason. His incompetence in not spotting the leak earlier would earn him the wrath not only of his superior but also of the Seers' Council.

'You're sure of this?' Hoban asked, realizing that this was not the time for recriminations.

'Yes.' The engineer could not meet his gaze.

'Marshal!' Hoban called. 'Are the beacons ready?'

'They are,' Karuna replied, coming over to join them, a puzzled frown on his face, 'but I thought—'

'There's been a change of plan. We're going to release the water now.'

'But we haven't checked all the channels yet,' the marshal pointed out.

'We'll have to take that chance,' Hoban stated. 'The dam here could break at any moment, and unless we coordinate all the others, this whole thing will be a disaster.'

'All right,' Karuna said, becoming businesslike now that he was aware of the situation. 'I'll send runners to the inspection teams, and inform the Chief Seer.'

'Better tell the Empress and her son too,' Hoban advised. 'They won't want to miss this.' He turned to the guilt-stricken engineer. 'Get your team ready to breach the dam on my signal. If it's going to burst, I want it to be controlled precisely.'

'Yes, Commissioner.' The man was eager for a chance to partially redeem himself.

A little while later, in their exactly predetermined sequence, the floodgates opened.

Terrel had grown up surrounded by madness, but he had never encountered anything remotely like this. Even if the Ancient's warning had not alerted him to the water's approach, he would have been able to sense it from the creature's increasingly demented thoughts and emotions. Five torrents were heading towards various entrances to the mines, in a synchronized assault that would soon generate a deluge underground.

To Terrel's dismay, the elemental's response had been to panic. It was evidently incapable of rational thought when it came to dealing with the approaching magic and, as it became more and more frenzied, Terrel's own predicament grew ever more perilous. Until then, even when the creature had moved around him, he had floated in relative comfort. But now he was being pulled in all directions with a violence that was becoming frightening. If it got any worse it was possible that he would be torn limb from limb. The reports of some of the miners' horrifying deaths began to seem less far-fetched.

Trying to think logically in such circumstances was almost impossible, but Terrel knew it was his only hope. He was the only one who could talk to the Ancient, and he had come here to avert just such a disaster. He knew that the creature was being driven insane, but he was also aware that, in one sense, it was no more than a child – and there was no telling what it would do when it was finally overwhelmed by the threat to its wellbeing. The potential violence he'd already sensed would spiral out of control, and – with the immense power it clearly possessed – that was a terrifying thought. The fact that the flooding would drown both Terrel and Alyssa seemed almost a minor consideration.

The next thought to surface in the boy's beleaguered mind was that the Ancient's reaction to the attack made no sense. Surely a creature capable of diverting the course of the Empire should be able to defend itself against a mere flow of water. Indeed, it must already have done so – under less frenetic circumstances – because Terrel was sure that it was responsible for Betancuria's drought. So why was it helpless now? How could magic he could not even sense be so potent?

Maybe not all rivers run downhill.

Somehow, Alyssa had found a way through the turmoil, but he could not work out why she should have repeated Elam's mysterious suggestion. All rivers *do* run downhill, he thought. That's just common sense. He tried to talk to Alyssa, but if she heard him she was unable or unwilling to reply, and he was left to his own devices. Around him, madness lurched and spun chaotically. *Why* do rivers run downhill? he asked himself. For the same reason that objects fall to the floor when you drop them. There is a force that pulls them towards the ground. An invisible force. And yet he was floating, not falling. Was it possible that . . .

The next moment Terrel was waving his hand around frantically, hoping that the glowing talisman might attract the creature's attention. At the same time he was shouting, trying to break through its terrified confusion.

You don't have to let them hurt you. You can stop this. Listen to me. I know what I'm talking about. I drank the water, remember. You can save us!

Relief flooded through him when he sensed a small chink of sanity in the Ancient's deranged armour, and knew that it was listening. He had no need to explain what was necessary; once he had convinced the creature that the situation was not hopeless, the information was there in his mind, ready to be taken.

A moment later, Terrel felt himself falling. Upwards.

He collided gently with the roof of the cavern, feeling as if *he* had gone mad, then hung there like an enormous bat. Twisting round, he looked down and saw that he and

Alyssa were the only ones left in the cave. The Ancient had vanished.

At first none of the onlookers could believe what they were seeing, but as they glanced at each other and saw their own disbelief reflected in their neighbours' eyes, they knew that this was no hallucination. Close to the centre of the mining area, hundreds of objects – mostly pieces of rock – were rising slowly into the air.

At the same time, something equally strange was happening to the water in the channel leading from the reservoir. Near the town it was still flowing, but further out it seemed to have grown sluggish, and was swelling upwards as if a giant wave were forming. Swirls of mist floated above the water. And then – slowly at first, but with increasing speed – the man-made river began to flow *uphill*, back towards the lake.

Water bulged and eddied, caught between two opposing forces, while the astonished spectators could only stare in amazement, mesmerized by the bizarre spectacle. Further from the mines, the laws of nature were evidently still operating, and the water that had been forced back into the reservoirs threatened to overflow their banks. When a sudden tremor shattered part of the retaining wall across the old river bed, the failure of their plan became inevitable. No one could tell whether any water had reached the mine shafts, but if it had, it would obviously not be enough to inundate a single seam, let alone the entire underground complex. As the lake emptied itself in the wrong direction, reports began to come in from the other reservoirs – and they all told the same story.

By the time the rocks, which had risen so far and then simply floated in midair, fell back to earth, the picture was complete. The monster had beaten them.

Kamin was trembling, looking round at the horrified expressions on his companions' faces. There was nothing any of them could do now. This had been their last hope. The islands' doom was sealed.

CHAPTER FIFTY-ONE

What's going on? Alyssa asked. She was perched, upside down, next to Terrel on the roof of the cavern.

I think — I hope — the elemental's found a way to stop the water reaching us.

Did you tell it how?

I suppose so, yes. But you gave me the idea.

Excellent! she exclaimed. *Then it'll trust you. You can—*

Alyssa didn't get the chance to finish her thought, because just at that moment the world righted itself. As the bird fluttered into the air, Terrel felt himself being pulled down towards the rocks below. It all happened so quickly he didn't even have time to scream, but he knew that if the fall did not kill him he would certainly be badly injured, and would have no chance of ever climbing out of the mine. Trying to protect his head with his arms, he braced himself for the impact — which never came. Instead his fall slowed gently, and he came to rest in a protective refuge of darkness. The Ancient had returned.

The creature was still agitated, but the madness was

gone, and Terrel knew, without having to ask, that it felt safe again – at least for the moment. He also sensed the beginnings of gratitude, a comradeship based on their cooperation. Alyssa had been right; there would never be a better time for him to try to persuade the elemental to reprieve the islands.

You're safe now, he began tentatively.

There was no reply as such, but Terrel gained a strong impression that the Ancient expected the evil magic to return. It clearly believed that although it had won the battle, the war was far from over. It might have begun to regard Terrel as a friend, but humanity in general was still the enemy. What was more, it knew that it could not cope with the sorcery by itself, and therefore intended to keep Terrel permanently by its side.

When the boy reacted to the idea of becoming a prisoner again with horror, the Ancient responded with a mixture of puzzlement and irritation, and Terrel had to try to convince the creature that he was still a friend. But he could not give any genuine reassurance about the water. He also believed that the authorities would try to repeat the flooding, and – if that proved impossible – that they would find another way of attacking the monster. Because of the very nature of his contact with the Ancient, lying to it was not an option. On the other hand, Terrel could not just remain there in limbo, waiting either for the creature to lose faith in him, or for his own physical existence to be threatened by more mundane considerations. Presumably, if he was forced to stay down in the mines for too long, he would simply starve to death.

I can make them take the magic away, he claimed, as confidently as he was able. *I can make them leave you alone altogether.*

Even as he spoke he knew that the elemental was aware

of his inner doubts, and he sought to justify his claim — both to the creature and to himself.

If you give me a sign, something I can show them as proof that you're willing to strike a bargain— He broke off when it became clear that the Ancient did not understand the concept of a bargain, and then tried to explain. *You want to be safe, but so do my people. What you're doing to the islands will hurt us, like the magic will hurt you, and unless you stop, they'll go on trying to harm you. But if you agree to let the islands return to their normal course, then they'll have no reason to attack you because they'll be safe too.* He paused to see if the elemental had taken this in, and encountered the thoughtful silence again. Wondering whether this was a good sign or not, he waited for as long as he could, then pressed on. *If you were to slow the rotation, just a little, they would*— *Yes, that's right, the spiral.* He was beginning to have faith in his own proposal now and, just as the glamour affected other people's view of him, so his growing certainty was influencing the Ancient. *That would be enough for me to persuade them to leave you alone. Then you wouldn't need the collision with the mainland. You'd be safe here. The islands have been stable for hundreds of years, and the sea wouldn't be able to reach you. That way we'd all be safe*, he ended emphatically.

Once again he was left alone with his thoughts as the Ancient withdrew into silence. When it returned, Terrel's hopes leapt. The bargain was made.

A moment later the darkness shifted again, and all around them the mines shuddered briefly. Although he had no idea how it had been achieved, Terrel knew that the Empire's rotation was already beginning to slow down. The change would be imperceptible at first, but would become increasingly obvious as time passed — and that would give him the leverage he needed to convince the

eers to leave the Ancient alone. He also knew that the el-
mental would keep its side of the bargain as long as the
humans did too. There was a chance that Vadanis might
survive after all.

Thank you, Terrel said. *Now I have to return to the surface and tell them what's happening.*

To his horror, the response to this was a blank denial. It
had decided that Terrel was to stay where he was, that his
presence was necessary in case the creature's enemies tried
to attack it again. It believed that the boy could pass on the
essential information from where he was.

No! Terrel objected. *I can't do that. I need to talk to
them.*

He simply could not get the idea across that he was
unable to communicate with the outside world from his
current position, and no amount of pleading had any effect
on the Ancient's decision. Terrel was left to wonder how
the seers could honour a bargain they did not even know
had been made.

t was because *we* weren't there!' Adina declared furiously.
f it hadn't been for the incompetence of your engineers,
e'd have been able to play the parts assigned to us by
prophecy.'

The ignominious failure of the plan to flood the mines
had frayed the tempers of all those involved, and the council of war was becoming acrimonious. The prolonged earth
tremor that had interrupted their deliberations at noon
had done nothing to improve anyone's mood.

'I'm not sure what you could have done,' Kamin began.

'Jax is the Guardian!' the Empress exclaimed, gesturing
dramatically towards her son.

'Your absence was unfortunate,' the Chief Seer conceded wearily, noting that she had not been able to specify

what their roles would have been, 'but there was no time to send for you. Fate decreed that you play a different part. What is done cannot be undone. The point is to decide what we are to do now.' He did not really think it mattered what they did next, but – in public at least – he could not allow himself to show the despair he felt.

Adina subsided into her chair, and Karuna took up the argument.

'Surely the creature's reaction confirmed that it *is* afraid of water?'

'It also demonstrated that it was quite capable of defending itself *against* water,' Fauria pointed out.

'Exactly,' Adina hissed.

'Yes, but only by resorting to extreme measures,' the marshal countered. 'It might not be capable of doing so again.'

'You don't think it will have recovered by the time the reservoirs are full again?' Kamin asked.

'Possibly, but we may not have to wait that long,' Karuna said. 'If we're able to attack it in a more subtle manner, water might still be an effective weapon.'

'It seems to me,' Dheran announced, in his usual languid manner, 'that we have little alternative. Other weapons have proved ineffective, have they not?' The Emperor rarely attended meetings such as this one, and his presence was a sign of just how desperate the situation had become.

'That's true, Your Majesty,' Kamin admitted, then turned back to the soldier. 'What do you propose, Marshal?'

'Steam,' Karuna replied and then, seeing the mystified expressions around him, he hurried to explain. 'A relatively small amount of water produces a huge volume of steam. If we can start a large fire at the bottom of the main shaft, and then drop water on it from above, the effect will be explosive. Steam will be driven through the tunnels at high speed. We may not be able to drown the creature, but perhaps we can scald it to death.'

There was a pause as the others considered the merits of his proposal.

'Won't the steam just come back up the shaft?' Fauria asked eventually.

'Some will,' Karuna replied, 'but the rest will be forced into the other tunnels.'

'What do you think, Hoban?' Kamin asked.

The commissioner had been silent until now, uncomfortably aware that the failings of his men had been at least partly to blame for the earlier fiasco. Now he found it difficult to even consider new ideas. After what he had witnessed that morning, he felt he would never be sure of anything again.

'There are supplies of lamp oil at the bottom of the main shaft,' he said hesitantly. 'We can use that to start a fire.'

'And once it's going we could add more oil from the top,' Karuna suggested.

'And how do we propose to get the water there?' Kamin asked. 'Judging by what happened earlier, I don't think it would be safe to use the channels.'

'We can use what's left in the reservoirs,' the marshal replied, 'but transport it in barrels. That way it's possible the creature won't detect the water until it's too late. I can get my supply officers onto it immediately.'

'Do a test run,' Fauria suggested. 'If the monster doesn't pay any attention to one barrel, there's every chance it'll ignore them all.'

Karuna nodded, approving of the seer's idea.

'Agreed,' Kamin said. 'In the meantime, I want the dams repaired so we can begin collecting river water again. We should keep our options open. If the steam injures the creature, then perhaps another attack from the channels would be more effective.' He glanced at Hoban, who signalled his agreement.

'And this time,' Jax said, speaking for the first time since the meeting began, 'I don't want to be left out. I didn't get to see anything this morning.'

'You'll be kept fully informed, Sire,' Kamin told him.

'Good,' the prince responded. 'And I think I should be the one to empty the first barrel. Don't you agree?'

The Chief Seer was aware of the Empress looking at the boy with an expression on her face that was a mixture of triumph and alarm. Her son's demand had obviously both pleased and frightened her, and Kamin wondered spitefully whether she'd have the courage to accompany Jax on such a dangerous mission. Somehow he doubted it.

'I agree,' he said.

Terrel was beginning to feel that his position was hopeless. Struggling did him no good, and he'd been unable to make any sort of contact with Alyssa, but until now he had refused to admit defeat. Every so often he'd tried to renew his exchange with the Ancient, but it had reverted to a modified form of its earlier indifference and would not respond to his pleas. There was no way for Terrel to judge how much time had passed since he'd entered the mine, and it was only when he began to grow tired that he guessed that day must have become night. He fought sleep for as long as he could, but in the end he just could not stay awake.

He dreamt of rushing torrents of water, of dark clouds of oily smoke and explosions of flame and steam. Fire burst from within the earth, from his own hand, and from his eyes. He flew within the spiralling winds of a tornado, saw the ocean churned into mountains of white pray, and caught a glimpse of the mainland drawing terrifyingly close, the collision only moments away. Fighting these images of destruction, trying to deny their reality, only made them worse. The sheer scale of the impending disaster left him breathless, as mountains split in two, huge crevasses swallowed whole towns, and plains buckled and cracked as though the surface of the land were paper thin. He heard the dying screams of countless victims, saw homes razed by fire and flood and avalanche. He watched as the sky grew dark with dust and ash, so that the sun was obscured and a deadly cold followed the catastrophe. And above it all, only the moons remained serene, unchanging – except for the Dark Moon, whose ominous shadow spread so that it filled the heavens.

Moon's blood! Are you always so melodramatic?

The enchanter's return did not really come as much of a surprise, but it startled Terrel nonetheless. Even so, he was glad to be distracted from his apocalyptic vision – even by his tormentor.

What do you want? he asked, knowing that at least he now had the measure of his opponent.

Me? You're the one who made the link.

I was? Terrel thought, then threw off the blinkers worn by his dream-befuddled mind, and cursed himself for a fool. This was his chance.

Will you do something for me?

Why should I? the enchanter replied suspiciously.

The elemental wants to be left alone, Terrel went on, ignoring the question. *If we promise to do that, it'll stop the lands spinning – and that means we won't collide with the mainland. So you need to go to the soldiers or the seers, whoever's in charge, and make sure they don't attack it again. Do you understand?*

I understand, but why should I believe you? The en
chanter's curiosity was plain, in spite of his sceptical words

It's already started, Terrel replied. *Do you remember th
quake a few hours ago? That was the first part of the slowin
down. The elemental caused it, as a sign of good faith. Get th
seers to check. It shouldn't take too long for them to confirr
that the rotation is decreasing.*

Why can't you tell them yourself?

*Because the creature's taken me prisoner. It won't let me g
until it's sure it's safe.*

The enchanter laughed, obviously delighted by Terrel'
situation.

I still don't see why I should help you, he said eventually

Because it will save Vadanis! Terrel yelled in exaspera
tion. *It'll probably save your life too – and you'll get to be
hero in the process.* He could tell from the thoughtful silenc
that followed that his enemy liked this idea.

Why should they believe me? the enchanter asked. *I mear
how am I supposed to know all this? I can hardly say that yo
told me it in a dream, can I?*

Come to the mine shaft then, Terrel replied. *Climb dow
a bit, if you want. I can make sure it's safe for you. Just don
bring any water! Then you can say the creature made a bar
gain with you. When the seers realize the islands are startin
to return to normal, your claim will be proved.*

As long as we continue to leave the monster alone?

*Exactly. It'll probably mean you'll have to seal the centr
part of the mine complex permanently, but that'll be a sma
price to pay.*

And you're happy to let me take the credit for all this? th
enchanter asked. *What do you want in exchange?*

Terrel's heart answered for him. Once they were fre
he knew that Alyssa would have to leave him in order 1
rest from her long imprisonment in the stonechat's bod

But he was hopeful that now the elemental was his friend — and its safety was assured — he'd be able to persuade it to release her from her coma. And if the real Alyssa was going to wake up at last, there was only one place Terrel wanted to be.

I just want to go home, he said.

CHAPTER FIFTY-TWO

'What have we got to lose?' Jax concluded. 'If it doesn't
work, we can always go back to Karuna's plan.'

It was a valid point and, despite his initial misgivings,
Kamin could not help but be impressed by the change in
the prince's attitude. If he really went through with this, he
would be displaying a quite unexpected degree of bravery.

'Are you sure you want to go alone?'

'Yes. I'm the Guardian. No one else would be safe,' Jax
replied. 'Just make sure there's no water anywhere near the
shaft.'

'Of course. When do you want to go?'

'Now.'

Kamin hesitated for a moment before asking his final
question.

'Have you told the Empress about this?'

Jax smiled.

'She's still asleep,' he said.

Did you hear any of that? Terrel asked. He was awake
again, still floating in darkness.

The Ancient's response was intriguing. It had evidently been aware of the boy's dream, but hadn't been sure how to separate illusion from reality, what *had* happened from what might. Terrel tried to clarify the situation, telling the creature that the unconscious mind was capable of imagining events as well as seeing them. At the same time he tried to emphasize the genuine nature of his agreement with the enchanter. The fact that this other person was also his enemy confused the elemental, and Terrel had to explain that sometimes it was to everyone's advantage to deal with one's enemies rather than fight them. He was rather pleased with himself for having made this point, because it was obviously relevant to the Ancient's own predicament. However, it was only when the creature inquired whether the enchanter would really come that Terrel knew his explanation had been understood.

I hope so, he said, then urging himself to be more positive, he added, *I'm sure he will.*

As Jax made his way to the entrance to the mine, he tried to carry himself like a hero. Inside, he was trying to decide if he was being a complete fool. Which way is the mask pointing now? he wondered, recalling the insulting performance that had made him so angry. The prince could not help thinking that he might be walking into a trap. Although instinct told him that Terrel's offer had been made in good faith, he was worldly enough to know that instinct was not infallible. There were any number of possible explanations for the offer rather than the one he'd been given, but if it *were* true, then the rewards more than justified the risk. In any case, he was committed now. To turn back, having come this far, would destroy his reputation for good.

At the head of the shaft, Jax turned and glanced at the

group of soldiers who had accompanied him part of the
way, waved confidently to them, then steeled himself to
enter the mine. The light from the lamp he carried revealed only the topmost part of the ladder and the walls of
the shaft. Everything else was pitch black. *I'll just go
down to the first platform, and wait there for a while,* he
reassured himself. Even that seemed a daunting prospect
but he made himself climb on to the rungs and begin his
descent.

When he reached the ledge, he set the lamp down and
looked about him. Picking up a stone, he dropped it over
the side – then wished he hadn't, because he had to wait
an interminable amount of time before he heard the distant
clunk as it hit the bottom.

You don't have to come any further.

I've no intention of— How did you know I was here?

The elemental told me, Terrel replied. *Are you ready?*

Ready for what?

*I'm going to ask the Ancient to slow the rotation again, so
you can prove you've bargained with it. This place is going to
shake a bit, so you'd better hang on to something.*

No! Jax screamed, sure now that he *had* walked into a
trap.

You'll survive, Terrel assured him, sounding amused.
You're a hero, remember?

The horrified prince clung to the rungs of the ladder,
flattening himself against the wall, as far from the edge of
the platform as possible. Beside his feet, the lamp began to
tremble – which made the light flicker alarmingly – then
bounced over the stone floor, toppled over the rim and
disappeared into the abyss. Terrified and in almost total
darkness now, the prince could only hang on desperately
and wait for the quake to end. Although it only lasted for
a few moments, he was soaked with sweat and his finger

ad cramped painfully by the time the earth grew still
gain.

It's done.

Jax scuttled up the ladder as fast as his shaking legs
ould carry him, and breathed a huge sigh of relief when
e reached the open air. Several guards were standing
uite close by, having come forward ready to offer their
elp, and the prince put on a brave face for their benefit.
or their part, the soldiers were delighted to see him
merge safe and well. They'd all been alarmed by the
arthquake, and had not relished the idea of going down
ato the mine to rescue him.

y the time he addressed the gathering, Jax had recovered
is composure. Now that it was over, he appreciated how
uch his ordeal had improved his standing among the
ers, the soldiers and the rest of the court. He *was* a hero
ow – and if the rest of what Terrel had told him was
ue, his status would soon be legendary.

Behind him, Adina basked in her son's reflected glory,
ut inside she was seething. She had only woken when the
arthquake had struck – which meant that, once again, she
ad been excluded from a crucial event. Sooner or later,
meone was going to pay for that. In the meantime, she
uld only listen with all the others as Jax told his tale.

The prince's claim to have spoken to the monster was
reeted with silent awe, but when he outlined the nature of
e bargain he'd agreed with it, the atmosphere in the
amber became charged with a mixture of emotions.
oremost among these was hope, but it was tempered by
degree of scepticism. It was left to Kamin to articulate
e feelings of the entire gathering.

'Gentlemen,' he began, looking at his fellow seers, 'our
sk is clear. If what the unknown entity has said is true,

the change should be apparent within a few hours. W
must make every effort to measure the islands' course a
accurately as possible, as *soon* as possible.' For a fleetin
moment he wished that Lathan was there, but then dis
missed the thought. This was not the time for wishfu
thinking, and there were other capable mathematician
among their number. 'In the meantime,' he went on, 'n
attacks of any sort will be made on the creature, and a
water barrels are to be brought back outside the perimeter
He paused, looked round at the renewed hope on all thei
faces, and felt his own despair melt away. He had a goo
feeling about this. 'It only remains for me to pass on th
heartfelt thanks of the Seers' Council, the court and all th
people of the Empire to Prince Jax. His courage and enter
prise have shown that part of his prophesied destiny
about to be fulfilled. I have no doubt that this is but th
first of many triumphs for the Guardian.'

Jax did his best to smile modestly as the onlookers ros
to acclaim him and the room filled with cheering an
applause.

CHAPTER FIFTY-THREE

hey've agreed.

The enchanter's voice broke into Terrel's endless de-
lium. He no longer had any idea how long he'd been
spended in the swirling void. Whether it was because of
s exhaustion, or his hunger – or simply because of his
natural predicament, Terrel was close to madness now. He
d moments of lucidity, much as Alyssa did, but for the
ost part his mind was full of images he could not explain,
oughts he could not understand. Although his body was
t in pain, he was tormented nonetheless.

What? he mumbled, trying to grasp at the straw of
nity offered by the intruder.

*The seers have confirmed that the rotation is decreasing
d the islands are slowing down. They'll leave the monster
ne as long as that continues.* Jax didn't know how the
ers had reached their conclusions, but they were appar-
tly quite sure that if the changes went on as they were
w predicting, Vadanis would not collide with Macul
d the islands would eventually return to their normal
nderings within the Movaghassi Ocean.

That's good, Terrel responded weakly.

To show their good faith, the enchanter went on, *they'*
going to seal this area of the mines. You'd better get out soo
unless you want to be buried in there too.

Jax had intended to go down the shaft again – as far
the first platform – to pass on this news. It had not bee
necessary for him to do this, and some of his advisors ha
tried to dissuade him, but he was beginning to *feel* like
hero now, and it seemed like something the Guardia
ought to do. He was bolstered by the fact that Terrel w
no longer relevant. Jax's own position as the Guardia
was unassailable now, and his twin had been forgotte
even by those seers who had secretly wanted to try to fir
him. However, when he had reached the mine, and looke
down the shaft, he saw some wisps of smoke and decide
to deliver his message from where he was.

Tell the monster what we're doing. We're going to keep o
end of the bargain.

Terrel did not bother to explain that he wouldn't nee
to tell the Ancient anything, that whatever he knew wou
be passed on to the creature without any effort on his pa
He sensed his old adversary leaving the mine, and kne
that the only battle he had left to fight was the one for h
own survival.

Will you let me go now? he asked. *If you don't I'll die, a*
then I wouldn't be able to help you anyway. The bargai
agreed now. You don't need me any more.

The elemental's response was a long time in comin
and Terrel was about to renew his plea when the darkne
shifted violently and he fell heavily on to the floor of t
cavern. He lay stunned for a few moments, but then h
return to the world he understood gave him the ener
and willpower to overcome his fatigue. He looked round
he scrambled to his feet.

Alyssa?

She came flying from a shadowed corner of the cave, attering in delight.

Terrel! What's been happening? I've been so worried!

It's a long story, he replied, smiling as she alighted on his oulder. *But it'll have to wait. We have to get out of here 'ore they seal the shaft.*

He stumbled towards the cavern's entrance, and Alyssa ok to the air again. At the mouth of the tunnel, Terrel rned back to take one last look at the Ancient.

You'll be safe now, he said, though he didn't know ether it could hear him now that he was outside its undaries. *We all will.*

The creature did not seem to respond in any way, but rrel knew that his purpose had been achieved. He had nmunicated with the elemental; he had learnt from it; d in the end – in some small way – they had come to derstand each other.

Goodbye, he said quietly, then picked up his lamp, ich was running low on oil now but still burning, and de his way into the tunnel.

Alyssa went ahead of him as before, and although he ald not remember the route they had taken, she was ver in any doubt. As tired as he was, Terrel was able to ke good progress as he followed her. But when they ched the last tunnel, the one leading to the main shaft, : air was thick with smoke, and ahead they could see a ll, flickering glow. The smell was the same as the one t came from his lamp, but a hundred times stronger.

There's a fire, Alyssa reported, as Terrel coughed and his s began to water. *It's not that big, but I think it's been ning for some time. The smoke's too thick. We can't get ough that way.*

Where, then?

I don't know yet. We'll have to find another spiral.

They retraced their steps for a while, until they came
a junction. They were discussing which route to take wh
a sudden draught came from the direction of the Ancien
lair and blew into one of the other tunnels. Without he
tation they chose to go that way.

Their journey to the surface was long and arduous. C
several occasions they had to work their way past obstac
partially blocking their path, and Terrel sometimes had
crawl along on his hands and knees, but the wind alwa
guided them onwards, and they never questioned
advice.

Eventually, daylight glimmered ahead of them, and th
gave them the impetus to go a little faster. They emerg
more than half a mile from the central mound. Seve
groups of soldiers and engineers were at work in t
mining area, but none of them were close enough to noti
the new arrivals.

You need to rest, Terrel said, knowing that their parti
was inevitable.

Yes, Alyssa replied. *I'll join you again as soon as you
far enough from here.*

No, he told her. *Go back to the haven. You'll be sa
there. I asked the elemental to let you wake up. I'll get ba
as soon as I can, and I'll see you there.*

Alyssa said nothing, and Terrel took her silence
assent.

I . . . I couldn't have done this without you, he said aw
wardly.

We're a team, she replied. *Look after yourself, Terrel.*

You too.

Neither of them wanted to say goodbye, and in the e
Alyssa simply took wing, climbing swiftly into the s
Terrel watched until she was lost to sight, running throu

the other things he wished he'd said – if he'd had the
ne, and the courage.

vo days later, Terrel went to sleep in a real bed for the
st time in a long while. He had begun his journey north,
t was still no more than ten miles or so from
tancuria – and yet he considered himself to have been
·y fortunate. He had escaped from the mining area
detected, and his luck had held on the road, where he
l managed to find both sustenance and shelter.

The tavern he was staying at that night was full of both
als and travellers, and almost all the conversations in the
· had concerned the recent events in Betancuria. Many
the tales were already wildly inaccurate, but Terrel had
de no attempt to correct the rumours or even to join in
h the talk. He had been busy enough waiting on tables
l helping out in the kitchens. His reward had been a
al and a bed for the night in a tiny attic room.

For the last two nights he had slept soundly, unaware of
r dreams, but now he felt himself sliding into familiar
ritory. The red tide ran more strongly than ever and,
ile the pain and hatred were still there, there were
er, more subtle torments added to its inescapable
ault. There was a sense of loss, of betrayal, of a deep
ness that he could not understand. The waves of the
nson ocean thundered in his ears like a giant heart-
t – and then he knew that this was not a dream but a
mory.

Yet he had always remembered it as he remembered
ams; in fragments that made no sense by themselves; in
feeling that he had seen or experienced something
ore, without knowing when or where. But it was not a
am. He had not even been asleep. If he had been, the
n in his arm and leg would have woken him. No, he

had not been asleep, he knew that now. He had been wait
ing to be born.

The soldiers came for him at dawn. The door to his room
burst open, and he was dragged from his bed and led
away. The guards ignored his protests – allowing him only
enough time to gather together his possessions – and the
few people who witnessed the arrest averted their eyes, no
wanting to get involved. The captain of the patrol set him
on a horse and tied his wrists to the saddle, and then the
entire party rode away.

Terrel soon realized that they weren't going back to
Betancuria. Nor were they heading north. As far as he
could judge they were travelling southwest, but no one
would tell him where they were going or why. The captain
was grim-faced and taciturn, and his men would not talk
to the boy at all. Most of them would not even meet his
gaze.

Their journey took three days, with the captain pushing
his men and their mounts hard, as though he were anxious
to be done with his duty. Terrel was guarded constantly,
even when he slept, and for most of the time his hands
were bound. When at last they reached a small town on
the coast, Terrel guessed from the attitude of the soldiers
as they approached that this was their destination. They
stayed that night in cramped barracks, and as he lay in the
darkness, the boy wondered why Alyssa had not come to
find him. Had she returned to her own body in
Havenmoon? Or had her overlong stay in the stonechat
restricted her in some way? He had no way of knowing,
and – now that he needed her more than ever – he missed
her all the more. He was helpless without her. Even the
glamour was useless under the constant scrutiny of his
guards.

The captain shook him awake early the next morning.
'Here,' he said, thrusting a letter into Terrel's hand.
'I'm told you can read.' His tone implied that he found
this hard to believe but that he didn't really care either
way.

Terrel opened the letter with some trepidation. Was
this to be the explanation for his arrest? And if so, why
bring him here to read it? He glanced at the bottom of the
page, and saw that it had been signed by 'The Enchanter'.
He knew then that he'd been betrayed. With a sinking feeling
of dread in the pit of his stomach, he read:

Terrel,

I never really thought you would manage to
escape from the mine. I'm actually quite glad you
did. You obviously made some sort of pact with the
monster, which was probably a good idea for all our
sakes. We wouldn't want to annoy the elemental,
would we! Once again you've proved yourself to be
unusually resourceful, and that's why I had to send
the soldiers after you. I knew the dreams would lead
me to you sooner or later, and they did. In a way I
shall miss our encounters, but I don't suppose we'll
ever meet again.

Farewell, brother.

Brother? Terrel thought, his mind reeling. I have a
brother? And he's my enemy? Why?

'Who's this from?' he asked, looking up at the captain.

'I have no idea,' the soldier replied. 'I'm just following
my orders.'

Later that morning, when Terrel finally realized what his
punishment was to be, he was plunged into the darkest

despair he had ever known. To have gone through all the horrors of the last few months and then, just when he had thought they might be at an end, to be faced with the worst of them all, was unbearable. He knew now why they had come to this remote part of the coastline. He was to be sent into exile.

As the law decreed, he was provided with a quantity of water and a meagre supply of food. But the raft looked barely seaworthy, and – with no means of sailing it, or even steering – he would be at the mercy of the ocean's tides. But one thing was certain. With the latest change of course taken into account, he would have absolutely no chance of making his way back to Vadanis. Once the off-shore race had carried him out to sea, the islands would be moving away, back towards the centre of the ocean – and leaving him in their wake.

When the time came, Terrel was cast adrift upon turbulent waters, and the terrified boy could only cling to the raft as best he could, for fear of falling overboard and drowning. When the worst of that was over, and he was riding upon the slow swell of open water, he could only watch in helpless disbelief as the islands – the only home he had ever known, and the place that held everything that was dear to him – began to dwindle into the distance.

He was too stunned even to cry, and he felt a terrible numbness seep into his entire body – and into his spirit – as the ocean currents carried him towards a distant barbarian shore.

EPILOGUE

lyssa's long dream was in its fifth month now, and there
as still no end in sight. Although she had not wanted to
ash Terrel's hopes, she had known that the elemental
ould not release her yet. She had not even wanted it to.
'he haven was still a place of misery and fear, and she was
etter off as she was. Besides, it was not yet time.

Her separation from the stonechat had been a great
lief, both to her spirit and to the bird whose form she
ad usurped for so long. It had taken her several days to
cover, and she was still not sure she had the strength to
ke another living shape. But that was not what was wor-
ing her now.

The ring's failure puzzled her. In the past it had always
uided her – sometimes in unexpected ways, and not
ways as quickly as she would have liked – but it had
ever let her down before. Now it told her nothing – and
t that was impossible. Terrel was not dead – she would
ave felt that separation and gone looking for his ghost –
t he was nowhere to be found. He had simply vanished.

Earlier in her dream, before she had learnt to borrow the

lives of animals, she had told him that she would wait for his return — but now she knew she would do more than that. Her second vow was spoken in words she knew he could not hear, and it was as much a promise to herself as it was to him.

You're not alone, Terrel. I still have your ring. And I don't care what I have to do, or where I have to go. I'll find you, my love. I will find you.

Orbit titles available by post:

❑ Ice Mage	Julia Gray	£6.99
❑ Fire Music	Julia Gray	£6.99
❑ Isle of the Dead	Julia Gray	£6.99

The prices shown above are correct at time of going to press. However, the publishers reserve the right to increase prices on covers from those previously advertised, without further notice.

orbit

ORBIT BOOKS
Cash Sales Department, P.O. Box 11, Falmouth, Cornwall, TR10 9EN
Tel: +44 (0) 1326 569777, Fax: +44 (0) 1326 569555
Email: books@barni.avel.co.uk

POST AND PACKING:
Payments can be made as follows: cheque, postal order (payable to Orbit Books) or by credit cards. Do not send cash or currency.

U.K. Orders under £10	£1.50
U.K. Orders over £10	**FREE OF CHARGE**
E.C. & Overseas	25% of order value

Name (Block letters) . . . .

Address . . . .

. . . .

Post/zip code: . . . .

☐ Please keep me in touch with future Orbit publications

☐ I enclose my remittance £ . . . .

☐ I wish to pay by Visa/Access/Mastercard/Eurocard

Card Expiry Date